PEDIGREE CRUSH
WITH A TWISTED GENE

About the Author

Born in South Shields, Tyne & Weir, Katherine Black spent most of her years in the Lake District.

She now lives near Bolton with her dogs, a lazy Chihuahua and a neurotic terrier.

Find Katherine online at
www.katherineblack.co.uk

Also by Katherine Black
A Question of Sanity
Leverage
Nowhere Boulevard
Dark Around the Edges
People on the Edge

Also by Kat Black
Lizards Leap
Keepers of the Quantum

PEDIGREE

CRUSH

WITH A
TWISTED GENE

KATHERINE
BLACK

NIGHTSGALE

Acknowledgements

Special thanks to Peter J. Merrigan for all his hard work. More than an editor, he is a best friend.

Chapter One

28th May, 1973

He shuffled down the corridor. Clutching his Scooby-Doo lunchbox protectively in his left hand, he looked confused. He always looked confused.

'Late. Late. Late.' He had an empty rucksack on his back. It was his and because it belonged to him it was important. He didn't have anything to put in it but he took it with him always, as a child carries a favourite blanket. The rucksack was all he had. It was his, something that grounded him into who he is, just in case he ever forgot.

He didn't have much. None of them did. Even their clothes got mixed up in the laundry process. Very often he got Andy Dixon's Y-fronts, and towels were a free for all. Simon very rarely went into the linen cupboard for a towel because he didn't like to wash much. He didn't like soap—he hated the feel of it, but on the occasions when he was forced to use it, even that had somebody else's scud on the top.

His cardigan was fastened wrong. An extra hole hung alone at the waistband and, to compensate, a lone button stood out like an on-off switch near his neck. Mrs Quigley had made him his favourite for breakfast – soft boiled eggs – and his shirt bore testament. His trainers were on the wrong feet, the laces undone and trailing. Every few steps he stumbled over them.

1

Gloria shook her head and tutted. 'Simon, look at the state of you.' Simon tried to look but his chin stopped him seeing much of his top half and his tummy hid everything from the waist down. As for his face, he couldn't see that at all. 'How many times have I told you to stay in your room until someone comes to check you over?'

Simon didn't answer for some seconds, his long brow furrowing as he mulled the question over. He gave a triumphant grin. 'A millionty-three,' he said as Gloria herded him back in the direction of his room.

He waited there, sitting on the end of his bed and counting to twenty. He got confused and jumped from thirteen to twentitty-one, missing out his goal of twenty completely. He wanted to hurry up and get to twentitty-one because it was a funny number and made him giggle. He wasn't sure what came after that and was aware that he'd probably got it wrong somewhere. He tried to work it out and when he got even more confused, he decided to go back to one and start again. But before he began the second scale, he forgot about numbers and started to think about days instead.

He knew it wasn't Monday because they went swimming on a Monday and he hadn't been swimming. He forgot to allow for the fact that it wasn't yet nine o'clock. And if it was Tuesday he would have been swimming yesterday and his hair would smell of chlorine because he didn't like having a shower after he'd been swimming. The water in the pool's showers was too cold and Jimmy always splashed him and called him Jelly Belly. He liked smelling his hair on a Tuesday. He would remember being in the pool and how much fun he'd had. Swimming, he decided, not for the first time, was one of his favouritest things, but it wasn't as good as eating cream cakes or ice cream. If he could go swimming and eat cream cake and ice cream all at the same time it would be his favouritest day ever. He wished that there were twentitty-one days in a week because then surely one of them would have swimming and eating cream cakes and ice cream at the same time.

Nobody had come to check him yet. He wondered if he should go and find somebody. Because nobody's comed to get me and someone might be giving away good eats out there.

Helen always came at quarter to nine. He felt that it must be later than that now. Simon was an optimist. He saw the good in every situation, and if there wasn't any he'd add the possible element of ice cream, or something else nice, and his trademark grin would attach itself to his face. When Simon smiled, nobody could be angry with him for very long. Well, except Mummy, but she was always angry about something. Gloria said he was a sunbeam. Simon liked being a sunbeam. Gloria didn't tell anybody else they were a sunbeam. Gloria might be missing me by now, it's been such a longer time. I'd better go and find her and tell her nobody's comed yet.

And so he shuffled off down the corridor again, tripping over his laces, smiling his smile and trying his best to see if he could smell ice cream or even sausages.

3

Sausages were easier to smell than ice cream. Ice cream was a real hard smell to smell and you had to almost have your nose in it before you could smell it proper. Sausages were good, too, and he'd forgotten that he'd just had his breakfast.

Gloria was still clearing away the breakfast things when Simon reappeared. It was only three minutes since she'd taken him back to his room. She understood that three minutes was a long time to Simon. Gloria understood most things when it came to her kids. She patiently took him back to his room and promised him that she would get somebody to come right away and sort him out. She suggested that he might like to draw a picture until Helen came.

Simon thought that was a smashing idea. It was not something he would ever have thought of for himself. He had to be told what to do all the time. He didn't just do something. That was one of the things Mummy got annoyed about. Gloria didn't like Mummy much. Simon wouldn't ever think of drawing a picture by himself, but he was clever enough to know that Gloria didn't like Mummy.

Gloria led him over to the desk in the corner of his room. All the children had a desk in their room with coloured pencils and paper. It wasn't his, though, like his rucksack. His thick tongue stuck out of his mouth and he drew a big brown flower with two red leaves at the bottom and a snail climbing up the stalk.

As much as he struggled to work out what his routine should be from one moment to the next, Simon

4

functioned on order. He didn't always know what was right, but he instinctively knew if something was changed or different—or just plain wrong. He didn't like anything to be different, it upset him. Because you don't have chips on a Thursday, do you? No, it's mashed potato on a Thursday. He thought that something bad might happen if you had chips on a Thursday when it should be mashed potato. Thursday was mashed potato day.

This morning wasn't right, though. Two things had happened that upset Simon.

The first was that Helen didn't come into his room to check him over before the bus came to pick him up. Helen always came at quarter to nine because the bus would arrive at five to. Simon couldn't tell the time and he always got anxious that she'd be late and he always went looking for her, but that was all part of it being right. That's the way it was.

That morning somebody new came into his room. She said hello and put out her hand for him to shake. Simon knew how to shake hands. He liked shaking hands. Sometimes he shook hands with Helen or Gloria and it made him giggle, but not when they were trying to fold sheets. The new Helen said she was called Anna. Anna was pretty and smiled big but he wouldn't shake hands with her. He wanted to wait for Helen to come. But if he waited for Helen to come he'd be late for the bus now because it must be after quarter to nine. It was bad. He moved from one foot to the other and wouldn't look at Anna or shake hands with her.

Anna told him that Helen couldn't come just now. She said that Helen was sad about not coming to see him off but she'd had a bit of a problem with James. Everybody had a bit of a problem with James. He got mad. He got mad a lot more than Simon did and sometimes he hit people, too. Simon was scared of James.

Anna said, 'I'm sure Helen will be all right but she's had a nasty knock to the head and has gone to the hospital just to be on the safe side.' All the while she was talking she was also undoing Simon's buttons. He found that distressing. He was distressed that Helen was hurt too also. It wasn't nice that Helen was hurt too also. If Anna had a little more experience, or had known Simon and his ways better, she might have said something different to explain Helen's absence. With every word she said, he became more agitated. He moved from one foot to the other and made a deep moaning noise in his throat. Anna kept talking to him softly, trying to ease his discomfort but the foot changing became more insistent and the moaning was getting louder.

Gloria rushed into the room without knocking. That was very bad. Simon knew it was very bad because at Great Gables people always knocked on other people's doors. That was called good manners. Gloria said so herself and here she was coming in without knocking. It was bad for sure. It was a very bad day.

'It's all right now, Anna. I'll take over here. Thank

you for stepping in like that.' They talked in low voices. 'Yes, yes, she'll be all right, I think, but best not to take chances with these things. Head wounds can be funny.'

Simon didn't think head wounds were funny at all. He thought that they probably hurt a lot and that was nothing to laugh about. Gloria coming in like that without knocking was distressing, but not as distressing as a new helper sending him off or Helen getting hurt. It was still one more thing to get upset about and Simon moaned louder. Without warning, he brought his left hand up and hit himself hard on the side of the head. Gloria caught his arm as it raised a second time. 'No you don't. Come on, my bonny lad, let's get you sorted. It's all right, now. I know that was a bit scary but everything's back to normal now.'

'Not back normal now,' said Simon. 'Late bus now.'

'It's okay, Simon. The bus will wait for you. It doesn't matter, don't worry. We're only a couple of minutes behind.'

'Not five to nine.'

'No Simon, it's not five to nine, it's three minutes to. What's two minutes between friends, eh? It's no biggie. Tom's holding up the bus for everyone.'

'Bad, bad,' said Simon, in his upset voice. 'Not five to nine. Late to bus. Big bad. Big bad. Bad for sure.'

Gloria gave up on fastening his shoes, intending instead to distract him from his tantrum by walking him to the bus, hair uncombed and laces trailing. Better to have that this morning than face another one throwing his fists around. Simon was only thirteen but he was a big lad with plenty of bulk to fling his weight behind. Gloria thought he was probably the gentlest soul on earth but, like many Downs Syndrome sufferers, he could fly off the handle if he was angry, frustrated or frightened.

It was during the first lesson after lunch that it dawned on him what day it was. They had PE that day. It took almost half of the lesson to get all the pupils into their blue shorts and white vests, and then almost the other half to get them back into their normal clothes. The actual lesson only lasted ten minutes. Simon knew that Mummy came on the day they had PE and that distressed him.

Simon loved his Mother. She was always there waiting for him in his room when he got off the school bus but she distressed him. He was agitated, as always during the PE lesson, his mood would worsen throughout the afternoon and only subsided into a quiet stillness when the visit was over and his mother gone. He worried a lot on PE day. PE day was bad for worry.

After PE they had an activity lesson before home time and Simon tried every week to learn to be clever really fast, so that his mummy would like him. He tried so hard to do well in that lesson, but only seemed to succeed in covering himself in glue or paint or flour which made his mummy even more cross.

He made her a clay pot that he baked in the oven and painted. She said it was lop-sided. He made her a flower out of tissue paper and glitter. She said it was ugly. He made her a love heart and decorated it with real daisies. She forgot to take it home with her and Simon found it on the floor. The daisies had wilted and he felt sorry for picking them and making them die.

That day they made biscuits in class. It was a lot of fun and they smelled really good when they were baking. It made all the children hungry and Miss Brown said that if they were very good and made a great job of decorating them with icing and Smarties, they could each have one to take home. Simon really, really wanted to eat his biscuit with the other kids on the way back to Great Gables. There were only enough for them to have one each. Simon wanted to eat it a lot, but he saved it for his mummy.

She was waiting in his room when he got back. She was always waiting in his room. She didn't like it in the lounge or along the corridors where she might see the other children. She said they made her feel sick. Simon sometimes wondered if he made her feel sick, too. Simon had felt sick once and it wasn't very nice. He shuffled down the corridor a little faster than usual. His big moon face had a huge grin and his tongue protruded from his smiling mouth.

He walked into his room. 'Mummy biscuit,' he announced proudly, shuffling towards her and holding the present out before him.

She pulled a funny face and put it straight in the wastepaper basket. Simon was sad. He would like to have eaten it himself.

'Really, Simon, you can't expect me to actually eat that. Where have your hands been?'

Simon thought about that. He thought about all questions seriously but sometimes couldn't work out an answer. He looked at his hands – they were on the ends of his arms, the same as they always were. He wondered if Mummy meant to ask, 'What have you been doing with your hands?' which was a different question altogether. He remembered that he had put one of his hands down his trousers quite a lot that afternoon because he had an itch, but he couldn't remember which one it was that he'd scratched his private parts with. None of this seemed to have anything to do with his biscuit that was now in the wastepaper basket. He was still pondering his hands and his biscuit, looking sad and confused, when his mummy slapped him on the arm. It wasn't a hard slap but it made him jump. Maybe she slapped him because his hands had wandered off on their own for a little bit when he wasn't looking and that's what she meant by her question.

'Will you pay attention? I'm talking to you, Simon.'

He looked up slowly. His tongue bulged over his lower lip and his big almond shaped eyes looked empty. That was the expression that his mother said she hated most of all. She told him that she couldn't bear to look at him and she focused instead on her watch.

Only another hour and fifty minutes and she would escape her son and his smell of maternal neglect.

Chapter Two

Some might argue that an infant returning to the Lord deserves rays of brilliant sunlight and the Hallelujah Chorus sung by the angels. This wasn't that kind of funeral. It was a sombre occasion, a ceremony in black, as only a Catholic funeral knows how.

Violet Postlethwaite was still a young girl, though the strain of the past week and the black clothes and veil had given her the appearance of a woman fifteen years older. She was called Woods now, had been for the past five months, but people round those parts took to change slowly. So to them she was, and pretty much always would be, little Vi Postlethwaite.

She had elevated opinions of herself and very firm opinions about her name. She shuddered if anybody dared to call her Vi to her face. 'My name,' she'd declare icily, 'is Violet. Vi-o-let, three syllables. It is the name I was given and, had my parents wanted me to be called Vi, I'm sure they would have seen fit to christen me thus, in the sight of God.'

Her grievance with the name Postlethwaite was even worse. She hadn't been married long to Donald Woods and, on returning from their honeymoon, they'd moved into the small public house, just outside Windermere, run by Donald's parents. Local dialect was very neatly divided through the middle of Windermere.

11

Anything Bowness and south was still Cumberland until Cumberland leaked into Lancashire, but north of Windermere the Cumberland dialect really kicked into its wellies. Violet had been horrified the first time she'd heard Postlethwaite contracted to produce the sound Postlethut and was glad that she'd taken her new name of Woods. Even these yokels would find it difficult to tamper with that. Donald wasn't good for much, but at least he'd had the sense to be born with a reliably dependable surname.

She wasn't thinking about names as she stood beside the damp hole watching the coffin being lowered. She wept into a fine lace handkerchief and threw a small amount of earth on to the top of the white casket lid.

'God bless, my darling,' she sniffled, before throwing her head back and wailing, 'My baby. My poor, dead baby.'

Molly Davis, the Woods' cleaning lady, sobbed even louder. 'It was a lovely service,' she would tell everybody later.

Georgina and Arthur, Violet's parents, were the epitome of dignified mourning. They stood shoulder to shoulder with their daughter, lending her their support and strength. Donald was pushed out. He loitered, slightly apart, ashen and confused. In his turn he dropped a handful of earth into the grave but only after Monsignor Burton had urged him to. Donald had expected the soil to sprinkle like icing sugar on the top of a sponge cake, but Windermere earth is predominantly clay and it clumped in his sweaty hand and fell to the coffin lid like a stone landing with a resounding thump and Donald jumped as though he had been hit in the chest by a rock.

Georgina's head shot up, glaring at her new son-in-law. Her lips pursed tightly and her black eyes peered at him. She looked startled, like a malevolent crow, as she shook her head in slow exaggerated movements. Again Donald had disappointed. Donald felt that Georgina blamed him for the mud on her new court shoes, for the escalating price of home-cured ham and for the fact that it was raining. But what she could never blame him for was the death of the child.

Donald didn't want to get married. He'd never really wanted to put Violet in the unfortunate position that they had had to get married. If truth be told, he didn't like her very much. He hadn't liked her on sight and his opinion of her had never warmed. He'd been pushed into taking her out by his enthusiastic parents. Violet herself had made all the other decisions; he just went along with them because he found that, where Violet was concerned, that was usually best. What really upset Donald was standing beside that gave, with those people, on that day with his own mother smiling at him. It was one of those smiles that were meant to encourage, but really it said, 'I'm sorry, I don't know what to say.' Perhaps what Donald hated the most was the fact that his parents were hurting. They didn't deserve this. They were good people.

Violet told everybody that the baby was brought to

his burial in what would have been his christening gown. 'Yards of pure white lace,' she said to anybody who would listen, 'adorning his poor tiny little body. What was Our Lord thinking?' She repeated this many times that day, along with, 'How could He take our angel, our sweet, precious angel?'

Whispers carried back through the church from pew to pew. It was the tradition in these parts to go for open-casket funerals. Why then had they chosen to keep the baby's coffin closed? But nobody dared mention it to the family. 'Well,' said Maisy Roach, 'It wouldn't be right to ask, would it?'

'Mebby's it were a really ugly babby,' said Jack Dawson.

'Aye, or 'appen it 'ad summat right wrong with it like. 'Appen it were that spiral biffica, there's a lot a that abart.' Maisy sucked in air through her teeth and tutted and they all nodded their heads in solemn agreement.

No expense had been spared on the funeral. Usually, Arthur clung onto his wallet as Georgina ripped it from his hand with vigour but, that day, he just looked shifty and sad—and scared.

Willoughby's had taken care of the funeral. The family rode in a black Rolls Royce with red brocade curtains at the windows to shield their tears from curious eyes. The coffin was brought to the church in a carriage with a glass mantle. Four ebony stallions, with black plumes on their heads, pulled the carriage, their hoof beats tolling perfect time along the cobbled streets. Mister Willoughby himself headed the procession. He walked in front of the carriage, stamping the tempo into the road with his cane, raindrops reflected in the calyx patterns from the crystal orb on the top. He wore a black coat to his knees, a claret cravat and a black top hat, but mostly he wore dignity and respect. It was what the family had paid through the nose for.

Monsignor Burton ran out of prayers, his hands ached from being spread, upturned to God at chest height. His thin, reedy voice sang the final lament. His left knee throbbed with a deep arthritic pain from the damp weather. 'God be with you,' he said for the third time. 'Go in peace to serve the Lord.' For the most part the mourners had dispersed. They left quickly with a taste for sherry and salmon sandwiches with the crusts cut off. The family didn't seem to know what to do. They looked down on the tiny coffin, shaking their heads and searching their hearts for guilt.

Jack Murray gave an apologetic cough, his hand fisted at his mouth. He didn't know how best to disturb them and he was terrified of Georgina Postlethut, but time was getting on and Stinging Nettle was running in the three o' clock at Chepstow.

'Jack,' said Arthur, turning to shake the large man's hand, but he couldn't look him in the eye. 'Thank you for coming. And please, thank everyone at the lodge for the floral tribute. It's right grand.'

'It's nothing my man, nothing,' grunted Murray. His eyes examined the same pebble that Arthur seemed to find so interesting. 'Terrible business, terrible. Of course'—cough—'we've had another whip round'—

cough—'for…um…Well, there's a small monetary gift for Violet. It'll be presented at the lodge on Monday. We'll see you there, yes?'

Arthur heard raindrops bouncing off the lid of the coffin. They shook hands and, without another word, the president of the Windermere branch of the Freemasons Society walked away, wiping the shaken hand on the seam of his suit trousers.

Like the family, for his part in the scandal, he wouldn't sleep easy in his bed that night.

Chapter Three

After the funeral, life settled down quickly for Violet and Donald. Violet wasn't happy to rest on her laurels for long. Before meeting Donald she had a life plan mapped out. Getting pregnant at nineteen wasn't part of that plan. It wasn't even in the small print at the bottom that said she should always be able to rely on her mother and father for financial help in any unexpected eventuality. Nowhere was unexpected and unfortunate pregnancy mentioned and Violet felt violated.

Donald had worked at Borrowdale Quarry for eight years. He was happy. His friends were there and he got to work outside in the fresh air. He always joked that he had a full membership to the cheapest gym in the country. His work wasn't far from Derwent Water Lake and he spent eight hours a day playing Peeping Tom to nature at her most alluring. He was a worker and both management and his co-workers respected him. His body was brown and taut and his job made going home to Violet just about bearable.

As soon as it was seemly to do so, Violet arranged meetings with estate agents in a thirty-mile radius. They looked at bed and breakfast establishments, public houses and hotels at the cheaper end of the market. Violet saw no reason at all why they shouldn't commit to four hundred thousand pounds worth of mortgage right away. They were young. They had their whole life ahead of them to pay it off and, with a sizeable down payment from Daddy as a late wedding present, they'd manage. Donald's head swam. Four hundred pounds was more than he'd ever owed to anybody in his life. Four hundred thousand wasn't a millstone, it was an entire mill house—and the town surrounding it—tied about his neck. It was in the days when being a millionaire still meant something, and four hundred thousand pounds was a tremendous amount of money. Donald's protests fell on grit and concrete. He couldn't make Violet see sense. However, the mortgage companies fared better by simply refusing to fund her whims. She alienated several brokers who'd been willing to allow them a more manageable mortgage before she finally agreed to downgrade on her ambition with the bank's money.

Luck was with them the day they found the small hotel on the outskirts of Windermere. It wasn't on the lake edge as Violet wanted but otherwise, it was beautiful. Structurally it was sound but it needed a lot of work and modernisation. Mrs Finch, the vendor, was an elderly widow with money. Since her husband had died, she'd found it increasingly difficult to manage alone and the good reputation of the hotel declined. Her glass back was telling her it was time to hang up her apron and let Glenridding Mount go.

For all her bombastic nature, Violet was canny. Instinct told her she needed the old lass on side, so she turned up her charm oven to four hundred degrees and coated her natural brusqueness with honey. Each room seemed to her more old-fashioned and dingy than the last. The only place where she felt the ambience of the place was in the kitchen, fitted with a huge Aga. She was bursting with a desire to voice her plans. Walls out, décor changed, complete overhaul, Little Bird Finch thrown on the scrapheap. But she held herself in check, cooing in all the right places and complementing the vendor on her charming home.

One thing that was genuine was her instant love for the place. Glenridding Mount had Mrs Violet Woods' name written all over it. She soon had the old crow eating out of her hands.

Donald went along to the viewings reluctantly. He was happy in his work and, frankly, the thought of spending not only his leisure hours, but also his workday close to the bosom of his lovely wife appalled him. To an outside eye, Donald Woods was a wimp, the blueprint of the stereotypical henpecked husband. Anybody studying them saw that he only gave his lady so much rope, and when he was ready to reel her in he kept her on a short tether—and a muzzle. When the farce began, he had no intention of giving up his job to begin a new trade as a hotelier. It was an occupation that he was untrained for and hadn't the first clue about how to begin. Some might say it was cruel to let his wife look for something he had no intention of buying her. But the way Donald saw it, Violet was a woman who needed something to occupy her mind. She was somebody who bored easily, and an idle Violet was likely to turn to gossiping, and spouting malice around the town. This way, Violet got to play with her fantasy and Donald got some peace and avoided the relentless nagging about a hotel that they couldn't afford.

It surprised him more than anybody when he fell in love with the Glenridding Mount. He became enthused with Violet's plans and found himself adding his own ideas. Violet had an eye for detail and surprisingly good taste. Donald saw polished floors, restored oak beams and a new bar that he might just feel at home behind. He was caught up in the moment. He rode piggyback on Violet's excitement. The normally frugal and reticent Donald couldn't believe what he was saying when he heard himself putting in an offer, right there on the first viewing, standing in the kitchen beside the old blue Aga.

Violet couldn't believe it either. She hadn't expected that. Donald's way was to go home and talk it over if she decided to change their brand of toilet roll. He'd clearly been outside in the sun too long but she wasn't about to knock it. She squealed like a little girl when their modest offer was accepted. She was, after all, not quite twenty. Donald had never seen this side of her. She threw her arms round his neck and hugged him fiercely right there in front of Mrs Finch.

Donald wondered, as if it was the first time that he'd seen them, if Violet had been named for the colour of her eyes. Her plain, ruddy complexion looked softer and pinker. Maybe it's just the lighting in this old kitchen, he told himself. He surprised himself again with a genuine feeling of affection for his wife. He hugged her to him and felt that, just maybe, they would be happy there.

The hotel sale went through; they got it way below the market value. But even in the busy and exciting months ahead, the Wednesday and Sunday rituals remained rigid. Violet wouldn't waver and wouldn't relent. Every Wednesday afternoon she went out at noon and didn't return until after six. Sunday's belonged mainly to God. Violet attended Mass twice on a Sunday, Donald refused to be hauled along with her more than once a day. For appearance sake, and to make his wife happy, he attended early Mass, but that was it. That was as far as his religious devotion would extend and he stubbornly refused to budge. The other Sunday ritual he would have no part of at all, and nothing Violet said would change his mind.

Right through the bitterly cold winter months, through the delights of spring and into the heavily laden summer, Violet went to the cemetery with flowers every Sunday, immediately after lunch. She would spend an hour at the grave throwing out the previous week's blooms and arranging the new ones. Grieving relatives talk over their loved ones graves, telling them their news, just feeling close to them. Violet never uttered a word unless to speak to a passerby. She did what she had to do and then knelt at the graveside in prayer. She stayed only as long as she needed to, to be seen doing her duty, and then she left, returning home many hours later after attending to her private business.

Despite being a spoiled brat, hard work came easily

to Violet. She had exacting standards, and very shortly after opening, the hotel was booked up months in advance. They were soon in a position to take on more staff. Violet hired and fired with gusto. As hard as she drove her staff, she drove herself more, in an almost manic need for perfection.

After their second year, they not only broke even, but their bank balance was healthy enough for expansion. Violet was ambitious, she could never be satisfied with enough and would always want more. They extended their property once in that year and twice more in the following three years.

Donald found his niche, not as a hotel manager, but as grounds man. He loved the land and tended the acreage with pride. He took to entering competitions with his flowers and vegetables and his work and hobby became intermingled. Violet hired a chef and a manager with experience and reputation. The Glenridding Mount Hotel gained a star a year for three consecutive years.

While the Woods' empire was busy building, things weren't slacking on the domestic front. Almost nine months to the day of the funeral, Violet bore a son. She saw this as a purely solo endeavour. If she had to admit to Donald having any role to play at all, then it was as an extra, a cameo role, soon done with and out of the way. Violet wouldn't have wanted him there anyway, getting in the way and making the place look untidy. Having babies was women's work.

She gave the final almighty heave that would

propel the infant into the world. Apart from a few grunts of exertion, the labour had been silent. She bit down on her fists when the cramps chewed into her raw nerve endings and made her want to scream. She felt the procedure was unbecoming enough without any wailing and gnashing of teeth. But as she felt her second child slither into the world she became hysterical, crying for her husband, terrified that it might be like the last one.

'It's a boy, love,' said the midwife, smiling.

'Take it away. Take it away,' she whimpered. 'I don't want to see it until...' Her voice tailed off.

Donald was brought into the delivery room. He barely noticed the blood and amniotic waters on the floor. He didn't look at the child. His first concern was for his wife who needed him for the first time ever — and would never need him again. She groped for his hand and clung to him, vulnerable and pale. She couldn't cope if it was like last time.

Only when the midwife had cleaned the baby and convinced her that he was beautiful, and beautifully normal, did Violet take her son into the crook of her arm.

She examined the grizzling face. She looked at his forehead, peered into the baby's eyes and followed the contours of his tiny face to his mouth. Without care or gentleness she ripped at the blanket the midwife had wrapped her son in, exposing him before her. She had to know. She needed to be sure.

The midwife urged Violet to put him to her breast

but she ignored the woman. She spread the baby's hands in turn, scrutinising each one closely, back of the hand, palm, back of the hand again. She wasn't counting the fingers or marvelling at the beauty of something so delicate and tiny. This wasn't her son— not yet, not until she'd made sure. She was looking for a larger than normal space between the fingers and thumb. She was looking for a thicker than normal tongue. She was looking for hooded, myopic eyes.

'Vi, love, he's perfect. He's our boy,' said Donald.

'You said that about the last one,' she spat back at him. Her eyes never left the child crying stiffly in her arms.

Donald cradled his wife and son until he felt the tension leave Violet's body in a flood. He was perfect. She wept silent tears onto his soft head.

This was her son.

She named him Simon Peter, after the first Apostle. It was a name befitting a child who would mature to greatness, for Violet had no doubt of this. Simon Peter was the rock of Jesus.

Simon Peter was her rock.

Two and a half years later, another son was born. Violet was disappointed. He should have been a girl. She'd planned for a girl and expected a girl. Violet and Georgina blamed Donald for producing a son instead of the daughter they both so badly wanted. It takes a real man to make a girl. Violet took a few days to love this one. But she reasoned he could be great too: her Andrew, the second Apostle of Jesus.

Less than a year later, in her compulsion for a daughter, Violet gave birth to twins, both boys. She was resigned to having sons now. They were her boys, her beautiful, perfect boys. A girl would be different, would stand out. Yes, she decided, boys were best, all uniform, all wonderful in their own special way. Her Apostles. Jesus had no time for girl Apostles and neither, she decided, did she. The twins were called James and John after the third and fourth apostles. A tradition had been set. Donald was scared. He was often seen to pull at the corners of his moustache, a sure sign that something was troubling him. Where was it going to end, this churning out of children? Did she plan on going for the full twelve? He hoped not. Dear Lord, he joked, please make her stop before we get to number ten. Surely not even Violet could christen a child Labbaeus Thaddaeus.

Violet completed her family two years later, with her last son, Philip. She was a staunch Catholic and didn't believe in birth control. When she came out of hospital after the birth of her fifth son, she moved directly into her own bedroom. She had lain down and made her children and she was done with all that stuff now. Sex was a perfunctory business, and she'd never taken to it. Donald sighed, having to accept what he couldn't change. It was nice while it lasted, he thought.

Violet felt as though she'd been pregnant forever. Now that she was finished with it—and sex, she needed a new challenge. She went back to hounding the estate agencies and took to viewing grand Lakeland hotels, way beyond their budget. The difference this time was that she had history. The Woods had an excellent record of accomplishment and their reputation preceded them. The brokers fell over themselves to throw money at them.

Violet was viewing, but she wasn't buying. She knew exactly what she wanted, and was determined to wait to get it. She viewed many and found them all lacking. She knew that when she saw it, it would be the one for her. And when she saw it, she was proved right. Donald had no say in the matter; his voice was a chirp in her ear. It wasn't just the name of the hotel but that did seem like the hand of God pointing their way ahead. The Halcyon Woods Hotel stood on the water's edge of Windermere in twenty acres of its own woodland and lakeside splendour. Violet waited for news of harsh times in the hotel industry and, when an outbreak of foot and mouth disease hit Lakeland ground in the summer of sixty-six, effectively slaughtering tourism, she pounced.

They made an initial offer of four million and settled on £4.8m. It was a colossal amount of money and while Donald took to night sweats and insomnia, and the brokers pulled at their ties and wiped a thin film of grease from their collective foreheads, Violet slept soundly and dreamed of chintz coverlets.

Financially, things were tight for the next few years. It had been a tremendous gamble, but one that only Donald lost sleep over. Violet was far too occupied making it work to have time to fret.

The boys grew under a strict regime of firm

discipline. Violet treated her children in the same way that she treated her staff. She expected things to be done when she first asked, for them to be done properly and, the hardest thing her staff, her children and even her husband had to live up to, everything had to be done to her rigorous standards.

The boys had the perfect playground to grow up in. There were always guests' children to make friends with, and yet Violet's boys—always Violet's boys, never Donald's—were given no time to play and were discouraged from engaging with the guests.

She dressed them alike and expected them to be spotlessly clean at all times. 'Appearance,' she always said, 'is of the utmost importance in our profession. And you, my darlings, are my ambassadors. Remember your position at all times and make Mummy proud.'

The Woods boys grew to love Wednesday afternoons in the school holidays. Donald had shorts and t-shirts hidden in his garden shed for them to change into the minute that Violet left. She still went out every Wednesday. The kids would fell trees with their father or play football on the lawns. On a Wednesday afternoon they were allowed to get dirty on the strict understanding that they would clean up before Mother's return. Violet was always too preoccupied on those evenings to notice that they collected most of their scrapes and grazes on a Wednesday.

But into every week a Sunday must fall. What they enjoyed mid week, they paid for on the Sabbath.

They rose at five thirty to bathe. Violet would fill

the enormous tub in their quarters and a conveyor belt system was operational. As one got out of the bath, the next was ready to step in, starting with Philip, because he was the youngest and therefore needed the most help. James, the more dominant of the identical twins, always made John go after Philip because the youngest boy often peed in the bath out of sheer wickedness. John still had to get in the bath water, now, slurried by another brother's scum and by his turn the water was too cloudy to see if James had also peed, but it wasn't so bad if you didn't get in straight after Philip.

By the time it was Simon Peter's turn to get in the bath, the water was black and cold. SP, as the lads called him when their mother wasn't listening, perfected bathing without ever getting into the bath, but every so often Mummy would check behind his ears and then he'd be for it.

The boys hated their Sunday outfits. Violet faced down the tears and tantrums, the screaming and bawling. She never raised her voice much, but she spoke to them in a tone three parts ice to two parts venom. They didn't refuse her wishes. It wasn't done.

They would present for inspection at six thirty. Being Catholics they weren't allowed anything to eat until after Mass which began at seven-thirty and could go on for two hours if Monsignor Burton had a fire in his belly to preach about. The brothers would stand in line looking miserable, but that wasn't allowed either. Violet chided them to straighten their hats and their faces before leaving the house. 'And for goodness sake, men, smile.'

She had earned the nickname Mother Duck around town. She was a regular sight on a Sunday morning, marching down the street in her stout church brogues. Her five children marched behind her, in single file, starting with the eldest and ending with little Philip, who found it hard to keep time and sometimes had to run a bit to catch up.

The matronly woman and her five offspring were a remarkable sight and if ever somebody compiled a list of the Windermere eccentric, Old Mother Duck would be right up there at the top of the list. Violet was proud of her standards.

'Standards,' she said, 'are everything.'

She felt that she was a respected member of the highest Lakeland society. And indeed she was highly respected as a shrewd and determined businesswoman. But when it came to the way she treated her children it was a different matter. There wasn't a mother in town who wouldn't like to take those poor l'al lads into her arms for a cuddle.

She wore black for church, right down to the brogues on her feet and the lace veil on her head, folded back for marching, ready to pull over her face when she entered the House of God. Childbirth had not been kind to her and Violet was broad in beam and bosom. By comparison, her boys were all slim and gave the appearance of being easily broken.

She had their clothes handmade. They hated the straw hats the most, but only marginally more than the burgundy and grey striped blazers with the tacky gold buttons. Their outfits were finished off with grey knee-length shorts with creases you could cut paper with, long grey socks and black shoes, which the boys would clean on a Saturday night until Violet could see her face in them.

Nobody knew for sure whether the boys learned to walk first or to march. They had a car so Donald could have driven them to church, but Violet wouldn't hear of that. Regardless of weather or temperament, every Sunday those boys would be marched through the town to Our Lady of the Lake Catholic Church. When they passed the house of their paternal grandmother, Violet would order, 'Eyes right, boys, and salute to Grandma.' The children would dutifully turn their heads as one, raise their right hands and salute in unison into their grandmother's lounge window.

Donald's mother hated it. She loathed seeing her grandchildren demoralised and had begged Violet not to do it. 'They're only children, Violet. Let them be.' But Violet saw it has her duty to the town to show them that her boys were the best behaved and the most beautifully mannered children ever raised. Grandma Mary had long since made sure that she was never in the proximity of her front window on a Sunday morning. Violet saw that as no deterrent, and commanded the boys to salute regardless.

As children do, the boys learned to adapt to their mother's ways. They were well fed, almost never spanked and had musical and holiday privileges that most boys their age didn't. Violet loved them even more than she loved her double string of cultured pearls, and showed them off to all the right people just as often.

She was grooming them all to be altar boys and if Monsignor Burton was too busy to see how good they were, then Violet was sure he would hear about it.

Chapter Four

Mass was over for another week. The Woods boys were starving. Violet ordered the meal to be brought to her quarters. Sunday lunch was as religious as seven thirty Mass. No menial waiter was allowed to serve this meal; it had to be brought by the head chef himself.

Succulent pink beef, roast potatoes—crispy on the outside with a hot and fluffy centre—red wine and garlic gravy made with the juices from the tenderloin and infused with thick double cream. The meal could have been good, it should have been good, but hanging over them was the Sunday curse. The boys drew out the feast as long as possible, while the meat turned to cardboard in their mouths.

On getting home from Mass the whole family changed out of their Sunday best before sitting down to eat. Endless prayers were said over the tureens, while the head chef, Marcus, with eyes rolling and feet shifting, rubbed his lower back as it ached. He worried that the meal would cool and he'd be sent back to the kitchen with it amid a torrent of screaming abuse from the Madonna Violet.

When at last Philip, who was the star of the show when it came to holding up the proceedings, had shovelled the last Brussels sprout into his unwilling mouth, the second course was over. He screwed up his face and chewed until the food became water because he couldn't face the thought of swallowing the foul vegetable. Violet allowed nobody to leave until every plate at that table was empty and the cutlery laid neatly to rest, side by side like a little old couple in their grave. There was no table chatter; children should be seen and not heard. Apart from polite requests for the cruet set to be passed, the meal was taken in silence. Sunday lunch was a chore for the boys and their father. Only Donald rose from the table with a joyful heart. He'd attended Mass with his wife and sons. He had smiled dutifully as he paraded her around on his arm and passed time with the wealthier parishioners. When he rose from that table, he did so a free man. Donald didn't hold fast to much, but from day one he had steadfastly refused to go through the Sunday afternoon ritual with the rest of his family. He felt sorry for his sons but at least they were spared the worst part of all. They didn't know what he knew, so it wasn't so bad for them. When it came to Sunday afternoons, Donald was of the firm opinion that it was every man for himself, and he was far too concerned with getting his own backside out into the sunshine, or breeze, or even snow if that's what the weather had in store for him. Donald found peace in his gardens. While his wife lived life in the fast lane, wired on nervous energy and flying into rages over un-Brassoed brasses, Donald breathed. He had two gardeners under him now; the place was too big for one person to cope with. He was a thinker, sitting for long periods on his bench by the water's edge and planning his perennials and herbaceous borders. For the most part he was a content man.

Lunch finished, they would file out of the room while Marcus waited, still standing to attention, ready to call his team in to clear the table and relay for afternoon tea.

The boys would change out of the gabardine slacks they had worn for lunch, and back into their Sunday best. They would each get their emerald cushion, crafted in the finest crushed velvet with leather underside. Violet had had them hand made for a purpose. They would march back in procession with all pomp and formalities, to the church.

On a good day the sorry pantomime would be over in an hour but if there was an audience, Violet would wallow, dabbing at her eyes with a lace handkerchief. Once, when dignitaries from the Bishop's party had visited, she had wilted in afaint to the nearest bench and, when attended to, told how her heart breaks for her Lovely Angel now returned to the Lord Above. But not before she'd made the boys sing a rousing chorus of *All Things Bright and Beautiful*, in four-part harmony, around the graveside.

'Philip, don't be so tone deaf, dear,' she hissed over the headstone. 'Mime, dear, mime.'

Gerald Sawkins had been walking his dog through the cemetery that day and Andrew suffered weeks of torture at school. Children were unable to forget watching a band of little soldiers, in straw boaters and striped blazers, singing *All Things Bright and Beautiful* while their mother waved her walking cane like a baton.

Beginning with Simon Peter and ending in Philip,

the boys were expected to come forward and tell their Lovely Angel all about the week just passed. Once, Andrew had asked what their Lovely Angel was called.

'What's he really called, Mummy?' It had been puzzling him. Apart from around the grave on a Sunday afternoon, the boys weren't encouraged to talk about their Lovely Angel.

Violet had turned stricken eyes on him that day, they shone with unshed tears, but beneath the watery sheen there had been something akin to malice. Andrew wasn't sure what the look was, but he knew well enough when to leave it alone.

'When the good Lord, in His infinite wisdom, decided he couldn't bear to be without our Lovely Angel beside him, he reclaimed him quickly. We had him only a second before he was gone. He is, and always will be, our Lovely Angel, taken back to heaven to look down upon us. He is too good to have an earthbound name.'

John was dying to point out that even Jesus had an earthly name and that surely their Lovely Angel wasn't gooder than Jesus, but he'd seen the look in his mother's eye. He bit the words back before they came sprawling out of his mouth and got him a slap around the head. It was as well that he did hold his counsel because he would have received not only the slap but a hundred lines illustrating the correct use of the words 'better' and 'good' for his trouble.

The prayers would come next. Prayers for their Lovely Angel and prayers for the hungry in Africa, though Violet never did really approve much of Negroes and secretly felt that starvation was their punishment for having the audacity to be born coloured. But one had to be seen to be doing one's bit and one never knew who was passing when one had their eyes shut in supplication and prayer. She was just thankful that Windermere had not been invaded by any Negroes.

The boys always had to sing, *The Old Rugged Cross* before leaving, because Mother said it was such a rousing song to leave their Lovely Angel with. She said that he would surely be warm and snug in his grave, wrapped in the lyrics like a shroud. The boys didn't like to think of their Lovely Angel lying in his grave. John was the most inquisitive of the boys. He often wondered how long it took a body to decompose. What would our Lovely Angel look like now, he wondered, if we dug him up and opened his coffin? How would he smell? They were questions that haunted him at night and he would wake from nightmares, convinced he would see the stain of earth on his hands.

The boys were all agreed that Sundays were the worst day of the week.

Chapter Five

The church brogues were a little too big, the leather stretched and shapeless with ample feet that had forced their way in and out of them every week. The tweed skirt had to be held up and cinched tight with a belt. The double string of pearls hung almost to the waistband of the skirt.

'It's so difficult getting clothes to fit these days,' said the false, cultured tone.

Makeup lay strewn across the glass top of the kidney-shaped dressing table. 'Now, then, which lipstick shall I wear today? Something subtle, I think. Oh dear, I don't have anything subtle. Cherry Bomb Explosion number sixteen, yes that sounds about right. It'll just have to do.'

The evening meal was ready. The boys were assembled at the table and standing to attention behind their chairs until grace had been said and they were given the instruction to sit. Violet pursed her lips in irritation; she was always tense on a Wednesday evening. What made her mood black this week was the fact that Donald had refused to come in to eat again. This was the third meal he'd missed that week. Violet was a staunch believer in the adage, 'A family that eats together, stays together,' and she had no intention of letting any of her family escape. She glared, first at her husband's setting, and then, at the only other chair that didn't have a boy standing behind it. Where was he? He was her most sensitive son, the one with an artistic personality, prone to tantrums and flares of temperament. He was the one who would go off by himself to find somewhere to read. He liked to be alone.

'Oh, for goodness sake, go and get him,' she said irritably and to nobody in particular.

The child nearest the door replied with a courteous, 'Yes, Mummy,' and left the room, remembering not to run like a hooligan in his mother's presence. The boy, who would one day become a Master forger knew that his brother would be for it because he was late for a meal. Violet didn't hold with people being late to her table, she didn't hold with anything on a Wednesday. He wanted to find his older brother and bring him to the dining room fast. Once he knew he was out of his mother's earshot he called his name and ran down the corridor, his slippers flapping time on the cool Mediterranean tiles.

The foundation was messy and took awhile to rub in. It stuck to his hands and he had nothing to wipe them on. If he left handprints on any of his mother's fine bathroom linen she'd know somebody had been in her room. That would be crime enough, but Lord forbid she ever discovered what he did on a Wednesday afternoon when he knew she was out for hours. It didn't bear thinking about. He went into the en suite bathroom and washed his hands carefully in the basin. He covered the top of the soap in Autumn Glow foundation and then

38

had to wash the soap as well as his hands. That got soap all over his hands again so he had to wash and rinse several times until he'd got rid of all the suds. He could see that it wasn't all glamour being a girl. He sat back down at his mother's vanity unit and applied a layer of pressed powder. He chose pale blue eye shadow; it brought out the lilac of his eyes. He kohl'ed his inner eyelid with black liner, rouged his cheeks with pink blush, reddened his lips with Cherry Bomb Explosion and finished the look with a thick application of black mascara. The end result looked sultry and feminine. He didn't look like a boy playing with makeup, but a girl with a practised hand. His high cheekbones and full lips made the perfect canvas for his art. Anybody seeing him for the first time might have queried why she was wearing her mum's clothes, but they would have thought she looked beautiful.

He lamented his mother's lack of fashionable clothing. Serviceable tweeds and polyester slacks were the norm for Violet Woods. She had a large selection of special eveningwear for socialising with the Lakeland elite, kept in polythene from the dry-cleaners. How he longed to get hold of those dresses with the black lace and sequins.

He'd been doing this for months now. It was more than just an urge, it was a compulsion. He twirled in the full length mirror, satisfied with his look. Now that he had finished with the intense concentration of putting the makeup on, another part of his mind was taking over. Mother had just one fine item, one piece of feminine clothing that he adored.

Donald, hoping to rekindle their love life, had brought home a pair of delicate French knickers one Valentine's Day. Violet was appalled. It just wasn't a man's place to buy underwear. It wasn't seemly. They had a terrible row. After forcing him to tell her where he'd bought them, Violet said that she wouldn't be able to shop in Kendal ever again. Donald argued that a large place like Debenhams in Kendal was hardly likely to remember one nondescript man buying a pair of knickers for his wife.

'Donald.' Violet had admonished. 'Please don't use that word; it's vulgar and most unchristian for a gentleman to be talking about a lady's under garments in such terms.'

Violet was shocked by her husband's behaviour. Valentine's Day — what piffle, she thought as she stuffed the baby pink knickers to the back of her drawer and out of sight. She was happy with her Marks & Spencer underwear in a hundred percent cotton with breathable gusset. Anything else just wasn't hygienic.

The cross-dressing boy had no idea where the knickers had come from but he was delighted that they had. He wore them under the frumpy old skirt. They felt decadent and the heavy silk lining under the tweed was forcing the smooth satin of the panties against his young body. His penis, on the cusp of puberty, was rock hard, his heart racing as he posed this way and that. He felt the cold material moving against his turgid penis and it felt wonderful.

He lay on his mother's bed and pulled the skirt high on his slim thighs so that he could see himself grown under the sheer material of the French knickers. They were just like boxer shorts really, but without the fly. But boxers had never felt this sumptuous. He fantasised about wearing the satin under his school uniform. The thought was dangerous and exciting. He could only do it on days when he wouldn't have to change for PE. It would be his special secret. He would never have the courage do actually do it, but just the thought of it was enough to make him want to touch himself. He did, tentatively at first. But instinct overtook him and had taught him how to manipulate his penis within a fistful of baby pink satin. And that's when the new fantasy was born. It was an idea so wrong and so sinful that it put interfering with oneself into the baby-sin bucket. It was wrong. It was dirty and wrong, but it drove him mad with the thought of doing it. His whole body tensed as his hand flew. He felt a strange tightening in his stomach and, seconds later, he experienced a sensation that was new, a little bit scary and all encompassing. He had his first ever ejaculation and it left him shocked and quivering.

His mind was in turmoil. He'd made a mess in his mother's panties. Surely he would go to hell for such a sin. His penis was flaccid now, but his mind was still turgid. The idea that had formulated as he interfered with himself wouldn't leave. He cleaned the mess and washed the underwear under the tap. What was he going to do with it now? He couldn't put them back in her drawer, soaking wet. He couldn't put them on the radiator to dry.

In desperation, he flushed them down the toilet. Imagining them getting stuck in the piping and flooding out the entire hotel. He was scared as he tried to cover his tracks. What if Mother found out? He felt guilty and dirty but he lamented the loss of the satin knickers. He put his own pants back on. He was shaking and hadn't had time to replay and think about what had just happened. He intended to take the makeup off but he needed to sit down for a moment. He lay back on the pillows of his mother's bed, still in her blouse, wearing her pearls and her makeup. He closed his eyes to think and seconds later he drifted into sleep. He dreamed of hotel rooms filled with sensual female clothing and in his sleep his body reacted again.

He heard somebody calling his name. In his dream, he was dressed in lace underwear, a sable fur coat and high heels. The voice was pulling him out of the soft fur; he didn't want to come out of sleep. It was nice. He heard his name again and opened his eyes. He was awake. The bedroom door was opening. He panicked. He mustn't be caught like this.

The bothers stared at each other. Neither of them spoke. The cross-dresser with the painted face and pearls dangling in his lap was the first to drop his eyes. He looked at the erection pushing through the skirt, alerting his brother so that his eyes, too, focussed there.

The forger tugged at his hair, the way he always did when something upset him. His brother could see that he was shocked and disgusted. And the fact that he didn't mock or tease the cross dresser showed that it went too deep for that.

'Get out. Get out.' the cross-dresser hissed as though the intruder was the one in the wrong. He was angry, the rouge on his cheeks standing out on his pale face, his bright red lips pursed in temper. His blue, lidded eyes flared angrily.

'I'll cover for you. Hurry up and come down, you're late for dinner and Mother's furious.' The forger closed the door behind him and walked back to the dining room, buying himself as much time as possible to make up an excuse for his brother's absence. He could have stayed a few moments to help tidy up the room so that his mother wouldn't know anybody had been in, but he didn't want to see his brother taking off the painted face. It was obscene and seeing it come off would have been too reminiscent of it going on, and he wanted no part of that.

The Cross-dresser arrived at the table, grey with fear and apprehension. Was his dirty secret out in the open, exposed for them all to make of it what they would? Or was his brother as good as his word? His pallor served their purpose well and backed up the story that he had been sick. Mother showed maternal concern for half a minute, asking if he was all right before firing a barrage of questions at him to find out what he'd been eating while she was out. Had he been at the fruit trees in the orchard? Had he taken sweets from one of the guests?

Had he been associating with dirty children from the estate who might have countless untold and horrendous viruses and illness? She was hungry and impatient to eat and finished her inquisition by telling him how disappointed she'd be with him if he vomited at the dining table. The matter, as far as she was concerned, was closed. He was well enough to walk, therefore he was well enough to eat the meal the good Lord—and the kitchen staff—had provided for him.

When Mother turned her attention to the tureen of roasted parsnips, two pairs of eyes met over the table. The forger dropped his gaze. And the secret that was shared between them remained just that, a secret. A third pair of youthful eyes caught the look. The eavesdropper realised something had happened and he made a mental note to find out what it was from his brothers later, but a game of cricket was organised for the evening and the vibes he had seen crossing the table were forgotten by the time the meal was finished.

Over the following week the cross-dresser's mind was congested with the fantasy of going into the guests' rooms to steal clothes and makeup, some nice jewellery, too. It was the middle of the summer holidays, the hotel was booked solid, the weather was hot and the women were walking round in flimsy dresses and shorts that showed all their thighs. He took to sitting in one of the Chesterfield armchairs in reception. He watched the women passing through the foyer, his penis pushing hard against the material of his shorts. He wasn't very interested in the women and girls, mainly how they dressed and carried themselves. He studied their styles, the way they moved. The way he wanted to look and move. He made notes about which guest occupied which room and the fantasy of sneaking through them and stealing their pretty things became a burning desire.

The following Wednesday took an age to come. He sat at breakfast that morning with two spots of high colour to his cheeks and an uncomfortable erection hidden under the table. It was still a dream. He had no intention of actually doing anything. For another hour and a half it was just a fantasy borne in the mind of a young pubescent discovering himself.

His brother's were cycling to Fell Foot Park for the day. It was perfect; they'd be gone for hours. That left him alone to trawl the corridors of the vast hotel undetected. He'd learned that young boys have an uncanny knack of passing unnoticed among adults. He could check in the register to see which guests had left their keys, and had gone off for the day. It would be easy to take his mother's master key from the hook in her private office, nobody would notice. But it was just a dream. The others tried to get him to go with them, but he said he wanted to finish the book he was reading. The forger looked at him accusingly and he slopped orange juice from his glass. His mother was too preoccupied with her own Wednesday thoughts to notice.

He waited for a long time after the other boys had gone. His mother left before them and he checked that his father was still taking some fresh produce to the local market that day. He walked around the upper storeys of the hotel for the first hour, talking to the chambermaids and mentally marking their progress along the corridors. He saw a couple leaving room 506. They were full of chatter about sailing on The Swan across Lake Windermere. He watched them go round the corner, listened to the lady's clicking heels descending the stairs, and his heartbeat quickened in his chest. He walked by their room and tried the door. It was locked. This was the defining moment. The second that turned his fantasy into reality. He was going to do it.

Getting his mother's key was as easy as he had expected it to be. Checking the hotel keyboard proved more difficult, but he bided his time until the receptionist was called away. He slipped behind the desk and into the general office where an enormous board with hanging keys covered the back wall. Guests were encouraged to leave their room keys at reception when they left the hotel in case of loss. The pegs were two thirds occupied with room keys and a volt of adrenaline shot through his body.

He contemplated cycling into town to have a copy of the master key made, but he had no money. He had lots of time, but didn't want to waste any of it by going into town. He had far more exciting things to do. And anyway, he promised himself this was a one off. It would be too risky to do it again, just today, just once. Only today. He'd have to make sure he found lots of the right things first time.

It would have served his purpose well to be able to jot down the vacant room numbers but that would have been too dangerous. If he was observed, difficult questions would have to be answered; he contented himself with writing to memory the first five numbers under the pegs with keys hanging from them.

Making sure the chambermaids were nowhere in sight and that the corridor was clear of guests, he rapped on the first door. He hadn't a clue what he would say if anybody answered and was ready to run at the slightest noise from within. He was terrified. His mouth was dry and tasted metallic and he could feel his heartbeat through the artery in his throat.

There was no answer; with trembling hands he let himself into the room. It was empty. The bed was made and everything was neat and tidy, despite the chambermaids not having got that far on their cleaning rounds yet. The only sign of habitation was the towelling dressing gown, hanging on the back of the door and the neatly folded, *Observer* newspaper, beside the bed.

He was disappointed, a quick search of the drawers showed that, despite it being a double room, only one person inhabited it, a man. He rifled through the guests' belongings, making as little disturbance as possible. In the shallow bedside cabinet drawer, he found some lose money, about two pounds in all. He almost took it. He picked it up and felt the weight of the coins in his hand. There might be enough to pay for a duplicate key but it would be stealing. He was going to steal, he had every intention of stealing, that's what he'd come for, but he wanted to keep his sins down to a low number, and taking actual money seemed worse and more sinful than taking somebody's old clothes and stuff. He put the money back, checked to see that nothing was out of place and after peeping around the door to see that the corridor was empty, he slipped back out of the room, locking the door behind him.

The second room was better. The bed was made but the place wasn't as tidy as the last room had been. Damp towels were thrown on the end of the bed. Mother wouldn't approve of that. He picked them up, folded them and put them neatly side by side on the towel rail in the en suite bathroom. He stepped over a pair of tiny black panties; they were scrunched up and had been worn. He felt a jolt at the thought that if there was one pair, then there would surely be more. He didn't like the thought of touching underwear that had been used. What kind of a lady left her dirty linen on the bathroom floor? He crossed the room, but the thought of those tiny panties drew him back. He picked them up. He rubbed them through his hands, liking the soft feel of them. His fingers found the double layer of the gusset. His penis jerked and rose in his pants as his thumb was the first digit to find the stuff. It had stiffened in the crotch of the panties and it cracked as he bent the material. He saw the white staining, and a tiny flake of something that had once been wet but had recently dried, fell onto his hand. He pulled the underwear up to his nose and rubbed the stained part across his nostrils. The smell wasn't strong, almost undetectable. He had no idea whether it was female stuff or male stuff that had leaked from the woman, but he knew that it was the smell of sex. He'd pulled on himself everyday since that first time. He wanted to do it now. He had to squirt his own stuff on top of the stain that was already there. The need to do it was unbearable but he might be caught. He stuffed the panties into his pocket, forced his mind back to the real job in hand, and breathed heavily as he waited for his boyhood to shrink back into itself.

The room was an Aladdin's cave of treasures. Bottles of exotic creams and lotions, shampoos and bubble bath filled the shelves in the bathroom. The vanity unit had perfume in fancy bottles and makeup left out. Bracelets and necklaces were strewn amidst the lipstick and blusher. The people in this room had left in a hurry. The wardrobe was hung with shimmering dresses and elegant trouser suits. And, joy of joys, the top drawer of the dresser was filled with nylon stockings and sinful lingerie.

That first day he only took a few small things. He took a necklace with pretty blue stones set in a crescent shaped pendant, a chiffon scarf that smelled strongly of a sophisticated perfume, two pairs of sexy panties and a pair of stockings. It was only later, in his own room, that he discovered that you had to have something to hold the stockings up and he had no idea what that something was.

From another room, he took more panties and a black lacy bra. And from a third, he took a broach in the shape of a heart and a pink underskirt. He was tempted by a bottle of perfume; it looked expensive and had a French name. The bottle was so pretty he wanted it, but when could he wear it? Somebody would notice that he had ladies perfume on. He didn't have to wear it though, did he? Just having it, owning it, knowing that it belonged to him would be enough. It would be there. It would be his. He could smell it and imagine what it would be like to dab some on the pressure points of his neck. He felt the stirrings of sexual arousal again and hovered with the perfume bottle in his hand. The things he had taken might not be noticed immediately if he was lucky. He reasoned that the jewellery might be expensive; he had no way of knowing what was good and what wasn't. But jewellery was so small that somebody might not notice that a piece was missing until they came to want it. He knew that his mother wore the same perfume every day. *J' Taime* by Estee Lauder. His mother would notice if a bottle was stolen, but then his mother would probably notice if a hairgrip was out of place. He wanted the perfume. It was so pretty, so feminine—and too risky. He left it, taking instead some lose change that had been thrown into an otherwise empty trinket dish on the vanity unit and a pale pink lipstick. He didn't take all of the money that was there, and hoped that fifty-three pence would be enough to have the key replicated.

That was the year that The Halcyon Woods Hotel

experienced a spate of thefts. The proprietor, Mrs Violet Woods, made several statements to the police and to the local press, saying that she would not rest until this despicable thief had been caught and taken to book. It had to be a member of staff. The police were ruling nothing out, and at that stage, they had to assume by the nature of articles stolen, that it was a female member of staff, probably one of the chambermaids. The staff were all fingerprinted and released without charge. It was a terrible business and not good for the hotel's reputation.

The day the police came to take statements and fingerprint all the staff, he was ill. He vomited several times, guilt rising with the gorge from his stomach. He waited in his room, expecting the police to come for him at any moment, but they didn't come at all.

They returned several times over the following months. He assumed that the police hadn't worked out that the spate of thefts coincided with the school holiday but they had. The focus of the investigation shifted to the casual staff that Violet employed in the holidays to help out with the seasonal rush. They tracked the school holidays for several terms and then, when the Windermere secondary school let out for their summer break, there were no thefts. It blew the police theory out of the water. There were a few small incidents two weeks later when Guildmarten Head public boy's school had their term end. These rose to another full on assault of guests missing property as the long summer months unfolded. The case was never solved.

He felt invincible. The stupid police were too dumb to catch him. He was purposefully sloppy, leaving little clues for them to pick up, but they never associated the thefts to the son of the proprietor. He was beyond reproach and the Woods` boys were never formally questioned.

He was caught once. That had been hairy. There he was, not only in somebody's room, but rifling through the woman's knicker drawer when her stupid husband walked in.

He'd been marvellous. All the guests knew the children of Mrs Woods. The man recognised him. While he demanded to know what was going on, the cross dresser stood up and stammered, pretending to be confused. He wasn't frightened. This was the first time he'd ever been caught since his brother found him in his mother's clothes, and yet he was calm and composed. He fed the man a line about his mother asking him to come up to Mrs Burton-Graham's room for her spectacles. He said he was very sorry and could see that he had mistaken room 432 for 423 in his haste. The man clapped him on the back and said what a fine boy he was, how he was a credit to his mother. And that was the end of it. He was concerned that the tale would get back to Mother, but it didn't.

He was untouchable.

It was after that incident that he used the facilities. He would shower in the rooms, take long bubble-baths and use the guest's cosmetics in-situ. He dressed in their clothes, ate whatever edibles were left in their rooms and made himself tea with the tea-making facilities.

He had his secret room. The attics in the hotel were immense. Room after dingy room sat at the very top of the house, most of them empty and unopened in years. The boys had been forbidden from going up to the attic years ago when they were young and played hide and seek up there. Mother considered it a dangerous place for them to be. And then they grew up and although some of the rooms were used for storage, most of them were empty. He'd taken one of those. During the police investigations only the staff were suspected. None of the workforce lived in, so the hotel was never searched. He had fixed external and internal locks to the door in case it was ever found. He had the only keys. It was risky and he knew that one day his room would be discovered, but nobody would ever link it back to him.

He found his greatest treasure. He entered a guest's room and almost hit the ceiling with shock. There was somebody there, sitting at the dressing table. It was only when the shock faded that he saw that it wasn't a person at all. It was a polystyrene head with a long auburn wig attached. It was beautiful. He had to have it. He'd become selective over the months. He no longer took indiscriminately. Clothes had to be designer. Perfume had to be the best. He never used it, but had a collection of fine fragrances that he knew would be his to wear one day. His tastes in jewellery had refined, he took only gold and precious stones. He would have traded his entire collection for that one wig.

He put it on and felt the long curls cascade down his back. He masturbated on the woman's bed, naked apart from the fabulous wig. In that wig he was a woman.

His need for danger and excitement were more enhanced too. He had stolen for over three years. He was fifteen and his mother didn't terrify him the way she used to. Part of him wanted to be caught, but another part still craved his mother's love and pride. He hated the fact that he yearned for her approval.

Two weeks before he went away to begin his chef training, he decided to go out with a bang. He'd be caught, but he needed the excitement. Just as he had played with his ideas that first week before he committed any crime, he fantasised about the way his coming out as a cross-dresser would go.

They had a talent contest scheduled for that night. The entire hotel was to be there. His mother in her finery, his father in a suit, all his brothers, the ones with stubble, shaved, the ones without, their faces gleaming. It was a charity bash and Mother was so good at charity.

He dressed with care. He wore stilettos and walked on them with more grace than many women that he'd seen. He wore stockings and a short skirt, a bat-winged top that was currently popular and a wide belt, almost as broad as the skirt beneath it. He spent more time than usual putting on his makeup and when he donned the wig, he truly felt like a natural born woman.

When he walked through the hotel, heads turned.

Everybody looked at the stunning woman; it was that kind of look. He walked past his mother's table. Looked right into her eyes. She glared her disapproval. She didn't hold with hussies flaunting their bodies for men to be tempted. She didn't like strumpet in her hotel. Two of his brothers were talking to girls at another table; they looked up as the stunner passed by. The other two brothers were standing at the bar. They stared as he walked between them with a polite, 'Excuse me, please.' It was a buzz. Nobody recognised him. He was a butterfly in the light, a chameleon—he was untouchable.

Chapter Six

18ᵗʰ July, 1979

The residents didn't go on trips very often.

They weren't called children on Hathaway wing. Simon didn't like moving to Hathaway when he was eighteen, he was happy on Bronte. He was very worried that Mummy wouldn't be able to find him. She always waited in his bedroom. But it wasn't his bedroom anymore. It belonged to somebody else. He worried that his mummy belonged to somebody else, too. Maybe part of him even wished she did, and that made him feel bad. Simon loved his mummy and was a bad boy for thinking bad things. Sometimes, when she was shouting at him, Simon imagined his mummy burning in a big orange fire. He tried really hard to not think bad things about her because she often seemed to know what he was thinking and if she knew he was watching her burn in a big fire, she would be mad with him again. She pinched him sometimes, when his tongue flopped out, and he couldn't help that. Simon couldn't imagine what she'd do if she knew about the fire stuff. He was good at imagining fire stuff, but not good at knowing what Mummy would do. He just knew that she was always mad at him.

They were going on a big bus. But it was Tuesday. They always banged drums and tangerines and sang *This Old Man He Had One* on a Tuesday. Simon didn't want to go on a big bus, he wanted to go on the school bus to school and bang drums and sing *This Old Man He Had One*. Sharon Peat always got sick on big buses that went far. Gloria said they weren't going far, only to Lancaster and that Sharon would be fine, because she'd given her a tablet. She said he'd like it at Williamson's Park. But it was Tuesday. He moved from one foot to the other, and Gloria sighed and gave him a tablet, too.

David, one of the helpers, pushed Simon from behind while Gloria and Helen pulled him from the front. He didn't want to sit on the fifth row back; he always sat on the second row. That's where he sat when he went to school. Mike didn't mind moving from the second row seat. He couldn't talk and he didn't mind about anything much. Simon sat quietly on the bus. His eyes glazed and his tongue lolled out of his half-open mouth. He thought about drums and hummed *This Old Man*. Gloria sang it and some people joined in until Sharon started to be sick. It wasn't the same without drums and his blue tangerine, anyway.

Williamson's Park was lovely but there were too many hills and lots of steps and his legs hurt. Gloria said he'd complain about the colours in paradise. Simon had never been there so didn't know if he'd like the colours or not, but he knew that he was hot and that his feet were hurting.

They had a picnic in the shadow of the Ashworth Memorial building. It was a beautiful day. Sharon had stopped being sick and wanted lots to eat but Gloria wouldn't let her have lots because they still had to go home in the big bus. Simon thought that Sharon should walk home, because she made the big bus smell really bad.

After lunch they went to see the butterflies. The butterfly house had some lizards and bats and was hot. Simon liked them but was glad they couldn't get out of their homes. Gloria was fascinated by all the plants but Simon didn't like the way the butterflies were just there, not fastened up or tied down or anything. He wondered what it would be like if one of them fluttered near his face. He gave his low moaning noise that sometimes came just before and during an epileptic fit, but sometimes he did that noise anyway so Gloria held his hand and promised him that nothing would hurt him. Up to that point they had only seen little butterflies. Rounding a corner, they saw an orchid, but the beauty of the flower faded next to the enormous butterfly that was resting on it. Simon couldn't understand how something so big didn't make the flower bend all the way over until its head fell off.

Gloria was in her element. She scrambled through the guidebook that had a section on identifying all the species of butterfly. It cost her three pounds ninety-nine at the door and Simon thought that was probably more than a pound. He wasn't impressed. Gloria let go of his hand to find the big butterfly. Simon was scared. If the big monster fluttered near his face it would cover him completely and he might not be able to breathe. It was hot in the butterfly house and he could feel his chest tightening and thought that he'd drown.

A man called Callum was taking them round. He was a guide and told them all about the different species of animals and flowers. He was very interesting and Gloria listened to him while scrabbling through the book for a picture of the massive butterfly. She liked to do things herself sometimes and didn't wait for the man to tell them about it. Simon was bored. He was hot and uncomfortable, too, and he was uneasy and nervous, all symptoms that led to his agitation.

'Ah, here we are,' said Gloria, grinning like a fool. Couldn't she see the danger? 'It's a Goliath butterfly and guess what, Simon? It's the second biggest species in the world and has a wingspan of almost a foot. They can only be found in Indonesia. Aren't we lucky to see such a beautiful thing right here in Lancas —?'

The butterfly chose that moment to flex its wings. It fluttered, once, like a tablecloth lifted in a breeze and then it rose resplendent into the air. As it lifted, Simon saw its ugly little face and realised that butterflies aren't pretty at all, it's just an act they put on to fool people they want to drown. The butterfly had the face of a bluebottle only much, much bigger. Its beady little eyes peered into his and the long black things called antennae twitched towards his face.

They hadn't seen the birds yet. As if on cue, there was an enormous batting of wings that Simon thought was coming from the butterfly. Simon didn't like wings, they sounded dry and feathery. The hot house smelled bad. It smelled old and green and rotten. He knew the butterfly was big but he couldn't understand that it could make so much noise just by flapping its wings. If he'd looked up he would have seen the real culprits, but Simon was transfixed on the butterfly that was coming to suffocate him.

The miniature murmuration of starlings rose as one. They did a circuit of the hothouse before looping the loop and swooping down on the visitor's heads. People squealed in delight as the birds landed on them hoping for pickings from the specially prepared bags of birdfeed. The cheeky birds were gentle but greedy and they dive-bombed the visitors with aeronautical precision, never missing their mark.

Simon didn't have a bag of food but he waved his arms in the air and that attracted the bird's attention. Three of the starlings flew towards him. He wasn't moaning now, he was screaming. The birds landed on him, two on his arms and one on the top of his head. They were screeching. The noise was cacophonous, echoing in the stillness of the hothouse.

Gloria tried to calm him, but he was a large man-child in a frenzy of terror and easily fought her off. People stopped what they were doing to watch the Downs bloke having some sort of fit. Mothers grabbed their children to them. The world slowed down.

Callum ran towards Simon, their female Goliath was right in front of the Mongol's face. She was their most valuable exhibit. He made three steps while Simon thrashed. The starlings took flight and rose into the air, adding to the mayhem, their wings beating, beating, fluttering and beating. The noise was too loud, amplified in his rush of adrenaline. Simon beat them off, catching one on its tail feathers and knocking it into a spin. It landed safety on the floor, shook itself and rose again to perch somewhere high up and safe. Still there was the beating in his ears, loud droning. Too hot, the place was too hot. He couldn't breathe.

His arm came down fast, smashing into the valuable Goliath. She fluttered to the floor and lay twitching for a second, broken. Simon didn't notice. He was too far into his panic to see. His feet pounded on the dying butterfly, ripping its delicate wings and turning it to dust on the floor.

The crowd gasped. Gloria moaned just the way Simon did when he got upset. A piece of green wing with a black, 'eye,' blot looking towards him hung over the front of Simon's shoe.

Callum reached out to Simon. His fingers made contact with the sleeve of his shirt. Simon batted him away as though he was just another butterfly.

He was running for the exit. He didn't mean to knock the children over. He didn't see them. All he could see was wings flapping around him. All he could hear was the beating, thrumming boom of wings. All he could feel was his terror. He pushed a little girl. She lost her balance and her father's arm shot out too slowly to catch her. She teetered for a moment on the brink of the edge before falling with a loud splash into the water with the Koi carp. A warder jumped in to save her before she was hurt or came to any real harm. Simon came into contact with four children, innocent children, and several adults, all of them with wide frightened eyes, all fighting to get out of his way. The children were knocked to the ground, into water or bashed into walls. Adults screamed about assault and yelled for the police to be called.

Callum was chasing him. He saw the beautiful Goliath, so gentle, so serene, cut down and killed by the Mongol. People like that shouldn't be allowed out in public. They should be locked up and kept away from decent folk. He had cared for and tended all the butterflies for four years, but the Goliath was his favourite. He didn't tell any of his mates, but he called her Lotus, sometimes she'd rest on him and he talked to her. People would say he was mad, but he liked to think that she knew him and waited for him coming in each morning.

He was so mad that when he got hold of him, he was going to punch that stupid retard's face. All Lotus ever did was make people happy. What had the spastic ever done to make anybody happy with his fat body and mongy face? Where was the beauty in that great useless lump of humanity?

He caught up with Simon by the face painting stall. Clowns and tigers, monkeys and vampires, turned to stare with wide, innocent eyes. A second throng of panicked parents, sensing danger, drew their young into their embrace.

Callum, tears of anger and loss stinging his eyes, let out a bellow and flew through the air towards Simon's legs. He caught him in a rugby tackle and Simon turned to face his danger before going down on his back. The rucksack he always wore protected his back from the hard concrete, but his head made contact with a sickening crunch. Again the world slewed and Gloria was in time to see Simon's head bounce off the paving. He'd bitten his tongue and a line of spittle and blood hit Callum in the chest. Simon's eyes were wide and pleading for mercy.

People screamed, a crowd forming a circle around the action. Ghouls moving forward to better see what was happening. Callum straddled Simon and drew back his right arm to punch him full in the face.

He stopped mid swing, appalled at what he was about to do. Beating a handicapped person. All the fight left him and his fist fell to his side. People jumped at him to pull him away. He rolled off Simon and held out a hand to help the boy to his feet.

It was too much. Simon's eyes flickered erratically before turning up and rolling backwards, showing only the whites. His body jerked and spasmed. Pink, foamy spittle frothed out of the corners of his mouth. He made the low cow noise. It looked as though a demented puppeteer was pulling at his arms and legs to make them jerk. But Simon was away from it all, he was in the peaceful place.

He woke up several times in the hospital. He'd taken a nasty knock to the head and done more damage during the seizure. He asked for his mummy and Gloria promised to get her.

But Mummy was too busy to come. It was Tuesday,

not Wednesday, so she didn't have a window.

When she did come, she was angry. She called him names and said that if she'd known what he was, the good Lord could strike her down stone, stiff dead, but she'd never have had him.

Simon didn't blame his mummy for not wanting him for what he was. It was horrible being a butterfly killer.

Chapter Seven

Violet hated watching the boys become men. One by one they slipped through her fingers and were not just her boys, but people in their own right. She had held them to her, protected them from the world. They were little projections of her, innocents in need of firm management.

She stood open mouthed and speechless the first time one of them had risen in front of her and openly defied her command. He knew his own mind, that boy of hers. He was her strong one. He was a fifteen year-old hippy the first time he stood, hands on hips, furious points of crimson on his cheeks and said, 'Mother, I will not have time to practise my trombone tonight. I have other plans.' Where was the wheedling voice? 'Aw, do I have to?' It was the most rebellious thing any of them had ever said to her.

He didn't sound like her son, this gruff-voiced man-becoming with determination blazing in his eyes.

'You will do whatever I tell you to do, my boy.'

'I'm sorry, Mother, I don't want to argue with you. But I've had enough of practising my trombone every night, followed by another hour on the violin, followed by a third of homework before bed. From now on, I'll play when I want to play. I've put in the practice. Since I was eight years-old I've practiced my music for two hours a night, five days a week. Surely music is supposed to be a passion, something inside you. I'm coming to detest my music. You are driving me to hate it.'

'How dare you stand there hurling your unfounded accusations? Do you have any idea how much I've spent on you and your brothers, so that you can attain the high standard you have as competent musicians? All I ask is a little hard work in return. A little dedication, is that too much to wish for? A little loyalty from my own flesh and blood. That awful rock and roll babble that you try and call music is rotting your brain, child.'

It was the same old tired guilt trip, she knew she relied on aged material, dredged up every time one of them dared to disagree with her, but it had always worked before.

'And, what's more, I think it's time we all had our own bedrooms. All our lives we've had to share. Will you please at least think about it, Mother?' He left the room, his too-long-for-his-body legs taking giant strides across the Axminster carpet, his broadening shoulders flung back and defiant. He left her standing there, mid-lecture, without waiting at attention to be dismissed. 'Fucking bitch,' he said, too far from her and too low to be heard.

'Come back here right now. Don't you dare walk away from me. You just wait until I tell your father,' she yelled after him. That was a first, too; Violet had never relied on Donald for back up in any situation. She had never needed to.

She lost him that day. In standing up to her, he

made the transition from boy to man. He stayed, until he was sixteen and school was finished for good, but he was the first of the Woods` boys to leave home. He knew the day he left that he would never live under his mother's smothering control again. He went to college and, from there, to university studying mathematics and the sciences. Watching him leave home broke his mother's heart for ten minutes, but she recovered nicely in time for the seven-thirty pensioners' bingo.

The day of the argument, he stormed to his room, resolute and determined that he would continue to make a stand against Violet's bullying ways. Not knowing what to do with his allocated music practise time, he took apart a transistor radio that had broken months before. He loved anything technical or with working parts and he broke down every component of the radio that could be taken to bits. He cleaned each piece on a soft cloth and assembled them methodically in front of him. He gave thought to putting it back together. His fingers worked deftly. Instinct, more than memory, told him where each component belonged and in a short time he was turning the dial on the old fashioned radio to find a station. His mood was calm and tranquil; he was doing what he loved to do.

The first station he found came alive beneath his fingers in a hiss of sibilant static. A song was playing that he didn't know. He wasn't listening to it. He was too busy being pleased with himself for fixing a radio that half an hour earlier had been destined for the dustbin. Something happened to him that afternoon, sitting on his knees on the bedroom floor, his eyes glowing with calm and quiet pleasure, the words coming out of the radio seemed to be sung just for his ears. He straightened and listened closely.

If I could save time in a bottle,
The first thing that I'd like to do,
Is save everyday 'til eternity passes,
So I could spend each day with you.

That single verse held his future in its melody. As though a light had shone through the ceiling and slapped him on the head, he knew what he was going to do with the rest of his life. The hippy, who that day had stood up to his domineering mother, was going to make time.

Violet was wary of him from that afternoon. He was different. He had a grown-up confidence and wasn't as malleable. She was frightened that this new found independence would rub off on the rest of her children. She had their futures written, their careers mapped out. They would follow their parents into the family business. She wanted all of her boys to work in the hotel, all in positions of responsibility, pulling together to make it better than it already was. The Halcyon Woods Hotel was a family affair and she fully intended to keep it that way. Her boys would be allowed to go off and finish their education at university. She would even permit them a year to play on the continent—and find themselves— if she had to. That was the fashionable thing. But it was always understood that the boys would return after their year out, funded by Violet as a bribe, to take their rightful positions in the business. They had been groomed for it since they were old enough to stand. One day, Violet and Donald would hand over the reins of the company to their children. It was already written.

The fraudster was her clever boy, although she didn't know he would become one. He was happy to slot into the role his mother had carved out of the lodestone for him. He had no ambition or dreams of his own and was willing to float on the prophecies of Violet. After all, it was in his best interests to do so. The fraudster did all his wrong doings well away from his mother's sight. He never challenged her in any way. He passed from boy to man without a cross word. It was never once threatened that he would be struck from the parental heritage. He worked hard at manipulating his mother, while all the time keeping her sweet. He went from public school to university, reading mathematics and science like his brother, but alongside those subjects, he crammed hard to fit in an accountancy course and a degree in hotel management. His life-road was charted and he saw no valid reason to veer from it.

Like his brother with the preference for pink, he took stupid chances. Occasionally, when the bar areas were deserted for whatever reason, the fraudster would swoop in, calculating as a magpie, and steal from the till. It was two years before security cameras would be installed but, by the time they were, the first four Woods boys were all pursuing their education elsewhere. There were sackings, and raised indignant voices when the tills were found to be down. Violet had no time for the innocent until proven guilty clause that the rest of Britain clung to as being right. If money could not be accounted for in one of the Halcyon Woods tills, then whoever had control of that till, at that time, was removed from her employment. Along with the other spate of thefts, the finger of accusation never stuck its bony presence in any of her children's faces.

The eavesdropper was her thoughtful boy, but didn't care for others. Thoughtful was the only adjective she could find to suit this son who wasn't always a nice person—sly would have fit him better, but Violent stuck with thoughtful. She didn't like to see any unpleasant traits in her little men. Sly and cunning were two words that would have fit equally well, but she didn't like those at all. This boy flapped his ears at private conversation, pressed himself against closed doors to listen, and told tales out of school. He held no allegiance to anybody and was often labelled a grass and a turncoat by his brothers. The first sign of trouble, and without any form of discipline or torture, this one would sing like a canary in spring for the pure joy of doing it. He had a head for facts, but never used it for storing anything useful. All of his learning was deleted in favour of an empty head, in which to store gossip and salacious tittle-tattle. When he was twelve, he kept a journal. He was obsessed with filling it. Book after book was dutifully written and then locked securely away in his personal safe. For three years, when asked what he wanted for Christmas and Birthdays, he said he wanted his own safe to keep his personal stuff in. the other's wanted one, too, but for them it was only a whim. Violet sent men to manufacture a hole in the wall big enough to hold a small safe. He kept a picture of his mother over it and joked that it would deter any would-be safebreakers. His brother's all had a crack at opening the combination on the safe. They were never fewer than three numbers away from success.

He knew things.

And what he knew, he wrote in his journals.

He was her favourite boy. The one who would never leave her. He was devoted to his mother. He wanted to be like her in strength and character. His childhood had not been easy, but he felt that it had made him the fine man that he came to be. In truth, he wasn't a fine man at all. He was a mummy's boy, precious and pathetic. He debated at the debating society and came out with a swelled head, after shouting everybody down until he was hoarse. It didn't matter if his opinion was a valid one, only that he was heard. One by one, the other members stopped attending the society.

He made patches for clothes, he wanted to be a hippy like his brother, but his mother wouldn't let him grow his hair past his collar. He wasn't allowed to sew the patches he made onto his clothes either, so he made them with the intention of selling them to other people at festivals around the country. But his mother wouldn't let him go to festivals—rough places, full of dirty drop outs, she said—so he made his patches and kept them in a bag in his wardrobe. He liked to sit in the hotel foyer cutting pieces of felt and sewing them together, but Mother said he looked like a sissy, sitting in public sewing, so she made him go to his room, as though making patches was something to be ashamed of. He collected things, too. Beer mats and beer towels, stamps and patches, pin badges and dead insects, Super Cars cards and later, real super cars as they hit the market.

He took eggs from the nests of roosting birds.

He would have made the perfect bookworm, but he didn't like books. Reading took too much of his attention and he had no opportunity to voice his opinion. So he didn't enjoy reading at all. The only other thing he liked doing was talking at the guests. He'd hang around reception and then pounce. Sometimes he saw them poking their heads round the graphite pillars in reception before running very fast out of the door and down the drive to freedom. It didn't matter, and he wasn't offended, he'd catch them on their return.

Violet would stand at reception glowing with pride as she watched her friendly son, deep in conversation with a party of hotel guests. He was her ambassador and his arms would gesticulate with enthusiasm as he signalled the air or slapped the table for emphasis. This was the last of her children still at home. She wouldn't let him go—she wouldn't. He was such a good boy, this one.

The gambler liked to play cards. What started as a little bit of fun became a nuisance. He had to be stopped from looking for likely people to trap into a game of Newmarket for pennies. The gambler liked two things. He liked girls and he liked money, the latter because he discovered that money could buy him girls. He was fourteen when a fiver and ten fags bought him his first blow job. Suzie Philips had met him after their last period of the day. They found a quiet place in the Woods at the back of the hotel. She'd never sucked anybody off before, but the gambler had nothing to compare it to as far as good blow jobs went, and he blew like Old Yeller under high pressure build up.

She tried to kiss him afterwards but he didn't want any of that. 'I've got to go now,' he said, backing away and putting distance between them. 'I'll see you in school tomorrow.' He was a disgusted when he saw her trying to clear her throat and making little coughing noises but, if the price was right, he would definitely do it again.

'Hey, what about my fags and money?'

He walked back to her, pulled a crumpled five pound note out of his trouser pocket and handed it to her. He took a ten pack of Embassy No. 1 from the inside pocket of his school blazer, opened the cellophane, took a cigarette out of the pack and lit it, 'One for the road, babe.' He'd heard James Dean say that in a film. He thought it was cool. 'That was great, by the way; I need a fag after that. See you tomorrow.'

He threw the packet with the other nine cigarettes to her. She tried to catch them but failed and had to scramble in the fallen leaves to find them. He swaggered as he walked away and never looked back until he was sure that she'd left. He doubled back and met Pete Walker and Jamie Dodd at the clearing, they'd come out of the cover of the trees.

'You jammy bastard,' Pete said. 'I can't believe she just did that. She went with Robbie Jones and wouldn't even let him touch her tits.'

'I've still got a fucking hard on,' moaned Jamie. 'It's not fair, you get sucked off and we have to fucking pay for it.'

'Don't bet if you can't afford to lose. And speaking of which, gentlemen, I do believe you have some settling up to do.' The gambler was smiling. This was one of the best days ever.

The boys dug into the pockets of their school pants and pulled out their money. They coppered up two pounds fifty each and handed it over to the gambler. Jamie put his hand into his blazer pocket and brought out ten fags. He took the cellophane off, took one out of the packet and lit it. 'One for the road, mate. I need a fag after—'

The gambler snatched the lit cigarette from between his lips and put it in his own mouth. 'Some men are born to win and others will always be losers.' He grinned, turned his back on his mates and walked away, making sure that his strut was cool and his manner confidant.

At the other side of the clearing in the woods, a fourth boy was sitting with his back against a tree. The eavesdropper was writing furiously, his hand flying across the page. He had a sly smile on his face.

Violet was in her office, mornings were a time of brisk efficiency where none of the staff dare hardly breathe. It was her custom, from nine until luncheon, to review the mail, deal with customer complaints and meter out staff discipline.

Thumbing through the post, one envelope caught her attention, it was plain white, household brand and unremarkable in itself. What made it stand out was that it was typed—badly. The margins hadn't been set properly and the formatting of the address was misaligned. Whoever had typed this wasn't proficient in clerical skills. If it was a job application it would be going straight in the bin.

As she read the single sheet of paper, the colour drained from her face.

I know about your handicaped son.

Put fifty quid, in used ten pound notes, in an empty After Eight box.

There's a bin outside the nut house, just by the bus stop.

On Wednesday, when you go to visit, put the box with the cash inside the bin, just before you get on the 5-15 bus.

Do not tell nobody.

Do not go to the police.

If you unregard this letter

I will ruin you.

Violet pushed the letter into her pocket and took the rest of the day off. She read it many times over the course of the day. There was only one P in the word handicapped. Unregard was a word that Violet had never come across. But the thing that she couldn't get her head around was the sum of money that the blackmailer had demanded. Fifty pounds was a ridiculous sum. Violet assumed that the letter meant fifty thousand pounds, but it was specific— fifty pounds. Could the imagination of the blackmailer really be so limited? It had to be one of the staff at Great Gables, it couldn't be anybody else. They had promised to protect her identity from the general staff, it was enough that they had to know that she was the boy's mother. She would have them all sacked. They were useless anyway. But she didn't— when the time came, she didn't say a word. She treated herself to a small box of *After Eight* mints and gorged on them, making herself feel sick but not stopping until the box was empty. She wanted to feel sick.

The Eavesdropper was in the park across the road. There was a concrete tube, whether the council felt that it constituted modern art, or it was some flight of fancy of a psychologists idea of stimulation for young people, or if, indeed the council workmen had just dumped it when their job was done, wasn't clear. Youths smoked in it at night. He had a clear view of the bus stop from where he crouched.

Violet looked agitated. She had her crocodile skin handbag hooked over her arm and was holding her white gloves in the same hand. Every few seconds she would look around, up and down the street and into the windows of the care home, as if they held the answers that she was seeking. As the bus came around the corner, she opened her bag as though she was going to take out her fare. She pulled something out of it and turned to put it into the waste bin at the side of her before boarding the bus. The eavesdropper watched the bus pull away and saw his mother's gaunt, but fleshy, face pressed up against the window, staring towards the home.

Three weeks later he sent a second letter, this time asking for a hundred pounds, a week after that— a thousand. It was more money than he'd ever seen before. He took it out of his safe and counted it at night. He loved the feel of it, the sound of it, even the smell of it. He imagined buying his own casino. It was his dream.

During this period, Violet was distracted. She wasn't eating properly, skipping meals and then gorging herself on chocolates and biscuits long into the night. She didn't sleep and often she got up an hour after retiring to walk the corridors and sometimes the grounds at night. Every payment had escalated. It was well within her means for now, but if it continued, she'd be ruined. She had to go to the police. It couldn't continue. She'd be outted publicly as the mother of one of those people. She couldn't stand it.

The gambler knew that his brother was up to something. The eavesdropper was always shifty, it was inherent in his DNA, but he'd been acting oddly. The forger had noticed it too. He was scribbling in his stupid diaries more. On Wednesday afternoons he didn't walk home with the others anymore. He said he had somewhere to be. The gambler thought he had a secret girlfriend, until he found a crumpled type written envelope on the floor by his bed. It was addressed to their mother. That night, after dinner, the Eavesdropper sloped away to his room. The gambler followed him and waited for the familiar, beep, beep, beep of his safe mechanism opening. He held his ground for another few minutes and then burst into the room.

The eavesdropper was sitting on his bed surrounded by money. More money than the gambler had ever seen. The eavesdropper tried to cover his stash with his quilt, but it was too late.

'Fuck, will you look at all that money. Where'd ya get it?' He looked at his brother. 'What are you up to?'

He wouldn't say. The gambler dragged him off the bed and straddled him on the floor, picking up his head and banging it onto the carpet. Still he wouldn't tell. He looked as though he saw stars, and he was crying, but he wouldn't utter a word about where the money had come from. The gambler helped himself to most of it. He left him a few quid, but not much. 'Can you get any more?'

'The eavesdropper shook his head.' He hated the

gambler. He wanted to kill him. But mostly he just felt relieved. He'd almost been caught. The gambler still asked, from time to time, where the money had come from, and he bullied him to find out if there was any more. The eavesdropper knew how to make money. It was so easy, but he wouldn't do it to his own family again. He was honing his art and turning his attention to the community. He wrote everything he saw and everything he heard in his diaries.

Chapter Eight

Andrew knew the day he left for University that he never wanted to come back to the hotel as a resident. He intended to complete his education. He even intended to take the year out after his second year, but it would be done on his terms and under his own steam. He'd broken away from his mother on the day of the argument over music practice and, they both knew it. Andrew became a man that day and there was no going back.

It wasn't long before he wished he could be a little boy again, protected and coddled by his overbearing mother. Kept safe and out of trouble.

When he came home in the summer holidays of 1984 he had finished his second year at university. He was worn and troubled. Violet didn't know that look. She was used to the hungover, cannabis induced, appearance of him and his brothers when they came home, usually with an entourage of hangers-on for summer break, but this was different. Andrew was edgy and introverted. He looked frightened but wouldn't talk to his parents about his problems.

He was a man weighed down with guilt and secrets.

Andrew left home and Violet and Donald didn't see their son again for over five years.

It was the Thirteenth of October 1989. Everybody knew the date. It was branded into all the staff's brains because it was Violet's birthday. Simon Peter—SP—was stomping around in a foul mood. He was on the warpath and everybody was wary of crossing him. Everything had to be perfect, all arrangements adhered to, the staff beautifully turned out and looking fresh and efficient, every attention to detail considered and acted upon. SP's shrapnel voice rang through the kitchen, the dining hall, the ballroom and reception. The man gave the impression of being everywhere. He held a clipboard on his arm, ticking off jobs as they were done, and adding new ones at an alarming rate as they occurred to him. Fag breaks were foregone and coffee cooled in staff room mugs as yet another bouquet of flowers arrived and needed arranging.

Julia Morgan was on reception that afternoon. She was sick of being told, 'This isn't right, that isn't right.' Julia prided herself on doing a good job, as she kept telling Linda Bell, who was working reception with her,

'If he shouts at me just one more time, I'll ram his clipboard so far up his arse that he'll be chanting out his orders falsetto without even having to look at it.'

Linda laughed. 'You'll have a job mate; I bet his arse is so tightly clenched that it would take a JCB to prize it open.'

They were still laughing when they saw the couple who had wandered in from the street. They were used to the hippies, Windermere, although exclusive in Lakeland society, still had its element of undesirables, people who, according to Violet, lived in packs like wolves and roamed the streets in their beards, beads and peculiar odours. She had put a large sign on the hotel entrance, next to the one that said *No hikers: boots and backpacks must not be brought into the hotel.* The hippy sign said *No Hippies: Patchouli oil must not be worn in the hotel. Anybody caught in possession of illegal substances, will be prosecuted.*

The Halcyon Woods Hotel did not encourage hippies.

The couple looked tired, as though they'd travelled a long way. She was heavily pregnant and he supported her and their possessions, which were packed in the forbidden backpacks. Either they had been too weary to see the sign or had chosen to ignore it. She wore two plaits and men's boots; he had dirty hair past his shoulders and an unkempt beard that covered most of his face and chest.

'May I help you?' asked Julia stiffly in a voice far removed from the one she had been talking to Linda in just moments earlier. She didn't add, 'Sir,' and there was no welcoming smile to accompany the clipped words. Snobbery, like malice, is an emotion that spreads like infection, but Julia was too caught up in her position of assumed power to notice that.

The man opened his mouth to speak, but SP was already homing in like a torpedo.

'You people can't come in here looking like that. We have a dress code. There's a sign,' he finished, as though that explained everything.

The hippie's narrow eyes opened wider and the sun-bronzed crows-feet wrinkled into his hairline. 'Well

SP, you pompous old bastard. I see the old lady has taught you well.' Despite the insult, the words were warm and the man smiled broadly through them.

SP stood with one arm, half raised, a barrier as he tried to herd the couple back towards the main entrance. He furrowed his brow and then he burst into laughter. People quietly reading *The Times* in the Chesterfield sofas looked up in irritation. They were amazed to see that the cause of the unruly commotion was none other than one of the Woods' blokes.

'Andy? Is it you?' he grabbed the filthy traveller in a suit-crumpling bear-hug. 'Where the hell have you been, you sod? We hoped you were dead,' he laughed. 'What the hell are you doing here?' He held Andrew at arm's length and looked at him, checking that it really was his brother and not some impostor hoping to take his place. 'Come on, come into the kitchen quick.' Julia and Linda looked at each other with open mouths as SP shouted at them over his shoulder 'Not a word to anyone.'

'Yes, Mister Woods,' they chorused. Old Witchy Woods wasn't going to like this.

James was the head chef at the time. It would be another two years before the court case and gossip, and Violet sent him to exile in London. SP was dragging the man by the arm towards the kitchen yelling James' name at the top of his voice. 'This is going to be the best present ever for Ma, she's going to be stoked. James, James, look who I've got here.' They disappeared through the swing doors. 'You are going to have a shave before the party, though, aren't you mate? You do niff a bit,' were the last words the receptionists heard or saw of SP and the stranger.

The pregnant woman was left standing alone in the middle of Reception with the two overstuffed backpacks at her feet. 'Um, you'd better sit down, I suppose,' said Julia, confused. 'Can I get you a glass of water or anything?'

And that was how the prodigal son returned.

Andrew and his new wife were hidden until the present giving and for once Violet was speechless and her tears were genuine. Violet was delighted to have her son returned to her and thanked the Lord many times that evening. Andrew refused the tuxedo that SP tried to insist he wear. 'My days of being told how to dress are long over, bro,' he said, thinking back to the straw boater and striped blazer days. He wore the least creased and dirty of his own clothes, a pair of khaki shorts and a cheesecloth shirt that bore just the merest olive stain from their fruit picking in Greece the previous summer. He wore battered Jesus sandals, but his feet were clean, his toenails clipped and his beard partially tamed.

Like SP, Violet had not recognised Andrew as he was led to her table during the party. Her lip curled with disgust.

'And here's the biggest surprise of all. Look who's come home especially for your birthday.'

'Hello, Mother. Surprise.'

And then there was hugging, crying, and more hugging. Mother duck had her little ducklings all present and correct and around her once more. John was back home on holiday from his work in London and that night the champagne flowed. All ills were forgotten, old scores laid to rest and misdemeanours brushed under the red carpet for the evening.

Violet hated Beth, Andrew's wife, on sight, not least because of the huge swelling that she carried and flaunted in front of her. 'You're going to be a Grandma, Mother,' Andrew said, glowing with pride. The girl was in her final month; her breasts were swollen and heavy, readying themselves to nourish the infant to come. She wore a thin sundress and no bra, her panties were visible through the sheer material and the way she flaunted her condition was shameless. She wore flat espadrilles on her feet, the laces climbing bare sun-browned legs. Violet even managed to find fault with them and said they were indecent and the type of things that only a shameless hussy would wear. But, for this night only, though her expression said it all, she kept her opinions hushed and shared them with only a select few.

'So, am I to assume that you are married?' she asked with just a touch of ice to her tone.

'You may indeed, Mother. You may indeed. Been married this past three years. May I introduce Mrs Bethany Woods to you? Your daughter-in-law, my wife and the mother of my children, of which there are several and will be many more. And long may I hope to enjoy making every one of them.'

'Really, Andrew, there's no need for that kind of talk here,' said Violet shocked. Andy grinned at a blushing Beth; he had always loved to wind his mother up. 'You have children? I'm a Grandmother and you never bothered to so much as send us a postcard. Shame on you, boy.'

'Oh come on now, Ma, this is a day of celebration. Save the recriminations for another day. We've come a long way to be here tonight.'

'Tell me about your children.' Her voice was frosty and hurt, but her eyes burned with curiosity.

'Let me see if I can remember them all. It'll be a first if I can reel them off without missing anybody out. We have Rainbow Viola, she's the eldest. She's almost five. We call her Raino, and I tell you, Ma, bossy. Phew she's a madam.' He gave a little laugh and winked at James sitting on his right.

'She's a lot like you, you'll love her.'

Violet did the maths and bristled. She shot a revolted look at the illegitimate girl's mother. She decided at that moment that Grandchild or not, it would be impossible to love a child conceived out of wedlock.

'And then there're the twins, Denim Sky and Storm, both girls and both, not surprisingly, four years old.'

More of them, thought Violet uncharitably. It's a bastard epidemic. 'What kind of names are those for children?' She nearly said innocent children, but they were hardly that with being born the wrong side of the brush. 'There's nothing wrong with good strong names out of the holy book. What are you going to call this poor child when it's born? Sludge?'

Even Andrew had to admit that was quite witty for his caustic mother.

'Touché, Ma,' he replied with a good-natured grin. Opposite him, Beth seethed. 'We worship the elements, Mrs Woods. We see it as an honour to name our children—'

Andrew cut in before she could say any more. Beth could be opinionated about her beliefs. It was one of the things he loved about her. That, he thought, and the ability to give the best blowjob in the civilised world. But his mother had a lot to get used to and their lifestyle was just one of them. 'Ladies, lets drink to life, love and togetherness. They lifted their glasses, Beth's filled with orange juice, everybody else's with champagne, and while the two women sharpened their tongues, the toast was made.

Philip, ever the peacemaker, tried to break the tension in the room. 'Wow, another of my brothers all grown up and married. James was the first. He married a lady from London, didn't you mate? And just last year SP tied the knot. He and Ros are just coming up to their first anniversary.' Everybody ignored him. Violet hadn't finished grilling her second son and his loose wife.

'You must show me your wedding photos, Bethany. I'd love to see them, seeing as how Andrew's father and I weren't invited on the actual day.' She gave Beth a sickly smile.

'Oh, there weren't any photographs, Mrs Woods, it wasn't that kind of a wedding and we only invited people who we really wanted to be present.'

Let it go, thought Andrew, please just let it go. Violet opened her mouth to speak. Oh well, here come the fireworks.

'We had a special and unique ceremony, Mother,' he cut in. 'We married on the top of a volcano in spring.'

Violet's mouth fell open and she sat for a full ten seconds resembling the laughing clown at Blackpool Pleasure beach. She turned her head, mouth still open, from side to side, but there was no laughter coming from her. For those few seconds, she even forgot to breathe.

'What? You weren't married on consecrated ground? What in the name of the Lord was the priest thinking?'

Andrew shifted in his seat. 'Actually, Ma, there was no priest. We were married by an elder of our commune.'

Even Beth could see that he wasn't explaining things very well. She was passionate about her beliefs, maybe as passionate as Violet was about her Catholicism. 'Andrew and I are Pagan's. He denounced all ignorant religion when we purified in a sweatlodge together. We don't hold with false Gods, we worship the old ways before modern religion was founded. Our Gods are the sun and moon, the tides and the seasons. We were married by pagan law in a ceremony of light and petals.' At this point her eyes were dreamy as she remembered the breeze blowing the fragrant petals all over them. 'It's not actually called marriage, in the traditional sense of the word. Our ceremony was called a hand-fasting. We are joined in the ceremony for one year and one day, or for as long as both partners want to remain so. 'We were naked too, so photographs would have cheapened it.'

Violet lost her dignity. She screamed and ranted. Each time she ran out of insults, she returned to her favourite. 'You witch. You evil, horrible witch. You took my God-fearing son and made him believe all your rubbish. You took my innocent boy and seduced him, you...you...Methuselah.' Beth sat quietly, not saying a word. She didn't agree with raised voices.

It was at this point that Violet swooned and had to be helped to her bedroom.

The boys suggested that Donald should go to her. She'd had a shock after all, but Don was having none of it. He knew that somehow, at some point, and in some way, the fact that they had produced a heathen son would all boil down to being his fault. Sometimes Violet was best left to her own devises and he figured that this was probably one of those times. Besides, his son was home, and he had some partying to do.

The night was a tremendous success, from everybody's point of view except Violet's. They partied late into the night and ended up having a drunken sing-song, huddled round a fire that Andrew insisted on building on the lakeside. 'What about the mess?' said

Donald 'It'll burn the ground. Oh Sod it, let the fire commence,' he slurred. Plenty of time to lament his singed grass tomorrow.

Things were tense again, when, bolshy with ale, James teased Phil. 'That's it now Phil, we've all succumbed to the spell, except you. You're the only one left who isn't married. We've never even seen you with a girl. You know what I think, don't you? I think you're gay.'

'Get stuffed, James, Phil said. 'Just because you like to go around in a dress,' James coloured, it was a subject that the family avoided talking about. James was married now and all of that unpleasant stuff was behind him. He had Rhona and had settled any silly confusion that he had suffered. Philip felt guilty for bringing it up again, but he'd had his mother whining on at him about grandkids earlier. Then SP had asked him if he was seeing anybody yet. He felt left out and secluded at family gatherings. He was always the one on his own. The brothers had man-talks, moaning about their wives. Phil wanted a woman to complain about, too. It wasn't the first time that James had called him gay. He looked up about to apologise, just as James jumped him and the brothers sprawled onto their backs in the grass.

The party dispersed after that. The cold night air drove people back into the cosy warmth of the hotel. Watching their breath dance in the air made the guests long for warm beds, with fluffy duvets and central heating. Soon only Donald, Philip and Andrew were left. Philip sensed that Donald wanted to talk to his son alone. They had a lot of catching up to do, so after shaking Andrew's hand and reiterating how good it was to have him home, Philip headed for his bed in the early hours.

Left alone, the two men sat for in companionable silence. Andrew took rolling tobacco and papers out of his shorts pocket and rolled a cigarette. He would have preferred a joint, but in deference to his father, he contented himself with a roll-up. He concentrated on the task while his thoughts drifted. He licked the paper and made sure that the finished product was smooth and even before putting it to his lips and lighting it. He offered the pouch of tobacco to his father, and although Donald hadn't smoked for over twenty years, he took it from him and attempted to roll a cigarette. The paper tore under his callused hands and tobacco spilled to the floor. They both laughed. 'It's been a while since I've done this, son.' Andrew took the fixings from him and rolled a second cigarette. 'Your mother would kill me if she knew.' They laughed again.

'It's going to freeze tomorrow, lad. Look at that rag around the moon.' The conversation was sparse and held no substance, but it wasn't stilted or awkward. They were two men, sitting by a fire in the moonlight, happy with each other's company.

'So what are your plans, son?' asked Donald as he stubbed the end of his smoke out on his precious grass. 'Are you staying awhile?'

'Nope,' answered Andrew. He was in no hurry and took the last draw on his smoke before elaborating. 'No, we're not staying awhile. This is home dad. I've seen the world, seen some fantastic places and lived some crazy dreams. And now I've come home,' he finished. 'If you want us, we're back for good.' He emphasised the word 'us', letting his father know that if his wife and children weren't accepted into the family, then this wasn't the home he was looking for. 'She's a good woman, you know.' Neither of them had mentioned Beth since she had kissed her husband goodnight hours earlier. He wasn't asking his father to like his wife. He was stating a fact, in the same lazy way that they'd talked about the weather.

'Aye lad, aye, I reckon she is.' Donald put his hand on his son's knee and gave it a little pat. He coughed, embarrassed and moved his hand to the grass, picking at an imaginary weed. 'Reckon your mother's just going to have to look beyond her blinkers. So, what are you going to do? Any ideas?'

'Were going to look at property tomorrow. We've left the kids at the commune in France. We need to arrange collecting them. Home has to be right, Dad, you know? It has to have the right feel, to sit well with nature. I need a place with outbuildings that can be used as workshops. I've build myself a name as a pretty good watchmaker. I do clocks, too. Beth's an artist. We need a studio for her, space for the kids, and a barn to turn into a shop. I'm looking at buying a working farm, you know so that we can put something back into the land.'

Donald didn't answer for a second or two. 'Sounds

expensive,' he said at last. 'Clockmaker, eh? That's a fine occupation, lad.'

'Oh, we've got money, Pops. That's not a problem. And I don't mind if the place needs work. We'd like that, doing our own place up the way we want it. We're in no rush to have it done and we'll be comfortable while we work on it.' At this point his voice turned bitter. There was hardness to it, something below the words that Donald couldn't work out. 'We've got more money than we'll ever need.'

Donald was about to press his son to explain. Andrew was troubled; something was on his mind, but the heavens opened and raindrops the size of pennies dropped from the sky, soaking them through in seconds. The rain would take care of the dying embers of the fire. They ran drunkenly for the hotel laughing like kids.

Andrew's words came back to Donald as he waited for sleep to take him. The lad seemed to be doing okay financially. He had a lovely, feisty wife, a family, and yet something wasn't right. The way Andrew spoke, it was as if his money was a curse.

We've got more money than we'll ever need.

Chapter Nine

'Where's the damned artichoke? Morley, you snivelling moron, stop playing with yourself and get the artichoke here now. I told you to prepare it ten minutes ago.'

Keith Morley wiped his nose on his kitchen whites and blushed to the roots of his ginger hair. 'Yes Chef,' he muttered.

'Yes Chef, yes Chef,' mimicked James in a whiney voice. 'Just get it here now, dickhead. If you're not up to the fucking job, get out of my fucking kitchen and don't come back.' He was screaming at the top of his voice again. 'Bloody hell, it's not as if I ask you to do anything challenging, is it? Did your mother fuck the village idiot to have you? Fuck me.'

The young boy with the tearstained face crossed the busy kitchen carrying a bowl of prepared vegetable. James snatched it from his hands and Keith Morley turned to scuttle back to the relative safety of the prep area.

James poked the artichokes with a finger. 'What the hell is this?' he bellowed. 'Oi, Moron, get back here. Do they look crisp to you? They've gone limp. You've taken so bloody long doing them that they've wilted. You're a waste of fucking breathing space.' James had taken Morley's surname and morphed it into Moron. The nickname had stuck from day one.

Keith turned back to the enraged chef. He was crying again and hung his head.

94

'Look at you. You're like a whipped dog. Why are you so soft?' Keith didn't respond, but he raised his eyes, silently pleading with James to lay off him. 'Answer me, you pathetic cretin. Why are you so bloody soft?'

'Dunno Chef,' whispered Keith.

'Go and prepare another bowl. Go on, get out of my fucking sight.'

'Yes chef.'

Keith ran back towards the prep station without another word.

James threw the bowl of artichokes at him. The stainless steel bowl smashed into him in the middle of his back and fell with a clatter on the tiled floor. The food spilled and fanned in a semicircle around him.

'Clean it up, arsehole.' James was red in the face and sweating with the exertion his tantrum had brought about.

The new boy was suffering the fourth hour of the first day in his second week at The Halcyon Woods Hotel. He didn't think he could take much more.

Marcus had taken to James when he first met the lad as a rebellious three year-old. In busy periods, the Woods' children were not allowed in the bustling hotel kitchen, but between shifts, when it was quiet, Marcus always had time for them. He would give them cake and tease them as he prepared the bread for the next shift. Sometimes he'd give them a piece of pastry to roll, or a small bowl with cake ingredients to hand-mix. It was a passing fancy for all of the lads except James. The kid loved to be wrist deep in butter and flour. He learned to knead dough before he could recite his alphabet and Marcus enjoyed teaching him new things as his ability matured.

As a teenager, it was easy to see that he had a flair for cooking that couldn't be learned. Marcus always said that true chefs were born with flour in their blood and even at that age, James had the making of a remarkable chef. It was obvious that he would go straight into the kitchen when he left university, just as Simon Peter would go into hotel management. The difference was that the eldest Woods' boy had been groomed to take over the family business from the day he could walk. With James, it was a gift that he already possessed. He could make food sing.

Marcus was happy to take him on as his apprentice, but his pleasure was short lived. The cheeky young lad had become a surly, bad-tempered thug. From day one, James was difficult. He was eager enough to learn the rudiments of his trade from Marcus and was a keen and able student. He loved to bake the bread and cakes and produce fine and exotic pastries. He had flair and imagination, often marrying flavours that only the foolish or incredibly brave would ever think of putting together. He was creative and temperamental, both signs of a good chef. What he couldn't do, was take criticism or discipline. After his regimented upbringing, he should have been used to following orders, to knowing his place and observing the rules of his rank.

He wasn't.

After nineteen years of being repressed, first by his mother and then by masters of school and university, the boy was done with being told what to do. He was the son and heir, if not of the hotel, then certainly of the kitchen within it. Because he was Violet's son, he considered himself to be the master and Marcus a lowly employee. It caused heated debates and bruised egos on both sides.

Violet bribed Marcus heavily that first year. A dramatic increase to his salary made coping with his apprentice's inflated ego bearable. On a weekly basis, he flew into Violet, and later SP's office, threatening to walk out, but he never did. A bonus usually slaked his feelings of being undermined.

With SP as hotel manager, he and James fought bitterly until some months later, SP learned not to interfere in any way with the running of the kitchen. He stopped querying invoices and left his brother and the head chef to sort out their own hierarchy. At the same time that Violet and Donald gave the running of the hotel to their eldest son, they called a meeting with Marcus. The chef who had served them loyally for many years had become one cook too many in the broth. He was given a hefty golden handshake and two months notice to leave. His final day would coincide with the official end of James' apprenticeship. Marcus had enough saved to buy his own restaurant, a dream that contentment in his work had always kept on the fringe of his fantasies. James walked out of his apprenticeship and into the head chef position of his parent's hotel.

Marcus had taught him well. By the end of the second year of training, he had learned everything that he should have done in his third year. Marcus was an excellent chef— but James was better. The transition was a smooth one.

With a certificate of power, James was a bully. He persecuted everybody who came into his kitchen. What had been controlled while Marcus was in charge, was left to run wild when James took the reins. The turnover of staff in the hotel kitchen was rapid. Only the very strong-willed survived more than a couple of weeks. The pay was above most in the county, but it had to be to keep the few loyal staff that could tolerate working for James, he was an artist of extreme highs and volatile lows. The kitchen ran like clockwork, standards were everything, and anybody who couldn't keep pace was dispensed with. He had inherited his ambition and willingness to work hard from his mother. But like an unwatched pan, James was never far from boiling over.

Things came to a head the day after the artichoke incident. James was in a foul mood. A fillet of veal had been returned to the kitchen with a complaint of it being tough. James wasn't working the main meals that day, but he took any complaint personally and saw it as an attack on him. The kitchen staff were in line to catch the fallout, he didn't single Keith out. Morley just managed to irritate him more than the other members of his staff.

James resented the apprentice. Morley flew through catering college as a grade-A pupil. Oh his first day in the kitchen, he had dared to suggest that James might want to prepare a skate the way Morley was shown at college. James couldn't believe the audacity of the little cunt. How dare he come into his kitchen showing off his school-taught ways? Morley had the makings of a decent chef. He should, by right of his qualifications, have gone into the kitchen on a second-chef salary, but James made it company policy to start all of his staff at the bottom. If they had what it takes, they rose quickly through the ranks in a matter of weeks. If they didn't— they were out. Keith didn't mind starting on veg prep. He knew of James' reputation and wanted to please him and rise to second chef on merit. He had all the knowledge and all the skills. What he lacked was the flair and impulsiveness that makes a great chef.

From that first hour, and Keith's fatal error, James decided he didn't like the lad and would bring him down.

Morley knew what hotel kitchens were like; he'd done his placements. It was all screaming and temperament one minute and then best buddies in the bar when the shift was over. James was in the bar talking to some people after Morley's first shift. The lad, in baggy jeans and Adidas T-shirt, excused himself and tapped James on the shoulder.

'I'd like to buy you a drink, James, just to show there are no hard feelings and to say that I understand why you were so tough on me today.'

The lad was only two years younger than the head chef. In other circumstances they could have been brothers or drinking buddies. The look on James' face told Morley he had just made his second big mistake. From that moment on, war was declared.

On the second day James took Morley down. He broke first his spirit and then his will to live. By the time the shift ended, Morley didn't know if he could face another day working for the spiteful bully. He saw the week out in misery, becoming increasingly withdrawn. By day four, he had no confidence left. He'd been making stupid mistakes in the kitchen, things he would never have done in college. He was emotional, burst into tears several times during the course of the workday and wanted to turn things around and prove himself worthy of the job. It wasn't about pleasing James; it was about showing that he could do what he'd been trained for. He stopped sleeping had headaches from the stress and exhaustion. By the first day of the second week, he was a shadow of the boy he'd been eight days earlier.

The last day of Morley's life wasn't a happy one. Several times he'd been at the biting end of Chef's temper.

'Moron, get the eggs on.'

'Yes Chef.'

'Moron, you gay boy, prepare the garnish.'

'Yes Chef.'

'Moron, do me some onions. Did you hear me? I said do me some fucking onions.'

'Yes, Chef.'

'Moron, Where are the tuna? Get them over here now.'

'Yes Chef.' Keith took the pan off the hob and hurried across the kitchen. He was about to put it on the board next to James when the head chef turned round and collided with Morley and the hot pan.

'You stupid, dumb, fuckwit. What have I told you about walking round with fucking hot pans? You really are a useless fucking tosser aren't you? Get me some spinach.'

'Yes Chef.'

Morley was preparing the spinach when an almighty roar echoed round the sterile cavern of the immense kitchen. 'You stupid, incompetent wanker. You fucking little queer.' James ran up behind Morley and grabbed him at the back of his jacket collar. Knocking the boy off balance, he dragged him backwards across the kitchen and to the large range of different sized cooking rings. One glowed an intense red, throwing out a blanket of heat. 'Look. Just look at it. You've left it on, you imbecile. Surely, basic kitchen safety tells you that you don't wander off and leave a ring burning. You need to spend less time sucking your boyfriend's cock at night, so that when you come to work you are aware of what you're fucking doing.' He grabbed the sobbing boy's left hand and forced it down onto the burning ring. There was a fizz of burning flesh. Keith screamed. His hand was in contact with the ring for a split second, but it was long enough for it to burn into the meat of his palm. James had lost it. He was out of control, sheer bloodlust clouding his vision and his rationale.

'You're finished in this hotel. Do you hear me? I'll see that you never work again.' He pulled Morley away from the stove and rammed him hard against the seven-foot freezer. Morley was holding the wrist of his burned hand and screaming in terror and agony. Lucy ran to get SP, while Dave, the commis chef, and Darren, the kitchen porter, tried to pull James away from Morley. James turned, punching Dave Hill full in the face. Pandemonium erupted in the kitchen. SP came in ranting at his brother. He and James fought in the hotel kitchen, knocking dishes and utensils onto the floor.

Lucy looked for Morley, she wanted to check his hand, assess the damage and call for an ambulance if necessary. He had slipped out when the violence distracted everybody's attention. She assumed he had gone home to lick his wounds.

Morley ran from the kitchen and out of the rear entrance of the hotel. He didn't stop running until he was surrounded by the cool greenness of trees. The woods were deep. Tears rolled down his face and he was white and shaking. The pain throbbed in the palm of his hand and up through his arm to the shoulder. He was in agony, body and mind abused and debilitated. James had taken the last of his confidence and made him believe that he was useless. His feeling of failure hurt more than the circles of pain radiating from the centre of his palm.

102

With his good hand, he slid the knife from the sleeve of his kitchen whites. He'd hidden it there, when SP and James were arguing. He listened for any sign that he'd been followed. All he could hear was birdsong. A squirrel stopped in the path ten feet in front of him to observe this trespasser to his territory. Even here Morley felt that he didn't belong. He backed against the trunk of a tree and slithered down until his buttocks came into contact with the cool, damp moss. He worried about staining his whites. James would go ballistic if he marked them. Morley gave a rueful laugh. What could he do to him now that he hadn't already done?

He sat for two minutes contemplating the eight-inch blade and solid wooden shaft of the knife. He felt no fear. What he was about to do meant nothing; he had gone beyond worrying about something as slight as his own death. His only concern was that he would be found before it was over. His only fear, that he'd have to see James Woods' face again.

He cut calmly and professionally. He might feel useless, but he could still prepare a cut of meat. He bit deep into his wrist just below the base of his hand. He winced but only slightly, in truth the pain of the incision was nothing compared to the pulsating throb of the burn. His arm was resting against his thigh, palm up. The knife was so sharp and his compulsion so strong that he cut clear through his arm and into his leg with the force of penetration. The knife tore through muscle, tendon and cartilage. He had to wrench it back to make

103

the downward pull. He grunted with the exertion of removing the point of the knife from his femoral artery on the inside of his upper leg. That was a mistake, but an added bonus nonetheless. The cut to his leg was insufficient to do much damage, but it gave him the idea to improve on it. He stabbed the knife hard into his thigh, doing incredible damage with the butcher's blade. This time it did hurt and was far worse than the deep throb that it had been going into his arm. He cried out, clamping down on the noise in his throat so that he wouldn't be heard. He made a second cut to his wrist, less aggressively this time. There was no pain, shock had gone to his brain and shut down the valves that sent messages to the nerve endings. His cutting hand was weak. He even forgot about the agony of his burned flesh. He was deep in concentration. There was a lot of blood. His knife hand was trawling through it. His whites spread with a deep crimson stain that washed through the material the way a wave washes up a shale beach. The blood was warm and felt pleasing. Satisfying. He was mesmerised as it poured both from his leg and bubbled through the wound in his wrist. He wondered if he had already done enough, but didn't want to take any chances. The knife was the best. Eight inches of brutal stainless steel that could cut through a rabbit neck, releasing bones from their anchorage with a single chop. Going clean through the underside to the back of his arm had been no trouble at all. He felt the weakness enervating him. His eyes had black spots dancing somewhere to the left of his vision. He went to work fast. It only took one more movement. The knife was already home, He drew it smoothly through the flesh of the inside of his lower arm from wrist to elbow, neatly separating his meat into two fillets, attached only by the layer of skin on his outer arm and bones. As delirium claimed him, his final thought was of suitable herbs and sausage meat to stuff in his arm before cooking could commence. He died beneath the bough of an oak tree, a disgruntled squirrel his only witness.

Violet took over and did what Violet always did when James went too far. She bought everybody off. Silence cost her dearly on that occasion and even she had to admit that James had become a liability. SP wanted to force James into anger management counselling, but Violet wouldn't hear of it. The Woods family did not air their dirty laundry in public. The inquest heard that Keith Morley had been suffering a depression. Girlfriend trouble was hinted at, subtly suggested by Morley's best friend who also worked at the Halcyon and had been bribed by Violet. A verdict of suicide was heard, and that was the end of it. Everybody has their price; Violet knew this to be a statement of fact. She bought loyalty, and after Morley's death, she bought silence. 'Dinky' Johnston, Morley's friend, hated himself, he hated the hefty bonus cheque in his back pocket, but he couldn't stop a smile playing at the corners of his mouth as he dreamed of the hi-fi he was going to buy from Currys. And then, he remembered that his best friend would never listen to it with him. He was dead and Dinky was weighed down by the solace of his thirty pieces of silver.

James was finished at The Halcyon Woods. It would be many years before he could return. Mother funded his first solo venture, a nice little restaurant of his own. 'Somewhere near Marcus. You like Marcus, don't you dear?' Yes, London would be far enough away. Violet cried as she waved him away in his Jaguar XJS. She'd packed him some macaroons for the journey. He liked those.

Chapter Ten

A two pound deficit and eight pound gain were jointly to blame for Julie's bad mood. The two pounds was the couple of quid she was short on the fantastic jeans she'd just tried on, and the eight pounds was the half a stone—at least—that she had gained which prevented her doing the buggers up. What's a girl to do when trauma as gigantic as that blight's her life? She might be getting fatter but she wasn't bloody stupid; the answer was obvious. She had no alternative but to go to Salvanna's for the lunchtime special. Once her diet was broken enough to indulge in spaghetti bolognaise drowned in melted cheese, what harm would a full-fat latte on the side do? It took her half a minute to talk herself into it and half of that was spent asking herself if she had the guts to eat alone. She decided that once she got in there, she'd ring her sister and offer to treat her to lunch, if she was up for providing a bit of pig-out moral support.

The restaurant was busy but not oppressively so. Wimmin-what-lunch and the business exec crowd filled three quarters of the clientele capacity. Julie was gratified to see another woman sitting alone, until her companion came back from the toilet. What the hell, she thought. She was hungry, they served food, and it was less shameful than throwing herself off the dock's bridge and expecting the recovery divers to lift her, and her extra half stone of weight, out of the slimy green water.

She squeezed herself between one of the close tables and a pushchair, pausing to glare at the child with the mitt-full of deep pan Margarita. His wide blue eyes a striking contrast to the tomato red of the rest of his face. He looked as though he'd been massacred—a self-proclaiming prophesy if the brat touched her camel-coloured jacket with either of those filthy hands. She caught the mother's eye and quickly changed her expression into one of those sickly ones, reserved for the parents of young children, the one that said she'd probably like one of those too, one day.

She felt as though she had shot from a size fourteen to a sixteen overnight and there was no way that she was going to go from a sixteen to a size oh-my-god-how-did-that kid-get-in-there.

The bloke at the next table was eating alone. As she sat down, he looked up from his newspaper with a half-interested glance of curiosity. He didn't actually look at her and they certainly didn't make eye contact, so she had no need to smile or say anything. A weary waitress was manoeuvring through the tables towards her. She had menus tucked under one arm, pencil and jotter at the ready. Julie ordered her latte to fight away the afternoon chill and the weight gain depression. She said that she would order food when her friend arrived.

Emma, her sister, declined the offer of a free lunch. She had a man coming to fit blinds. Julie was going to plead desperation due to the gained weight and tragic demise of the jeans that had never been hers. But she was well aware that the man at the next table was within earshot of their conversation, hell she could lean over and snog him without lifting more than her left butt cheek if she had a mind to. Vanity demanded that she only suggested once that Emma leave the blind man to it, and go AWOL. After using precious phone credit, she resigned herself to eating alone.

The man at the opposite table was causing her some problems. Apart from an initial glance, he hadn't once lifted his head from his paper, but even so, he was causing her to moderate her choices. If he hadn't been sitting there she could have put the hard word on Emma *and* she could have had spaghetti bolognaise for lunch. However, there was no chance of eating that in public now. She opted for the safer risotto; it still came smothered in melted cheese, so that was good. Her mood demanded heaps of melted cheese today.

The table was getting on her nerves. Every time she shifted position, the short leg rocked to the floor. Maybe leprechauns escaped from Ireland and roamed restaurants in the night cutting an inch of every fourth table leg. Julie came to the conclusion that it was the grand plan the Irish had to overthrow the British. Boi jimminy, we'll bring them down boi way of their toibles so we will, Paddy. She was smiling as the waitress returned with her lunch.

The food looked good, but it was no use, the damned table was driving her nuts. She folded a cardboard coaster and, being careful not to dangle her hair in the food, she leaned over the table to put the coaster under the wobbly leg to balance it.

As she bent down she caught the edge of the table with her elbow. It caused it to slew towards her. She was aware of the plate of hot food sliding forwards, but couldn't get up fast enough to stop it.

She watched horrified as the dish slid towards her face. At the last second, instinct drove her to drop her head. The food emptied into her hair. She was aware that she was screaming as she brought herself upright in the chair.

The man at the next table saw what was going to happen. He leaped from his seat and less than a second after the contents of the dish spilled all over Julie's head, he emptied his pint of lager on top of it. He let the glass go and it dropped to the floor, shattering in a ricochet of broken shards. Still less than a second had passed since the first splash of hot food hit her. He was in with his hands, clearing the mess from the top of her head before the burning reached through her thick hair and on to her scalp.

'Keep still, I'm a first aider,' he said it to Julie before addressing the room in general. 'Get me water. I need to cool her head.'

When the food dropped, the place had erupted into activity. Waitresses hovered and people vacated their seats at the tables nearby as glass and food splashed towards them. As if to add to the humiliation, a second drink was thrown over Julie's head followed by a jug of water. She stopped screaming, there was no heat or pain, only plenty of fluid and mess. She peered at her world through two strands of lank, dripping cheese as the man, with a penchant for drowning strangers in restaurants, pulled lengths of stringy mess from her hair.

She was embarrassed, humiliated and pathetic and, at a loss for what else to do, she began to cry.

The restaurant, presumably worried about legal suits, was wonderful. They helped mop up the debris, waived the bill and gave her complimentary vouchers for dinner for two, with wine, on the house. The man, not satisfied with initiating the first public drowning in Barrow for a hundred years insisted, despite all of her protestations, on taking her to hospital to be checked over. 'Head burns are serious things,' he said several times. 'You can't be too careful.' Julie just wanted to escape from all the curious eyes and was too upset to argue. She allowed herself to be led out into the street, looking like hell and still snivelling into a Salvanna's paper serviette. If the child wearing the pizza mask was impressed that a grown-up could get more food on them than he could, she didn't notice.

People looked at them as they walked the short distance to his car. He had his arm protectively around her shoulders, the taboo of intimacy between strangers broken down in the Age of the New Samaritan.

He insisted on going in with her when she got to the hospital. Worse, he insisted on staying until she had been seen and given the all clear. 'Might as well see the job through to the end,' he said.

Who the hell does he think he is?

Julie was grateful to him for what he'd done, but was still smarting with indignation about the way he'd done it.

When she went in to see the registrar on A&E duty, she found out exactly how lucky she'd been. He told her that if it hadn't been for two intervening factors, she would be left very seriously burned indeed. She had long, very thick hair, which had protected her head from the scalding. The Samaritan's quick-witted reaction stopped the food from burning through the hair to her scalp. If it hadn't been for these two saving graces, she would have been horrendously scarred for life and would never have been able to grow hair over the scar again. As it was, she walked away from the incident humiliated but, apart from being wet and dressed in risotto and cheese, completely unharmed. The enormity of what *could* have happened hit her and she trembled.

The man, who introduced himself as Philip Woods, said that he would see Miss Spencer home safely and insisted that she had a calming brandy to steady her nerves. Despite being commended vigorously by the doctor and nurses he was surprisingly self-effacing. He said anybody would have done the same thing in a similar situation.

He saw her into the house and insisted she shower and change into her night-clothes even though it was only four o'clock in the afternoon. 'You've had a nasty shock and need to rest,' he told her, still playing his role of medical competent to the hilt. Here was a complete stranger fussing around making coffee in her kitchen and opening the bottle of brandy he'd bought on the way over, as though it was all perfectly normal. She felt uncomfortable showering with him in the house. He could be anyone. And here she was at her most vulnerable, naked and covered in soapsuds. He didn't seem the type to be anything but a gentleman, but then, what type is an axe murderer or pervert? Although she didn't feel at risk, nonetheless, she locked the bathroom door and didn't linger. Normally, she wore a short silk dressing gown for lounging, but despite the mild weather, she chose her heavy, hooded velour gown and made sure it was firmly belted over her Pooh-Bear pyjamas.

Julie didn't have any brandy glasses. In fact, she'd had a few disasters with glasses over the previous months and the option was one half pint glass, or coffee mugs. Philip was appalled that they were drinking brandy from chipped mugs and for some reason that set Julie off into peals of irrational giggles. Philip saw nothing funny about the situation and put her silly giggling down to delayed shock setting in. He'd only had the tiniest drop of brandy because he was driving. He was uptight, but he was kind and considerate. She was grateful to him for all that he'd done for her that day.

It seemed only right and proper that she invite him to join her for the complimentary meal and that was how their relationship began. No fireworks or love at first sight. No wild palpitating heartbeats. Just risotto

awash with lager, and brandy out of chipped Easter
bunny mugs.

Chapter Eleven

He looked at her and deliberately changed the subject. 'Should we go out for a drink tonight?'

She wasn't letting him off the hook this time. 'Phil, why do you always look so uncomfortable when I ask about your family?'

'I don't.' His eyes shifted to the right, unable to meet her inquisitive gaze.

'Yes you bloody well do.'

'Julie, please don't swear; it makes you sound common.' He could look at her now. He wasn't the one in the dock anymore. He'd done a clever sleight-of-hand illusion, and she was standing there, with her right hand on the metophorical bible, under the steel grey eyes of the prosecution.

Julie Sandra Spencer, it is alleged that on the sixteenth of May, nineteen ninety one, you did utter a profanity, that proves, beyond any shadow of a doubt, that you are the common, sewer mouthed, trollop that he always suspected that you would prove yourself to be. How do you plead?

'I'm sorry,' she said, hating herself for rolling over and showing her belly. This was her house, dammit, and she could say what she fucking well pleased. What she did say was nothing. She lowered her eyes to her plate and ate in silence. Phil didn't like a lot of chatter when he was eating. She forgot that sometimes.

Her father broke wind loudly from the sitting

room. Her mother whined a half-hearted protest. Phil didn't comment.

He looked at his food, forked through the cheese and coleslaw on his baked potato. She wasn't sure whether the look of sheer disgust on his face was for the food, or for the woman so beneath him that he'd taken as a girlfriend.

Her plate was almost empty when he spoke again. 'Are you going to eat all of that? You've put on weight since I met you.' It was a simple statement with no inflection or tone but the rebuttal stung like a slap. Putting her cutlery down and remembering, as an afterthought, to place them neatly side by side, she took their plates to the sink. She was scraping leftovers into the bin and running water to wash up. He didn't like the plates left after a meal, better to wash them immediately, he always said, and then it's done with. She almost didn't hear what he said next.

'Perhaps it is time you met my people,' he mused. Just that, no more. He was watching the news on the portable television in the tiny dining room. Wiping her hands on a hand-drying towel, not a tea towel—never a tea towel. She opened her mouth to say something but he put his hand up for silence, palm facing her, a barrier, a brick wall, a command. My people? Pompous bastard, she thought, who does he think he is? Jesus?

'You know what,' she said, seething. 'Why don't you, get up off your sanctimonious arse, and do the washing up yourself.' She flung the towel at him and flounced upstairs for a bath, but she did remember not to slouch in her temper, he hated a sloppy posture.

'We'll go to Mother's on Saturday,' he shouted up after her. 'Find something suitable.' Find something suitable for what? To wear? To give as a gift? Or to murder my boyfriend with? What did one wear for a first meeting with a bloke's parents anyway?

Philip was impatient; he wanted to get away before the tourists blocked the road. Julie insisted they stop off at a florist to buy his mother a large bunch of chrysanthemums, a fitting flower to give on a first time meeting with the parents. Violet and Donald lived at the hotel, though Violet had delegated most of the day-to-day running of the place over to Simon Peter when she made him the hotel manager. Violet spent her days playing bridge and chatting over coffee with the affluent guests. She and Donald had a suite of rooms overlooking the lake and life was cosy and comfortable.

The first thing Julie noticed as they were invited in were the vases of fresh flowers dotted all over the place. It seemed the lady of the house had a passion for delicate orchids and elegant lilies. The flowers that Julie had brought looked bulky and bulbous; they didn't fit in with the general ambience at all.

'Hello Mr and Mrs Woods, nice to meet you,' said Julie. She tried for a warm smile but it died on her lips under the scrutiny of the other woman. She gave Violet the flowers. The older woman thanked her stiffly and her face cracked momentarily in a forced smile, but Julie felt no warmth under the cool gaze.

'So, you're our Philip's bit of stuff then, eh?' Donald

said.

He had changed during the time he'd been married to Violet. It had been a slow and subtle changing, but he bore little resemblance to the mild man who had plodded along and was happy with his lot. His wife's views and opinions had rubbed off on him. After years of sharing a life, if not his bed, with her, some of her manner and attitude must have leaked onto his crisp, starched shirts and contaminated him. Donald contracted it and was a far more outspoken man.

He didn't bother to mask his top to bottom scan of her. It wasn't the leery body scan of a middle-aged letch, it was a sizing up of his son's girlfriend to see if she was worthy of a welcome into the Woods' social circle. He shook hands with her noncommittally. 'Hardly a slip of a lass, are you? Like your grub, do you? Well, it could have been worse. You could have been a darkie. Don't like those wogs, I don't. Ought to send them all back to where they came from.'

Julie sat stiffly, perching on the edge of the sofa, while Violet went to make tea. Julie hated tea. Phil knew she hated tea but he didn't say anything to his mother and Julie felt that it would be rude to ask for coffee instead. Phil and his dad, sitting on opposite armchairs, made small talk. Julie was ignored as Donald told Phil about some work he wanted a hand with in the hotel grounds. They discussed when it would be done, what tools they'd need and how long it would take. Julie felt invisible.

Violet returned with a tray. The tea set was Royal

Doulton, fine china with a small handled cup that rattled on her saucer. She handed Julie a cup and said, 'We don't have smoking in here. If you'd like to smoke I can show you to the terrace.' The words were hard and clipped, disapproval slipping out on the back of every syllable.

Julie laughed, it was a nervous reaction. 'Oh that's all right, thank you Mrs Woods, I don't smoke.'

'You don't smoke? Oh, I thought you would.' In those last five words, Violet summed up everything she thought about the girl in front of her. The insult was barbed and deliberate.

Tea was served and, as if on cue, they peppered her with questions about her background. She told them openly and honestly about her home, a modest council house on a Barrow estate where she lived with her parents and two sisters. She had never been ashamed of her roots and was proud of the way her family had helped one another through some difficult times. Her mother was a dinner lady at the local primary school and her father had taken voluntary redundancy from the shipyard five years before when his back was bad. He hadn't been able to work since and probably liked to drink a little more than was good for him. They were good parents and Julie was happy.

Donald asked her about her work, though she felt sure that Phil would have already been well-grilled on that, and pretty much every other subject. She told them about her job as an assembler of electrical components at Oxleys in Barrow.

'Factory work? Really?' said Violet glancing at her son as though he'd suffered a serious loss of his common sense. 'Never mind, dear. Perhaps something better will come along one day. Didn't you do well at school?'

Julie had been a good guest. She was well mannered and polite. But she was getting fed up of having one thinly disguised put down after another flung at her while her boyfriend sat by and didn't say a word in her defence.

'No, Mrs Woods, I didn't do very well at school. I messed around when I should have been learning and I wasted every academic opportunity I was given.' She could see Phil cringing. He was flashing eye signals at her to shut up. This wasn't what she was supposed to say at all. 'I might one day,' she went on, 'regret the time I wasted. I might feel stupid and dim for not having any qualifications, but at the moment I have a job that I enjoy. I work a full week and earn my living honestly and respectably. I've got some fantastic mates and I'm happy. Phil and I haven't talked about any future plans, so for the time being, I'm happy and don't see any reason to change.'

'Philip. His name's Philip. We don't hold with name shortening here. And I think it's far too early to be thinking about plans for the future, dear. You're only — what? Nineteen, wasn't it? You haven't even begun to live yet, child. I'd like to think Philip would marry one day, but there's plenty of time yet. And I'm sure that one day you will meet a boy of your own age and want to settle down, too.' Julie thought she detected a hint of panic in her adversary's eyes at the thought that this cuckoo in the nest might have designs on her son. She disguised a smile and was about to wind the woman up maybe just a little bit when Phil spoke in her defence.

'Don't underestimate Jules, Mother.' Julie could have kissed Phil, right there in the drawing room. 'She's very bright. She can play the piano and guitar and she has a lovely singing voice. She's a wonderful artist, too, and can draw just about anything she puts her mind to. You'll have to show Mother some of your portraits, love. She made that dress she's wearing today.'

Violet sniffed. 'Yes, I can see that. You should have lined it dear, it would have been quite a nice little dress if you'd lined it.'

Julie was impressed at first that Phil had spoken out in her defence. It was lovely to hear him put into words the things that he admired about her. But as he went on his voice took on a wheedling, beseeching quality and she realised that it wasn't her that he was defending at all, but himself and the choice he'd made in a girlfriend.

'The others have all had wives and girlfriends. Why shouldn't I have one, too?' he muttered sulkily. Julie was shocked. The opinionated and insensitive man had turned into a five year-old child, desperate for his Mother's approval.

'Really, Philip,' his mother spoke to him sharply. 'You do get the silliest notions. Of course we're not saying you can't have a friend. You're twenty six years old; it's not up to us what you do. I'm sure Julie is a nice girl, in her own environment, we just feel that she's a little young for a man of your age.'

'We have a reputation,' Donald cut in. 'A certain social standing that has to be upheld. You running round with a slip of a girl, well, it doesn't look right, that's all. No offence, lass,' he finished, glancing at Julie.

'None taken,' said Julie, nonetheless offended.

They didn't stay long after that. The atmosphere was tense and Julie kept throwing furious looks at Phil. He made the excuse that they were calling in on friends on the way home and that time was getting on.

'Thank you for your hospitality, Mr and Mrs Woods. It's been nice meeting you,' she lied.

She shook hands stiffly with them both.

'Goodbye, lass, I hope your dad finds work soon.' Donald was relieved that she was going, but his wishes sounded sincere.

'Goodbye, Julia, dear. Do come again,' said Violet sweetly, gushing insincerity from every pore. She had drawn out the 'ah' on Julia.

'It's Julie, Mrs Woods. Just plain Julie.'

'Quite, dear,' said Violet.

Chapter Twelve

Three months later they bought a house.

It was a good house on Jesmond Avenue. Nice neighbourhood, upper-middle range of the price bracket. Philip was pleased with his purchase. He fronted most of the deposit and as the security credit checks were all run on him, the house went in his name only. That was okay, Julie didn't care about all that money and paperwork stuff, as Philip assured her it would be his house but their home. They were going to be happy there.

There was only one black cloud marring their horizon. Philip couldn't seem to find the courage to tell his parents he was leaving home. Through the exhilarating and tense weeks of the house sale going through, he was borne down with the extra worry of how his parents would react. He put it off first for days, then for weeks and finally for the full three month it took for the house to be officially theirs. She said they would go and face his parents together. How bad could it be? But Phil wouldn't hear of it. He knew all about waving red rags in front of raging bulls.

They went to pick up the keys together. It was supposed to be the day they were moving in. There was a hold up with the other people and instead of picking up the keys at nine in the morning; it was three in the afternoon before they took possession of the little pieces of brass that would let them into their new home. It was the perfect excuse for Philip.

'You move in today, love, and make everything nice. I'll talk to the folks tonight and join you tomorrow.' She hated the idea. This was the start of the rest of their lives. They would enter that house together, or not at all. It was more than that, though; instinct told her that if she'd moved in alone, he might never have joined her. She wasn't mercenary and didn't see the benefits of such an arrangement. They only had two days booked off work and one had been wasted. Common sense, and Philip bringing his greater will to bear, decreed that they'd leave the house move until the weekend. They celebrated with a champagne dinner that night, but the mood was broken and a tense atmosphere lay between them. Julie wouldn't have cared if they had to work the whole night through. She'd looked forward to this day for so long and now she was going home, to sleep in the same single bed that she'd slept in every night of her life.

Phil didn't talk to his parents on the Monday night. He couldn't find the right moment. He didn't talk to them on the Tuesday or the Wednesday or the Thursday. They were moving into the house on the Friday.

Each of those evenings they'd hit the shops and spend money lavishly, giggling as they piled the house high with beautiful things. Every night the bubble would burst and they'd each go back to their own homes. Julie's parents were diplomatic. They said it was a big thing for him, and to give him time and be understanding. She tried, but it was difficult. Julie gave him the them or me ultimatum.

He told his parents on the Friday morning, blurting it out over the breakfast table. It didn't go well. He left his mother sobbing and his father yelling. He had never defied them before.

Julie didn't have a lot of money, but when her Auntie Mavis had died, some money had been put in trust for her. She hadn't touched it when she turned eighteen, she had no need of extra money but she drew every penny of it out. Philip was broke, all his money had gone on the house deposit, so Julie's inheritance was spent furnishing the house. She had good taste and was amazed when Philip took a back seat and gave her almost a free rein when it came to buying furniture and fittings. She found that out of character for him. He could be very demanding and she hated to formulate the word, because once said it couldn't be withdrawn, but Phil was controlling. With something as big as his first ever house, Julie expected him to be picky to the nth degree, but on the contrary, he let her buy pretty much whatever she wanted. It was the spending spree of a lifetime carried out over several weeks. As Phil's wages came in those first few happy months, more was added to the pot. He was generous, denied her nothing and she had the time of her life spending money like water.

Phil was twenty-six, Julie just nineteen; neither of them had lived away from home before. Once the novelty of 'keeping house' had worn off and the pin money had run out, things were difficult. They had to tighten their belts and the first sign of things to come insinuated its way into their paradise.

They would come home from work, tired and fractious. Phil was used to a meal on the table; Julie had never cooked in her life. When he was on early shifts, Phil would do all the housework. He finished at three and when Julie walked in at half five she would be greeted by the smell of pledge and home cooking. On these days, Phil ran his home like an army base, everything just so, everything done properly.

When he worked a full day, the weave of his ordered life unravelled at the seams. Julie wanted to sit and relax when she got home from work. Phil wanted his tea and a clean house, just as his mother had always provided at the hotel. But, this wasn't the hotel, this was a house with dust on the units and the breakfast dishes still in the sink. He found it difficult living in a house and having to do everything for himself or rely on Julie, who didn't do things the way he wanted them to be done. The washing piled up. He hated that. He could see the sheen of dust on the units. It enraged him. Julie was in the habit of leaving clothes on the bedroom floor. He couldn't tolerate it.

They fought.

Things had not improved between Phil and his parents. He didn't see them at all for those first idyllic three months before the money ran out and the arguments started, but one day he had to ring them about some paperwork that he needed to collect. He said he and Julie would call at the hotel that evening. He always picked Julie up when they finished work. They'd go to Windermere. He saw no reason why there had to be any animosity.

'Don't you dare bring that gold digging tart to my home. Don't you dare, you little bastard,' Violet screamed down the phone.

Phil sat down heavily on the chair beside the telephone. He was rocked. He couldn't believe what he was hearing. Never, in his life, had he heard his mother swear at him. He hung up in a daze. He didn't go for his paperwork that night. But the row with his mother coincided with the first big fall out with his girlfriend.

The next time Phil spoke to Violet was when he rang to tell them that he was marrying Julie.

And, there was the S word. Julie was confused and didn't understand. He knew that, but when she came to him, insinuating with her ripe body that she wanted to be intimate, he couldn't help freezing. Her curves disgusted him and the thought of doing it terrified him.

That's why he proposed.

To buy some time.

In the first days of their courtship she had been all over him. It shamed him and made his cheeks burn the way her chaste kisses had become open mouthed and demanding. He didn't like that. He felt as though he might be swallowed up into the slightly sweet, slightly sour-tasting mouth. Sometimes when they said goodnight, she'd rub her body against him, her breath harsh and her eyes wanton. It scared him. He didn't like the feel of her breasts pushing into him. He felt the hard points of her nipples against his body when she embraced him and he felt filthy. He'd noticed she wasn't even wearing a bra.

He was horrified when she brought the subject of sex up. She actually said it, like a strumpet.

'Don't you want to make love to me?'

He certainly did not. 'Of course I do.' The thought was abhorrent.

He felt hot, the room was stifling. He wanted to run, aware of his testicles contracting and his limp penis tortoising its way back inside his body. He'd heard that it was wet and that a woman is slimy down there and smells of fish. Why the hell would anybody want to subject themselves to that?

'Of course I want you, baby,' he lied. 'It's just that, well, you know. I'm a Catholic. It's not allowed.'

She eased off then. Didn't get herself so het up. He was relieved, and maybe that's why he let her push him into buying the house. Maybe he thought the problem of the S word had gone away and she wouldn't expect to do it. He felt that he'd made his feelings clear.

He was wrong. It was obvious the day that they went to buy beds. He didn't mind her having a double bed. It was okay when she talked about the bedroom. Of course she could have the biggest room, which was fine by him, he'd already picked himself the attic room with the sloping roof and skylight that shone shafts of bright sunlight down on him in the mornings, and framed the beautiful vista of the stars at night. He suspected that she had other ideas, but he hated confrontation. He never voiced his opinions on the bedroom arrangements. Like telling his parents about moving out, he felt that the whole sleeping together issue was something that he'd have to work up to.

He never said a word until bedtime on their first night of living together. She went up for a bath and while she was preening and pampering herself, he crept up the second stairs and got into the snug single bed that she had bought for guests.

It's better this way, he reasoned to himself, no embarrassing scenes. She'll get the message now.

But she didn't get the message at all; she said she was hurt and confused to find him fast asleep in the attic. She didn't understand.

'What are you doing in here?' she asked, tears forming in her eyes. 'Aren't you coming to bed?'

He thought it was obvious that he was already in bed, and he would have to talk to her about knocking before she entered his room. He needed his privacy.

She was almost naked, she had on a thin white negligee and he could see the form of her, even in the pale moonlight coming through the window. Her breasts were full and the nipples stood out against the cold, enormous. His eyes betrayed him by travelling lower to the patch of darkness pushing against the fabric of the night-dress. His small penis shrivelled smaller and lay flaccid against the cushion of his testicles. He flattened his arms against the duvet, hiding himself from her.

She smelled of shampoo, and shower gel, talc and deodorant and some cloying sickly perfume. He just wanted her out.

'Go to bed, Julie, we'll talk things through in the morning.' Her head hung and she went to the door and she was just closing it behind her when he called her back.

'Julie?'

A smile came to her lips and the tears froze on her eyelids. She was framed in the doorway, backlit by light from the hallway and spotlighted in the glow of the moon. He saw her completely then, the swell at breast, stomach and hip, the thatch of dark hair between her legs, the want in her eyes. He was repulsed.

'In future, would you mind knocking before you come into my room?'

The next morning he came down to breakfast as though nothing had happened. Julie was already up, curled miserably into the plush armchair with her legs pulled under her. Her face was puffy with red eyes from crying most of the night and the double bed had been left undisturbed. She was confused and unhappy, she felt unwelcome in his house. Julie wanted her mum.

She wanted to talk it through. Didn't she understand that he just plain didn't want to do that? For the second time he fell back on his religious beliefs and said that he couldn't have sex out of wedlock. She pushed and wheedled and before he was totally aware of what he was doing, he'd grudgingly agreed that, yes, they should get married so that they could make love. She said she understood and he bought another few months in his own little bed looking at the stars.

'Jules and I are getting married, Mother.'

Chapter Thirteen

Her answer was a long time coming. He knew she was still there, he could hear her inhaling deeply on the other end of the telephone connection. The silence was laden with disappointment, her disappointment of him, and his feeling of being small and useless. He thought he was going to have to break the nothingness between them and be the first one to speak. He had cleared his throat nervously and had even stammered the first syllable of, 'Say something, please, Mother,' a couple of times when she cut in on his ineptitude to even manage basic vocabulary.

She spoke slowly and quietly. 'Put her on the line.' There was no please. The ice in her voice froze any argument he might have put forward. A bigger man could have tried to protect his wife to be, but he pointed the handset towards Julie.

'She wants to speak to you,' he mumbled in the voice of a chastised child.

She took the telephone from him. It was slick with the sweat from his clammy palm. 'Hel...'

'Are you pregnant?' Julie winced at the attack in the form of words. Four syllables, three words, and yet she felt as though the woman, who was soon to be her mother-in-law, had punched her in the face and knocked her to the floor with a single blow. It was only words that she had been struck with, and yet she straightened her posture and clung on to the door beside her for support against the assault.

'No, Mrs Woods, I am not pregnant. I—'

'Liar,' Violet spat. 'You must be pregnant. Why else would you be rushing into this ridiculous notion of marriage? My son's not a fool. He won't marry a low-grade trollop. Or is it just that you're scared, missy? Is that it? Hmm?'

Although she had asked a question, she had no intention of giving Julie an opportunity to reply. Barely pausing for breath, she launched herself into a full-blown rant, spitting out accusations like poisoned darts from a blowpipe. 'Are you scared? That's it, isn't it? You're scared that any day now, my Philip will look at you and see what you really are. He'll look at you and see filth, won't he? And we know what will happen then, don't we? He'll kick you out into the same gutter that he pulled you up from. Oh, I can see what your game is. You saw my poor son and your greedy little eyes lit up. You saw a great big pound sign and you grabbed at it, like any common little whore would.'

Philip was hovering half way across the room, tugging on his hair the way he always did when he was upset. Although he was over ten feet away from Julie, and the words were tinny and distorted by the telephone line, he could hear every word that his mother said. She had called him a bastard the last time they'd spoken. Now she was flinging insults at Julie. He tried to take hold of the telephone, and lowered his head so that his mouth was close to the receiver, but Julie wouldn't let go.

'Oh really, Mother. I think—' Julie held up a hand to silence him. She didn't even try to excuse herself from the tirade on the other end of the phone. She spoke directly to Phil without bothering to cover the handset for privacy.

'No, love, it's all right, let her speak. She needs to do this. Let her get it all off her chest.' Phil let the tension go from his body with an audible sigh. He was relieved not to have to try and get between the two strong women, better to let them sort it out themselves.

'Let me speak? Let me speak? Why, you condescending, crass, little bitch. How dare you assume that I need your permission to speak. Who the hell do you think you're talking to? I could buy and sell your stinking family a thousand times over.'

'Stop right there. You can say what you like about me, but leave my fam…' Violet cut her off as though she'd never spoken.

'But you know that, don't you? You know that if you don't get a ring on your finger, my son is going to see you for the gold digging tramp that you really are. Don't think I don't know what's going on. He's a meal ticket, isn't he? And you're going to take him for every penny you can, bleed him dry and then cast him aside when you move onto your next victim. Well, I'm telling you now, girl. This wedding will not take place. It isn't going to happen. Do you hear?' Her voice had risen to a shrill screech.

'Right, Mrs Woods, you've had your say now let me have—'

'Over my dead body. Do you hear me? Do you hear me?' Violet was screaming into the telephone, the last remnants of self-control lost in the rage of her tantrum. 'Don't mess with me, girl, because I'll crush you like a woodlouse.'

In other circumstances Julie would have found this funny. Even in the drama of the moment her mind wandered and she wondered how a woodlouse would crush. She missed the final barrage of the bitter woman's threats and was brought back to it with Violet screaming at her to put her son back on. Phil lolled beside her, looking diminished.

'I want you to go to Dr Watkins to be tested for AIDS,' were the first words she spoke when Phil muttered 'hello' into the handset.

'Oh really mother now you're being...'

'She could be riddled with disease. You don't know who she's lain down with before you, do you? I'd hate to think that you've caught something dirty from her. Oh, Philip, please go and get yourself checked out. You've always been such a sensible boy. Why are you doing this to me? How could you hurt me so, after all that I've sacrificed for you?' Phil's eyelids drooped and his posture slumped as he settled in for a heavy dose of Violet's pain and disappointment. 'You said you'd never leave me. You were the one who was going to stay home and look after me. We've always been so close, Philip. How could you let this trollop come between us like this? I swear, this marriage will not happen. I forbid it. Now tell the girl to go back where she came from and come home immediately. We can sort out the mess you've got yourself into buying that silly little house. Come back to your family and be forgiven, son, because I'm telling you now, if you don't, you are going to lose us all. And for what? Eh? What is so good about this fat, low grade bitch that you'd give up your own family for her?'

'Mother, please. It doesn't have to be like this. If you'd just give Jules a chance.'

'Never. She will not set foot over my door, and as long as you are with her, neither will you. I hope you'll think it's worth it son, because you've broken my heart. Your father, brothers and I will not be attending this sham of a wedding.'

She ranted some more, sobbed some more and feigned illness, but the latter was only a momentary hiatus while she restocked on new and previously unused insults. Philip learned that his mother had quite a talent for profanity and gutter talk. Julie sat quietly by, listening to the tinny voice spouting poison, willing Phil to stand up to his mother. She heard the names the foul woman called her, but remained seated; breathing slowly and thinking about the flowers she wanted to plant in the garden. If we marry in early May, she thought, the cherry and apple blossom will be out. That'll be nice for photographs. She said nothing, hoping that Phil would jump to her defence at some point. And then Violet got started in on Julie's family again.

'The father doesn't work and the mother's a

domestic, Philip. They're scum, scrounging off the state and living a life of filth and squalor.'

It was as though a bomb had been placed under the pink cherry blossom tree. Julie, sitting pretty beneath the boughs in a white dress, saw the blossom explode and she was on her feet wrenching the telephone out of her fiancé's hand.

'You nasty, venomous old cow.' She screamed, slamming the telephone into its cradle hard enough to cause a tremor to ripple through her carpal tunnel.

They argued that night. It started when Phil turned to her and said in a cold voice, 'I won't have you speaking to Mother like that,' and finished some time after midnight when Phil stormed up to his bedroom in a sulk.

Julie didn't feel lonely lying in bed on her own that night. She didn't cry into her pillow, confused and rejected. She seethed, furious with Phil for taking his mother's side. Sleep was a long time coming.

The distance between them was tangible the next morning, the air thick with resentment. Julie made plans for her wedding, wondering all the while if she even wanted to get married, and Phil sulked. As she was leafing through a brochure of wedding cakes, she paused and examined her reasons for going through with a wedding to a spineless man who would never protect her when she needed him to. She loved her new lifestyle. She loved her house. After living on a rough council estate all of her life, after tasting a better life, she didn't want to go back to what she had been. She was ashamed to recognise that her motive was more mercenary and sheer bloody-mindedness than love. There was no way she was going to let the old cow win this one. She, Julie, was going to marry Philip, and if that pissed on Violet Woods' parade then all well and good. Somebody had to stand up to the evil old trout and if her future husband couldn't do it, then she was going to marry him and teach him how.

Philip was great at sulking over short distances, but he couldn't go the mile. 'I'm making a coffee, can I get you one?' he said at three thirty. The frost was still in the air, but she sensed some slush dripping from the edges. She hadn't made lunch, so they both did without. At teatime he went to the kitchen and made chicken with pasta and a cracked pepper sauce. It was her favourite and they ate from trays in the lounge, something Phil normally hated. That evening they picked out a honeymoon in Corfu but Julie still went to bed alone.

The following day she had just finished washing up after their evening meal and they were settling down to watch some TV. Julie went into the lounge to answer the phone, but Phil was already there, pulling a face at being disturbed. His telephone voice was evident by the time he'd put the handset to his ear.

'He-llo,' he chimed. Around both strangers and on the telephone he sounded like the most easygoing bloke in the world.

'All right, Spud. How's it going?' It was SP. He'd called Phil Spud for years, but nobody could remember the origins of the nickname. 'What's going on, bro? Mum's fucking furious.' It was only around Violet that they spoke with cut-glass pronunciation. 'What's all this about you getting married? Bit of a rush, isn't it? Hell, we haven't even met the girl yet.'

'You've heard then? Listen, SP, are you going to come?'

'Whoa. Slow down man. In fact, that's what I've rung up to say. Why not just slow down. Mum say's this girl—what's her name? Julie? Mum says, she says, she's not pregnant or anything, so what's the rush? Why don't you just wait a while? You've not known her five minutes. We're worried about you, Spud, and don't want to see you made a fool of, that's all.'

'Made a fool of? What the fuck are you talking about? Who's making a fool of me, SP? You're judging her before you've even met her just because of what Mum says.'

'I don't like my Mum being hurt like this, Phil, she was crying to Ros for two hours today. What the hell are you playing at?' His voice, although still cajoling, had taken on a hard edge.

Phil's voice echoed his resentment. 'Look, I don't like Mum being hurt either. All I want to do is marry the girl I...All I want to do is marry Julie, and if you don't want to come, then bollocks to you, that's fine, but the marriage is going ahead. Sod the lot of you.'

'Come down off that bloody high horse of yours a minute, will you? If my littlest bro is getting married, then of course we'll be there, all the lads will, you know that.'

'And Mum and Dad?'

'Well, Spud, that might not happen.'

'Well stuff them then.'

'She's pretty raged up you know, and the old man just wants a quiet life. My guess is, he'll try and talk her round, but, well, you know what she's like. So what's the big hurry, Phil? Why are you digging your heels in on this? If you waited and gave everybody a chance to get to know her, I'm sure things will calm down. Why do you have to get married on the rush? You've only known her six months for Chris sake, and six weeks is a ridiculously short space of time. How can you arrange a marriage in six weeks? Doesn't it make sense to do things properly? Why not set a date for next summer and we'll have a bash to be proud of? Or are you hiding something? Come on, tell us the truth, is she up the duff?'

Phil spent the next ten minutes convincing SP that Julie was not pregnant. He blushed as he admitted that they hadn't even slept together and that they had separate bedrooms for the time being. He explained that he wanted to do things properly. Julie was furious and could have hit him for talking about their personal life so openly.

'Look, Spud, let me be honest with you. We're worried. What's this with the mental illness thing? What exactly is wrong with her? I'm not judging or anything but if we can understand, maybe what you're doing won't seem so mad.'

'What?' Phil spluttered into the telephone. 'There's nothing wrong with her, what are you on about? Who's saying that? What the fuck? What mental illness?'

'Mum says she's been in Dane Garth. Said she thought it was drugs-related, something to do with heroin, or something.'

'Oh, she's gone too far this time. She's talking a load of bollocks, man. Heroin! I've never heard anything so ridiculous.' He was shouting now. Julie had been following Phil's side of the conversation, and at that moment, just until the shock set in, she thought the situation was hilarious. She laughed.

'She said what?' she spluttered. 'I've never done drugs in my life.'

On the other end of the telephone SP heard what Julie had said.

He lowered his voice to a whisper. 'I'm guessing she hasn't got AIDS either, then.'

'No she has not got bloody AIDS.' This time even Phil could see the funny side, and the three of them shared the joke.

SP tried to persuade Phil and Julie to change their plans and have the reception at the hotel, but Julie wouldn't hear of it. She wanted this to be her wedding, organised her way.

She asked to speak to SP before Phil hung up. 'Hello, Simon Peter.'

'Oh fuck the formalities, call me SP, everyone does.'

'Look,' she went on. 'I know you think this is too soon and all that, but I do love your brother, you know?

I suppose, I just want to say thank you for giving us a go. It means a lot to Phil, well, to both of us. Thank you.'

Julie was hurt. She wasn't a bad person. How could Violet make up those horrible lies about her? She went into the garden and dug around the plants in her herb garden looking for miscreant weeds. She talked to her baby chives, they were growing well but they had grown long and leggy, bolting for the sun until they couldn't sustain their own weight and had slewed to one side. Julie didn't want them to look untidy. She supported them with fresh soil while asking the more robust Basil why anybody could be so cruel. Phil brought her coffee and they sat at their table on the patio enjoying the garden. It was bitterly cold and he put his cardigan around her shoulders. He praised her efforts in the garden and said that she was doing a good job. She basked in his praise. He told her not to worry and that everything would work out just fine. She tried to believe him.

James rang the same evening. He began the conversation with, 'Way to go, bro,' and then continued, 'have you lost the plot, or what? It's okay shacking up with a drug-crazed loony for a bit. Hell, I've bedded a few of them myself, but fucking hell man, wanting to marry one? If you were here now, I'd shake your hand. It's the first time you've ever bested me as the black sheep of the family. When did you grow a pair of bollocks? Jesus, I bet the old girl had a cow. Wish I'd seen it. Is she a goer then, this Julie?'

For the second time that night, Phil explained the situation and James was disappointed. But he good-naturedly assured them that he wouldn't miss the wedding for the world. 'Hell, there's bound to be a punch up somewhere along the line, bud. Count me in. I'll travel up from London the night before with John, if he's coming. You can guarantee he won't want to miss out on a party.'

Andrew was the next to ring. SP had already filled him in on the anti-climax of their mother's vicious tongue.

'Hey, Phil. I'm sorry about all the hassle you've had, bruv. I've just called to say that I hope there's an invitation to this wedding for us.'

And so it was arranged. The wedding was going ahead and all the Woods' boys would be in attendance. Julie didn't feel accepted by this hostile family, but she did feel that maybe a few bridges had been mended before too much damage was done.

They didn't hear from Mother Woods again until soon after the invitations had been sent out. Phil had invited friends in Windermere and word spread that the youngest of the Woods boys was getting married and, what's more, it was taking place in a registry office.

People stopped Violet in the street to fish for gossip about this startlingly low-key marriage. She flew home that day in a rage. She tried to get Donald to do the dirty work for her, to let it be understood that this was his idea and that he'd put his foot down to make his wife comply. Indeed, Donald had done his damnedest to make Violet change her mind about not attending their son's wedding. It broke his heart to think that he wouldn't be there to shake his youngest son's hand and wish him all the best. He didn't approve of the girl, either, but it was Phil's choice and, rightly or wrongly, he had made it. To this point, Violet had been immovable. Donald had resigned himself to the fact that if he wanted a continued peaceful life, he would have to stand resolutely beside his wife on this one. He wanted to go against her wishes, but this was too big a fight for him to take on. The gossips were already out in force; it wouldn't do to be seen to be at war with his wife, and if he went against her, he knew for a certainty there would be war.

She flounced through reception in a fury. Mrs Hughes-Norris was knocked out of her path as Violet muscled her way through the WI brigade with elbows out and murder in her eyes.

'Something must be done about this wedding,' she said to her husband when she reached their suite.

Donald was rarely immovable about anything, but on this point, he faced his wife down and flatly refused to do her grovelling for her. Had Violet been less involved in herself at that moment, she might have seen an unusual expression tiptoe across her husband's face. He listened with his arms folded across his chest. His mouth worked hard not to let the minuscule curl at the edges of his lips turn into a full-on grin, his eyes shone. He'd never seen Violet eat humble pie before and he wanted to see if it could be done. He was going to enjoy this. He had tried to push for a run out to see the couple and sort this silly mess out face to face, but that was going too far and Violet was having none of it.

'He-llo.'

'Philip, My daaarhling. How are you both? How is Julia?' Violet enthused in a voice flooded with insincerity.

'What is it, Mother? If you want another fight, we're not interested. You said some vile, terrible things about Jules. How could you?'

'Oh, yes, I know dear,' her voice remained bright and not in the least repentant. 'Your father and the boys have told me off already about that silly misunderstanding. You must tell Julia to be more precise about things dear. Still, never mind that, it's not important. Now then, dear, time is moving on you know. If we are going to make this wedding the Event of the Year, dear, we are going to have to get on. Now then, the first thing we've got to do is cancel that horrible registry office. What were you thinking, Philip? How beneath you. Sometimes I despair of you boys, I really do. Now, wait until you hear this. It was almost impossible, I grant you, and there had to be some radical changes made. But—are you ready for this, dear? As a special favour to me, Monsignor Burton has agreed to attend your wedding at St Mary's though of course father McDonnegal will be leading the service. We'll have the hotel at our disposal, of course. There now, what do you think of that?'

Julie, who had her ear pressed against the

telephone and was fighting for the handset with Phil to hear what Violet was saying, couldn't believe what she heard. Phil stood there like a plank listening to his Mother muscle in. He didn't say a word. Julie was the first to speak. She addressed her comment to Phil, but was in no doubt that Violet, and indeed most of the neighbours, could hear her.

'No way. No bloody way is that wom..'

Violet gave a little chuckle. 'Oh, she's such a one, that Julia of yours. Tell her there's no need to thank me, dear. I'll pick her up at ten sharp tomorrow; we'll have to have her measured for a dress.' Her voice dropped slightly, 'Given her dimensions it might take some time, dear. It really is most inconsiderate of you, giving me so little time to arrange an entire wedding, and not just any wedding. The Wedding of the Year, dear. Now, you two lovebirds just leave everything to me. Cheerio.' And with that, Phil was left listening to a broken connection, and Violet was gone.

'Well, thank you very much,' screamed Julie, wheeling round to Phil in fury. 'Why didn't you tell her that there's no way I'm going with her to get my wedding dress? In fact, while were on the subject, why didn't you tell her that while she's welcome as a guest, she's having absolutely nothing to do with the organisation? Why didn't you tell her, Phil?' she finished on a sob.

Phil's mouth had stretched to form a thin lipless line. He spoke to her in disgust. 'You're hysterical. Calm down and when you're ready to have a civilised

146

discussion, then we'll talk.'

'She called me an AIDS ridden junkie with mental problems, Phil. How do you expect me to react?'

He retreated to the quiet of the study.

She was hurt. She sat on the sofa staring at the television but taking nothing in. she couldn't understand why Phil wouldn't stand up to his mother. Gradually, her blood pressure dropped, her breathing returned to normal and she went from rasping sobs to the occasional dry hitch. It wasn't Phil's fault that his mother had rung, she could see that. She had turned on him irrationally, she could see that too. She took him a cup of coffee, remembering to knock on the study door and wait for an answer before going in.

'I'm sorry, love,' she said, going up behind him and putting her arms around his shoulders. She felt him stiffen beneath her touch. 'I know this isn't easy for you and you must feel stuck between us. Can we talk now, please?'

'She's my mother, Julie. Why can't you let her in? Have you any idea how hard that must have been for her?'

Julie wanted to say that it wasn't easy for her either but she held her counsel. 'If I go tomorrow, she's going to take over. This is our wedding. It's supposed to be the best day of our lives. I want us to arrange it ourselves. I don't mind getting married at the registry. I like the fact that it's going to be small and intimate and that we're paying for it all ourselves. I don't want her to take over, Phil.'

'Oh, well, excuse me here, Julia, I didn't realise you were the elite when it came to producing a wedding. Have you any idea how many weddings Mother's managed. She's done celebrities.'

'What did you just call me?'

'What?'

'You just called me Julia.'

'No I didn't. I said —'

'You did. You called me Julia.'

'Don't be ridiculous. Anyway, my mother's wedding plans might not be good enough for you, but I think it was very generous of her. You're going to make her look a fool in front of her priest if you snub her. And frankly, *Julie*, I won't have that. I'm telling you, either you let my mother in, or the wedding's off. And what's more, I expect you to show some gratitude. So, what's it to be? Do you want to marry me, or not?'

She tried to keep her temper. He was still angry with her. He had every right to be but she was angry too. 'I'm sorry, Phil, but that's just it. Your mum produces weddings; she choreographs them like a stage production. That's wonderful if it's what you want. But I just want us to say our vows with the people we care about behind us and then have a bit of a do afterwards. I just want it to be special. I know we had no choice but to do it on the cheap, but you know what, it's exactly the way I want it.'

'Have you once stopped to think what I want? Have you once asked me if I want a dirty little two-bit affair? Has it even crossed your mind that unless I'm married in the sight of God, as far as I'm concerned, we won't be properly married? I went along with you because it was all we could afford and yes, dammit, I wanted to please you.' He omitted the fact that the main reason he agreed to marry her was to keep her out of his bed. 'Things are different now. Mother is offering us a proper marriage, done in the correct way.' The anger went out of his voice and she felt his shoulders slump. 'That's what I want, Julie.'

She turned things over through the night. Insomnia was a new but frequent bed partner these days. At first, she stubbornly resisted the thought of that woman having anything at all to do with their wedding. It felt as though having her making arrangements was to give the wedding the kiss of death before they even made it to the alter. And then some of Phil's words came back to her, 'Have you any idea how hard that must have been for her?' Julie smiled and hugged a pillow to her. The thought of how hard it would be for Violet to watch her favourite son marry a woman she detested, filled Julie with a delicious feeling of power. Even better was the fact that she would be paying for it all. Hadn't one of her main accusations been that Julie was a gold digger? She could learn her part and, she decided, she was going to play it to the hilt. It would have to be a grand wedding, because Julie knew that Violet's position in the community was everything to her. It would be a wonderful, lavish and expensive wedding, with all of Julie's down to earth family and friends in attendance, and Violet would be paying for every penny of it. Let the old bitch have her way, thought Julie. I'm going to love every second of it from this moment on. And, while I'm having the time of my life, she'll hate it and be suffering.

She slept soundly dreaming of wedding cake and victory.

Chapter Fourteen

It was six thirty in the morning. Julie was sitting in the garden as the sun rose on her wedding day. The enclosed back and side garden of their house was enormous and she was sitting on a bench made out of three large rocks. She was sipping at her first coffee of the day, it was piping hot and calming. She loved this seat in this part of the garden. Phil had made it for her; she had chosen the position because it had the best view over the rest of the garden. It was a simple piece of furniture, half ornamental and half functional. He'd made it from three large rocks taken from Roan Head beach. He'd found the flat, broad seat that lay horizontally across the top and then it had taken weeks of beachcombing to find two tall pieces of rock that were similar enough in size to work into legs. She'd insisted that it was put under the boughs of the huge cherry tree in the bottom left hand corner of the patio. The ground before her was littered with thousands of cherry blossom petals. The cherry blossom was her favourite tree, she loved its delicate, pale pink petals but hated that it only flowered for such a short time. She looked ahead to her first photograph later that morning when she had put her dress on. She'd sit under the tree with her train arranged around her, and fresh petals would be falling as the shutter closed.

She thought about Phil at the hotel. Following with tradition, he'd spent the night there with his best man and long-time friend, Chris Wattle. She smiled as she imagined his entire family trying to talk him out of marrying her. She could almost hear them saying, 'It's not too late to back out, Spud.' But she knew that he would hold firm and be standing at that alter when she walked down the aisle. Her fiancé was a stubborn man. He wouldn't let himself down.

But would he let her down? That was the question that she asked herself as she sat under the tree. Did he really love her? More to the point, did she love him? She thought that she was in love when they'd moved in together, but months of sharing a house came with all of his obsessive compulsive habits. She'd met a man who was easy going and mellow. In reality, he wasn't like that at all. He was resolute and controlling. She felt that he was possessed by the Catholic religion. And then there was the question of sex. She could understand that he wanted to go to his wedding bed a virgin. She was not. And while she understood and respected his religious beliefs, there was a little nagging voice at the back of her head that told her that things might not change after the ceremony. Whenever she'd mentioned him moving into her room—their room—after the wedding, he changed the subject.

Do you love him? She could hear the voice inside her head as clearly as if she'd spoken the words out loud. She ignored it and thought about her dress.

Do you love him?

She listened to the birdsong as the morning chorus practiced singing her to her wedding. She would have smiled at her inner child if that child hadn't grabbed the bars of her cage and rattled it so thoroughly that she couldn't ignore what she already knew.

No, she didn't love him. But she wanted to, so that was something. She felt that with time, she could learn just how he liked the cutlery drawer arranging, and she would remember to turn all of the labels of the tins in the cupboard to the front. They just needed to grow together a bit. He would smarten her up and make her more conscientious and particular about things and she would loosen him out. She did believe that they could make a good marriage from a troubled start. It wasn't all about flouncy dresses and home-grown confetti trees. If she'd truly believed that it wasn't going to be a happy marriage for both of them, she would never have gone through with it.

She felt cheated. She should have been ecstatic. She'd written it into her wedding plan, this cup of coffee, sitting under the cherry blossom, feeling ecstatic. She did feel excited about the day and the honeymoon to follow, but bowled over by true love and excitement at embarking on a lifelong union with her husband, no. It wasn't like that. She made her first vow of the day. It was a private one. She vowed that, no matter what, she was going to be a good wife.

They'd had drinks the night before. Several empty wine bottles rested on the worktops in the kitchen. Phil wouldn't like that. He hated an untidy home. Lisa and Emma, her sisters, had stayed over, along with Anne Wattle, the best man's wife, at Phil's insistence. Julie had only met her once before. She was a quiet woman, almost silent. The three of them had spent all night trying to involve her in conversation and not let her feel left out, but it had been awkward. Julie hoped that at least one of her sisters would be downstairs before Anne.

An hour later, the kitchen was buzzing with excited conversation. It was still only eight o'clock and she wasn't getting married until one. Phil had asked her not to drink too much the night before. He said it was for her own good because he wanted her to enjoy her wedding day with a clear head. It had seemed sensible advice. Anne was teetotal and drank only orange juice. Lisa and Emma had both come downstairs with hangovers after being called by Julie two minutes after Anne made an appearance. Emma, the sensible one, suggested bacon butties to soak up last night's wine. Lisa, the forward one, suggested Anne make them. Anne, the silent one, cooked.

After eating, Anne tidied the house and washed up while Julie's sisters fought over the bathroom. Julie was to be the last of them to be ready and Anne said that she would take her turn after Lisa and Emma, or after Julie, or whenever, she said she really didn't mind. The hairdresser was arriving at eleven. Julie spent a long time up to her neck in bubbles in the bath, her last bath as a single woman.

Another woman arrived to do their makeup and when she had finished Julie had never felt so beautiful, in fact she had never once in her entire life felt attractive at all until that moment when she looked in the mirror. She felt that she had been masked and turned into somebody that she didn't know. She felt shy when she stood in the middle of the living room in her wedding dress. Phil's mother had tried to buy a dress that was frumpy and unflattering to her larger than average shape. Julie knew that she had done it on purpose to score points, to be able to say to her cronies, 'Well, of course, dear, I did the best that I could with what I had to work with. Despite it costing four thousand pounds, nothing could make her look anything other than what she is. I did try.' Julie had fought her in the towns and on the beaches. She told her that she wouldn't be seen dead in any of the dresses that Violet had picked out for her. She had stormed out of the shop, giving Violet more cause to tittle tattle about her to the bridal wear proprietor. Julie had refused to return until her wishes had been listened to. Far from opting for a big fat ugly cloud of net that made her look like Antarctica, she opted for simple sophisticated elegance. Her dress had a fitted bodice that, when laced, lost an instant three inches of her waistline. The skirt was a shift of heavy satin, straight-lined and flattering to the bigger lady. The train swirled around her feet and she'd chosen a full veil that fell to her waist. On her wedding day, Julie Spencer looked beautiful.

Her parents arrived, and cried. The wedding party went into the garden and Julie sat on the bench at the end of the patio with her father standing above her, one hand resting protectively on her shoulder. The photographer arrived an hour earlier and had been setting up his equipment in the garden. It was all perfect. How could this wedding not be blessed when everything had fallen into place just as she had wanted it to? She put all the thoughts that she'd had that morning down to wedding day jitters.

At twelve thirty, a white Rolls Royce, adorned with deep purple ribbons to match her colour scheme, pulled up outside the front door. The neighbours had all gathered to see the bride leave. Julie felt like a princess.

At the church, standing in front of the massive oak doors, she was scared. The knave was cool and peaceful, her husband-to-be was waiting for her on the other side of the doors and yet she wanted to stay where she was and collect her thoughts. So he had turned up. His mother, the family, hadn't talked him out of it. She was surprised that they hadn't succeeded. Nobody gave her the 'not too late' speech. They told her how lucky she was and how she'd fallen on her feet. She realised that she was bloody amazed that her future husband had turned up to marry her at all. She felt grateful. The organ took up the opening strains of *The Wedding March* and her father held out his arm to her. Showtime.

As they walked past each pew, the people turned to look at her. Aunties that she hadn't seen for years beamed their gummy grins and, on Phil's side, people that she'd never met before looked at her curiously, wanting to see the disgusting, drug addled creature that Phil had taken up with. When they reached the front of the church her mum already had a tissue up to her face, dabbing at her eyes and sniffing loudly. Violet's reaction was very different. As Julie approached the alter she locked eyes with her future mother-in-law. In that unguarded second before she rearranged her mask, the look in Violet's eye was one of pure hatred. In that split second, her lip curled away from her teeth in what appeared to be a snarl. Julie knew that no olive branches had been laid, no alms arranged before her. There may have been a veneer applied to their relationship for the sake of appearances on this one day, but the battle swords were drawn. The four brothers and their spouses stared, neither warmly nor openly hostile, just bland vacant stares. Simon Peter was only concerned with his own appearance and looked bored. Andrew was disinterested; he was failing valiantly in an attempt to keep his children under control. James' eyes swept over the yards of satin and lace and then journeyed back up Julie's voluptuous body; they came to rest on the bodice with a sneer. John's glance rested on Julie for only a second before straying to Lisa. He looked her up and down with lust in his gaze and his partner Gaynor's expression hardened and fixed pointedly on Jesus on the Cross. Jealousy leaked from her posture and hatred for Julie, who had the pretty sister, grew in the pit of her stomach.

As the procession came to the alter railing and Richard, Julie's dad, delivered her to her husband-to-be, and Philip beamed, the choristers stood. Philip tried to squeeze out a little tear and very nearly succeeded. Julie did feel emotional as the soloist's soprano voice sang *Ave Maria.* At the final refrain, the choir joined in and the music was striking. At Violet's express insistence, Monsignor Burton had been wheeled out for the day. He hadn't left his monastery in Keswick for over five years. The Benedictine monks cared for him and the old priest was well into his late nineties. He spent most of his time in service, or dosing in the monastery gardens and was as nutty as a squirrel's stash. The clergy had refused point blank to turn the poor old gentleman out of his routine. It would confuse him, they said but Violet would hear none of it. As well as writing several letters of appeal to the Bishop himself, she turned up on the monastery doorstep to plead her case. She told them in no uncertain terms that the Monsignor had Married Violet. He had served at the Christenings, and First Holy Communions, of all five of her boys. She wept into her handkerchief and said that if he wasn't in attendance at the marriage of her youngest child, then as long as the monsignor was alive, the wedding couldn't go ahead. The clergy pondered this statement at length to determine if the crazy old coot was making a death threat. In the end it didn't matter because the gilt edged cheque that she discretely handed over — towards the monastery funds—salved their holy conscience.

The Monsignor was slumped forward in his wheelchair at the side of the congregation, conducting his own personal mass in Latin to an audience of none. When he forgot which part he was up to, he simply went back to the beginning and began again. Violet said later that it had been most unfortunate and she deeply regretted her insistence that he be the guest of honour. At several points during the service, proceedings had to halt because he'd hit a particularly rousing part of his service and he'd fling his hands up and incant Latin at a far-reaching cry. It was only the restraints tying him into the wheelchair that held him in place and stopped him launching himself out of the chair to kneel at the appropriate times.

Everybody laughed politely, except Violet who was horrified, when Julie and Philip knelt at the altar and the brother's had written 'he' on the sole of one of Philip's shoes and 'lp' on the other.

The crucial point of the ceremony, the bit that people would talk about for months was the part where the priest asked the congregation, 'If anybody here knows of any lawful impediment why these two people should not be joined in holy matrimony, then let them speak now or forever hold their peace.' Donald placed a restraining hand on Violet's shoulder, manning up to stop his wife from disgracing herself, her marriage and her entire family. When Violet had changed her mind about boycotting the wedding she was still ranting and raving. She had promised every family member that when that time came she would stand up and denounce the wedding. At some point, the chambermaids had heard her making the same threat to Simon Peter and then the whole village knew what Violet had been planning. Julie and Philip knew because Violet had screamed the threat down the phone at her. Speculation was rife as to whether it would prove to be an empty and meaningless threat or not. After all, if Violet did say anything, she would only be making an unholy show of herself.

The moment came and Father McDonnegal laid down the gauntlet. You could hear a pin drop in the church. The outcome of the next thirty seconds meant a lot to Gary Yardley, one of the regulars in the hotel bar, he was running a book on it. Everybody's attention was focused on Violet. Julie had laid plans of her own and that's when she chose to show the village, and her new family, some of her mettle. As the priest spoke the words she was in profile to Violet. She removed her left hand from Philip's, gathered up her train and turned to face Violet. And there she stood holding her cascading bouquet of honeysuckle in front of her. Her expression was neutral, but her eyes were wide open, challenging. Violet had nothing. She coloured to the roots of her bronze hair dye. Her face was scarlet and clashed ridiculously with the Barbara Cartland hat of flowers and feathers spilling all over her head. Julie raised an eyebrow. Only seconds had passed since the priest had finished speaking, but as Julie held her ground, and Violet squirmed and flustered, it seemed much longer. After Julie raised her eyebrow, effectively slapping Violet across the face with her glove, the congregation let out their first held breath and drew a second. It was clear that she wasn't going to turn back to the altar until some response had been made.

Violet stared at her, silently imploring her to go back and continue the service. Still Julie waited. Violet cleared her throat. She made a sound that might have been a titter, or a chortle. Perhaps she attempted bell-like laughter but instead she spat out barbs from the wire. She smiled a sickly smile, pleading with her still, squirming uncomfortably in her seat, and turned to Auntie Dorothy beside her, rolling her eyes as though to say, Silly girl, she does so like her practical jokes. Her smile was forced and tight-lipped as she discreetly shooed Julie's attention back to the priest with a white-gloved hand. Even the priest had been holding his breath.

Julie lowered her eyebrow, nodded once and with a flick of her hair, she curtsied proudly to Violet, and turned back to the altar. Philip was stiff. When she took his hand and asked Father McDonnegal to continue he allowed it for the sake of propriety, but Julie knew he was furious with her for embarrassing his mother. He went through the motions, but Julie had ruined their day.

Philip played his part. When he spoke the last of his vows his eyes shone with love, but Julie saw the glint behind the sheen that wasn't visible to anybody else. When it came to exchanging the rings, Julie's fingers had swelled. Philip made several attempts but couldn't push the band past the fat below the second joint of her ring finger. They heard the brother's laughing at them in the pew behind. James guffawed. Philip was embarrassed and Julie was angry. It wasn't her fault

161

that her fingers had swelled in the heat. When the ceremony was over and the register signed, the priest was relieved. Philip was still sulking about his mother and Julie didn't know how she felt. She tried to analyse it while posing for photographs in the archway of the seventeenth century church. She felt a headache coming on.

Julie had been looking forward to her reception; she thought she would be able to relax. But the headache niggled at her while they ate the succulent roast beef dinner. By the main course, the niggle had turned into a roar. She felt sick and barely picked at the food that she had so looked forward to. Desserts were Julie's vice. She loved rich, sticky, creamy desserts. When the trifle was delivered to her plate she couldn't touch it. The pain in her head was blinding. She just wanted to lie down. She had only taken one sip from her glass. During the toasts she pretended to sip the vintage champagne. The noise of clattering cutlery, bustling waiters and conversation was deafening. She barely heard the best man's speech. When her father got up to speak she pulled her mind past the jack-hammer in her head to listen. He spoke from the heart and with love. He told Julie how proud of her he was.

Donald rose from his seat. He kept his words brief, welcomed Julie into the family and raised his glass in toast. He was stoic and dignified. What couldn't be killed had to be endured.

Julie's parents had saved to give them a hundred pounds. It wasn't much but they had worked hard for the money and Julie knew that it was more than they could afford. Phil's parents had paid for the wedding at a cost of thousands that meant nothing and the brother's had clubbed together for a cheap trinket. Julie took the insult and stored it.

After the meal, there was an hour of mingling before the evening entertainment got underway. Julie still felt terrible. The headache had turned into a full blown migraine and she couldn't bear it. She went from clique to clique, ensuring that everybody was having a good time. She carried her untouched flute of champagne with her and couldn't face a drop. She heard James' raucous laugh as the words of his conversation drifted to her. 'Yeah,' he said to a group of the hotel staff. 'I wanted to write "Help me," on one shoe and, "I'm about to be crushed," on the other, but the lads wouldn't let me.'

Julie took this additional insult and stored it. She left her party to go to bed before the first dance, before the cutting of the cake and before the party got underway. She threw up while still in the acres of restricting wedding dress and then hung over the toilet bowl dry heaving for nearly an hour. She fought to get out of the dress but she couldn't, it was like a straitjacket, restraining her and crushing her diaphragm. Fully dressed, she lay on the marital four poster and wanted to die. The day had been a disaster and she felt awful. Her head was pounding and she couldn't face even the smallest chink of light. She prayed that somebody would come by soon and untie

163

her from the suffocating wedding dress, but nobody did. Philip never came to bed; he stayed up all night partying with his brothers. Julie spent her wedding night ill and alone.

Chapter Fifteen

Julie had a terrible night. The wedding dress had cut into her and she couldn't breathe. The migraine had pummelled her until the early hours of the morning when she fell into a fitful sleep. She woke in a fugue. The curtains were heavy and lined and let in no light. It took her a moment to realise where she was. She thought it was still the middle of the night. It took her another moment to remember that she was a married woman. She turned her head to look at her new husband, but he wasn't there. It was ten o'clock. Why hadn't anybody called her for breakfast? Some of the previous day's misery washed over her but she refused to allow it access to her mind. She felt a little bit thick-headed but not unwell, the migraine had left her. Today was the first day of her marriage; they were going to Corfu later on their honeymoon. Things had got off to a bad start but that was behind them. She was excited. She jumped out of bed, fought with the damned dress and wrestled her way over to the window where she flung open the curtains and let glorious, bright sunshine flood the room. She rang reception to ask them to send one of her sisters. She wanted a bath before she went in search of Phil and needed somebody to untie her from the dress. The girl on reception told her that as her family had to check out of their rooms by ten, they had just left to travel home to Barrow. Violet had left word for them that Julie had asked not to be disturbed. Violet had thrown her family out as though they were any old guests. How could she be so cruel? Not stopping to check her appearance, she flounced out of the room to either find her husband or confront her bitch of a mother-in-law, whichever came first.

The desk clerk stared at Julie, but told her that Phil had passed out and was carried to John's room just before the guests arrived for their breakfast. She turned from the desk. Everybody milling around the reception area stopped to stare at her. Sharon paged Simon Peter to report a small problem in reception.

SP strode in and without saying a word he grabbed Julie roughly under the elbow and guided her across the room and to the lift. It only took seconds to open as it was already on the ground floor. 'What the hell are you playing at coming into reception like that?' He whispered, pointing at her dress. 'You look deranged. Who do you think you are, Lady fucking Haversham?'

Julie had no idea who Lady Fucking Haversham was, so ignored his question and posed one of her own. 'Where's Phil?'

SP pushed her into the lift. 'Make yourself decent, woman, and never come into my hotel if you aren't presentable again.'

The front of her dress was splattered in vomit. Her hair had come down from its wedding arrangement on one side and hung in vomit-stiffened tails. Her makeup, that had been so exquisite the day before, had run down her face. Her breasts, having nowhere else to go, partially spilled out of the top of the tight bodice. SP

166

was right, she looked deranged. As the lift rose, and in the tight confines, she could smell herself. She was ashamed.

The lift stopped on the top floor. As she squeezed her size and her dress out of the small door, three people waited to get in. The lift stank of stale vomit. She sobbed and ran along the corridor to John's room. There were other guests in the corridor, they all stared at her. John took ages to answer. 'All right, I'm coming.' He shouted as she hammered. She burst though the door as soon as it was opened. Gaynor was still in bed; she sat up and pulled the quilt up to her chin before curling her nose in disgust. 'Bloody hell, you look worse than we do,' John said, taking in the state of Julie. Phil was asleep on the small sofa. His shoes were on the floor and his stocking feet hung over the edge of the arm. He had slept fully clothed.

She berated him all the way back to their room. Phil said nothing, he was tight-lipped and silent. As she struggled with the key in the lock he had his hand over his mouth, he gruffly uttered one word, 'Hurry,' and then he pushed past her and ran straight into the bathroom where she heard him retching. The newlyweds may not have spent the night together but the toilet had seen plenty of action.

She flumped herself down on the bed to wait. She heard water running and realised that the selfish man had jumped straight into the shower before releasing her from the prison of the bastard dress which she had come to loathe with a passion. The aroma of his shower gel oozed itself under the bathroom door. She heard him towelling off and then brushing his teeth. If only he'd unfastened her she might have joined him in the shower. She could have shown him how wonderful it is to be washed all over by somebody who loves you. She felt that cleansing him before they made love for the first time would be an act that was almost sacramental and if it was good enough for Mary Magdalene, she had no qualms with it.

Finally, he came to her and undid the multitude of knots that held the laces of her bodice tight. She felt her body screaming for mercy as inch by inch of it was released to spill out of its tether. He told her that he felt a bit better after his shower. She suggested that they have a cuddle before packing their things and heading out. And as he flung the cases onto the bed he made a feeble excuse to leave the room, and then he was gone and Julie was alone again.

She dragged the underskirts from her body and stood in front of the mirror in her wedding lingerie, a second whalebone corset that had punished her for almost twenty-four hours. He hadn't even seen her underwear. The previous day, as she looked at herself in it, she had felt sexy and alluring, now she considered herself with a critical eye and realised that she looked ridiculous. Her breasts weren't even contained in the cups of the bodice, she had rolls of spare flesh under her armpits and the areola of both nipples was clearly visible where the garment had failed in its attempt to hold her up. The stockings, stretched beyond their natural elasticity, held only at the two points of contact with the suspender clips. The rest of them had dropped. Far from coming up to the tops of her thighs, they barely covered her knee caps. And she had deep indentations where the tight elastic had dug into her flesh. The partial loss of circulation had caused severe black bruising around the dents. The feeling of relief when she undid the suspender clips was instant, she could have undone them the night before, but the pain from the bodice had been so intense that she hadn't even noticed the discomfort from her legs. She struggled to undo all the hooks and eyes travelling down the back of the corset. Her fat arms ached and the effort of reaching high up her back and fighting with the fastenings left her out of breath, she had to stop and rest half way through. She was free; she stepped out of the French satin knickers and breathed. Her body had deep ruts where the whalebones had cut mercilessly into her, and she had gained inches of girth in ten seconds, but she was free. She ran a bath and let the softness of the hot water ease the pain. She was glad that her husband wasn't with her because she felt ugly.

She had dried and dressed in a simple pair of black trousers and a blouse when she heard Phil come back into the room. He knocked on the bathroom door and told her that they had to hurry getting packed and ready to go because his mother had asked them to join her and his father for a light lunch. Julie didn't feel as though they'd been asked anything, she felt as though she'd been summoned and that there was no option of refusal.

In Violet's quarter's, lunch had already been served. Violet perched stiffly on the edge of a sofa, so Julie took the other end and aped her. She sat with one buttock barely on the very rim of the seat, the other half of her enormous backside hung uncomfortably in mid air and her thighs had to cling to the leg of the sofa for support. She tried to cross her ankles and twist her lower legs to the left, but they were too large to contort in such a manner. Julie comforted herself with the fact that Violet was no skinny, either and probably looked equally ridiculous. Phil flopped into an armchair across the room; he was still nursing his hangover and looked thoroughly miserable.

Lunch was eaten from china side plates, croissants and sweet and savoury pastries. Julie smelled the warm bread and realised that she was starving. She hadn't eaten since breakfast the day before and could easily have demolished the lot. She took a croissant and a small slice of cheese. The crispy bacon looked delicious, too. What she wanted was two doorstops of fresh bread, half a pound of butter, a bottle of ketchup and the full plate of bacon with two fried eggs on top. She made do with the one croissant and the sliver of cheese. She raised it to her lips and bit daintily into it. Flaky pastry cascaded and sprinkled her knee and Violet's cream sofa. She didn't even look at Violet to gauge her reaction; she put the plate down on the occasional table beside her and took her chances with the rattling cup of tea in its delicate saucer, instead. They left half an hour later. Violet dropped an icy kiss towards each of Julie's cheeks, while never making contact and told Phil to 'uphold the family name,' whatever the hell that meant. Julie's stomach growled after being tricked into thinking that it was going to get fed.

Donald drove them to Manchester airport, the journey was long and uncomfortable and very little was said. He repeated often that yesterday had gone extremely well and both Julie and Phil agreed with him, despite it being one of the worst days of Julie's life. He and Phil discussed herbaceous borders and the predicted weather forecast in Greece.

At the airport she wanted to get some food but after a tour of every eatery in departures, Phil decreed that everything was far too expensive and said that he wouldn't pay their inflated prices on principal. He refused the in-flight meals because he'd once seen a documentary based around a factory where airport meals were produced. After seeing that, he'd vowed never to eat on a plane again. His principals were all well and good, but Julie was hungry and far from being elated at the prospect of their honeymoon she was in a bad mood and when she was hungry, she was nasty. Philip had control of all of their money, including the hundred pounds that her parents had given them. She asked him for enough to buy herself a sandwich and a bar of chocolate. He refused, saying that it was a waste of money, and that they were on a tight budget. She whined that she was hungry and Phil spent ten pounds on a raffle ticket to win the fancy sports car that was sitting in the middle of the departure lounge.

Julie had never flown before and was terrified when the plane took off. Phil was a seasoned traveller and held her hand tightly, telling her that it was fine and to just relax. He had taken the window seat and Julie had to strain her eyes, trying to see out of it to watch the earth slipping away from them. The in-flight movie was *Shallow Hal*. Philip said that it reminded him of her. He tried to explain that he meant it as a compliment, that you shouldn't judge a person on their size. Julie didn't appreciate the compliment and was embarrassed that the person sitting next to her smirked when he said it. In fairness she had probably taken up more than her fair share of the seating arrangements and he'd had to lean into the aisle for comfort. She was insulted by Phil's remarks. When the drinks cart came along he ordered a whiskey on the rocks for him and a vodka and coke for her. She would much rather have had a sandwich. She asked for a packet of nuts, the only food on offer with the drinks trolley. Phil glared at her, but bought them. They were tiny and she wolfed them down in three handfuls. They had cost one pound seventy five, and he sulked about it until they circled in preparation for landing, when they looked out of the window and got excited as they had their first glance of the island.

Philip was grumpy when they landed, and he had to wait with her to get their luggage from the carousel. He wasn't allowed to have a cigarette until they'd cleared customs and were outside the building. He'd gone several hours without one and he was as cranky as hell. They left the cool interior of the airport terminal and an unnatural heat, the likes of which Julie had never felt in her life, engulfed them. It was so hot that it took her breath away. Everything about the place, right down to the atmosphere, felt foreign. Julie loved it and was so excited that her former moodiness was forgotten. They boarded the coach and chatted with the other holiday makers for the half hour trip to their all inclusive complex.

Julie was devastated to learn that they had missed dinner when they checked in. They had finished serving half an hour earlier. The intense heat had dropped to a light Mediterranean haze as they'd travelled, and by the time they got up to their room it was chilly. The room was spectacular. Julie was delighted to note that there was only one bed; that would save any arguments or upset later. She saw Phil eye it with disgust. The bed was enormous and must have been eight foot or more across. Philip cast a hotelier's eye over the room. He ran his finger along the skirting, looking for dust. He checked the light fittings for cobwebs and he checked that the wardrobe had the requisite six wooden coat hangers per person. Julie was entranced, everything was perfect and she couldn't wait to sink into the deep bath before going to bed with her husband for the first time.

After contenting himself that the room met his approval, Phil went to the French doors and threw them open onto the balcony. He scoured the mini-bar and took out two bottles, whiskey for him and vodka for her with a mini can of Coke. He helped himself to the ice tray. Julie suggested that they go to the hotel bar instead of using the mini-bar in their room. She worried that there would be a hefty cost involved. Phil laughed, 'It's all inclusive stupid, everything's free.'

'Oh,' said Julie, smarting over the fact that her husband had just called her stupid, but again her mood was lifted over the wonders of Greece. Their balcony looked out over the beautiful gardens of the resort that led directly onto the beach only a couple of hundred feet away. They watched the waves lapping the shore and she felt a tranquillity and peace of mind that she had never known before. In that perfect moment she was truly happy. She loved the resort, she loved Greece and she loved her husband. Her stomach, probably thinking that it was never going to be fed again, had given up complaining and, far from feeling empty and uncomfortable, she felt a sense of not needing to eat every five minutes to comfort herself and find pleasure in food.

She looked over at Phil. For the first time in his life he had grown his hair to his collar. His mother had been telling him for weeks to get a hair cut and was horrified when Julie had put her foot down before the wedding and had told her that both she and Phil liked his hair longer and that he wouldn't be having it cut for the big day. He was looking out to sea and had a small smile on his face. He seemed happy but she wanted to hear him say it. 'Are you happy love?' she asked.

He turned to face her. His face cracked into an enormous grin and his eyes crinkled at the corners. 'Happier than I've ever been in my life,' he replied. 'I love you.'

'I love you, too,' she said simply.

'Come here and kiss me.' He leaned over and kissed her deeply, wrapping his hand in her hair and pulling her face in towards him. His mouth was wide and grinding and he pushed his tongue into hers when she gave a little moan of part surprise and part pleasure. His chair grated on the patio floor as he moved it closer to her and cupped her throat with his hand. He pulled his head back from her mouth and gazed into her eyes; his own shining with love as he looked at her. He picked up his glass and drained the last of the whiskey into his mouth. He pulled her face to his and kissed her again, gently drizzling the fiery liquid from his mouth to hers and chasing it with his tongue. That was the sexiest thing that he had ever done. She kissed him hard, wanting him so much that her loins contracted. She waited for the moment when he would pull away from her and make some excuse to get out of the room. She would let him go and would take to the bed alone. Then she would pleasure herself thinking of the moment when he spat whiskey from his mouth into hers, she'd make the rest of the scenario up until she released the need inside her onto her own fingers. She was so turned on and the months of waiting for Philip to make love to her had left her wanting. Despite being married for only twenty-four hours she doubted that her husband would ever make love to her.

Philip didn't pull away. He kissed her harder. His breathing altered and became laboured, but Julie had been here before. He often got breathy and sometimes she'd even felt his erection press into her for a moment, but at that point he always stopped and left her turned on and frustrated.

'Julie,' he moaned her name into her open mouth. He'd never done that before either. The word felt heavy and rich in her mouth. She felt a roll of butterflies turn a somersault in her stomach. She wanted him more than she could ever remember wanting a man before. Months of being deprived of any intimate physical contact other than a few kisses had set her on fire but she still expected rejection to come at any moment.

Philip lowered his hand from her throat. He cupped her breast. He had never touched her body before. He squeezed it in his palm and moaned into her mouth. He moved his head, kissing her neck, behind her ear and onto her throat. His hand left the outside of her clothing and she felt the warmth of his fingers driving themselves into the cup of her bra. She wanted him to take it off, to take all of her clothes off, but she daren't move or make any suggestions. He found her nipple; it was huge beneath his fingertips. He rolled it and she almost screamed out in pleasure. She sucked the flesh of his neck into her mouth to stop her crying out and alerting other holiday makers.

Partly for balance, she put her hands on his thighs. She stroked the skin of his upper leg as he dropped his lips into her cleavage. He kissed the cleft of her breast, his mouth just an inch from her nipple. She stroked him, achingly aware of his cock close to her fingertips, wanting to touch it but not daring to. She kept circling her fingers on his thigh. He grabbed her left hand and thrust it onto the front of his flies. His cock was there in her hand. He'd put it there. She could feel its definition. His mouth moved and captured her nipple, He sucked it hard into his mouth, for a second and then he roughly pulled away from her.

He grabbed her hand that was manipulating him through his trousers and thrust it away from him. He sat up straight, holding her hands firmly in front of him so that she couldn't touch him. She looked into his eyes, the first sting of tears tingling behind her lashes. She wanted him so much and he was going to deny her again. But she saw his lust mirroring her own. He rose abruptly, still holding her hands and went into the bedroom dragging her along with him. She almost fell over the chairs. He stood in front of her by the end of the bed and pushed her onto it. He wrestled himself out of his clothes and stood naked in front of her. She could see her husband for the first time. She wanted him.

He helped her out of her clothes until she too lay, shy and naked in front of him. She tried to cover herself with the bedspread, but he pulled it back, looking at her. 'What about the curtains? Somebody might see,' she said. He told her to stuff the curtains.

And then he was on top of her. He lay on her heavily, squashing her and forcing all of the air out of her body. He didn't attempt to give her any further moistening first, before trying to ram his cock inside her. She would have liked some more foreplay first. He couldn't find the way in and grunted in frustration. She put her hand down and guided him. He stabbed into her hard and forced his cock right inside her to the hilt. It was forceful and hurt, but she didn't complain and encouraged him on with little mewling noises. He had never made love before but natural instinct was telling him what to do. He tried to ride her but with every attempt he over judged it and his cock fell out of her again and she'd have to guide him back inside.

'Slowly,' she advised him. 'Take it easy and it will glide in and out and stay inside me.' That was better. He eased his cock in and out of her gently for a few seconds. As he learned how to control his movements while maintaining pressure inside her, he got faster again, until he was riding her hard and fast. She grabbed his arse and felt his muscles contracting as he drove inside her again and again. She was screaming out in pleasure. It wasn't the soft gentle lovemaking that she'd imagined for their first time but if this was how he wanted it, then she wasn't going to argue. It hurt like hell, but it was damned good. His balls slapped against her backside with every thrust and he was grunting with each forward stab. She begged him to suck her breast, but he ignored her. He was deeply concentrating on his own pleasure and she didn't mind that. It was his first time and she would guide him to please her next time. She dug her fingers into the flesh of his buttocks and helped him to drive into her while she rose to meet him with each thrust, tilting her pelvis forwards so that he got maximum penetration with each stroke.

He jerked his lower body and rammed her even faster, she felt that he was close to coming and she wasn't there yet. She tried to slow him down. But he would not be slowed. He was sweating, drips falling from his body onto her chest. A droplet fell from his forehead into her eyes, stinging them and making her blink. She forced them open despite the sting because she wanted to watch his first orgasm inside her. He was crying out, grunting, and his backside was moving so fast that it was blurring. Then he stabbed into her hard and held it for a second as the first spurt of his ejaculation burst into her. 'I'm coming, I'm coming,' he yelled as though proud of himself. She wanted to come too but she wasn't ready. She wanted to get her fingers between them to manipulate her clit, it would only take a few seconds and she'd be there with him, but she couldn't force his body up to get her hand inside. He thrust again and held his body against her as he continued to come in her. And then he flopped down on top of her, his cock slipping from its mooring. He was soaking wet with sweat and heaving exhausted breaths. She stroked his back, still moving her pelvis into his shrivelling cock and trying to maintain pressure against her pulsing clitoris. He rolled off her and turned on his side to light a cigarette.

She was at the point of no return, close to orgasm; her body was aching to come. 'Phil, touch me, please.'

She wanted him to put his mouth to her pussy and devour her, but with his load already leaking from her, she would never have asked him for that. That was something that she only ever wanted to either give or receive immediately after bathing. But if he fingered her deeply she could imagine it.

'What?' he asked, looking alarmed.

'Please, will you touch me just a little bit? I haven't come.' She blushed, feeling like a tart for asking him to give her sexual gratification.

'Oh, right.' He moved his cigarette to his right hand and lowered his left onto the soft triangle of hair between her legs. She grabbed at his wrist greedily and pushed his fingers forward until they were pressed against her wetness and then she ground her body into him. She forced two of his fingers to enter her and let the index finger of her own hand fall onto her clit and then she writhed and bucked until she came long, hard and vociferously a few seconds later.

She looked up at Philip. His lip was curled in disgust at what she'd just done. He stubbed out his cigarette, still looking as though he'd swallowed something unpleasant and then he excused himself and went to the bathroom. First she heard him washing and then she heard him vomiting into the toilet, and then she heard him washing again.

She turned onto her side, facing away from the bathroom and cried herself to sleep.

The following morning she was quiet over breakfast. She nibbled on watermelon. The huge fruit bar was alien to her and she felt very cosmopolitan eating watermelon for breakfast. However, delicious though it was, it was hardly sustaining so she had a slice of toast with scrambled eggs, a rasher of bacon, a sausage and a small spoon of beans. Phil ate twice as much, and once again she was struck by the unfairness of life that he could eat one potato more than a pig and remain like a lat, while she only had to look at a chip to gain weight. She drank fresh orange, something she only did at home when she had a hangover. She followed this with a cup of even fresher coffee, it was bitter and way too strong, but just the fact that real coffee was on offer with this sumptuous breakfast made her feel like a princess.

After breakfast they went for a walk around the complex, it was vast and nothing like Julie had ever seen before. Within an hour and a half of breakfast they had a beef pancake each, cooked on a griddle at the side of the path, by an ancient lady who sat cross-legged and could turn out a pancake a minute. They found the small all-night restaurant that remained open after the three buffets, the *a lá carte*, and the three themed restaurants had closed. All of the day's food wastage was re-fried, re-boiled or re-constituted to look like something else and was laid out for the all-nighters coming in from the clubs with a need to soak up some alcohol. Julie chastised Phil for not finding this little gem the night before when they came in starving; they could have had a nice snack in the moonlight. Phil said that it all sounded dodgy to him, he didn't fancy getting food poisoning. Julie pointed out that when they'd had a roast at home they always fried up the leftovers and had bubble and squeak. The hotel had four stars; of course everything had to be done to a certain standard.

They took sun loungers by the juice bar overlooking the largest swimming pool. Every hour they indulged in a different variety of fresh juice in a little plastic cup. Julie creamed herself with suntan lotion and then smothered some over her husband's back and legs. When she asked him to turn over, he was reluctant. When he buckled under her nagging and turned he had a sheepish look on his face and an erection. He covered it quickly with his paperback and, given that they were surrounded by other people, Julie left him to apply his own suntan lotion, to his own front, in his own good time. She was flattered about the hard on, though, and thought that he was really sweet when his cheeks burned and he muttered shyly, 'Sorry, but after last night, I can't help it. I had one at breakfast, too.' She couldn't have had a better lead-in to the subject that she had wanted to broach all morning.

'Phil, I heard you being sick last night. You know, afterwards?' He was embarrassed again. He tried to blame it on the dodgy food, but they hadn't eaten anything, and then the weather, but it was cool in the room by then, and finally he blamed the last throes of his hangover from their wedding night. She asked him if she disgusted him. He said of course not. He told her not to be so stupid, and then he buried his head into his paperback. The subject was closed.

They had a delicious lunch on the sun terrace. Julie had a salad that seemed to offer a million different dishes, with some potato croquettes and a piece of grilled fish. Philip had a meat feast. He filled his plate with ribs and beef stroganoff and all kinds of seasoned and sauced delicacies. Julie cheekily asked him if the food was arousing him, as it had at breakfast. He laughed and replied that it had nothing to do with the food and that it had been down to her. She slid a hand under the table and onto his leg. He stopped her mid-thigh, shocked. 'Julie,' he whispered, 'people will see.' He was shocked but didn't seem angry. 'Oh God,' he muttered, 'here we go again, what have you done to me?'

For dessert Julie had a spoonful of lemon mousse and half a slice of pineapple gateaux, and something else that was pink and indefinable. Phil had more meat. When they left the terrace, the heat hit them like a blanket. It was fierce and she felt lightheaded after the large meal. She suggested that they go and lie down for a little while to let their food digest.

They lay side by side on the bed. Phil had taken off his shirt and lay in just his shorts, Julie wore a loose sun dress. She grabbed his hand and he intertwined his fingers with hers. She had never been so happy in her life. She was completely at peace, any worries from home had been wafted away on a Grecian breeze and she felt a new tranquillity the likes of which was not possible in England. Phil was more relaxed too and she thought that she might be falling in love with her husband. She lay on the bed with her eyes closed, listening to the swish of the sea.

She would happily have drifted off but Phil was restless, he kept fidgeting and he was stroking her hand with his thumb. The movement over and over in the same place was irritating her skin and she opened her eyes to look at him. He was staring at her. His shorts came to a point in the middle and he had the biggest erection she had ever seen. 'It won't go down,' he said, sheepishly.

'Well, we'd better do something about it then, hadn't we?'

She straddled him and took the waistband of his shorts in her hands. She leaned forward and kissed him while he obligingly lifted his hips so that she could remove them. She wanted to kiss his body and suck his cock and then she wanted to sit on him and take pole position this time, but he wouldn't wait. He grabbed her roughly by the shoulders and threw her off him and onto her back. Their lovemaking was a repeat of the night before. He thrust into her vigorously and came quickly, leaving her wanting again. This time he was more willing to finish her off by hand, in fact he was keen and forced his fingers inside her, two, then three, then four until she was filled and he was hurting her. She told him that he was hurting and asked him to be gentler. He was crestfallen but removed two of his fingers. He shafted her with his hand and stared at her face and then at her pussy and the flesh of her belly wobbling until she came. She felt the cream of her orgasm running down his fingers and into his palm. Immediately afterwards, he withdrew his hand and wiped it on the corner of her sun dress. He seemed pleased with what he had achieved and although he phrased the question in different ways, he asked her several times if it had been good for her. She lied and told him that it was fantastic. He asked if he was the best lover she'd had, and she answered him with, 'Of course, you are.'

He left the bed to wash within a couple of minutes, but he didn't throw up.

After that he was at her day and night. His sexual appetite had been awakened and he was starving. As much as she tried to inject some variety into their sex life, he bucked against it. He was strictly missionary and always in a hurry. His needs were of greater importance than hers and he didn't want or need foreplay. He just wanted to get in there and come as quickly as possible, anything else bored him. He wanted the gift without unwrapping the present. By the third time he had stopped leaving her to wash himself, he said he liked the smell of her on his fingers and the feel of her on his Old Man. He didn't like the word cock, he said it was coarse. That second night of sleeping in the same bed, he didn't roll over and sleep with his back to her. He spooned her, wrapping one leg over her body and holding her into him so that she could feel his heartbeat through her back. At first she loved it, and went to sleep with her man wrapped tight around her. She woke through the night to find him lying on top of her forcing her legs open and his cock inside her. She was confused and disorientated. She didn't know where she was, and in sleep fugue she tried to fight him off her, but he grunted into her neck. He was extra turned on by the way he had woken her and he grunted twice more and came all over the top of her legs before he'd even got his cock inside her properly. She cleaned herself up and when she got back into bed, his arm and his leg came over her and pinned her in place. She woke again through the night. The bed was soaking with sweat. He had all of the sheet and his body was leaking like a watering can. Her back was dripping wet and freezing cold. She took a blanket from the wardrobe and wrapped it around her. She finished the night, dozing in a chair on the balcony. The sunrise over the ocean was the most beautiful thing that she had ever seen in her life. Her husband was crazy with desire for her and her world was good. Phil woke at eight and dragged her back to bed for more sex.

During the holiday, they went jet skiing and horse riding. The jet skiing was great fun, but she was nervous of the sea. She loved the speed of the ski and the sensation of bumping on top of the ocean with the sea-spray cooling her from the vicious heat. But as much as she loved it, she was scared of falling into the deep, cold water and was cautious when it came to turning. Phil rode well.

The man at the stables looked them up and down and said that he had a special horse for Julie, one with six legs. She didn't appreciate this jibe about her weight, but Phil thought that it was amusing. If she hadn't loved horse riding so much she would have taken her affront and left without giving them the benefit of their custom. They brought her a big horse and she had to be given a leg up to mount it. The guide expected her to be as accomplished in her riding skill as she was at mounting. Her weight did hamper her being able to vault into the saddle but it didn't prevent her from being able to ride. When he asked if any of the trek wanted to break away from the pack and follow him for a gallop she pulled her horse to the side. He told her that it might not be a good idea as the horse that she rode was very fast and needed an experienced hand. She held back, letting the man gallop across the sands with two other members of the trek and then she kicked her mount on. Her seat was accomplished; she tightened the reins and dropped her hands allowing her posture to fall forward so that she was looking between the ears of her horse. The ride was exhilarating; the steady pounding of the horse's hooves beat in time with her heartbeat. The sand flew by in a blur beneath her and the wind blew strong around her, giving the impression of even greater speed. She was flying and drew along side the leader of the trek and brought her horse to a steady canter, then a trot and then stopped. Back at the stables, the man praised her and she suggested that perhaps he shouldn't be so quick to read a book by its cover, but he didn't understand her. He responded by drawing her away from the crowd as they dismounted and suggesting that she join him the following morning for another ride, just the two of them. She politely declined and returned to her husband. She wasn't sure whether the guide had wanted to make another few quid from her and was offering a one on one session, presumably at an elevated cost, or if he had been coming on to her and was offering more than a horse to ride.

They hired a car and drove all over the island. Philip discovered a love for sex al fresco and joked that he quite fancied being caught in flagrante. They took a carriage ride through Corfu town and ate in a seafood restaurant just outside the bustle. The next day they drove to the beautiful monastery at Paleokastritsa where they listened to the choristers at evensong. Most of the tourists were long gone by early evening and they found themselves in the votive room, a small cave away from the main courtyard, the room was set with hundreds of red votive candles which gave the place an eerie glow. She whispered in his ear. She told him that she could slip out of her panties and put them in her bag. She wore a loose skirt. She whispered that she would hear anybody coming long before they got to the cave. She told him how much she wanted him and felt him stiffen against her leg. He still had very strong catholic beliefs. He said it would be a terrible sin. 'Lovemaking should be confined to the bedroom,' he said hypocritically, after he'd taken her three times, in various beauty spots, the day before. 'And then only for the procreation of life.' Julie pulled her panties down and stepped out of them. She wondered how much he truly believed this crap. She could hear his mother in his voice and very nearly went off the idea of being sexed in the monastery. It was religious in a funny kind of way to her, too. She felt that being made love to in such a holy place would somehow cement their relationship. It would be like a blessing from above. He'd put his hand up her skirt. 'But I want to be inside you so much,' he said.

'Do it,' she urged him on.

And then he had her up against the wall. He'd lowered the front of his shorts releasing his hot, hard cock and he drove it into her. A trickle of ice cold water fell onto her back from behind her as it travelled down the cobbled stones of the ancient wall. She gasped as the coldness took her breath away. She felt the trickle travel all the way down to her waist and he rammed her hard against the wall. He was inside her and hammering into her harder than he ever had before. It was the first time he'd taken her in a standing position and he seemed to like the extra leverage that being upright gave him. She was so turned on that she couldn't breathe. She bit into his neck, stopping only short of bruising him to keep from screaming out. He was grunting and she could feel that he was close to orgasm within seconds of entering her. This time, she was right there with him. She had gone from cold to coming in less than two minutes and the orgasm that ripped through her at the same moment as he came inside her was among the strongest of her life. It was all over. He pulled out immediately and covered himself. She went to the ladies to clean herself with baby wipes. It was the best sex of her life.

She found him at the cloisters. He had his head bowed and his hands lifted in prayer. Tears streaked his face. He lifted his head when she came and they walked back to the car in silence. He still didn't speak as they drove away and they were half way down the mountain when he said, 'You shouldn't have made me do that, it was wrong.'

'Darling, that was the best sex I've ever had in my life. How can that be wrong?'

He turned in his seat and snarled at her, 'Do you have to be so coarse?'

'I'm sorry; I didn't mean to be flippant. I know that your religion means a lot to you, Phil, but how can it be wrong when two people, who love each other, come together in the sight of God.'

He turned again from the twisty mountain pass and looked at her sharply to see if she was being smutty with her last remark, but she seemed to be sincere. 'But don't you see? That's just it. We were literally in the house of God.' he moaned. 'I've committed a mortal sin. How am I ever going to be able to atone for such wickedness? You don't get it, do you? I am going to have to go to confession and proclaim my sin. Have you any idea how ashamed I feel? I can't go to our church, I'm going to have to find one miles away. I wonder if it would count, if I found a church here and confessed to a Greek priest who couldn't understand me.'

Julie searched his face for humour, but he was deadly serious. She wanted to laugh at the ridiculousness of the situation, but she knew that it was important to Philip to salve his conscience. She wanted to think of something positive to say, something that would make him feel better, but she battled her sympathy against the feeling of hypocrisy that surrounded the incident. He hadn't been feeling his shame when he had her up against the votive room wall banging the arse off her. She opted to try and lighten the mood before the hand of God appeared through the fully white clouds and lifted them, car and all, off the road and dumped them in the sea. 'I wouldn't confess here if I were you,' she said. 'They'd probably take us out into the town square and stone us. I'm sure they'd take a dim view of fornication in their Votive Room. I'd take my chances in England and maybe say a few extra Hail Mary's before you get there, just to work off a bit of the penance in advance.' It worked. He grinned over at her and squeezed her hand.

'You really are a minx, you know. You're very naughty and a terrible influence on me. Was it really that good?' he asked.

'Hell, you betcha, it was amazing.'

They ate at a roadside taverna on a balcony overlooking the Agean. The excellent food assuaged Philip's guilt and he relived every second of their adventure in whispered tones. He confessed to her that it was the most exciting thing he'd ever done and would never forget it. On the way home he pulled the car over by a secluded copse and took her from behind over the bonnet of the car. It was a deviation from his strictly missionary moral stance and for the second time that day, despite being sore and tender deep inside her cervix, she came in unison with her husband again. When he wanted her in their room, after drinks in the hotel bar, she just wanted to sleep. She begged him for a respite but he nagged and whined and groped until she gave in. He took her on top, brutally, and she moaned and writhed and pretended that she was enjoying it just to speed him up. It was over quickly and when he tried to trap her in their sleeping position, she suggested she spoon him, so that she could stroke his back. He fell asleep quickly and she was able to move away from him and cocoon herself in the sheet. She remained dry and comfortable all night and slept soundly. That, she decided, was what she called success. Victory to the tired people.

Chapter Sixteen

They returned from their honeymoon tanned and happy. Donald picked them up from the airport to take them to the hotel. Julie felt as though she had been away from their house forever. As every mile took them closer to the Halcyon Woods, she felt her mood dropping. The honeymoon had been like a wonderful, sexy, loved up dream, but now, sitting in the car, it was as though Julie had ceased to exist. She reached for Phil's hand but, within seconds, he shook her off to indicate a point about jet skiing to his father.

Phil recounted every minute of their time away, bar the intimate stuff. He told him every conversation he'd had, every meal they'd eaten, and gave a blow by blow account as though he were under police interrogation. When they got into the hotel and met for drinks with Violet and the two brother's who were there, he went through it all from the beginning again. Julie didn't want to share the details of her honeymoon with his family. It was theirs, it was special and private. She realised that she was being petulant but Phil barely spoke to her all night. When he was telling his very Catholic parents about the monastery on the hill above Paleokastritsa, Julie couldn't resist butting in. 'Oh, you should have seen the votive room,' she said, her eyes sparkling. 'It was amazing, so spiritual. Something entered me in that room.' Violet seemed pleased with her spiritual birth but Phil didn't see the funny side. His lips straightened into a single, thin line. She'd seen the look before and knew he was angry with her. He was very sensitive about Julie's humour when it was aimed in his mother's direction.

That night, Phil stayed up late with SP and James. He drank too much. Julie was tired and wanted to go to bed, but the alcohol flowed and she left him to his drunken revelry and went to bed alone. She woke alone and bar the foo-foo dress and stale vomit, it was a repeat of the last time they'd stayed at the hotel. This time Julie breakfasted alone in the dining room and then went in search of her husband. Again she found him laid out on a brother's sofa, in a brother's room. This time he was in James' quarters. He sneered at her when he opened the door. 'Well, well,' he said, leering at her. 'Aren't you the dark horse? I've been hearing all about you. Let me know if you ever fancy giving the more experienced brother a run around the block.' He winked at her, and Julie felt sickened by his smutty innuendo. Of Phil's brothers, James was the one she liked the least. He was hard and nasty. He didn't like her and made no secret of the fact.

Julie glared at him but otherwise ignored his remarks. 'Is Philip here?' she asked frostily.

He opened the door wider to let her in; gesturing towards the sofa with Phil sprawled across it. 'Don't worry love. I was only joking. You're not my type.' His lip curled away from his teeth as he watched her kneel beside Phil and shake him awake.

'I suspect anybody willing to give out, would be

your type. I feel so sorry for Tammy being married to a pig like you.'

Phil was waking and had only heard Julie's response to James's slur. He was defensive of his brother. 'Julie, why are you speaking to James like that? Don't blame him for keeping me out all night. I did that off my own back.'

'Yeah, Jules, don't blame me. I'm a good influence, I am.'

'Go fuck yourself,' said Julie and regretted it when she saw Phil's face. He went into one of his moods and barely spoke to her for the rest of the day.

It was so good to get back to their own house, even if Phil only answered her when he absolutely had to. Julie had given her mother a key and had asked her to come in and clean the place up while they were away on honeymoon. The house was gleaming. Not realising that Julie and Phil didn't share a bedroom; Zoe had only cleaned the master bedroom. But it was made with fresh bedding and Julie couldn't wait to get into it. She wondered if her husband would be moving into her room now, or if he would continue to sleep alone. After sharing a bed with him for ten days in Corfu, she hoped that he would be going back to the privacy of his own room. She hadn't had a decent night's sleep since before she got married.

Phil dropped their cases in the hall and wandered from room to room. He went into the downstairs bathroom and turned in a circle. 'Julie,' he shouted 'somebody's been in the house. All of my stuff's been moved around.'

'Yes, isn't it lovely and clean? I gave mum a key and asked her to give the place a once over while we were away. I thought it would be a nice surprise for you to come home to.' Julie's voice came and went in clarity as she set to making coffee and tea in their immaculately clean kitchen. She was thinking about the last time she'd seen it, with champagne bottles, makeup products, the remains of a cooked breakfast, even though Anne had washed up, and all kinds of other general untidiness that Phil would have gone mad about.

'Mind you, considering the state of the place when we left, she's excelled herself. We can go and visit her tomorrow and we'll take her some flowers to thank her.'

Phil came into the kitchen. His face was scrunched up with rage and bright red. He slammed a can of deodorant onto the marble island with such force that Julie wanted to check beneath it for damage. In his other hand he had one of his shirts, presumably dirty, perhaps taken out of the downstairs wash basket. He threw it at her and when it hit her full in the face, and hung there, covering her like a Muslim lady's niqab, she could smell her husband in the material. She pulled it away, astonished. Phil was yelling. She'd never seen him so angry.

'Don't you ever, ever let anybody into my house without my permission again. Who do you think you are?'

'Your house?' she said repeating the question for

good measure. 'And here's me thinking that we were an equal partnership and that this is our house. What's the matter with you? Mum's done a fantastic job for us.'

'She's been through my things. I don't like anybody touching my things, do you understand?' His voice had dropped in decibel as he explained how he felt, but as he got to the end of his rant it rose as he was engulfed by his sense of injustice. 'What right have you got to give somebody that I barely know a key to my house? Anything could have gone missing.'

'Phil, you're talking about my mother,' she screamed. 'I can't believe that you've just accused my mother of stealing from us. What the hell are you talking about?'

'Well they're always hard up, aren't they? I want that key back. Today,' he emphasised. 'In fact, no, don't bother. Let her keep it, along with whatever else she took. You do realise that I'm going to have to have all the locks changed, don't you?'

'Don't be so fucking ridiculous. She's my mother. I'd trust her with my life. How can you say such horrible things? She only did this to help us. Fuck you. I don't know how I'm going to get passed the fact that you've just called my mother a thief. My mother wouldn't dream of stealing.' Her bottom lip quivered and she pushed past him to go into the lounge. It was spotless and smelled of orange zest. 'You petty bastard, who do you think you're talking about? This is my family that you're slagging off, we might not have lot of money, but how dare you.' She sat on the end of one of the plush red sofas and curled her feet up beside her. She held the cup of coffee between her hands, and sipped at it without tasting the comforting bitterness of the beans. She wanted to throw it at him.

He'd followed her through and was standing above her, still yelling. 'Come on, Julie, look at them, they live in a council flat. Christ, it's not even a full house with two storeys. It's not as though I'm actually saying that she took something, all that I'm saying is that they need the money. She might have been tempted, that's all. And I'll thank you not to swear. You know how it makes you sound like a cheap trollop, which goes to prove my point about the council flat mentality.'

'You snob. You fucking, bastard snob.' She put her coffee down on the table, not forgetting to take a coaster from the dispenser first. The mug was feeling far too much like a weapon. 'Leave me alone,' she said in a tight voice. She was working hard to keep herself under control. 'I don't want to be anywhere near you, right now.'

'See? Can't take it, can you? You can say what you like about my mother. My mother, incidentally, who paid for our wedding, but the moment that I dare to criticise the glorious Zoe, you take it personally. People in glass houses shouldn't throw stones.'

He stalked out of the room.

'You get back here. Don't you dare walk out on me you pompous dickhead. I have barely said a thing about your precious mother, considering that she called me an AIDS ridden, gold digging, heroin addict. But look at you, eh? Showing your true colours now, aren't you? Like mother, like fucking son. She's a money-minded, pretentious snob and you're just like her. You're certainly your mother's son. Go on, fuck off and sulk, cry baby. Mummy's boy.' Phil straightened his back. Jutted out his chin and left. Julie heard him going up the stairs and into his small bedroom. She burst into tears.

The next morning, Phil knocked on her bedroom door. He came in without waiting for a response. He had breakfast on a tray, and a hard on. He apologised and admitted that he'd overreacted. Of course I trust your family, he told her. She apologised too. They ate breakfast, had unsatisfying sex, as far as Julie was concerned, and put the argument behind them. Phil smiled at her and said that he'd be moving his things into the master bedroom that morning. Julie's heart sank.

It was their last day off before they went back to work. Julie worked in a factory making circuit boards and Phil, having broken away from the hotel after the fight with his mother, was a maintenance fitter and team leader in the shipyard. Before they left for their honeymoon, he had just applied for a promotion to foreman. He was looking forward to getting back to see if the interviews had been arranged. Julie couldn't wait to see all of her mates and was looking forward to getting back to work too, but they were still both struck with a bad case of post holiday blues. Phil took her out to dinner. The food was rich and he droned on about things which interested him and left her wishing the night would end, and then she remembered that Phil was moving into their bed and she wished that the night would continue forever. But she'd still rather have been at the pub drinking lager with her mates and having a laugh. She reminded herself that she was a married woman now, and that all of that was behind her. She had responsibilities and drinking poncy wine in a posh restaurant was one of them. It could have been worse. He might have taken her to dinner at the Halcyon.

She woke up the following morning wet from her husband's sweat, exhausted and nauseous. Philip had already left for work. She felt guilty for not being the perfect wife and getting up to see him off with a cooked breakfast. He hadn't woken her. She met up with Karen, her best mate, at the bus stop. The mid-May morning was gorgeous and the sun was shining. She told Karen all about their honeymoon, especially the sex, and she felt better.

'At least one of us is getting plenty,' said Karen with a laugh. She caught Julie's anxious expression and looked at her sharply, 'What's the matter? Isn't it good?'

'Not really. Well, yes, sometimes it's great. If I just want a quickie. That time in the monastery was the best sex ever. But it's just that, well, he wants it so often. He's at me for sex all the time and it never varies. He's in, wham, bang, thank you ma'am, and out and it's all over. And he's so rough.'

'Hell, don't knock it, mate. I wish I had a man who wanted me that much. Ed would choose the footie over shagging me, any day. Get it while you can, 'cause I promise you, that honeymoon period soon wears off.'

The bus pulled in to the stop and they got on. 'As to it being a bit boring,' Karen continued, 'I wish I had a virgin to play with. If it's boring, that's your fault, mate. You need to show him what you want.'

'Suppose,' agreed Julie, changing the conversation because the bus was crowded and she didn't want details of her sex life spread all over town.

Six weeks after coming home from their honeymoon, Julie discovered that she was pregnant. Phil, far from flinging his arms around her in delight, was shell shocked. 'How did that happen?' he asked in a daze.

'How do you think it happened, Einstein? You don't believe in using any form of contraception. I thought this was what you wanted.' She felt tears stinging her eyes. This wasn't going at all how she'd imagined it. 'We discussed it. You said you wanted us to start a family.'

'Yes, but I didn't think it would be so quick. I thought it would take longer. I've only just got my promotion. I wanted to save some money first. We've only been married a few weeks. How did it happen so fast?'

'God, Phil, it only takes once. If I'd known you were going to react like this I'd have gone on the pill.'

'That's a wicked thing to say. You know it's against my religion.'

'Yes, but it's not against mine. Oh my God, I'm

carrying a baby that you don't want.' She burst into tears.

Phil put his arms around her. 'Shush, shush now, don't be silly. Of course I want it.'

'You do?'

'Yes, of course I do. It was just a shock, that's all. I'm delighted that we're having a baby.' He picked her up, swung her around and whooped in delight. Julie dried her eyes. This was more like it.

They arranged a special dinner to tell their parents. Richard and Zoe were delighted. This was their first grandchild. Zoe cried and Richard beamed and hugged Julie. Richard pumped Phil's hand saying, 'Well done lad,' over and over again, making Phil blush and glance at his own parents.

After a curt, congratulations, Donald didn't react at all. They might as well have announced that they'd bought a new pan set in the Debenham's sale. Violet's face was grim. Julie had seen the same expression many times on Phil's face. She looked with distaste at her and only applied a false smile when she was addressed for her feelings by Zoe, who was still trilling like an excited budgie. Julie wondered if Violet was disgusted that she was having a baby or that her youngest child was no longer a virgin.

Every week, Zoe came to the house with a little set of vests, or a couple of bibs. Violet bought an enormous silver cross coach-built pram that took up most of the lounge. 'If I'm going to be pushing it, no grandchild of mine will be seen in one of those modern monstrosities.

All of mine had coach-built. There simply is no other option.' Julie secretly christened it her Big, Fat Gypsy Pram and bought a cheap stroller from eBay for when Violet wasn't around.

Phil was present at the birth when Victoria-Violet Woods was born. Julie was looking at him when the midwife put his child in his arms. His face was sullen. He'd wanted a boy. Despite Julie telling him that it could just as easily be a girl, he wouldn't listen. Phil only ever thought of his child in the male gender classification, any other flavour was not going to happen. He wanted a son and that son was going to have his name, Philip John Woods Jr.

Julie had said at the time that if it was a boy, she wanted him to have his own name, and his own identity, but Phil's ego regarding his future son would brook no argument. At each scan, he eagerly asked the technician what sex the baby was. Julie had explicitly had it written into her records that she didn't want to know the sex of their baby. She'd sneakily asked that Phil not be told either. If it was a girl she wanted him to have time to get used to the notion. Julie knew that the second he held his child in his arms for the first time, any thoughts he'd had about gender would fade into insignificance.

They didn't. Phil had planned for a son.

And he didn't want a girl.

Chapter Seventeen

Simon was anxious and grumpy and frightened. Robert was coming to visit today. He was Janet Metcalfe's brother and he was horrible to Simon and some of the others. Robert was even nasty to Janet and she was his sister. He called Janet a spastic. He didn't call Simon a spastic. He called Simon Mong-boy and pulled his hair when Simon walked past. Sometimes Mother called Simon, 'Mongol.' Simon wondered if Robert had been talking to Mother.

He stuffed all of his belongings into his rucksack as if he was leaving home for good. He had to pack everything down very hard. The hanging clothes in his wardrobe wouldn't fit into his bag so he'd had to just stuff them under his bed as they were. Robert had never been into his bedroom. He wasn't allowed, but Simon went through this ritual every time Robert was coming, just in case. Robert made Simon tell him what number his room was. And Robert said that he was going to come in through the middle of the night and kill him if he said anything to anybody. He couldn't risk him getting hold of Simon's best cardigan. That had Simon's name inside the collar. It didn't say Robert Metcalfe inside the collar at all, not.

Simon got frustrated when his thick fingers couldn't do up the zip. 'Concentape, Shimon,' he said to himself, but it didn't matter how hard he concentrated, the zip wouldn't fasten and his best cardigan with the zipper up the front and leather patches on the elbows bulged out of the top of his bag. His mouth was open, tongue protruding and as he worked on the zip he dribbled onto his hand. He looked up to see if mother had appeared by magic and was very pleased to see that she hadn't. He wiped his dribbly hand on his cardigan and went back to work. Simon had a short attention span and a short fuse. He needed things to work for him right away and if they didn't he would get mad. Now he was mad. Under normal circumstances he'd ask one of the carers to help him zip up his rucksack, but he couldn't do that. If he told Belinda or Jane about his zip, they would ask why he had packed everything into his rucksack. They were like that. They wouldn't just come up and say, 'Yes, Simon, of course I'll do your zip for you.' They wouldn't do his rucksack up and walk away again. That was too hard for them, like Simon trying to hide his stuff under the bed. It should be easy, but it wasn't. Simon had a picture of the end of the zip on his thumb and it was all red around it. If it didn't have to have the hurt around it, it might be good to have a picture of a zip on the end of his thumb, but Simon whimpered when he saw it. He heard Belinda walking Janet up the corridor outside. That meant that Robert and Janet's mum and dad would be coming. Simon panicked, he grabbed the zip and pulled on it really hard, and then he was holding the end of the zip in his hand and it wasn't attached to his rucksack any more. This was bad. 'This is bad,' said Simon, 'This is bery, bery bad.'

Jane came to take him to the dayroom for integration. Simon had stuffed the rucksack under his bed with all of his important things, and all of his not so important things too, bulging out of the top. He stood by his desk, moving from foot to foot and making his noise that sounded like a cow. His face was bright red and his big eyes were bulging out of his face even more than normal. Jane called his name. 'Simon. Simon, come on now.' But Simon didn't answer because he wasn't really there. His big body was there, and his trainers were there and his brown jumper that was really green was there, but Simon wasn't there. Simon was in his own place where he went when the world got too much for him. Matron came and made Simon come back. She gave him some medicine and he was put to bed to rest. Worrying about this gave Simon a big headache. See, Simon was happy that he was in bed having a rest, because it meant that he wasn't in integration getting his hair pulled by Robert and being called Mong-boy. But Simon wasn't tired. It was only half past after lunch and Simon wasn't supposed to be in bed having a rest. He was supposed to be in integration getting his hair pulled. It was a big problem and Simon fell asleep worrying about it.

When Simon woke up, Nancy was standing by his bed. He had been asleep for a long time because Belinda and Jane had gone home and Nancy and Anne had come on duty. 'Hello, sleepyhead,' said Nancy laughing. Simon smiled at her. 'Look, Simon, I've got a surprise for you.' Nancy stepped to one side and Simon wasn't smiling anymore. Robert was smiling. He was smiling his nice smile, the one that was supposed to show that he was good. Nancy was still talking but Simon wasn't listening.

'Robert has stayed a little bit longer today because Janet's mum and dad have taken her to the hospital to get some special shoes for her. Isn't that nice? When we told Robert that you were under the weather today he asked if he could come and see you for a bit. Isn't that nice?' Nancy winked at Robert and then said, 'Robert says that you're his favourite. Isn't that nice?'

It wasn't nice.

Robert had already pulled up the chair from beside Simon's desk. The chair doesn't go beside the bed, it goes beside the desk. That's where it goes. Robert sat down. Simon was frightened. He could feel his heart going thump, thump, thump.

Simon closed his eyes and made a big snore.

Nancy laughed again. Simon made all of the carers laugh. They said he had a good sense of human. 'Will you look at that Robert, he's having a joke with us. Come on you, sit up, I've brought you a nice cup of tea and two Jaffa Cakes. They're your favourite.'

Simon loved Jaffa Cakes and he hadn't had a lot of lunch because his tummy felt icky. Simon's tummy always felt icky when Robert was coming. He got upset on a Wednesday when Mother came too, but he didn't feel icky in his tummy then, just worried. Simon looked at his two Jaffa Cakes. 'Right, I'll leave you two for a bit. Robert, if you come to the kitchen when you're ready, cook will rustle you up a cuppa and a slice of cake.'

'Thank you, Nancy,' said Robert in his talking-to-the-staff voice. 'I will.'

Nancy shut the door and Simon wished that mother was here. Mother was scary and would shout loud at Robert and call him stupid. Mother would make him go away. Robert grabbed Simon's two Jaffa Cakes and stuffed one into his mouth, barely taking time to chew and swallow before he rammed the second one in too. 'Hey Mong-boy, aren't you pleased to see me?'

Simon didn't answer.

'That's not very friendly when I've gone out of my way to come and sit with you. Whatcha got in here then?' Robert reached over and pulled open Simon's underwear drawer. It was empty. He pulled open the drawer underneath that one and then the last one on the bottom. 'Hey, where's all your shit?'

Simon didn't say anything. But he was scared that Robert would look under his bed.

But it was all right because Robert had got bored of looking in drawers and cupboards. He looked at Simon's cup of tea. 'Aren't you going to drink your tea, Monger?' He called Simon Monger too, sometimes. Simon didn't want his tea. He was still worrying about his stuff and just wanted Robert to go away.

'Here, let me help you.' He picked up the tea cup and came towards Simon. Simon was frightened. Robert put his arm around Simon's head and hauled it up from the pillow and then he rammed the cup into his mouth, hurting him. He forced him to drink the tea, it was still too hot. Simon knew to wait for five minutes and then blow on his tea before taking a sip to see if it was the right tempica. Robert didn't care about the temperature; he just poured it all into Simon's mouth. It wasn't boiling hot at all, not, but it was still hot enough to make Simon struggle. The tea spilled all down Simon's front and Simon was upset. Some of the others spilled their tea and their food down their fronts, but Simon was *High End Retardation*. Simon was very careful not to spill anything down him because he liked being *High End Retardation*. It made him feel special but he would never be unkind and tell Janet and the others that she was a low end and that she had to get her shoes from the hospital. That would be unkind. He just kept his specialness to himself and looked at his everybody, white trainers sometimes.

Simon choked on the tea and started coughing. Robert sat back in his chair and laughed. 'Ugh, look at the mess you've made, you dirty retard. Can't even drink from a cup like normal people. You make me sick.'

Simon thought he might be sick. He couldn't stop coughing, not, and he was all wet. His pyjamas were all wet. His bed was all wet. And he couldn't tell. Nancy would think he was turning into low end.

Simon was still worried about his stuff. It was bery bad to tell lies. But it would be bery bad at all if Robert found Shimon's stuff. It had Shimon's name on it on a special label what Mrs Taylor, the housekeeper, did sewed in, 'There's no thing under the bed, not,' he said.

Robert laughed and knelt down to pull all of Simon's stuff out from under the bed. 'You fucking moron,' he laughed. Robert was sixteen but Simon still didn't think he ought to use the dirty words like that. 'I didn't even think that you'd hidden it all. I just thought they took it off you to stop you shitting all over it, or something retarded.' He was laughing very hard. 'You shot yourself right in the foot there, me old son.' Robert flung Simon's clothes all over the floor.

'Clothes do not live on the floor, Shimon. Clothing lives on hangers in the wardrobe.' Simon was distressed. He repeated this phrase over and over. Robert was opening Simon's red pencil case. Simon didn't like nobody touching his red pencil case. It had his name on it on the inside. Robert could see Simon's name when he opened it. It wasn't sewed in on a label, but it was wrote in black marker pen so that it wouldn't come oft. Robert started taking everything out of his red pencil case and looking at it. He put Simon's parker pen in his pocket.

Simon stopped talking about his clothes and changed his chant to. 'Shimon's red pencil case. Shimon's name on it. Marker pen. Not come oft.'

'Will you stop rabbitting on like a fucking retard,' said Robert. He came up to Simon with a red felt tip pen and waved it in front of Simon's face. Simon thought that he was going to draw a picture right on him. 'We draws on paper, not on walls, not' said Simon weakly. Robert laughed, if he had been going to draw on Simon's face he changed his mind. He pulled the away

210

back and Simon grabbed them and pulled them back up to his chin. Robert slapped Simon across the face and tears came into Simon's eyes. 'Don't do that, play nice,' said Robert pulling the covers back again. This time Simon didn't do anything. A tear ran out of his eye but Simon wasn't really crying; he was too frightened to cry. It was a tear from the sting in his eyes after Robert slapped him. He looked down at himself and the front of his pyjama top had come up a bit showing his big tummy. Robert grabbed some of his tummy and pinched it hard. Simon cried out because it really hurt him. 'Got a dick under all this flab, have you?' He flicked Simon hard on his tummy. Simon was confused. Dick was the handy man and gardener. He came three times a week on Monday, Wednesday and Friday, but he had his own bed in his house somewhere else. He lived with Missus Dick and didn't sleep in Simon's bed.

'Well, have you? Have you got a dick?' he started pulling at the front of Simon's pyjama bottoms.

'No,' said Simon, hoping that it would make him stop. Robert thought this was very funny and laughed a lot. 'Oh Mong-boy, you are grade-A priceless. Haven't got a dick.' He kept laughing all the while, pulling Simon's pyjama bottoms down. And then he took hold of Simon's willy. This was bery bad. If a stranger touches you *there,* you have to tell. But Robert wasn't a stranger and Simon couldn't tell.

Robert started writing something on Simon's willy. Simon couldn't read it, but he knew his letters c-o-c-k and then a gap, s-u-c, it tickled and Simon's willy started to get big, like it does sometimes, and then they have to up his tablets to stop it getting big. Robert got very angry. He yelled as though Simon had hurt him. 'Agh, oh fuck. You fucking filthy queer. Simon hadn't got mad and punched him. Maybe Simon's willy had got hot as well as big and it had burned him. Simon was too frightened to get mad. Simon just wanted him to go away.

Robert got even angrier. He made a big fist and grabbed a bunch of Simon's pyjama top in his hand. He was going to punch Simon right in the nose and Simon knew it was going to hurt a lot. He screwed up his eyes and waited.

Robert grunted and threw Simon back into his pillows. He turned around and punched the wall beside Simon's bed, making his picture of sunflowers nearly fall off. He leaned over Simon and roughly ripped his Pyjama top open. One of his buttons flew off and rolled under his chest of drawers. Mrs Taylor would be mad with Simon and would tell him off for not looking after his things properly. Simon didn't have his eyes closed anymore. He was terrified and could hear his heart going thump, thump, thump very fast. 'I want to smash your dirty fucking face in,' Robert said. 'I want to hit you so hard that you never get a hard on again. I want to ram your teeth down your throat.' He took the felt pen and wrote g-a-y, gap, b-o-y on Simon's bare chest.

Simon didn't feel well. He got a big pain just under his armpit. He felt sick. The pain was really bad. Really, really bad. Badder than any bad pain he'd ever had

212

before. His eyes went big and bulgy and he took a breath in and didn't let it out again. He was rolling on the bed and making a strangled cry in his throat but he couldn't get any sound out. Robert shouted, 'Oh fuck,' and grabbed a rubber from the pencil case. He tried to rub the red felt tip from Simon's chest. This wasn't just a fit; it looked like a fucking heart attack. He had to remove the writing before he called for help. The rubber wasn't working. He ran over to the sink in the corner of the room and rubbed Simon's flannel with soap under the tap. Simon was bucking and writhing and still clutching his chest when Robert started rubbing vigorously on his skin to get the marks off him. He cleaned his chest and then, repulsed and disgusted, he grabbed his penis and cleaned the obscene slogan from that too, before covering Simon up and pulling his blankets back over him. He'd left large, dripping wet patches on Simon and he had red marks on his chest, genitalia and face. It couldn't be helped. He was going to have to yell for help or Simon was going to die. He didn't give a shit about that, but he did care about his own safety. He didn't want to get the blame for this. Simon stopped writhing and lay still. His eyes were wide open and his tongue lolled from the side of his mouth. Robert screamed and nurses flooded the room.

Nancy pulled out Simon's pillows, laying him flat, and began CPR while Anne ran out to ring an ambulance. Matron came into the room and took over the chest compressions from Nancy while she covered Simon's mouth with her own and gave him resuscitation. They didn't notice Simon's wet clothing or the marks on his skin. Robert watched on, horrified, terrified and fascinated. Watching somebody die had been the scariest, most awesome fucking thing that he'd ever seen.

Chapter Eighteen

It was the evening of the annual awards ceremony for the Licensed Victualler's Association. Violet was nominated for three awards and was furious because the year before she had been nominated for four and had walked away with three of them. This year, the rumour mill had it that The Lakeside Hotel was going to walk away with the overall *Best Hotel in Cumbria* award. The die had already been cast, the decisions made, but since her invitation had come through and she'd seen that she was only up for the three nominations she had made her staff's life a living hell. The Best Hotel award rightfully belonged to the Halcyon Woods. She had umpteen certificates and a bloody great trophy to prove it. The trophy changed hands with each new recipient of the award, but it had been at the Halycon for five years running. The previous year she had been nominated for best restaurant, best bedrooms, best gardens and overall winner in show. She had won all but the bedrooms and the following day the housekeeper, all of the chambermaids, upstairs cleaners and laundry staff were given their notice. Violet said that the recession had hit, when in fact the Halcyon's trade had been unaffected by the great recession. She said that the family would be pulling together to undertake their own domestic duties. The staff didn't have a leg to stand on and, the following day, Violet advertised for twenty-one new members of staff.

This year she had only been nominated for Best Gardens, Best internal floral arrangements and best bedrooms. Violent stormed and blustered. She said that the award for floral arrangements was an insult. She felt that it was a made up award thrown at underachieving hotels when they couldn't think of anything else to award them. She felt that it was only a slight step up from the most original garden gnomes award, which most of the hoteliers saw as a bit of fun and tried desperately to win. When, eight years ago, Donald had wanted to enter into the spirit of things with a pair of caricature gnomes, in the style of himself and Violet, his wife had thrown them at him and had threatened divorce if ever a gnome of any description laid its fishing rod in one of her ponds. From that moment onwards, gnomes were barred from the Halcyon Woods establishment. Donald felt that Violet had a dim view of dwarfs as well as Gnomes after she had refused to take a weekend booking of them in July last year. 'All those little people weebling around and looking small,' she'd said. 'It would quite lower the tone.' Donald hadn't acknowledged her from behind his newspaper; he had given up trying to argue managerial decisions with Violet many years ago. 'And besides, they always have such sharp, pointed little teeth, dear. They often look quite ready to bite somebody.'

Donald took a moment to ponder this insight. 'Don't they have exactly the same kind of teeth as anybody else, then?'

'Oh no, dear, it harks back to when they were primordial and had to live by their wits to survive in the forest.'

'Oh,' said Donald. There was a lady who lived on Springfield lane. Donald once passed her a packet of Fox's mints that were out of her reach in the newsagents and they'd had a good chat about horses. She bought the mints to feed to her horse apparently. She was a dwarf but didn't seem to have sharp teeth and she lived in a semi in town. She didn't look as though she'd ever had to live by her wits in a forest. Donald felt it best to drop the conversation, because he'd never win.

It was important to Violet to create just the right impression at the ceremony that year. It had been somewhat of an annus horribilis in the Woods Dynasty. James had publicly split up with Tammy in a bar. Witnesses said they'd had to pull him off her. They got back together a month later, but it had been a nasty business and involved an unpleasant restraining order that didn't shed a good light on the hotel. Andrew had been involved in a misguided business deal. The police called it fraud and it made the newspapers. Violet said afterwards that fraud is such an ugly word. The watch maker in question should have been flattered that Andrew so admired his work that he wanted to emulate it himself. Bribes had been paid from the top rung of the civil service ladder to the bottom and Violet took her red lipstick a shade deeper to show her stiff upper lip in times of trouble. Later in the year again, James, still under the shadow of what Violet called the silly tiff with his wife, found himself the victim of a pub brawl. He'd had to defend himself against a pack of football hooligans. James stood in the dock for the second time that year and three teenage boys were awarded thousands of pounds in damages. When the terrible year was almost at a close, there was the humiliation when James was brought home by the police in a dress. Soliciting in town, the Police said, picking up men for money. It was all lies. They had it in for the Woods. Violet screamed victimisation but never very loudly when anybody official was around. That had been the greatest scandal of them all. James was a problem sometimes but seeing her boy standing in the dock accused of such atrocities when he'd merely been on a fancy dress night out was ridiculous. Her lipstick deepened by two whole shades and preceded her face into a room. Last year had been a bad one that the family needed to dust off and put behind them. This was the occasion to shine.

It took the combined effort of three of her son's and Donald to talk Violet out of wearing her fox fur for the award ceremony. Yes, it showed a certain prestige, but it also caused consternation whenever she wore it as people tended to be sensitive around the whole issue of fox hunting. 'Well, I didn't kill the blessed thing, dear,' was Violet's continual bleat. It took all of the tact and diplomacy that Ros could muster to talk her down and to help her choose something else befitting the grand occasion. Ros was the Halcyon Woods' secret weapon. She was the one person in the world who had a certain amount of influence over Violet. For some reason, Violet liked her eldest son's wife. She would take counsel from her and listen to what she had to say. She was employed as a bookkeeper for the business but her real talent lay in stopping Violet from ruining the Hotel with any one of her terrible ideas that could land them, if not in the Court of Human Rights, then certainly shown in an unfavourable light in the local press. Like the time that Violet had wanted to take the hotel more upmarket. She instructed the girls on reception to ask visitors for proof of their earnings and said that only people with an income in excess of one hundred thousand pounds a year should be allowed to make a booking or sign in. Luckily, on that occasion, Beth had discreetly rung up to Ros' apartment and asked her to come down and sort her mother-in-law out. Another time, Violet had wanted guests to take a medical before using the hotel pool and gymnasium, and she once decided that every guest should have their bags and person searched on leaving to see if they'd stolen anything. Ros was the calming voice of reason on each of these, and many more, occasions. She understood Violet and could handle her and talk her down. She was an asset worth her weight in gold because, since her retirement, Violet had too much time to sit and think and, these days, although she was still as sharp as a tack, some of her ideas were slewed and her judgement impaired.

The evening was unfolding as expected. Violet, still smarting from the slur of her nominations, was the epitome of graciousness, an act perfected over many seasons in hospitality. She simpered and cooed, flattered corporate ego, and complimented corporate ego's wife, before turning to the next bigwig and tittle tattling about who corporate ego's wife was currently sleeping with.

The family had their own table toward the front of the room. She had made grand donations to various charities for this place, but she was still unhappy with the position, and before they sat for dinner, she had Donald and two waiters angling the table differently, so that she had a clearer runway up to the stage. The salmon flotage starter was too dry, she said, the lettuce too bitter, the champagne too gassy and the wine too tart. The main course had just arrived at their table and Violet was delivering her opinion of the steak when her phone rang. She coloured because it was the height of bad manners to have one's phone turned on during these occasions. But Violet never turned this phone off. It never rang, but religiously twice a week she'd take it out of her handbag and put it on charge before putting it back in the inside pocket of her bag. That telephone had never been used, but it had never been once been switched off.

She rummaged in her bag, trying to locate the zip to the inner pocket. In her haste she was all fingers and thumbs and almost dropped it. She clasped the phone to her breast, trying to still the noise coming from it. 'Excuse me. Excuse me,' she said apologetically, scraping her chair away from the table and stepping backwards to collide with a waiter holding a tray laden with plates. The waiter was good and managed to sidestep Violet while maintaining balance of his load. 'Hello. Yes, this is she,' said Violet, ignoring the waiter and stumbling through the closely positioned tables towards the exit.

Violet returned to the dining room a few minutes later. She stood at the side of the room trying to get Donald's attention, but he was engrossed in his dinner and had forgotten all about Violet and the mysterious phone call. The boys were more curious. Phil was still questioning Donald about who it might be. He was more observant than the others, he'd seen just how shaken his mother had been when the phone rang. Her reaction was more than just embarrassment for her social faux pas. He saw that the phone she answered wasn't her usual one. She had never mentioned changing it and Violet never did anything like that without a performance that involved the entire family. It was Phil who noticed his mother jumping up and down in her ridiculous chiffon tent across the room.

'Dad,' he said, tapping Donald on the shoulder to drag his attention away from the plate. 'Dad, mum wants you. She seems het up.'

'Son, your mother's always het up,' answered Donald around a mouthful of rare Scottish beef, 'while this hunk of meat, on the other hand, is a rare treat to be savoured and enjoyed without your mother's acid stare turning it to leather under her shrivelling gaze. She can wait.'

Phil tutted in frustration and rose to go to his mother. He took her under the elbow and led her from the threshold of the dining room where she stood in the waiter's way, to the relative privacy of the corridor outside.

'No, no, Philip, I don't want you,' she said, swatting at him with her hand. 'Go and get your father.' She was pale under her thickly powdered cheekbones. She shook and seemed unsteady on her feet. He guided her into a pink velvet chair and motioned to a passing employee, demanding he fetch her a glass of water. 'I've got to go, Philip. I haven't got time for this. Oh, do stop fussing and get me your father.'

Having finished the last morsel on his plate and feeling the need to loosen his belt, break wind and perhaps get some air before dessert, Donald was less reluctant to move. 'What is it, woman?' he asked, as he got to his wife who had risen from the chair and stood by the main entrance to the hotel. 'Are you ill?'

Phil had followed his father out and hovered by his parents. He was curious to know what was going on, as was James who had come out to see what all the fuss was about. Violet pulled Donald away from her sons and spoke quietly to him. 'There's been trouble. The boy. He's in hospital, intensive care. Serious. I have to go.'

Donald's face clouded. Phil and James strained to catch what was being said but only picked up the odd phrase. Somebody was in a bad way in hospital, but all the family was here. James commented that it couldn't be anybody important, they were all accounted for, and yet their mother was badly shaken. Their father had straightened his shoulders. His body was stiff, disapproving.

'I've called a cab,' said Violet in a normal tone. 'You'll have to come for me in the car, after you've slept off your excesses. Make my excuses will you?'

'Where are you going mother? What is it? Who's hurt?' shouted James, but their mother had already turned, opened the door of the taxi that had pulled up and was climbing inside.

It was after ten o'clock when she arrived at the front desk of the hospital. She was directed to the ICU, but nobody offered to escort her. 'Young man,' she said to a porter wheeling a patient covered in blood along the corridor. 'Take me to the intensive care unit, immediately.'

The porter didn't realise that violet was talking to him. 'You there, are you deaf or an imbecile?' The porter turned, confused. 'Leave him, he's clearly drunk, he'll be quite all right there for a moment and this is urgent business. Intensive care?'

'Oi who you calling drunk?' slurred the patient behind a face full of swelling.

'What?' said the porter.

'Intensive care,' bellowed Violet.

'If you follow the arrows to the lift, madam, ICU's on the third floor, you can't miss it.' With that he came to an intersection and veered off, leaving Violet shouting at his retreating back.

There was a flurry of conversation at the nurses' station at the intensive care ward. The nurses and a doctor behind the desk were discussing cases and the nurses to the side of the desk were talking about their love life. Violet burst among them like a border collie into a flock of pigeons. She was out of breath. Her bunions were throbbing mercilessly in the stiff court shoes. She had walked further in the last five minutes than she had in the preceding month. She flung her handbag onto the top of the nurses' station desk and flopped on top of it. 'Water. I need water.' She croaked, lifting her head from her arms. One of the clips holding her hair piled on top of her head had come loose and a third of her hair had dropped to cover her face. Her red lipstick had spread from her thin top lip, to finish just below her nose.

The two young nurses beside Violet giggled. An older nurse struggled to bring her own face to order and then glared the girls into silence. 'Can I help you?' she asked, ignoring Violet's plea for hydration and adopting her businesslike smile that conveyed compassion and authority in equal measure.

'And you are?' asked Violet.

The nurse was taken aback and the smile dropped from her face to be replaced by a look that clearly said that she was the boss around here. 'I'm staff nurse Jeffries,' she said, motioning to her name badge. 'How can I help you, madam?'

'You can't. You won't do at all. I need to speak to

the man in charge. You there, young man.' She poked her finger towards the doctor who had his head immersed in somebody's records. He was out of range for her to make contact, but he raised his head to stare at her.

'Are you a real doctor, or one of those people who follow the doctors around the wards?'

Adrian Walker smiled. He could charm any old bird out of the trees and this buzzard was no exception. 'I am indeed a real doctor, ma'am,' he said. 'They even gave me a certificate to prove it. Now why don't you tell me what I can do for you.'

'I'd prefer somebody higher, but you'll have to do. Simon Peter,' she dropped her voice on the last word, 'Woods,' she said. At that moment the pager attached to the doctor's pocket sounded an urgent alarm. He looked down at it. 'I'm sorry, madam, this is important. I've got to go.' He patted her arm. 'Nurse Jefferies here will look after you. She's got a piece of paper, too.' He winked at Violet and took off down the ward in the direction of monitors sounding alarms.

'You've come to see Simon Woods?' asked sister Jefferies. 'Are you a relative?'

'I'm his,' Violet faltered, 'he's my...I'm his legal guardian.'

'Oh, right, well I guess that's good enough. Only next of kin are allowed in at the moment. He's very poorly, but we've got him sedated and he's doing as well as can be expected. I'll take you to him now. Don't be alarmed by all of the monitoring equipment, it's keeping him alive. He's asleep, but some people believe that they can hear you, so feel free to talk to him.' She was striding down the corridor as she spoke and Violet was struggling to keep up with her. 'I can't tell you anymore, I'm afraid, but a doctor will be along shortly.' She opened a door and admitted Violet. 'Make yourself comfortable, and when the nurses have a spare moment, they'll bring you a cup of tea. She motioned to the bell above the bed. 'Ring if you need anything.'

Jeffries closed the door behind her and Violet was left alone with only the droning beep of the monitor, the loud ticking of the wall clock and the noise of saline and morphine feeding into a drip bag for company.

The doughy white figure, in the white bed, in the white room, seemed less real than the small noises around her. She approached the bed and sat in the chair beside it. Before looking properly at her son, she eased her feet out of her shoes, raised one fat ankle and rubbed it. She would have trouble walking the next day. She examined the bunion on the side of her big toe, visibly red through the thick denier of her tights. She rose, poured herself a glass of water from the jug on the bedside cabinet, and then wondered if it had been pressed to her son's mouth. She screwed her face in disgust, lowered the glass without drinking, and sat back down. Only then did she look at her son for the first time. His chest rose and fell in time with the machine that breathed for him. His face was slack, eyes closed, fleshy mouth open, tongue protruding. Violet shuddered and willed with all her might for the heartbeat to stop. She wanted the shame to end.

She examined each piece of equipment, working out what each did, how it worked, what it was for. She saw that the drip feed worked by controlling a simple slide wheel. Taking it down would lessen the flow of drugs, sliding it up to increase them. The beeping monitor took its signal from the finger clamp, cradling Simon's thumb and recording his pulse. She looked at the door, listened for footsteps in the hall. Then she removed the finger clamp from his thumb and put it on her own. She watched the number's rising on the monitor screen, but they didn't sound any alarms. She was ready to transfer the clamp if anybody approached. Her own elevated but steady heartbeat, within the perimeters of acceptable levels, pulsed out static pictures on graph paper. The machine beeped like a contented robot and she studied the man that she gave birth to and felt the reflexive, familiar revulsion that she felt every time she'd ever looked at him. She could speed up the flow of morphine into his bloodstream, and then return it to its original position when somebody approached, but she doubted that it would be enough to kill him. She tested the tension on the nasal tube hooked up to the ventilator. The tube was fastened under his nose with a piece of Micropore surgical tape. She loosened it enough to allow movement of the tube, but not enough to show that it had been disturbed. She wondered if she could pull the tube out far enough to suffocate him, without it coming right out of his airway. She tested the theory by easing the tube out of her son's throat inch by inch. This was her moment, her chance. She could rid herself of this terminal disease that she carried on her soul once and for all. God would forgive her. Surely she had passed his test of burden after all of these years. In almost thirty years she had only missed two Wednesday visits. Staff and come and gone from the home, but she remained constant. She had greater longevity there than any member of staff. She had never failed in her duty, apart from the two occasions when she'd been too ill to attend. And for thirty years she had burned with hatred and shame. She pulled the tube another inch and he opened his mouth wider, although his eyes remained shut. He was unconscious, but his broken, imbecilic mind had the presence of self enough to still send messages to his nervous system to fight for life. She watched him gasp, choking on the air that he couldn't pull into his lungs. She watched as his impaired brain starved of oxygen and she waited for the stillness that would be her reward for bravery. He reminded her of a fish out of water, a big fat, bloated, ugly fish, gasping and flapping for a life that he hadn't earned and didn't deserve. He was making a gurgling sound; she felt the first stirrings of panic. What if she was caught? Her reputation. The WI. The Media. She would scream euthanasia from the dock, but could she take the risk? She might not become the people's heroine for such a merciful and selfless act. And at the very best, the secret that she'd guarded so carefully all of these years, the fact that she had a handicapped child, would be out.

She wanted him to die, but she wouldn't be able to live with herself if word was out that she had given birth to that.

Later, she didn't know if she'd already begun forcing the tube back down his windpipe when she heard the footsteps approaching or if the footsteps came first. But when she heard the nurse she had to act fast. The tube was a lot harder to get back down than it had been pulling it out. He made unearthly choking noises. The footsteps were almost level with the door. There was a wet mucus mark on the tube where it was three inches higher than it had been. She transferred the finger clamp. The monitor dropped, slowed, settled and was still settling when the nurse came in. Violet flung the top half of her body over Simon and feigned weeping. The nurse glanced at the monitor and rushed over to the bed. She guided violet up by the shoulders. 'Easy, love, you've trapped his monitor.'

She sat Violet in the chair and looked at Simon Peter's finger clamp. It was still slowing, but was steadier now. The nurse adjusted it. After a few more seconds it stuck in a slow, steady, one beep per second rhythm. 'Crickey, I think you'd knocked all the wind out of him there. I know it's upsetting, but try not to squash him, eh?' Violet looked up sharply, from dabbing her eyes. 'I mean,' the nurse continued, 'please, just make sure he's got plenty of air.' She realised that this was a dumb statement that highlighted her student status. The patient wasn't even breathing for himself, so it didn't matter how much air he had, but having that great lump lying all over him had certainly done something to the monitor. It was okay now though and she could see to the matter in hand, 'Can I get you a cup of tea or anything?'

Chapter Nineteen

'Will you please just see to Vicki while I put this wash on?'

'Oh, come on, Jules, just a quickie, I'm aching.' He reached for her as she bent to stuff the dirty clothes into the washer, one hand around her waist, the other grabbing roughly at her breast, which leaked milk all over his hand. He rubbed his erection against her buttocks. 'Come on, Mummy, turn around and give me some titty milk.'

She stood with Phil still attached to her. Picking up a packet of washing powder tablets, she crushed them hard in her fist before opening the packet. She wished that they were her husband's balls. He disgusted her. If ever a man needed castrating, it was him. 'Your mother's coming any minute now. Get off me, will you.' She flung him away from her, pulling down her disarranged top and bra with one hand while she opened the tablet packet and put them into the washing machine with the other. Phil was smelling the breast milk on his palm and she turned away before she saw his tongue come out to lick it.

She went into the living room where Vicki was crying against the bars of her playpen. Julie picked her up and cradled her into her shoulder. Vicki stopped crying, but every few seconds she gave a great heave as the residue of her sobs subsided. Julie stroked her angry daughter's sweaty head and swore that she saw reproach in the baby's eyes. 'I'm sorry, baby girl. Mummy had to get tidied up for Grandma coming. And as usual, Daddy's no help at all. We don't want to give her anything to crow about, do we sweetheart? No, we don't.'

'I'll just go and sort myself out again, then, shall I?' said Phil as he walked passed the living room door and stomped up the stairs in the direction of the bedroom and his stash of lurid porn. She hated it when he was on the late shift at work, he'd be pestering her again before he went out at two.

Seemingly forgiven for her abandonment to the playpen, Vicki was already reaching for Julie's breast. These days it felt as though everybody wanted a piece of her.

Grandma, as she insisted on being called by all three of them so as not to confuse Victoria, was already perched on the sofa, with the baby on her knee, when Phil came downstairs. He glared at Julie in the second before Mother turned around, and then, when she did, he smiled a simpering smile and dropped a light kiss on top of Julie's head. Julie felt a wetness on her scalp. The bastard had purposely spat into her hair. She imagined it burning, like acid. He'd be in a bad mood for the rest of the morning because she'd refused him sex, and when he pestered her it later, he would be even rougher than normal. She couldn't refuse him twice in one day.

When she'd made the tea, she washed up the teaspoon, dried it on the tea-towel and put it in the drawer facing the right way and ensuring that it sat neatly with all the others. Julie had learned a lot since leaving her family home. She had learned to cook and found that she had a natural flair for it, and she had come to enjoy it. Mostly it was the little things that she had to perfect and never slip up on. The first time she had stirred a cup of tea and left the spoon on the side of the sink, Phil had gripped the top of her arm tightly. He had screamed at her, called her a dirty whore, and stood over her while she had washed the teaspoon and put it neatly away. Her arm was dappled with dark blue bruises for a week before fading to a dirty yellow colour. He'd had a similar reaction when he saw Julie drying her hands on a tea towel. He yelled so hard that he damaged his throat. He didn't touch her, but he degraded her and called her names, before turning the blame on her family and upbringing. Hand towels were for drying hands, tea towels were for pots. She only needed yelling at the once. She got it.

The house, even with a baby in it, was kept spotless. Even the dust bunnies were banished to warrens beyond the property. There was not a node of dust, not a spot of dirt anywhere in their home. It was immaculate. As soon as something was used, it was cleaned. It was the way he liked it.

The strange thing was it became the way she liked it too. She really had changed. At her family home, she had been untidy. Clothes were taken off and discarded over the back of the bedroom chair, until it threatened to tip under the weight. As Mrs Julie Woods, she had become a different woman. Lisa came to visit them a few months after they were married. It had been so good having her sister there, but Julie found that she had to tidy up after her all the time so that it didn't irritate or upset Phil. After the first two days she was getting pissed off with her untidy sister herself. When she waved Lisa off, Julie had heaved a big sigh of relief and couldn't wait to get the duster out to obliterate any stray fingerprints that might have been left behind.

She had changed in other ways, too. Julie had always been a jeans, t-shirt and ponytail kind of girl. If she had to analyse her change of style to herself, she would have put it down to becoming a mother and growing up. But lots of women had babies without changing their entire personalities. She had taken to buying print dresses and skirts. She found herself drawn to delicate flowers. Her trainers had been replaced by dolly shoes, feminine and dainty. She was leg waxing and having six-weekly hair do's. Phil hadn't ordered her to do it; he'd never said a word. But on occasions, she'd felt that he disapproved of her dress sense, or lack of it. Julie's change of image was all tied up in a Martha Stewart fantasy. She had to be the perfect mother, and far more importantly, the perfect wife.

'Nice cake, dear,' said Grandma, 'did you bake it, yourself?' She had. She made everything from scratch. Phil didn't hold with processed food. He said it wasn't sustaining for a man to work on. She made roast dinners and baked cakes. She had given up work and now she cooked and cleaned and pottered in the garden.

'Guess what?' she'd said to Lisa on the phone one day soon after her marriage.

'What?'

'I'm doing plants.'

'You're what?'

She was really excited. 'Plants and stuff. I'm growing them.'

'It's called gardening, love.'

'Oh, yeah,' she'd said. 'I knew that.'

Phil had come home and complained about the state of the garden. She hadn't had a clue what she was doing, but she bought books, and then every few days she'd buy blubs, or seeds. In six months she bought her own poly-tunnel and grew all their own veg. She had a herb garden, flower beds, lawns—three in total including the front—so smooth you could play bowls on them. She had a tool shed and a potting shed, and she took advice from her father-in-law. This year, she had entered her first carrots at the local fête. They hadn't been placed, but her Victoria sponge took third and was awarded a blue rosette.

Since she was married, she hadn't taken a single alcoholic drink. Partly because Vicki came along so quickly, and because she was permanently breast feeding. She declined all offers of nights out from her sisters and old workmates until they'd stopped inviting her. Occasionally, she went shopping with her sister on a Saturday afternoon, but that was rare these days. She preferred being at home in her lovely house, in her lovely garden, happy.

Lisa and Emma, and even her mum and dad on occasion called her The Stepford Wife behind her back. She became Steppy and tolerated it with good humour. They never called her that in front of Phil, though, just like they never called Victoria Vicki when he was around. He didn't like it. In fact, wherever possible he preferred her to be given the full title of Victoria-Violet. Lisa called her Vicki-Vee because she said it sounded like a DJ's name, but Julie couldn't bring herself to say that. She never, ever used her daughter's hyphenated name. She felt that calling her daughter Violet or even a shortened form of it, would sour her child, but she had stopped shuddering when Phil used the full name, because that's all he ever called her, apart from when he was angry and then he would address her as The Child.

Julie detested her husband. She had grown to hate him after Vicki had been born. He had no interest in his little girl apart from when his parents were around, or there was somebody else that he was playing the devoted father for. When it was just the three of them, he ignored her. He never woke in the night to attend to her. He never changed a nappy. He resented her and was jealous that she took her mother's attention from him.

'Victoria-Violet loves her grandma more than anybody else in the world,' sang Violet as she bounced Vicki on her knee. Vicki had had enough and was struggling to get down, but Violet held her in a vice-like grip. There were going to be tears. Julie watched her daughter screw up her face in preparation for the first yell. She had her father's temper. She rose and put a plain biscuit in Vicki's fist to distract her. 'Does silly Mummy feed you nasty biscuits that are full of sugar? Does she, does she?' Violet crooned. 'Silly Mummy. Tell her, Victoria-Violet, silly mummy.' Julie thought that she might puke if she had to listen to any more of Violet's stupid baby talk.

'Oh, here, dear, take her from me. Grandma really mustn't get this coat dirty. Jaeger, dear.' She held Vicki out to Julie as though the baby was radio active. Phil stepped in and took her out of his mother's arms. He cradled her in the crook of his arm and kissed her on her cheek. 'Victoria-Violet is Daddy's little Princess, isn't she?' he said. Vicki flung herself sideways, extending her arms towards her mother. She dropped the sucked biscuit on the floor and grizzled. As Julie rose to take her from Phil she realised that it was the first time that Phil had touched his daughter in almost a week.

'You shouldn't give in to her like that, Philip, dear. She's becoming far too clingy for her mother. It's not good for her. She'll become a spoiled brat. Put her down in her play pen and let her be.'

Vicki was grabbing at Julie's breast. Ignoring Violet's advice, she left the room, sickened by the act that Phil was performing for his mother's benefit.

When she first brought Vicki home from the hospital Violet and Donald had come round for a visit. The baby wanted a feed, so Julie discretely covered her chest with a feeding cloth and put her daughter to her breast. She hadn't given it a second thought—her baby needed feeding and she was there solely to provide for her.

'Take the child to the nursery and do that,' said Phil. Julie had never heard him speak to her so coldly and she thought she'd heard every nasty tone that the man possessed. His eyes were smouldering with fury. She looked up, shocked to find Donald pointedly looking out of the window and Violet with her head turned into the sofa and expression of deep disgust on her frosty face.

'The flowers are looking nice again,' said Donald. Julie, hoisted Vicki, covered herself and left the room.

'How dare you disrespect my parents like that,' Phil raged after they had left. 'I cannot believe that you brazenly exposed yourself to my father like a fishwife. I will never live this down. How could you? You filthy, dirty whore. I would make you get on your knees and humbly beg their forgiveness if it didn't mean bringing the disgusting spectacle up again.' He was clearly thinking about doing so. 'No, it's best just left now. But if you ever embarrass me in front of my parents like that again, I will never forgive you. If you were a Christian woman you'd go to confession and beg for your soul to be cleansed of such wickedness. He stormed from the room without another word. The upside was that he never pestered her for sex for nearly a month after that. He said that she disgusted him, but he still lay in their bed beside her, masturbating at night.

Julie thought back to that incident when she sat in the nursery chair feeding Vicki. She could hear their muffled voices from downstairs and she felt content. How could Phil not love this precious child?

'Grandma and Grandpa are leaving now, Julie,' Phil shouted up the stairs.

'Okay, see you next time. Thank you for the bonnet,' Julie shouted back down. She heard Phil's feet pounding up the stairs. She knew from the footfalls that he was angry again. He flung the door open, startling Vicki and making her jump in her mother's arms. She whimpered, but didn't remove her mouth from the nipple.

'Have you no manners?' he hissed. 'Get down those stairs now and say goodbye to my parents properly.'

'I'm in the middle of feeding your daughter, I can't just pull her away,' she hissed back.

'Put the child down and do it.' He didn't wait for her to respond and grabbed Vicki roughly from her mother's arms. As the suction from around Julie's breast was released, Vicki's rosebud mouth came away with a loud smacking noise. She instantly began to wail. Phil put her roughly in her cot. She hadn't been winded and wasn't finished feeding.

If Donald and Violet hadn't been waiting at the bottom of the stairs, she would have fought against this indignity bitterly, but under the circumstances it was better not to make a scene, it would only be held against her by all concerned. She glanced at her screaming baby and left the room, covering her breast as she went.

'No need. Really no need,' said Donald as she appeared around the bend in the stairs with a smile ready on her face.

'Every need, Dad,' replied Phil, hammering the point home that they had had words.

Violet's mouth dropped open to gape as she stared at Julie. Julie had been about to embrace Donald in the customary, awkward goodbye hug before moving onto Violet, but Donald had also seen what had happened and busied himself with his hat, holding it in front of himself like a shield.

Julie looked down to see a sticky wet patch covering the front of her top. Still full, her swollen breast had lactated. She felt a small river of it trickle to her navel.

'Go and clean yourself,' Phil spoke to her like a dog, further humiliating her.

Julie went back to Vicki. She lifted her gently from the cot, crooning to her all the time. Vicki latched on to her mother's breast, comforting them both. Five minutes later Julie was singing softly to her daughter, who had hold of her little finger and was staring up into her mother's eyes. Out of the blue, Julie remembered the look on her Mother-in-law's horrified face when her breast had leaked onto her top and she started laughing. Not getting the joke, but finding it funny anyway, Vicki laughed too and mother and daughter shared a special moment before Julie had to go downstairs to face her husband's latest fury.

Chapter Twenty

Julie padded downstairs in her dressing gown. The smell of toast and percolating coffee hit her before she got near the kitchen. Phil headed her off on the threshold; he had a white tea-towel folded over his arm. 'Ah, Good morning, Madam, may I escort you to your table, where breakfast is about to be served,' he said, guiding her past the kitchen and into the dining room where the table had been laid. He pulled out a chair and Julie sat down and he pushed her chair in. Before going back into the kitchen, Phil bent and dropped a kiss onto the top of her head. 'Happy anniversary, my darling.'

It was a beautiful May morning, warm enough that Phil had thrown the patio doors wide open. The sun was shining, the garden was coming into bloom and Julie identified a starling, wood pigeon and a cuckoo amongst the riotous birdsong. The birds were as happy as she was that the long and bitter winter was over. They were going to Morocco later that morning but the excitement of that wasn't the only reason for the little fountain that rose somewhere in the pit of her tummy and burst into a million tiny champagne bubbles of happiness.

She loved her garden, it had become her pride and joy, but she also loved this room and the lounge that opened through a door to the right and was kept for visitors. The dining room was the only room in the house that was wallpapered. She'd seen it in the shop and knew that it was made for this room. It had a pale blue wash with a light yellow stripe on the bottom of the wall, and above it was the wonderful buttercup print. Delicate yellow flowers adorned the walls, just like her dresses, and brought the outside garden inside. The dining table sat twelve, made from solid oak, with matching chairs that had high backs and screamed grandiose. The chair cushions were upholstered with a blue and yellow print. The dining room displayed her Cappo Di Monte collection. She had over forty pieces, most of it bought at auction for a song. In stark contrast to the delicacy of the rest of the room her tableware was Tunisian. She had fallen in love with the Tunisian style and over four trips to the country had brought back an extensive range of tableware and crockery, all in vibrant red, blue and yellow. Her glassware was all lead crystal and, when they had guests for dinner, which was often, Julie's table was always complimented. Her style was an extension of her and she felt that she wore it well.

Every week they bought three bunches of flowers along with their shopping, two large mixed bunches for the living room and lounge, and a delicate drop of carnations for the dining room table. She alternated the colour of the carnations weekly. This morning, by her place setting, was a huge bouquet of gardenias, freesias and red roses. A card was propped against her juice glass, with a jeweller's box in front of it. They had been married for six glorious years and every single day Julie wished that her husband would have a heart attack and die.

She was happier than she'd ever been in her life. She had taken to being a wife and mother better than she could ever have expected. She loved being married; she just hated her husband and would like to have replaced him with a better spouse. As she reached for her card, she smiled a smug smile, remembering the voices of doom on the lead up to her wedding, prophesising that it would never last.

To my darling wife, with love always and forever, Philip xxx

Her card to him bore similar words of love. She wondered how often he had wished her dead.

Vicki, who was a blessedly late riser in the mornings, ran barefoot into the dining room and flung herself into her mother's arms.

'Stop running in the house,' Phil yelled at her from the kitchen.

'Mummy, Mummy, the sleeps are all used up now aren't they?' At this, the wide smile froze on her face for just a second, in case it had all been a huge grown up joke and she still had another five million sleeps to endure.'

'They have indeed, my darling. And where are we going today?'

'Mocco,' the little girl screeched.

'Yay, Morocco,' yelled her mother, tickling her daughter and causing gales of giggles.

Phil arrived with two plates in his hands and a dish for Vicki. 'Proper behaviour in the dining room please,' he said sternly, glaring at his daughter. 'Go and sit down nicely now, please, Victoria-Violet. Have you washed your hands?'

'Yes, Daddy.' Julie watched part of her little girl's bubble burst. 'Daddy, we're going Mocco today. Would you pass me the Wice Cwispies please, Mummy?'

'How many times do you have to be told, it's Mor-Occo. What are you doing? Don't give her that rubbish this morning, she won't eat her eggs.'

Julie had taken the cereal dispenser and was pouring a few into the bottom of a clean bowl for Vicki. 'Can't she have both? It's a special day.'

'No.'

'Why lay them out on the table then?'

'Because it looks good, doesn't it? I wanted everything to be perfect. Aren't you going to open your present?'

'Oh, darling, it is perfect. It's wonderful, thank you for going to all this trouble.' She reached for the jewellery box. This would have been the perfect morning if he hadn't been so uptight. Vicki could never do a thing right when he was around. He was always at her. Trying to muster her earlier feeling of happiness and force down the resentment that was rising, she opened the box. A tiny pair of diamond and sapphire earrings winked out at her and she gasped in delight. They were beautiful.

'Why you got a pessant, Mummy, is it your burfday?'

'No, darling, it our anniversary. Today your daddy and I have been married for six years.'

'Wish you mother a Happy Anniversary, Victoria-Violet.' Phil was still growling.

'Happy Amme…' her brow furrowed into four little creases as she floundered. 'What is it, Daddy?'

How could he not be absolutely enchanted by his daughter's chatter? Julie marvelled every day at each new thing she came up with. Their daughter was bright and her thirst for knowledge inexhaustible. Julie laughed. 'Don't you worry, sweetheart, it's a great big word.'

'And she'll never learn to talk properly if you don't encourage her. You let her get away with being lazy.' He turned to face his daughter. 'Ann-e-ver-sary. Say it.'

Victoria giggled. 'Like Aunty Annie,' she said, referring to one of the helpers at her pre-school.

'Say it.'

'Ann-e-ber-sary'

'Versary'

'Versary.'

'Put it together.'

'Put it together.'

Phil sighed and closed his eyes. 'Say anniversary.'

'Ann-e-versary.'

Julie cringed, and pop went another champagne bubble.

Chapter Twenty-one

'So, Jamaica lived up to all its expectations, then?'

It was January and Julie, Phil and Vicki had just returned from some winter sun. 'How much longer are you going to live like this, Toots?' It was a familiar question and Lisa had asked it many times. 'It breaks my heart to see you so…so…' she struggled to find the right word. 'Cowed.'

'See how you didn't say unhappy or miserable or depressed? You still don't get it, do you? I am happier than I've ever been in my entire life. This is everything I've ever wanted and more. You think he bullies me, but I can handle him, you know. He is a small price to pay to have Vicki and all this.'

'But the sex stuff. You've just spent the last ten minutes telling me how bad it was on holiday, nearly put me off my sandwich,' she said, motioning to her empty plate.

'Even that's not so bad once you get used to it. The thing with the sex is not to fight it. I've perfected the sixty second blow job to an Olympic standard. Honestly, nine times out of ten, that keeps him on an even keel. We rarely have full on sex these days.

'It's no way to live. The man's a monster.'

'It's my way to live and it works for me.'

'But you could divorce him and take him to the cleaners. Why are you so bloody stubborn about it? Your promise means nothing.'

'It means everything.'

'You know it's going to come to it one day. Are you really going to throw away everything?'

Julie thought back to the golden promise she had made her Mother-in-law in the early days of the bitter fights and arguments. Violet had called her a gold digger. Said that she'd crawled out of the gutter. Said that Philip was nothing more than a meal ticket for her. Julie had promised, on her life, that if ever her marriage went sour, she would leave with nothing more than the clothes on her back.

She answered her sister's question. 'Yes, I am. I'll walk out of here empty-handed without a second's hesitation.'

'God, you're so stubborn sometimes. Bloody hell, girl, for what you put up with, you've earned every chrome washer in this place. It's Vicki-Vee's heritance. You can't deny her that.'

'I would rather my daughter grew up with dignity and integrity than a silver spoon. If I walk out of here with her and we have to struggle for awhile it will be character-building for her and she'll always know that her mother did what was right. A promise like that can't be broken. Anyway, shush, it's not going to come to that. Things are fine.'

Sensing a feeling of friction building between them, Lisa changed the subject. 'So, how's Woodzilla been?'

'Not so bad lately. She adores Vicki and she's taken to calling me "Dear," so maybe after six years of marriage she's realised that I'm not the monster that she had me painted.'

'She's such a fucking hypocrite. How can she pull our family to bits, when she's got a prostitute in a frock for one son, a fraudster for another, and a friggin' sex addict for a third.' She pointed upstairs to where Phil was asleep from his night shift.

'Shush, you'll wake him,' said Julie, just as the living room door opened. He'd crept down the stairs and had been listening at the door. As she heard him coming in, Lisa hastily grabbed her cup and side plate off the coffee table. Julie had no idea how much of their conversation he had heard. His voice, when he spoke, was cool and gave no indication of the fury he was holding beneath the surface. 'Well, look at Miss Lisa, sitting on my sofa, eating my food and drinking my coffee, and slagging off my family. I think it's time you ran along home now, don't you?' He ripped the coffee cup out of Lisa's hands and threw it against the far wall. Coffee dregs dripped from the muted mauve paintwork and ran in two trails down towards the carpet. Lisa stood and put her coat on. 'Get out,' Phil said in a controlled voice. 'Get out of my house and don't ever come back.'

'Will you be all right?' she asked Julie, and her sister nodded. 'I'll ring you,' said Lisa, glaring at Phil before beating a hasty retreat.

Phil waited for the squeak of the garden gate before speaking. 'Am I such a bad husband?' he asked.

'No, of course not.'

'I give you everything you ask for. I work eighty

hours a damned week to keep you happy. And you repay me like this. Don't you love me?'

'Of course I do,' she lied. 'Look, I don't know how much you heard, but it's just our Lisa mouthing off. You know she's got a big mouth.'

He walked over to her and Julie shrank back in her seat. Philip grabbed the front of her fleece and pulled her towards him. 'Liar,' he hissed. 'I've never hit a woman in my life but I could wring your rancid neck right now.' His eyes were blazing and Julie was scared. Phil worked up some spittle in his mouth and spat it full into Julie's face before throwing her back into the chair. He stalked out of the room, leaving Julie to wipe the soiling from her face.

She was glad that Vicki was at school. She had been quiet lately and Julie was worried that the fights between her and Phil were scaring her. She went into the kitchen for a dust pan and brush for the broken crockery and a wet cloth to wash the coffee from the wall.

In many ways, Phil was the perfect husband. He was right, he had become a workaholic. When Julie had met him he was a fitter on the shop floor. From that he elevated to foreman, and now he had a white collar job in the offices that allowed them an extravagant lifestyle. He worked five twelve-hour shifts instead of three or four and often went into the office on a Saturday and Sunday, too. Phil loved his work, and despised his daughter. He kept out of the way.

They had three foreign holidays a year, that year

they had already been to Morocco and Jamaica. He never denied Julie, or indeed Vicki, anything. If they wanted it, it was available. A tin containing an emergency float of one thousand pounds was kept in the back of one of the kitchen cupboards. It was there to pay for anything that cropped up between visits to the bank. Julie had never lived with financial security. Her childhood had always been clouded by her parent's money worries. They regularly had debt collectors and the loan woman at the door. Julie had taken a part time job working in the kitchen of a nursing home and she loved it. Her money was her own and Philip never asked her about it or asked what she did with it. She was able to help out her own family from time to time. She would take money from the kitchen tin, but she always made sure that she replaced it on pay day. Once a month she went into the mortgage broker's on Duke Street. The mortgage was an endowment and came out of Phil's bank on the fifteenth of every month. He left the finances to Julie, secure in the knowledge that everything was paid up and on time. He never looked at the biannual statements from the mortgage people. At the end of every month, Julie would make a second, equal monthly payment on the house. It came from her own wages and was her secret gift to Phil. It was her kick in the teeth for Violet. When the mortgage came to an end years before the final payment was due, she wanted to be able to say, 'See? I did that. I doubled the house payments so that we would be free of debt earlier. Now call me a gold digger.' With every extra payment Julie felt ten feet taller.

There's was a difficult and unhappy marriage, but Julie's life on the whole couldn't have been better. She was a loyal and faithful wife and a loving mother.

Mrs Calvert walked across the schoolyard as Julie was re-fastening Vicki's coat properly and getting the first barrage of words about her day at school. 'Mrs Woods, hang on. Can I have a quick word, please?' She looked up, startled, and rose to meet the teacher.

'What is it? Is everything all right?'

'Oh yes, I'm sure it is. If you'd just like to come to my office, I won't keep you long. I've arranged for Miss Finch to watch Victoria for you.' Despite the head teacher's light tone, it sounded serious. Julie was worried.

In her office, Miss Calvert pointed Julie to a chair and produced a buff file. She looked at it for a moment before speaking. 'Our role as teachers is not only to impart knowledge, Mrs Woods. We are also there to look out for the wellbeing of all of our children. We are trained to spot sudden or even gradual changes in behaviour.'

Julie had sat forward, alarmed. She clasped her hands in her lap. 'What is it? What's the matter?'

The middle-aged teacher smiled warmly. 'Don't worry, I'm sure it's nothing, but you see, that's why we want to talk to you now, so that if something is wrong we can sort it out.'

'Okay,' said Julie, wishing that she'd get to the point.

'Victoria has always been an exemplary student, Mrs Woods. A real credit to you. She's very well behaved in class, one of the top students. And that in itself is part of the problem, you see.'

'It is?'

'Miss Finch, as you know, is Victoria's form teacher. How can I put this? She is concerned that in some ways, Victoria is almost too good. Her manners are so tight that they seem to suffocate her. Am I making sense?'

'Not really,' said Julie, rudely.

'Okay, let me read you part of this progress report from Miss Finch. "Victoria is too stiff. She seems too polite, too clean, too well mannered, too everything. It's as though she only allows two-thirds of herself to come out. The impression I have is that Victoria is holding her personality in check." Now, I know,' the head continued, 'that this may seem silly to you. How can a child be too good but—'

Julie interrupted. 'What a load of rubbish. There is nothing wrong with Vicki's personality. She's fine. How can you haul me in here to complain that my child is too well behaved? I've never heard such rubbish. And while I am here, Miss Calvert, perhaps I can draw to your attention what happened yesterday. Millie Green called my daughter a bitch. I won't stand for that.'

'Mrs. Woods, you are taking this all wrong. I'm not here to make you feel as though we're criticising you. I just wanted to take this opportunity to have an informal chat with you to see that everything is okay. As to the incident with Millie yesterday, we are aware of it and I believe Miss Finch has sent a letter to Millie's parents. Mrs Woods, you have a lovely daughter. She's a joy to teach. We've seen how you are with her in the yard and she talks about you all the time. But, she never mentions her father at all.'

The teacher stopped talking to let this information sink in.

'Well, that's because he works a lot.'

'I see. As you know, Mrs Woods, Victoria's a real chatterbox. But both Mrs Finch and myself have noticed that when we mention her father, Victoria becomes distressed.'

'That's absolute rubbish. What are you saying? Let me get this straight, are you accusing Philip of something here? Are you suggesting that my husband is abusing our daughter?'

'No.' The teacher said this firmly. 'No, Mrs Woods, please get that idea out of your head. That's not what I'm saying at all. Please don't think that for a second. Victoria is a happy little girl, she's showing no symptom's of being abused in any way.'

'Oh, you've been looking for them, then.'

'We watch every child in the school, Mrs Woods. Vicki no more or less than anybody else. It's our job to be observant. She's showing none of the usual symptoms of being abused, but she is showing signs of domestic distress.' The teacher picked up an exercise book from the desk.

'Because she had noticed some changes in Victoria's behaviour, Miss Finch set the entire class an exercise.

She asked them to think about the best time they'd ever had with their daddy, and write about it.'

'Wait a minute.' Julie was furious. 'The teacher set the whole class a lesson just to trap my daughter into saying something bad about her dad?'

The head mistress didn't answer. She turned Vicki's book upside down so that it would face Julie and she pushed it across the table.

Vicki had written: *Daddy + mummy + me went to Jamaker. Mummy made sand casuls wiv me. Mummy an me lafed when we got ower feets wet. Mummy and me dansd on the beech.*

Miss Calvert watched Julie's reaction carefully.

'Well,' blustered Julie. 'Vicki and I have a lot of fun together. It doesn't mean that she doesn't have fun with her dad, too. She just remembered that day in her head, that's all. Philip is a bit stuffy. He's not the type to play in the sea or build sand-castles. Does that mean that he's not a good father?' Julie felt tears stinging the back of her eyes and fought to keep them contained.

Miss Calvert pushed a box of tissues across the desk to her. 'When Miss Finch asked the children to write about a time with their fathers, she expressly asked the children to think of a time when their mother's weren't there, a time when they were having a good time alone with their dads.' She let the implications drift in the room.

'He's a wonderful father. He works all hours to give Victoria the life that she has. I'm sorry; I don't know what else to say. I'm hurt that you're making my husband out to be some kind of monster. He's not. He's really not.'

'I don't mean to upset you Mrs Woods, and we're honestly not suggesting that something bad is happening at home. I assure you that's not the case. If we had any real concerns, this chat wouldn't be happening and the meeting would be far less informal. We've just noticed some tension between Victoria and her father that we wanted to make you aware of, as is our duty. All we ask is that you speak to Victoria yourself and maybe we can talk again in a week or two.'

Julie left the headmistress' office, reeling. Half of the way home she seethed in indignation, mentally defending her husband and deeply resenting the slight against him. The other half she thought about just how much she'd buried her head in the sand where Philip and Victoria were concerned. She acted as peacemaker between them, always trying to keep the equilibrium. She went through life hoping that Phil would ease up and find the joy in his daughter that she had. Sometimes she counted days. The other week she counted six days during which the only time he had spoken to Vicki was to tell her off. He was at her constantly, pulling her up on her manner's, making her sit up straight, be quiet, talk properly, eat nicely, not drag her feet, pull her dress down, pick her toys up, fasten her shoes, not swing her legs into the furniture, sit properly on the chairs, and a multitude of other minor complaints. When he talked to Vicki he had a tone, he used a certain disapproving, strict tone of voice when he asked her to do something. He only ever talked to her in two ways, in the strict tone asking her to do something, or shouting when he was telling her off. He never just talked to her.

Since starting work, Julie had noticed a change in Vicki herself, but she'd tried to swallow it and pretend that it was her imagination. If she was going to be late home and Phil would be there when Vicki came home from school, Vicki would throw a tantrum. It was rare that Phil picked her up; he was always at work so that Julie couldn't do a late shift. On the odd occasion that he did, Julie thought that it was a good thing for Vicki. Of course the child would have a tantrum; it was out of the norm for her to have her dad there when she got in instead of her mum. Children liked order and bucked against change. She didn't like Julie not being there for her. Julie didn't want her growing up spoiled so ignored her crying. She would pry her off her legs when she went out of the door. She was grateful when Vicki was at school when she left for work. She wouldn't tell the child in advance if her dad was picking her up. Vicki asked her every day if she would be there when she came out of school and every day Julie said that she would. Phil only picked her up about once a month, if that. Julie firmly believed that it was good for both of them.

When she got in from work, Vicki was always in bed asleep. She'd ask how she'd been and Phil would always say, 'Fine, no problem.' The following day Vicki would be clingy and whiney, but that was only to be expected. Julie would assure her that she'd be there after school and Vicki would settle down.

Julie's head was banging. She'd been trying to work through the headache but it had become worse as her shift progressed and now she felt nauseous with it, too. She was told to go home and get some rest, an offer that she gratefully accepted.

She put her key in the door and went into the living room. She could hear the television in the lounge at the back of the house. They had a long coffee table in the living room that Vicki ate some meals on if they weren't eating in the dining room, or she'd use it to draw or do jig-saws on. Julie would pull it into the middle of the room for her and when not in use it fit snugly into an alcove at the back of the room. Vicki was sitting bolt upright at the table, facing the wall. She didn't turn around when Julie entered.

'Vicki, I'm home, darling. Don't I get a hug?'

Vicki turned around. Her cheeks were streaked with tears. 'I can't, Mummy,' she said from her little plastic chair. 'I'm not allowed to move until bedtime.'

Julie was by her daughter's side; she pulled her into her arms and carried her over to the sofa where she sat with her on her knee. Phil still wasn't aware that she'd come home and was watching telly in the lounge.

Julie held Vicki's hand in hers. It was like ice.

'How long have you been sitting there like that, darling?'

'Since I came home from school, Mummy. Daddy

always makes me sit here and I have to be real still and quiet until bedtime.'

'Have you had your tea?'

'Daddy makes me a cheese sandwich when I get in and gives me a drink of juice.'

'That's all you've had?'

Her little girl nodded her head solemnly, big tears watering her eyes. 'Don't tell on me. He'll be mad.'

'No he won't, sweetheart. Don't you worry. Now you go up and put your jammies on and I'll make you some tomato soup and toast soldiers before you go to bed, how's that? She held her daughter close and kissed her hair.

'I don't like it when you leave me, Mummy,' Vicki jumped down off her knee smiling, and Julie patted her on the bottom as she skipped across the room.

'I promise you, sweetie, I'm not going to leave you anymore. I'm sorry.'

Julie waited for the door to shut before going to confront her husband. He had heard the living room door opening and closing and met her at the threshold to the kitchen.

'What the hell's going on?' she shouted at him. He looked guilty.

'What do you mean, what's going on? Nothing's going on. What are you doing home, anyway?'

'I walked in to find out little girl sitting in a corner facing the wall. She was crying her heart out because you'd told her that she wasn't allowed to move. What have you been doing to her Philip? She's your daughter.

How can you not want to love her with everything you've got?'

'Is that what she said,' he laughed. 'Well, the little liar. I think we've got a problem, sweetheart. Victoria-Violet obviously resents you going out to work. She's trying to play us off against each other.'

'Don't you dare blame any of this on her, you cowardly little man,' she emphasised the word little. 'You have no right to call yourself a father. You haven't even fed her.'

'Don't be so ridiculous, of course I've fed her. She's been pushing your buttons, Julie; the little bitch has been lying through her teeth to cause trouble between us.' Julie recoiled and put her hands over her mouth. She couldn't believe what her husband had just called their daughter. Had he ever said something like that to her face? He was still talking. 'She wants a good hiding, that's what she wants. I'll sort her out, lying and causing trouble. You've always been too soft on her, pandering to her every whim. You know what, Julie, if you want somebody to blame for all of this, you should start by looking in the mirror, woman. If I don't discipline the child and teach her some respect, she going to revert to her genes and grow up a low-grade whore, like her mother.'

She didn't think about what she was saying, she just reacted. 'I want a divorce,' she said simply, and pushed past him. She pounded up the stairs. Vicki's bedroom door was open and Julie saw her sitting on the edge of her bed looking terrified. She'd heard them arguing. What was a nice kitchen and Tunisian cookware in comparison to her daughter's happiness? She pulled a holdall from the top of the wardrobe in her room, mindful of her promise. She would return it later. She packed one change of clothes for herself. Then she went through to Vicki's room. 'It's all right, darling, don't be frightened. We're going on a little holiday, just the two of us.' She had a couple of hundred pounds left from this month's wages. It wasn't a lot but it would buy her a night in a bed and breakfast while she thought about her next move. Of course she'd have to go home, eventually, cap in hand to her parents. But the shame of her failed marriage burned inside of her. She didn't want to admit that she'd fallen short as a wife. She'd moved on from the tired council house on the roughest estate in Barrow. She'd grown accustom to better and Vicki had never lived the way she had as a child. Her parents didn't even have central heating. As she threw clothes into the holdall for Vicki, she realised that her family were right, she had become a snob. She hated the thought of going back to all that she had left behind. She worked hard for the things she had, was it wrong to want better than you were used to? Her mind was racing; she was haphazardly throwing Vicki's clothes into the bag and talking to her about the wonderful time that they were going to have.

'I'm hungry, Mummy,' said Vicki.

'I know, sweetheart, and you know what, forget silly old tomato soup, when we get to our hotel, we'll order in takeaway. Anything you want.'

'Takeaway, wow.' Vicki said it as though she was being offered Cinderella's castle. They didn't eat processed food; Phil insisted that everything in the home be cooked from scratch. Vicki had only ever eaten takeaway at her auntie's house, and because it came in exciting packages it was like the Holy Grail. She jumped up and down and chattered, trying to decide between a Happy Meal or chicken nuggets, or pizza, or sausage and chips.

Maybe they could afford a rented house. She only worked part time but Emma was at home with a small baby, perhaps Julie could pay her to have Vicki after school. Her mind was reeling with possibilities as she zipped her daughter into her warm winter coat.

She walked into the living room with Vicki under one arm and the holdall in the other. Phil was watching the television and barely even bothered to look up when she appeared.

'So, you think you're leaving me, then,' he sneered.

'No, Philip, I am leaving you.'

'You'll be back with your tail between your legs, begging me for forgiveness. I give it twenty-four hours. You're pathetic, you know that? Here I am trying to discipline the child to avoid situations just like this one, and you just mamby-pamby her all the time. Go on, go if you want to. I'll be better off without the lot of you. You only hold me back.'

She went over to the pot where they kept keys and odd coins and took her car keys.

Philip raised his eyebrows. 'Oh, you think you're

261

taking your car, do you? Think again. The car stays with me.'

She could have kicked herself for allowing him this victory. She threw the car keys at him, catching him on the cheek. Vicki started to cry and Phil wiped at the bleeding scratch on his face.

'That's assault.'

Julie had to swallow hard. She so badly wanted to scream at him to fuck off, but she held Vicki in her arms and the child was already terrified. She had to make do with a less than satisfying, 'Get lost, Philip.' She went over to the phone to ring for a taxi to take them into town where they could find a bed and breakfast for the night. She picked up the receiver and dialled as Phil rose from his seat and walked over to them. Vicki shrank back into her mother's arms and clung to her tightly.

Phil grabbed the phone out of her hand and pressed the disconnection button before she had finished dialling. 'My telephone, I do believe.'

'You monster, you fucking monster,' she whispered, hoping that whispering it would make it less likely to stick in Vicki's memory banks. She had her face buried in her mother's hair so that she didn't have to look at her father, and witness the fight taking place between them. Julie's arm was aching with holding her.

'What's in the bag?' asked Phil.

'Nothing of yours,' Julie spat back. 'Some things for Victoria and a change of clothes for me, that's all. Surely you can't begrudge me that.'

Phil adopted a mocking sing-song voice. 'I'm telling you now that if I ever leave, I'll walk out of here with nothing but the clothes on my back.'

Julie dropped the bag. It landed on Phil's feet. She straightened her aching back and stared into his eyes. 'You disgust me,' she said to him before dropping her handbag next to the holdall and walking out of the door with nothing but her daughter in her arms.

The bitterly cold night air hit them and she stormed down the road with Vicki. She'd have to put her down soon because she was heavy, but she needed to calm her first. She'd left her purse with all of her money and her bank cards. She could neither pay for a bed and breakfast, nor a takeaway. She had three choices. She could go to her parents, Lisa's or Emma's. Her parents and Emma lived on the same estate, but Lisa would have been her port of choice because she was the most likely to have money, so that Julie could borrow enough to get Vicki her takeaway. She was annoyed that her stubborn pride had meant her breaking her word to her daughter, but she felt victorious that he hadn't got the better of her. She felt that she'd come out of it the winner. But he wasn't trudging through the streets at eight o'clock in the middle of January with nowhere to go. Lisa lived in the opposite direction of Emma and her folks. What if she wasn't in? Emma had kids and was always in, and there was a spare key to her mum's house in the coal shed, but Lisa was a single woman and often went out at night.

With the takeaway heavy on her mind, Julie made

the decision to go to Emma's house. Vicki would love playing with her cousins, Jack and Scott, and she loved Ruby, the baby. It might just take her mind off things until Julie could get her bearings and decide her next move.

After her late night, Julie let Vicki stay at home the next day. At three o'clock in the afternoon Lisa's doorbell rang. She went to answer it. Julie heard raised voices at the door.

'I've told you. She doesn't want to see you. Now do one, will you, or I'll call the police, you fucking abusive bastard.'

'I want to see my wife.'

'Well she doesn't want to see you.'

Julie went into the hall. Phil stood on the doorstep holding a massive bouquet and a teddy bear that was bigger than Ruby. He held them out to her, grinning.

'Julie, this is ridiculous. You're behaving like a child. Come home.'

Emma was ready for tearing Phil's eyes out and loaded up on another barrage of verbal missiles to fire at him. Julie, told her to give them a minute. They needed to talk.

'So by protecting my child, I'm behaving like one, am I?'

She saw a flash of anger glint in his eyes, but he controlled it. He took a second, breathed deeply and apologised. 'Julie, I'm so, so sorry. I want you to come home where you belong. We were both stubborn. We both felt that we were in the right and it got out of hand.'

'How can torturing a little girl ever be right?'

'Oh, now you're exaggerating. Come home. We'll discuss it. I'll do anything you ask. I promise you with all my heart. I'll change. I'll be the father that you want me to be.'

Half an hour after he arrived at Emma's house they pulled into their drive. Once inside, at Julie's insistence, Phil sat Vicki on his knee and apologised to her. The second insistence was a takeaway, anything that Vicki wanted. They bought enough food in to feed an army and had a wonderful family night in. Phil played on the floor with her. He bristled, but controlled himself when Julie said that as a special treat she could have more than one toy out at once. Phil didn't raise his voice or talk to her in his usual tone for almost five days and the slip back into what they, as a family, considered normal, was a gradual slide.

Chapter Twenty-two

They had been summoned. Violet met them in reception, 'Victoria-Violet can go and feed the ducks with her daddy, and you can come up to my quarters with me, Julie, we need to discuss what you are going to wear for my party. I hope you don't mind my saying so, dear, but the dress that you wore last year was quite inappropriate. I thought maybe rose organza. Come along, dear, come along.'

Julie turned to Phil, pleading with her eyes for some kind of rescue. None was forthcoming. She bent and kissed Vicki on the top of her head and then spoke to her husband. 'Watch her near the water. Hold her hand. She gets excited when the ducks come to the edge. Thinks she can swim the way they do, I think,' she laughed. 'Don't let her get too close to the water. If you spread some crumbs around, the ducks will come out onto the grass.' It had been six months since she'd returned to him, but some hurts go deep and the trust that had been lost was taking a long time to rebuild brick by wobbly brick. Julie followed in her mother-in-law's wake, leaving Phil standing at reception with the excited child.

Vicki put her hand in his, 'Come on, Daddy, let's go to the kitchens and ask Uncle James for some stale bread and cakes. There a brown one called Herbert,' she chattered. 'He's very greedy, even more greedier than the three swans.'

'Either more greedy or greedier, not more greedier, it's ungrammatical,' he corrected her. He was on auto-pilot and didn't even think about the reprimand.

'Sorry, Daddy.'

They went to the kitchen where Uncle James lay a stretch of kitchen roll on the counter and sat her up on top of it. 'Don't you fart, Vicki. My guests have got to eat the food I prepare on here.' Victoria giggled. He gave her fresh cake to eat, and four slices of crusty bread and some of last night's cake for the ducks.

'Hey, bud,' James said to Phil after teasing his niece. 'Have you heard what I'm getting?'

'No, what?'

'Only a fucking ferrarri 458 Spyder. The greatest fucking car ever built.'

'No way. How can you afford one of those?'

'I've got most of it saved but the old lady said she'd let me have ten grand off my inheritance, now.'

'You jammy bugger,' said Phil. 'SP will be livid if you outdo him on a car.'

'I know. He's well pissed. Hey, come on up to mine and I'll show you the photos. I'm due a smoke break. He told the sous chef where he was going, and left orders for what he expected to have been done by his return.'

Phil turned to Vicki. 'You go and wait for me in reception, okay? I'm just going up to Uncle James' flat to look at something. I'll only be a few minutes.'

Vicki nodded.

'Hey, man, don't leave her down here on her own. Bring her with you. What's wrong with you man?'

'She's okay; she knows how to behave. Don't you girl?' Phil was annoyed at having his parenting skills questioned by his brother. They left the hotel kitchen, leaving Vicki to make her own way to reception. James winked at her on the way out.

In James' rooms he booted up the computer. 'Feast your eyes on this beauty and dream some wet dreams,' he said, clicking buttons and links. When the page advertising the car came up, he left Phil looking at it while he went over to his kitchenette and put the kettle on. He picked a joint out of an ashtray and lit it, inhaling deeply. Then he went over to the window and flung it open. There'd been complaints from guests about the smell of the pungent weed infusing the hotel corridors on the third floor. He offered Phil a draw on the spliff, but Phil declined. He had never done drugs in his life. He took out his tobacco tin and rolled himself a cigarette. James finished making coffee for them both. 'Better knock this down quick and get out to Vicki.'

'What's this about you lamping some bloke in the Sawn last week? Andrew was telling me about it.'

'Fucking tosser. Thought he was hard,' said James. They settled into opposite armchairs while James told his version of the events.

Philip took his cup and put it in the sink. He was irritated that he had to cut short his time with his brother because of the child. He only left in the end because James said that he had to get back into the kitchen.

Phil wandered down to reception. It was a Tuesday afternoon and the hotel was quiet. He wasn't worried when he searched reception to find that Vicki wasn't there. He was just mad. He asked where she was.

'I don't know, Mr Woods,' said Natalie. 'She was here about ten minutes ago.'

'Weren't you watching her?' Phil asked angrily, a note of accusation in his tone.

'No, I was sorting out the stationary order, nobody asked me to watch her.'

'Well even an idiot could see that she was unattended for a moment.'

'I'm sorry, Mr Woods but she was down here for over half an hour sitting in that chair over there,' she pointed. The receptionist raised her chin defiantly. 'I'm only the receptionist here, not a babysitter. I don't think it's my job to be looking after children.'

'Why you impudent...Look, if you want to keep your job, get over to the ladies' now and check to see if she's in there. I'm going to check the kitchen again.'

She wasn't there. 'I told you not to leave her there by herself,' said James. 'Look, she likes the music room. I'll go and check in there, you see if she's wandered outside.'

Phil left the hotel by the kitchen door and veered to the left. As he walked towards the south side of the boating lake he saw a guest running hell for leather across the lawns towards the front door. He felt the first prickle of apprehension crawling up the back of his neck.

He was still out of sight of the lake when he heard somebody screaming. He broke into a run. Time slowed, the faster he ran, the less ground he made up.

A man was standing in the lake up to his thighs. There weren't many people around—two or three others standing on the bank, somebody with a mobile phone to his ear, a woman screaming— his daughter floating face down in the lake. The man in the water was fighting with weeds that had wrapped around her body. Finally she was free and he was striding towards the bank. Phil was running down the hill towards the water's edge. The guy on the banking helped to pull the other man out of the water. They lay Vicki on her back in the grass and Phil watched as they knelt beside her and began resuscitation. Somewhere far in the distance, he heard an ambulance siren.

Chapter Twenty-three

Phil coped after his divorce. Julie left him with everything and life continued pretty much as it had before. He worked a little less and drank a little more. He spent a lot of money on prostitutes. One of his brothers taught him a long time ago that if you wanted sex, an easy way to get it was to pay for it. John had paid a schoolgirl five pounds and some cigarettes for a blow job. Phil was still a virgin at that point. He'd interfered with himself sometimes, and burned with shame and self disgust afterwards. He didn't want to have sex, he had no interest in it back then—it was dirty—but he liked having money. He'd sent notes to Suzie Philips, telling her that he knew what she'd done. He'd threatened to write to her parents and he had her bring him money to the same clearing that she'd knelt in to blow his brother off, until the Philips' family moved away and his cash cow was gone.

Phil's regret was that he came to sex so late. Julie was his first, but he soon experienced others and found that Julie wasn't very good at it. He'd grown up with so many hang-ups and had missed out on years of sexual gratification. He wondered what Suzie Philips was doing now. Maybe she'd made a career out of prostitution.

He couldn't believe that his bitch of a wife blamed him for the death of their daughter. It was a terrible, tragic accident; everybody said so, especially the coroner. So as far as he was concerned, she could go and fuck herself. If he was so lacking as a father, why had she left Victoria-Violet with him in the first place? Picking material for stupid bloody dresses had been more important than their child's wellbeing. If she wanted somebody to blame, maybe she should have looked in the mirror. And in the six months that followed, you'd have thought she was the only one who had lost a child. He was grieving too, you know. He told his mother that he doubted he'd be able to look at another duck again. Violet said that duck phobia was a terrible thing to suffer. She made a mental note to see that Chef never served duck when Philip was home.

Violet would miss Victoria, of course, but she had grandchildren coming out of her ears, what with James' flower-power brood. Losing one was a small price to pay to have her baby back in her arms. Philip came home a lot more often now and, without that awful low-grade woman dragging him down, he was so much like his old self. He seemed happier these days, too. Violet was philosophical and reasoned that everything had worked out for the best, really.

Phil had been distraught when Julie left him for a different reason altogether. He was beside himself with grief. When his wife walked out, she had taken something very precious with her. A lifetime of his hard work was gone and he would never get over the loss of it. The trollop had hired somebody to break into his safe. She had stolen all of his books and papers. Violet couldn't see why a load of old diaries mattered to him so much. Let her have them; it was only a bunch of books. But Philip couldn't get over it.

'It was my life's work, Mother.'

'But, darling, who's going to care about what you did in December 1986 or March 1992? At least she didn't get away with any money, or your house. Just let it go. Write some more little stories.'

'Little stories! Mother, they were historical documents. There were lists of people in there who owe me money.'

'What kind of people?' Violet asked. 'Who owes you money? What for?'

'That's not important. The fact is that there were things in that safe that can't be replaced or replicated, and now she has them. She had no right.' Violet didn't see what all the fuss was about, she could have taken everything, and at least he still had the house.

In truth, Philip was a man waiting for the hammer to fall. He stayed at his own house as little as possible, terrified of the knock at the door. He jumped every time the gate squeaked in the wind. On the rare occasion that somebody did come to the door, he wouldn't open it. He'd sneak upstairs and look out of the bathroom window, but it was only ever the postman or somebody to read the electricity meter, or some bastard wanting money for charity. As the months after Julie left passed, and he was still at liberty to walk the streets a free man, he feared his arrest less. He saw no reason not to continue where he left off. He cleaned off his trusty cameras and spent a thousand pounds on one of the new office computers. He taught himself how to use it and put a password on new documents that he could bury deep in files within the system. He liked this new way of working, it was far superior to ledgers and books. He opened spreadsheets and kept his books just as he had with his special fountain pen.

He lost a lot of business due to the theft of his evidence, but still managed to re-snare some of his old customers. In a small Lakeland town there was always somebody doing something that they shouldn't and new business grew as it always had. The eavesdropper was back in business and the figurative sign above his door read OPEN.

Two years later, in 2004, the biggest scandal to hit the Woods' family since James had been charged with cross-dressing prostitution broke out. With SP and James in charge, the men worked well together, SP running the hotel side of things and James enforcing full control over the kitchen and restaurants, pretty much as he had been doing for the last ten years. That year, one of James's favourite recipes came to bite them on the backside. It was called cooking the books. SP and James had been defrauding the tax man and creaming from the hotel profits for years. The auditors arrived mob-handed to undertake a thorough investigation. The books were taken, computers seized and every receipt, every wage slip and every penny in or out was scrutinised for discrepancies. SP and James were arrested and taken in handcuffs to the local station. Violet called Graham Bradson, the corrupt but trusted family solicitor. He met with Violet later the same day in her quarters. James had already been in a lot of trouble. He was looking at a long stretch. Over a family dinner, ramifications were discussed and re-discussed. Tempers frayed and some broke. When the summit concluded, it was decided that SP would take the fall for them both. They couldn't both be saved and James had the most to loose.

SP covered for his brother. They'd been stealing vast sums of money since they'd matured from shorts into long pants, but SP had never had any serious criminal convictions. Even so, the Prosecution Service wanted to make an example of him. The case was referred to Crown Court at Preston. He stood trial in front of twelve men strong and true, though four of the jurors were women. One of them fancied him, and at first wouldn't opt to convict. She couldn't believe that the man with such a kind face could knowingly commit fraud. She said that perhaps it was all an accident and that he'd fully intended to declare all of their income, but forgot. A couple of the other jurors commented that it was unfortunate they were selected randomly and not on merit of intellect. It took a full ten minutes of negotiations around a table for the lenient juror to change her mind and come to the same decision as the other eleven.

Simon Peter Woods showed no emotion when he was given a three year custodial sentence. He was away for just over a year and a half with time off for good behaviour but had a terrible time inside. His upbringing meant that he stood out from the other cons. He was bullied and victimised, beaten up on more than one occasion and his spirit was very quickly broken. Three months into his sentence, he tried to hang himself and after spending three days on the hospital wing, he was transferred to a different prison. The problem was never the other offenders, it was him; he was still different from the rest. The bullying picked up where it had left off, and SP had little choice but to change. He grew a hard skin and learned to brawl. He undid years of elocution lessons and taught himself how to drop his aitches.

He grew accustomed to food seasoned with spit.

Violet told the guests that her eldest son was in Hong Kong setting up another hotel and would be home when their Asian enterprise was strong enough to fly without a Woods figurehead at the helm. The locals all knew the truth. Most of the town knew that the Woods boys were rotten to the core. One after another, they fell by the wayside and turned to trouble.

When SP went away, Andrew wasn't given a choice. The family business needed him and as he was next in line to the throne, the role of office fell to him. He still managed his own business, though he passed on all of the legitimate stuff to Beth to maintain. Andrew was rich beyond measure. Nobody knew how much he had stashed away. When he first made his timepiece forgeries in his early twenties it had all been a game to him. He considered it an art to reproduce the watches and clocks from history. He had an aptitude for imitating Rolex and the modern greats. He saw his work as a compliment to the originals. He never did, and never had, cared about the money and most of it was unwanted, hidden in secret offshore accounts not to evade tax but merely because he didn't know where else to put it. The better he became at forging, the more he was in demand. As his name spread in the underworld, he came under the scrutiny of Maurio Rizzla, A mafia boss with a keen eye for business. It was said that he could fillet a man faster than a butcher could hang a beef.

Almost immediately, Andrew wasn't working for himself. He was forced into the Rizzla stable and became an employee of Maurio 'Razor' Rizzla. Razor fed him commissions and timelines in which to complete them. Andrew had never been a nine-to-five kind of man. He'd worked when he wanted to work. He'd slept when he wanted to sleep and he'd made love to free-spirited women as his loins led him. He didn't like answering to somebody else. The money was vast, each commission giving him more to swell his secret bank accounts. Razor paid him well, but demanded his loyalty and subservience.

When Andrew got frightened and tried to quit, Razor had him hustled into a van, driven to a disused warehouse at the centre of his operations and beaten up by four heavies. He got away and fled under the cover of darkness to the continent, where he lived in the communes, met Beth and had his children.

After years in exile, they came back into the country quietly, but then Andrew drew attention to himself by spending large sums of money on the expansive farm with acres of land and all of his workshops, studios and outbuildings.

He wanted to be an honest man, bringing his kids up well in love and compost and making Beth proud of him. He had his home, he had everything he needed. His plan was to keep the farm as a working venture of dairy, meat and arable land. The west area of his property he set up as a commune for wayward travellers passing through, allowing them to earn their keep, for as long as they wanted to stay and work the land.

It didn't take long for Razor to find them. He'd always known Andrew would return to the happy homestead and family pile sooner or later. He'd been waiting, patiently. He reeled Andrew back into his employ. Beth was pregnant at the time, so Razor bided his time before leaving Andrew a little reminder, something that would stay with him, just in case he ever forgot who was in charge.

One night, when Beth was tending a calving cow, she was jumped from behind and taken to Razor. He kept her prisoner and raped her several times over a period of twenty-four hours. Afterwards, he rang Andrew to tell him that Beth was in his bed. Beth pleaded with Andrew to help her. He could do nothing and when Beth was returned, the following day, with only minor injuries, the adoration she had for her husband had left her eyes.

Henry Stephen Woods was born nine months later, and his parents peered at him, looking for resemblance. He wasn't given a fanciful name like his brothers and sisters, or named after the elements and he carried a traditional name. He grew up darker than any of his siblings, but Andrew didn't hold that against him. He didn't blame Henry for who he was or who he came from.

Beth didn't want any more children. She wasn't as sweet. She loved less, complained more, and grew bitterness along with the herbs in plant pots on her windowsill. Andrew wanted to live the life of an honest farmer, but Rizzla owned him and he couldn't buy his emancipation.

When he was called to take on the hotel as well, it was his duty to rise to that right of passage. He worked day and night to manage his own life and fulfil Rizzla's demands as well as those of the hotel. The tax returns were filed correctly, the takings and profits had never been better, but Andrew didn't cope well with the responsibility. He'd shaved his beard, cut his hair and he wore a suit that made him feel like a corporate loser. He was used to wearing sandals because shoes pinched his feet. He hated the pomp of the hotel and longed for his land. Andrew lived by a calendar in as much as he did what the seasons told him in relation to running his farm. He took to counting the days until his brother could reclaim his position and, until then, he worried that he had yet another wage to deal with. Andrew knew only too well that money was the route of all evil, but as hard as he tried to denounce it and live a simple existence, he just made more. It was his personal curse.

Time dragged on in the Woods Empire. It was ten years since Julie and Philip had divorced. Violet had grown closer to Ros and relied on her more than ever to keep her grounded to reality. SP still stole and lined his pockets from the business. James still got into fights, beat his wife and wore women's clothes, seeking his sexual deviance wherever he could. Andrew still forged. John's gambling was out of control. And Philip blackmailed and became a rich man on the back of other people's misery.

In the cycle of sausages, beef was beef and nothing much had changed.

Donald died quietly while tending his garden. He would have liked it like that. The gardeners had all knocked off for the day and he was left digging out a few vegetables to make up a hamper for the Legion raffle that night. The pain came suddenly and he leaned on his spade and waited for the twinge to pass. And then he was gone, quick as that, without much drama, without anybody knowing, or any fuss. Just the way he would have wanted it. Dinner was eaten without Donald attending and Violet pursed her lips in annoyance. She had the waiter transfer her meal from the table to a tray and she ate it on her knee in the lounge. Donald's food was covered and put in the kitchenette oven to keep warm. After eating, she picked up a paperback and read for a while. It was only when the shadows lengthened and she'd had to turn on the reading lamp that she realised the time. Donald should have been getting ready for his lodge. The feeling of foreboding settled around her from the top of her head. It swathed over her shoulders and down her body. Something was wrong. Donald was never late for the lodge and he wouldn't dream of going without showering his garden mud away first. A fastidious man, he went to the weekly meetings in slacks and a blazer, with a small bowtie cinched tight at his neck. She called down to Ros. She was always her first point of contact in any dilemma or crises.

Ros sighed and dragged herself from the sofa. She was watching the concluding part of a crime drama on TV and resented that she wouldn't be allowed to see the ending. She had wasted her time making sure that she was cleared of her duties and ready to watch the first two episodes, because now she was going to miss the last part. She might as well have not bothered. Violet's call was insistent and she didn't have time to set up the box to record it.

She assured Violet that Donald wouldn't be far. Yes, she'd go and find him, right away. She had to dress, as she was just out of the bath and had settled for the night in her pyjamas. Poor Donald; she didn't blame him sloping off for a bit of clandestine time alone. He wasn't in the reception or lounge areas of the hotel. She stopped the porters and asked them to search for Donald outside.

The doctor who signed Donald's death certificate estimated that he'd been dead between three and four hours. The gammon had dried up in the oven.

Violet was lost without him. He had been there for the majority of her life. He kept her grounded and reined in her more colourful ideas. He had been her stake in the ground, her anchor that kept her fancies earthbound. After his death, she leaned heavily on Ros for emotional support.

Chapter Twenty-four

They say that life goes on. Julie went through the motions of going on. In the days after Vicki's death there seemed little point in anything. She had moved out of the marital bed and into the spare room. She was unapproachable, and Philip never touched her again, not even so much as a tap on the shoulder. At the funeral she refused to have him near her. He was flanked by his family on one side of the grave and she was flanked by hers on the other.

This time, instead of bolting and leaving him on gut instinct, she planned her move with precision. After three months of intense, debilitating, suicidal grieving, she went back to work fulltime. The home meant nothing to her and the garden lay to overgrow, neglected. Her role in life was to work. When she worked she stopped thinking and somehow that kept her alive when she had nothing left to live for.

In the early days she thought about taking her life a lot. She took an overdose one night and had to have her stomach pumped, leading to a three day stay in hospital and a compulsory six week counselling course. The counsellor was vapid, with huge eyes that screamed, 'Wherever you are now, I've been and come through it.' It might have helped her to rant about how much hatred she had for her husband. She could have discussed the many ways in which she fantasised about killing him, but she didn't. She talked enough about healing to fulfil the terms of her course and keep her from being sectioned.

She was her own counsel. The only thing that kept her putting one foot in front of the other and taking the next breath into her body — was revenge.

When she was strong enough to deal with it, Julie sought legal advice about commencing her divorce. She had an appointment with a solicitor who eventually refused to represent her.

She sat in front of the power horse's desk where a black granite plaque announced a black granite woman, Miss Monica Dupont. She was hungry, a self confessed man-hater, specialised in representing women in the divorce courts. Julie told her story, and with each point against Philip, Monica's smile was wider as she totted another thousand on the final settlement. Julie didn't exaggerate or embellish, she simply told the story of their marriage from beginning to end.

'The bastard,' Monica said when Julie had finished. 'You want revenge?'

'Oh, God yes, I want revenge more than you can ever know.'

'Lady, we are going to nail this bastard to the wall by his balls. I swear to you, by the time I've finished with him, he won't have a pot to piss in. We are going to take him for every penny he's got. You want the house, the car, half of his pension, what else has he got?'

'No.'

'I beg your pardon?'

'I want a divorce. I don't want a penny of his

stinking money. I'll deal with the revenge side of things in my own way.'

'I don't understand.'

Julie went on to tell Monica about the promise she had made to Violet. She spoke in a flat monotone when she talked about the horrible things that Violet had done to her.

'My God, all the more reason to hit them where it hurts. Listen to me. You are not a gold digger. You have earned every penny of what I'm going to get for you. For fuck's sake, woman, do it for your daughter.'

Julie was taken aback. She hadn't expected a solicitor to speak like that. 'I'm sorry. I don't want anything, only my own surname name back.'

'Then I can't help you. I'm very sorry, you have an excellent case, but if you won't let me do my job, then there's nothing I can do.' She had already stood up and was walking to the door to show Julie out. 'If you change your mind, please get back in touch and let me at him.' She smiled as Julie passed, but the contempt that Monica felt for her was apparent. A woman, who wouldn't financially strip a bastard husband to the bone, was a lower life form.

The second solicitor that Julie spoke to was an impassionate man. He had no qualms about representing her. He wasn't interested in hearing her tales of woe. He wrote down the salient facts, just enough to show irreconcilable differences, and ran with it. It was the easiest divorce he'd ever dealt with. There were no kids involved, no assets to split. Julie had clear grounds for divorce. The papers could be served quickly and then, six weeks and one day from the Decree Nisi, the Absolute would go through without question. Roland Johnson would file a few forms to the court, send out a couple of papers to the spouse, write a, Thank you for your custom and congratulations on your divorce, letter to the plaintive, and take his nine grand, plus expenses.

For his part, Philip didn't make waves. While they still shared a house, he was considerate enough to leave his coming week's rota out for her on a Sunday night. They spent ridiculous amounts of time at their respective jobs. Julie arranged her shifts to fit around his, so that, wherever possible, they were never in the house at the same time. She worked in the same nursing home that she had before Vicki's death, but had come out of the kitchen to work as a hobby therapist. She needed no qualification, but took courses as another means to keep her away from home and to better herself at the work she did. She found it soothing and it helped to stop her from going mad.

Occasionally it was impossible to avoid Philip and their lives collided. She would make herself something to eat and then take it with her into her room where she wouldn't come out until he'd gone. They met rarely, but when they did, Julie didn't look at him much. He made her puke. Once, soon after Vicki's death, when she had made eye contact with her husband, she had felt her gorge rising, and had to run to the toilet and purge her stomach. She didn't have to accuse him verbally, or lay blame for their daughter's death at his door, her actions did that for her, but that didn't stop her doing it.

When she passed the threshold to his room and knew that he was in there, she would stop at his door and rattle the handle to get his attention. Sometimes she'd do it deep in the night when she could hear him snoring. 'What's going on?' he'd say, snuffling himself out of sweet dreams, and she'd hiss through the door, 'Murderer,' just to keep it fresh in his mind.

She stopped the secret mortgage payments to his account. She stopped helping her family out of their financial crises. She ate at work mostly, and apart from her basic living expenses, almost everything she earned went into her leaving-Philip fund. She did have one necessary extravagance. Twice a week she studied. She used her office at work and from seven until nine in the evening she hired a private tutor who worked with her extensively and set her complex exercises to complete as homework. She bought newspapers to help her with her studies and read them cover to cover in her lunch breaks and when she got home in the evenings. Her life was full and busy. She allowed herself no time to dwell on things that were gone.

Three months after going back to work and six months, to the day, since Vicki's death, Julie went into her daughter's old bedroom. She remembered it as a nursery. She thought back to sitting in the peacock chair with her child at her breast during the three in the morning feed. It was her favourite time. Some parents hate that feed, but Julie loved it. It was when she felt at her most peaceful, with the radio playing soft music and Vicki all warm and cosy, staring up at her with blue eyes as she fed. The baby would make greedy gulping noises as she took from her mother and Julie had thought that Vicki would always be there to nurture for the rest of her life.

She also remembered when Vicki was five and they were lying on her Barbie bed together, Vicki's eyes were heavy as she fought to keep them open until the end of the chapter. 'What happens next, Mummy? Will Violet Beauregard be a blueberry forever and ever?'

'I don't know. Wait and see, shall we?'

'Violet Beauregard's very bossy isn't she, Mummy?'

'Yes, darling.'

'And she's called Violet, like Grandma.'

'Yes, she is.'

'And Grandma's very bossy, too.'

'Yes, she is.'

'Does it hurt being a blueberry?'

'Oh, I shouldn't think so. Now then, where were we?' Vicki's face was screwed up in thought and she wasn't for being derailed in her ruminations.

'It would be very, very funny if Grandma turned into a blueberry.'

Julie laughed with her daughter. 'It would, love, especially if she kept her bright red lipstick.' Vicki got giddy after that and Julie had to settle her again and, inevitably, Phil had shouted up the stairs that she should have been asleep by now.

It was another week before they visited the hotel.

Julie nearly choked on her teacake when Vicki had piped up, 'Grandma, do you like blueberries a really, really lot?'

'What a strange question, child. Where on earth did that come from? You say the oddest things out of the blue, dear.'

'Yes, but do you like blueberries?'

'Vicki, tell Grandma about the horse that we fed on the way here,' Julie said.

'No, Mummy, I need to know if Grandma likes blueberries.'

'I suppose I do. I don't dislike them.' Violet said, humouring Vicki.

'Bloody horrible things, dry all your mouth out,' Donald muttered from behind his paper.

Vicki gasped and put her hands over her mouth in delight. 'See, Mummy? She is, she is.'

'I am what? Victoria-Violet, do start making sense, dear.'

'Violet Beauregard is Grandma, when she was a little girl. What's it like turning into a blueberry, Grandma? Does it hurt?'

Julie smiled as memories of her daughter flooded her mind and tears of regret flooded her eyes. The room had been packed up after Vicki's death. Most of her things were taken to the charity shop. It was used as a store room. She picked up a small material doll with yellow hair, from the top of one of the boxes that hadn't been closed properly. Bringing the doll to her nose she was sad that she couldn't smell her daughter. She almost took it with her but that would mean breaking her promise and taking more than the clothes on her back. She didn't need a cloth doll to remind her. She put it back in the box and pressed down the flap and looked around the room for the last time. Julie didn't see the boxes; she saw the mobile over the cot. She saw the Barbie bed. She saw Vicki's brow furrowed in concentration as she struggled to tie her first pair of lace-up shoes. Julie closed the door softly behind her so as not to disturb the ghosts of times gone by.

She went out of the front door and posted her keys back through the letter box. She would miss her family, but she could live without them. The only real love in her heart was for her dead daughter. She hadn't told a soul that she was leaving. She had her handbag over her shoulder. Her handbag, bought with her money. It contained her purse, driving licence and passport.

At check in, the girl raised her eyebrows, though checking in without luggage was more common these days what with skinny baggage allowances and obese fines for exceeding them. Julie's only regret was that her divorce would take some time, so she hadn't been able to change her passport back to her maiden name. The papers were to be served to Philip that day. She had arranged for them to be handed to him at work, hopefully in front of the entire shop floor. She may legally still have the curse of the Woods' name hanging over her, but she intended to live her life as the uncomplicated and very free Miss Julie Spencer. But the unexpected happened; Julie found that the Spencer name didn't fit her either.

Chapter Twenty-five

She touched down at El Prat airport, Barcelona, and thought of her husband. While in flight, she had closed her eyes and spoken to Vicki. I love you with all my heart, my darling, she'd said, with her mind's voice. You know that I will never ever forget you. You gave me the happiest years of my life and I can never tell you how sorry I am that I let you down. They will pay Vicki, the lot of them. If it's the last thing that I do, I am going to make them pay in your name, my love. If I squeeze my eyes shut really tight, I can feel your little hand in mine now. I know you're here with me, chattering in my ear. But my darling, this is where you have to be a big brave girl. It's time for Mummy to move on. I will always love you, but I'm not going to be able to have these chats with you anymore. It's time for you to go forward, too, my love. I love you Vicki. And then she whispered aloud, 'I love you.'

The fat man in the seat next to her said, ''Scuse me?'

Julie glared at him.

She waded through the barrier of dry heat as she stepped out of the airport. She had left England at the drab beginning of another unpleasant winter. Along a wall to the left, furious pink bougainvillea grew from the floor to the roof and a little green house lizard winked at her from the stem without taking fright or preparing itself to run. The scent of mimosa from the flowering baskets tantalised her and she felt a wonderful, butterflying surge of adrenaline-filled excitement at the beginning of this new life.

She had allowed herself three glorious days to reacquaint herself with her favourite city, before she got down to the serious business of building a life. She'd booked into a cheap hotel away from the tourist quarter, right in the heart of the real Barcelona. Later that week she had an appointment to meet with a rental agent who was going to show her around some flats, and even one modest villa within her budget. Then she had three interviews already lined up, and later, a meeting with an employment agency, in case none of the interviews offered the right job for her.

She'd miss her family, but she thought of herself as a tree standing alone with neither blossom nor berries to offer. She didn't have a friend in the world, or a soul to talk to. Nobody knew where she was and she expected not to be found. Nobody would believe she had the confidence to set up life in a new country. They wouldn't consider looking for her at airports, and even if they did, they would automatically search the flight details from Manchester. It was the only airport that they had ever used. For that reason, she had taken the train to London where, hopefully, any trail they were following would fizzle to nothing. She flew from Luton. If by some miracle she was ever found, it was no big deal really, but she would prefer not to be. She wanted a complete sanitary cleansing from her old life. The date was 11th November 2002 and she felt as though she had been reborn.

On the day of her job interviews, she went into a newsagent to buy *Fama* and *20 minutos*, the same newspapers that she had been reading everyday at home. As she was leaving the shop she noticed the rack of scratch cards. She had never bought one in her life, neither had she ever done the lottery, though Phil had bought tickets a few times at the beginning of their marriage, before the novelty had worn off. On impulse, she bought one and handed over a euro. '*Buena Suerta, Señora,*' said the lady behind the counter, wishing her good luck with a wide smile.

'*Gracias,*' Julie replied, before telling the woman that she had come to live in their beautiful country. She loved any opportunity to try out her new language. They chatted for a few minutes in Spanish and Julie felt as though she belonged. She couldn't imagine wanting to be anywhere else but here.

Outside the shop she took a coin from her change and scratched off the panels on the card. She checked the three matching symbols, and then she checked them again. She turned the card over and read the instructions, in Spanish, on the reverse. And then, she looked at the front again, to see if, during the last minute, the three matching symbols had changed. She got a cab to the hotel in a daze. She had to ring a number to verify the win. She relayed the reference number on the scratch card, waiting for the call centre employee to tell her in a dispassionate voice, that she had made a mistake. When he did reply, surely something was lost in translation. She spoke Spanish slowly, but fluently. However, having a college professor enunciating every syllable with exaggeration was far different from hearing rapidly volleyed words, spoken in a regional dialect. She couldn't have just won A hundred thousand euro. It couldn't be. Julie only believed it when the money had cleared her new bank account and she drew out her first twenty euro to buy lunch, in a pavement café in the heart of the tourist quarter.

Over the next six months Julie's divorce came through. The first thing she did was toast herself with a slippery nipple cocktail in a beachfront bar, which she found that she really didn't like. Then she changed her name by deed poll. On 6th May 2003, Julie Woods signed her new name on a legal document proclaiming her to be Señora Consuela Vengarse. Vengarse translated into English as 'to be avenged.' The name pleased her.

On her arrival in Barcelona, she'd rented a very modest villa. Nothing ostentatious, but she loved it with all of her heart. With the hundred thousand euro winnings from her scratch card, she had enough capital to secure her a mortgage on a business premises for a bakery.

Returning home in the evenings to her villa was a joy that filled her completely. She was never lonely, not even in the early months before she had made friends. The villa was typically Mediterranean, open plan, with tile floors throughout to cool the air. She had decking outside the colonial doors on the ground floor, and a balcony along the first floor, front of the building. Her garden was modest, with established fruit and olive trees, and ample beds ready for planting, and she shared a pool with other tenants in the complex. She furnished it with beautiful things, and although it was a very different home to that which she'd shared with Philip, it was every bit as splendid. In retrospect, Julie wondered how she had loved such a stuffy, enclosed space so much, when the villa was so open, cool and spacious. Her life was coming together in ways that she never could have expected, and God loved her.

Her love of baking had flourished as her shop made money. The desserts in Barcelona were very different from a traditional English bakery. Consuela didn't consciously try to introduce English baking, merely pulled on what she already excelled at. She made Victoria sponge and in the early days, before she became too busy to think, as she beat the ingredients of each one, she thought about her daughter and, though her life was perfect, she remembered her hatred for the family who murdered her.

She made trifles and cheese scones. Once she was established, she had products flown in from England — English sausage, bacon and double cream. She extended her bakery to include a dining area for customers and she produced full English breakfasts in her traditional English café. She made time-honoured meat and potato pies, Cornish pasties and sausage rolls. The Spaniard's couldn't get enough of Victoria's Kitchen.

Consuela had never been afraid of hard work. She rose every morning at four and didn't get home until seven, and the weight fell from her obese frame, her skin coloured, turning deep brown in the sun. In six months she had made enough money to move to bigger premises with a larger bakery out back. Her life, she noticed was moving in six month increments, each one heralding a new change in direction and circumstance. She hired staff and soon the kitchens were operating twelve hour shifts, seven days a week. Soon she had to hire more staff and was wholesaling her products to other businesses. She bought a factory with offices above, and opened seven more Victoria's Kitchen bakeries across Spain. Victoria's Kitchen became a recognised brand, and Consuela Vengarse became a wealthy company director with enough profit in the bank to secure her future. She had moved into her own glorious villa with expansive gardens and her own pool. A woman in her own right, she had paid back her mortgages and owned her own corner of the world. All of this made her very happy, but it was only ever the means to an end.

Consuela made friends. She occasionally went out for drinks in the evening and discovered a taste for Martini. She had dinner parties, and while she missed having her distinctive Tunisian tableware, she bought less flamboyant, but nonetheless exquisite crockery from the kilns of Barcelona. She had wines from the Montserrat vineyards less than twenty miles away, and she cooked splendid meals for a growing mismatch of new friends.

While browsing an art gallery one Sunday, she met Jorge Vasquez. He took her to dinner and she thought, over her first Martini, about taking him to bed. She imagined his mouth roaming her body as she had her second drink, and after her third, the fantasy became reality when Jorge Vasquez took Consuela Vengarse to his bed. She called herself Whore-Hay's Whore, which amused him immensely.

Consuela was good at sex. She knew that. But she had never truly loved it before. Philip had always been an unsatisfactory lover. For the first time, she bathed in her sexuality, danced in it, and covered it in diamonds and gold. She could have let the past go. She could have just blanked it from her memory and lived out her days in blessed wealth and luxury. She had good friends, a good life, she was happy, successful beyond her dreams, but she had taken her new surname for a reason and Vengeance had to be hers.

The day she opened the telephone directory on Plastic Surgeons, her life changed again.

Part Two

Chapter Twenty-six

England was cold. She had forgotten just how much. Ten years under a Spanish sun had made her soft.

She'd sent a gilt invitation and there was never any doubt that he'd come. It was delivered in a classy black envelope to his office so that suspicions wouldn't be aroused at home. *You've been selected at random*...et cetera. She knew that the five hundred pound gift voucher, redeemable for casino chips, would bring him like a child to the Pied Piper, and just like the fable of Hamlet, she would make Violet's children follow wherever she damn well led them.

She was already at the roulette table. He took a seat three stools away from her. He looked nervous, a thin line of perspiration moistened his upper lip. His hands rolled the top chip repeatedly across his palm as he studied the board. The ball was spinning through the game in progress. He stared at it greedily, eyes dancing, body tense. The wheel slowed and dropped into number eighteen. The croupier dollied the losing bets home and a Japanese businessman collected his winnings. His friends jabberwockied animatedly in Japanese and jumped up and down like an annoyance of Furbies. They walked away from the table, heading for the bandits.

Consuela sat the next few spins out. That's what separated a seasoned player from a stag party. She watched the board, scrutinised the other players. Of the five men left in the game, she knew who were the chancers, playing straight up, thirty-five to one, and who was playing it safe with outside bets. She had John Woods pegged for a rouge-noir initially, leading to four corners when he started losing. He'd be a big man in the bookies, playing bravado on the gee-gees, but put him in a situation where the stakes were lethal and his bollocks would retreat like a kid's in a rugby scrum. He'd play evens bets.

He played two spins, betting rouge-noir and oods-even. She knew he would. Ten pound stakes and he lost both. He upped the ante, adding a second twelve, making his next bet thirty pounds instead of twenty. She was aware of him staring at her when he thought she wasn't looking. She didn't even have to put in any effort. He wanted her, simple as that. He wouldn't have the balls to make a move though. Her extensive plastic surgery saw to it that she was out of his league; she was unrecognisable as his former sister-in-law.

It was time to be noticed. She felt his eyes rest on her. It was only ever a matter of time. Gambling and women were his two vices, as she'd learned from reading Phil's diaries, and he couldn't concentrate on one to the exclusion of the other. Although it wasn't necessary, she stood up to place a three hundred pound straight-up bet. His eyes were on her legs. She posed for him for a second before resuming her seat. She heard his intake of breath. Three hundred on a thirty-five to one shot was ridiculous money. She lost with a matter-of-fact shrug of her shoulders. When the croupier had cleared her chips, she placed five hundred on the same number. She lost.

She had drawn the attention of every man at the table. She was the only woman, and was playing a suicidal game. A debonair suit on the other side of the table walked around and indicated the seat next to her. She had to get rid of him.

'Do you mind? Miss, I can't help but be impressed by a woman so stuck on her lucky number that she can lose big and not cry.'

John glared at him. The look was not lost on her. She knew that the brash man with the American Accent had just done what John would never have the guts to attempt.

The Yank put his chips on the table and went to sit down. Consuela pointedly put her hand on the chair to stop him moving in. She glared at the American; her expression froze him in his tracks.

'I mind,' she said in a heavily accented voice.

'Jeez, sorry Ma'am,' he tipped an imaginary hat, gathered his chips, and walked away, shaking his head.

Consuela turned to look at John Woods. He was caught in the trap of her stare like a naughty boy caught starting into the girl's changing rooms during PE lesson. He lowered his gaze.

'Won't you join me?'

She knew he'd heard her, but he kept his eyes on the board, playing with his chips, focussing on the spinning wheel and the ball blurring in front of his eyes. She knew him well—the husk in her voice was probably enough to give him a boner. She cleared her throat to get his attention. She was waiting for a response, looking at him with an open expression. He raised his head, feeling the weight of her gaze penetrating his.

'Excuse me?'

'Come. Sit next to me. Keep the wild dogs at bay.'

He might as well have done the comedic Stan Laurel gesture of pointing at himself and looking around to see if she was really talking to him, he couldn't have looked any more ridiculous. In his own environment he was a peacock. He was brash and confident, wooing the local girls and the guests in his parents' hotel. He bedded plenty, and flirted with more. Here, he was like a child thrust into an adult environment. He didn't belong and his bravado fell to his feet, while his dinner jacket suffocated him and his tie pinched at the collar.

'Maria Callas.' She held out her hand palm downwards. He clearly had no idea whether she intended for him to shake her hand or kiss it. In his confusion he clasped her fingertips and then didn't know what to do.

'John Woods,' he introduced himself and just a hint of his swagger returned as he realised that the other men, croupier included, saw that he had just pulled the most beautiful, and probably the richest woman in the room. 'You're very beautiful,' he added, attempting his killer smile.

'And you are very'—*small* is what she wanted to say, but she amended her words—'kind,' she finished, removing her hand from his.

They played three more rounds. Consuela lost them. He won two of them; modest fifty-percent chance wins, barely worthy of note.

'You're lucky for me.' He asked her to kiss his next chips. She obliged and then laughed as though he amused her. He lost, but she had emboldened him. He wanted to show off. He collected his meagre stash of remaining chips, three hundred and eighty pounds, small change in a place like this. He placed them all on his next bet, Two eighty on black, one hundred on evens, fifty-fifty all or nothing.

The ball span and he sweated. His eyes bore into the spinning wheel, willing the ball to land on black. He'd chosen it, he said, for the colour of her hair. They were playing *La Partage* rules, zero was the devil's rut. The ball span. Once that little sphere of luck, good or bad, came to rest, he'd either be puffing his chest like a peacock or he'd have to retreat to the cashier for more chips. He'd be drawing on his credit card. It was already overdrawn. He may well have to face the embarrassment of it being refused. If that were the case, he'd walk away humiliated. He needed to impress this woman. He wanted to get her into bed. He already owed a fortune to Monty Wheeler, his bookie. Gaynor was always whingeing about his gambling and the debt they were in. She was breathing down his neck and breaking his bollocks, and if he didn't win big soon, several other guys from town, big guys with pickaxe handles, were likely to be calling. All of his juggling batons were up in the air at once and soon he'd be out of his depth. Mother would have to bail him out—again. But tonight he just wanted to forget. He needed Lady Luck to smile on him with favour.

The roulette ball stopped spinning. It landed on number four. Black and Even, two wins. He'd just doubled his money. Consuela lost her stake and told him she was bored of losing and was sitting the next game out.

The croupier dollied her chips away and passed John's winnings back. He piled them up in front of him. He held the top one, a hundred chip, in front of Consuela's lips for her to kiss before sliding the lot onto black. The croupier set the wheel spinning and dropped the ball. 'No more bets, please.' The ball span and John felt dizzy with excitement. He closed his eyes waiting for the click-click-click of the ball settling, willing it to fall into a black slot.

'Ten black,' the croupier said. John let his breath out and opened his eyes.

Consuela smiled. 'You are having good luck, my friend. I like to surround myself with lucky people.'

In two spins he had just won one thousand, five-hundred and twenty pounds. He should take his money, walk away. But he was a fool. A wise man deducts possibility from probability, while a fool commits to folly. He pushed his winnings across the board. This time he put his entire stake on the second twelve. 2-to-1 odds. For every pound he bet, he would take back two pounds if he won, but winning on the second twelve was less likely. To take the money, the ball had to land in a slot between number thirteen and twenty-four.

Consuela purred like a cat. 'So daring, so reckless.' She ran a red talon along the inside of his wrist and he shivered under her touch. There was twice as much chance of him losing as winning this time. He felt sick. The night was working like a dream for him; everything about it was surreal. From him winning the mystery gift that brought him here, to the exotic woman—he'd forgotten her name almost as quickly as she'd told it to him—picking him over the American smoothy, to his getting luckier than he'd been in a long time. Just a couple more spins in his favour and he'd be getting into some serious money. It was just a case of having the balls, just being able to hold your nerve long enough.

His future was spinning in the wheel. Consuela made a huge show of being bored with the game. She took a file from her purse and filed her nails. John was strung out, his adrenaline causing the equivalent of a synthetic high, and he couldn't stand still. Sweat had dappled his forehead in polka-dots.

The ball stopped and he heard Conseula gasp before opening his eyes. Number twenty-one. Number fucking twenty-one. He'd won again. Four thousand eight hundred fucking quid. One more spin and he'd be walking away with twelve grand. If he could hold his nerve for two more runs he could leave the table with thirty-six thousand pounds that would go a long way to clearing his debts. Two more spins. Two more wins and he'd quit while he was ahead.

He was counting up his chips, piling them to move onto the board. He'd had better wins on the horses, but there was a skill in that; winning on roulette was pot luck and this wasn't a bad night's work at all. The way things were looking, there might even be a shag at the end of it.

As he moved his arm to place the next bet, Consuela laid a cool hand on top of it. He looked up at her.

'I'm bored.'

'Well, you run along and be bored somewhere else, sweetheart, and I'll catch you up in a few minutes. I'm on a roll here.' Stay or leave, he didn't care what she did, he'd just won nearly five grand, gambling was the only woman turning his head at that moment and Consuela was invisible to him.

'You're a fool, is what you are.'

He pulled his arm back and looked at her. How come she wasn't impressed? 'A minute ago you said I was daring.' He sounded like a sulky twelve year-old.

'A minute ago you were playing the game, now you're the desperate man, your eyes are flashing green, the colour of desperation, and the table has its hold on you. If you walk away now, you leave a winner. The next spin you will lose everything because the table knows it has you in its power. At first you bet for the fun in it. Now you're betting in desperation and that's an ugly thing to watch in any man.'

She was talking bollocks, but she had a point about

the possibility of him losing. She took hold of his super-human confidence in her palm and shook it. He was hesitating, unsure. He'd won nearly five grand. It was a lot of money to lose.

She shrugged and turned away from the table. She knew that he'd follow.

'Hey, wait. Lady, hang on, I'll come with you.' After stuffing his pockets with his winning chips, he regained some of his composure. This way he had some good winnings and might still get that shag. Whichever way you looked at it, it could only be a win. 'Let me buy you a drink for bringing me luck.' He made to walk in the direction of the bar, but Consuela hooked her arm into his elbow and led him towards the exit.

She kicked her shoes off as he closed the door behind them. Looking around the room he whistled. 'Wow, this is some hotel room you've got.' It was a suite comprising a bedroom, bathroom, dining room-lounge and balcony. They were standing in the lounge area and she motioned him onto the sofa. A gold hostess trolley was laid with a bottle of champagne on ice and several lead crystal decanters filled with amber liquids. 'Champagne?' she asked, lifting the dripping bottle from the bucket. 'Or would you prefer whiskey? Brandy?'

What he wanted was a long cold beer and to get back to that lucky table in town. 'Whiskey, please, Maria. That'll be great.' She had reminded him of her false name in the taxi on the way to her hotel as he tried not to stare at her cleavage.

She poured him a large one, a smaller one for herself, and sat at the other end of the sofa curling her feet up underneath her. He had his arm stretched across the back of his seat and she reached over and stroked him gently, making his arm tingle and clearing all thoughts of gambling from his mind in an instant as his other primal desire took control.

The telephone on the side table rang. She reached over to answer it. 'Who can this be, ringing me at such an hour? I'm not expecting a call. Excuse me.' She put the phone to her ear. '*Si, Señora Callas. Si?*' She spoke for a moment in Spanish before breaking into English, 'Thomas, my darling,' She rolled her tongue around the R and spoke in a richly accented voice. 'Of course I was going to answer your call; you know how busy I've been.' She motioned to get John's attention, in a show of good manners he'd picked up a magazine on the table when Consuela had answered the phone. She cupped the handset and spoke to him, 'Please excuse me one moment, I must take this, it's business.'

John made to rise. 'Do you want me to go? I'll—'

'No, please wait. Make yourself comfortable. I won't be long.' She walked into the bedroom, pushing the door carefully behind her. It remained ajar.

'Now Thomas, you *vieja cabra*, what is the great urgency?' She saw John's shadow fall across the room. As she hoped, he was listening at the door.

'Thomas, it is not a problem. *Si*, let me put up all of the money—oh you are stubborn, *Cabrio*. Why won't you let me? We don't need the third person. What does it matter that my interest will be greater than yours? Does that not just mean that I will protect our combined interest's better—okay, you win. I have a friend. I will talk to him. I'll get back to you with an answer by tomorrow night—*Si*, I know it's a perfect deal, five million turnover? Are you sure? And that's guaranteed? Yes, yes. I know all that. Now go, I am busy; this is no time for talk of business. *Chao, chao, caro mia.*' She rang off and stabbed a new telephone number in to the handset before putting her finger on the disconnection bar before the connection was made.

'*Hola*, Gregory? Darling it is I, Maria, you have missed me, *si*?—I know it is very late and I'm so sorry but this can't wait. Time is running out on this deal and I have a proposition for you that cannot wait even until the morning. Do you remember Thomas Barrington? That's right, one squiffy eye that doesn't know where it's looking and the other eyeing up any piece of skirt that's around.' She paused as though listening, and then she laughed. 'The thing is Greg, we need an investor—that's right the Faquad account. The one I told you about. Yes, it's a massive payout, but the thing is, we have to move quickly. I need an answer now—that's the good part. Twenty down and two million return by the end of the month, guaranteed—you will? Oh, that's wonderful. Will you do a bank transfer?—Oh, that's going to be a problem. You see, I can't get back to Spain in the next couple of days—Darling, you cannot afford to lose out on this. Oil prices are through the roof, we cannot fail—*Si*, I understand, but that's no good, it has to be immediate— Okay. *Si*, we will have to leave it, this time. Now don't you worry about it, there'll be other deals. I'll speak to you soon, kiss kiss.'

She sighed loudly, giving John plenty of time to get away from the door before she walked into the lounge. She sat on the sofa and picked up her glass, her brow furrowed. She clicked her long nails on the side of her glass, distractedly. 'I'm sorry about that, a small business problem that I had to deal with.'

John moved forward in his seat and smiled at her. 'All sorted out now?'

She sighed again. 'No.'

John laughed. 'I've got nearly five grand if it'll help you.'

Consuela laughed too. 'Unfortunately, my friend, it doesn't quite work that way.' She slugged off her whiskey in one swallow and moved cat-like over to the trolley to pour them a second glass.

John's mind was working fast. He could get the twenty grand she had mentioned on the phone. It would be risky, but he was pretty sure that he could get access to the old lady's accounts. He could borrow from the hotel and have it paid back before anybody noticed that there was a deficit. The accounts weren't tallied until month's end. It would be a simple loan. Maria was kissing his neck but all he could think about was clearing two million pounds in less than two weeks. 'Do you like that, Jonny?' she asked, trailing her lips across his neck and onto his cheek.' Nobody had ever called him Jonny before. He liked the way the name dropped from her lips in a husky Spanish accent. She was probably the sexiest woman that he'd ever pulled. He tried to concentrate. He turned his head and covered her mouth with his. She tasted of whiskey and lipstick and all things woman. Her hand dropped onto his chest and stroked its way up until she was undoing his shirt buttons. His cock should have been like a rod of steel by now, but he couldn't get those two million pounds out of his head. He pushed her away and looked earnestly into her eyes. 'Let me invest, Maria. I can help you.'

'Don't be ridiculous.'

'Why not? You want an investor and I've got the money.'

'Darling, I've already told you, five is not enough.'

'I can get twenty. I heard what you said on the phone, I'm sorry. You want a bank transfer.' He didn't care that he'd just given away his snooping. 'I can have the money in your account by start of business in the morning. I'm a sound investment. I own a large hotel in Windermere. Twenty grand is nothing.'

'It's out of the question. I don't know you. I might take you to my bed for a little pre-dawn workout, but I don't conduct my business with strangers. You have me all wrong, Jonny boy.'

'My name is John Woods; I'm a major shareholder in the Halcyon Woods Hotel in Windermere. Check me out. I'm good for it.'

'My business partner would never go for it, it's absurd. Out of the question. No, I'm sorry; I should never have even mentioned it.'

'I want in. What do I have to do, Maria? Tell me and I'll do it.'

She screwed up her eyes in thought, as though she was considering her options.

'I'll think about it. Go now, it is late.' She all but shoved him out of the door. He leaned in to kiss her and after a brief peck, she pulled away. She had him wriggling on the line. She didn't have to tolerate him slobbering all over her.

'How will I know? Shall I call you tomorrow? Can you give me a number?'

'No, come to my room at six; a banker's draft will not prove to me that your claim is a valid one. We have no business history so I'm afraid that it will have to be cash. Will that be a problem?' He shook his head. 'I will speak to my partner. Bring the money, but I am promising nothing. He may well refuse your offer. We'll see.'

'You're promising nothing except that the two million is guaranteed if we do go ahead, right?'

'Jonny, my darling, I thought you were a businessman. Surely you understand that there are no guarantees where money is concerned. But oil is liquid gold, prices have never been better, and we have the deeds of passage. Your two million is merely a beginning dividend in the first month, after that it will rise and nobody knows when the balloon will burst. Once you're in, you can reclaim your original investment in the first week or two as agreed, and let your profits accumulate for as long as you please, or you can withdraw completely with one clean deal.'

He kissed her again before she got him out of the suite and she tasted a sour tinge on his breath. Shutting the door behind him, she rested her back against it. A smile played around the corners of her mouth.

Violet looked at Graham Bradson with her mouth open. 'Don't be preposterous. That's impossible.'

Bradson looked uncomfortably at SP. The accusation was clear from his expression. 'I'm sorry, Violet, but I've been through the books a dozen times. There is nothing to account for that money going missing. On the fifteenth of the month, it was a Friday; you signed for an open banker's draft, at nine forty-six in the morning. That was then processed and rerouted to the hotels cash flow where it was taken from the safe, on the same day, in cash. The balance in the safe was correct, because the banker's draft had covered the shortfall.'

'I did not. I did not, I tell you.'

'Well somebody did, they used the password — he stopped short of repeating it in front of her son. They used your user name and password and had your mother's maiden name to pass through security.'

'It could have been any one of a dozen people.' SP was angry. 'Her password's The Old Rugged Cross. We all know it. I wouldn't be surprised if half of the girls on reception have been told. Knowing mother, she's probably given her details to one of the guest's brats and asked them to draw money out for her so that Ros doesn't find out about it. Are you aware that she donated three hundred pounds to The Sisters of Mercy's raffle, last month?'

'Quite, quite.' Bradson looked uncomfortable.

'Now maybe you can see why I wanted Power of Attorney. It's for her own good, she's a liability. I knew it was just a matter of time until something like this happened.'

'I am here, you know,' Violet said, in her most refined voice. She took a small sip of her sherry and hummed, *O sacred heart, O love burning*.

The police were brought in to investigate. It was a far cry from when the boys were young and impervious to blame. Apart from the youngest, the rest all had police records. Violet's sons, and SP especially, were under suspicion at once. This had SP's previous form all over it. Despite being questioned and scrutinised, probed and deeply investigated, SP came out of it squeaky clean, but one of Violet's other sons appeared on the radar. He was taken to the station for questioning. His fingerprints were all over the company safe. He could come up with no plausible excuse as to why he had been in the office, let alone the safe. He appeared on the CCTV cameras at the bank when he went in to collect the banker's draft. His crime was strictly amateur. He hadn't thought it out well.

Fergusson, the investigating officer, peered at him from the other side of the Formica table. The only sound in the room was the hypnotic whirring of the tape machine recording the interview. 'I ask you again, Mr Woods. Why did you steal the money?'

'I didn't.'

'Come on now, stop playing games, we've got you on camera at the bank. For the purpose of the tape I am passing over two colour photographs for Mr Woods to look at.' He slid the A4-sized photographs across to John. They showed him striding out of the bank with a stupid grin on his face. 'Why don't you just save us all some time and tell the truth?'

'Okay. Okay. I took it. But you're wrong, I didn't steal it. I borrowed it. It was a loan. I was going to put it back before anybody noticed that it was gone.' He rubbed his sweaty palms on his trousers.

'Taking money without the owner's consent is hardly akin to taking out an agreed loan, Mr Woods. Did your mother give you permission to go into the company's private safe and help yourself to the money?'

'Not exactly.'

'Define, "Not exactly" for us, Mr Woods.'

'No. No, she didn't know.'

'You didn't consult her?'

John looked at the table, ashamed. 'No.'

'So you stole twenty thousand pounds from the family business and then—'

'Borrowed.'

Fergusson sighed. 'We've already established that, in the eyes of the law, it was theft. What did you do with the money?'

John squirmed in his seat. 'There was a woman.'

Mark Fergusson and his partner, Pete Johnson, exchanged a look. If they had a pound for every time a perp confessed that a woman was at the root of their problems, they would be very rich men. 'Go on,' Fergusson said.

'Look, I'm a married man. Gaynor, my wife, she wouldn't understand. I have children. If I tell you what happened, please, can we keep it away from my wife?' He looked at the whirring tape recorder.

'Indeed,' Fergusson said. 'Women, eh? They very rarely understand. However, this is a police investigation, Sir. We have no interest in your inability to keep it in your pants. We just want to know the facts.'

Johnson spoke for the first time. 'Just tell us what you know, Mr Woods, and we'll do our best to decide what's relevant to the case and what doesn't have to become public property, so to speak. Just start at the beginning and, trust me, you'll feel better for getting it off your chest.'

'Two weeks ago.'

'What date?' Fergusson asked.

'I don't know exactly, sometime at the beginning of the month, I'd just renewed the car tax and insurance a few days before, so probably about the second or third. I received a letter through the post. Elegant, you know? Not your usual bill demand in a brown envelope.' He went on to tell them how he came to be at the casino that night and about his meeting with the Spanish woman.

'What was her name?

'Maria. Maria Callas.'

'The famous opera singer?' Johnson smirked. 'I thought she was dead.'

'What? What are you talking about?'

Fergusson chuckled. 'Did you meet Maria Callas, the deceased opera singer?'

'No. Well, I don't think so. She didn't say anything about opera, but she was rich. I didn't give it a second thought.'

Both policemen were laughing. Johnson composed himself and wiped at the corner of his eye. 'I think you've been duped, my old son. She saw you coming a mile away.'

John told his story. It sounded ridiculous when spoken aloud.

'And that was it?' asked Fergusson. 'You handed over the hotel's money and never saw her again?'

'I was supposed to meet her again, two nights after I paid.' He shifted uncomfortably on his seat and felt the heat rising in his face. 'She never turned up.' John was bright red. 'She had invited me to a party. Said she wanted to introduce me to the other business partner in an informal setting. Said that there would be lots of contacts there. That it would be good business for the hotel. I wanted to do it for the old lady. You know, because I'd taken the money without asking. If I brought some business in, money people, I'd be doing something right for once.'

The police officer's exchanged a look. 'Go on.'

'The party was taking place at the Adelphi Hotel.' He reddened further and dropped his voice. 'She told me that it was a fancy dress party. Said she was going as Jane, wanted me to go as Tarzan, like a couple, you know.' He paused. 'Security threw me out.'

The policemen smirked. 'There was no fancy dress party?' Fergusson guessed. John shook his head.

The investigation was conducted over the following weeks. Violet, on discovering that her son had stolen the money, tried to drop the case, but the police overruled her and said that they had enough evidence to bring their own case to court.

The croupier on duty that night had been paid off by Consuela. He remembered seeing the gentleman, but had no recollection of a lady, Spanish or otherwise. Consuela's money had bought his silence. The hotel checked their records and found that the gentleman was mistaken; room 703 was not occupied on the night in question. The police searched their computer's data for a businessman under the name of Thomas Barrington. They found a Thomas Barrington III living in a nursing home in Suffolk, but he was addled with dementia and made even less sense than John Woods.

Fergusson, who had taken a dislike to Woods, made a point of interviewing his wife. She had no information to give, except to confirm that her husband had gone out that evening and hadn't returned until the early hours.

Gaynor filed for divorce the following day. She was

used to his affairs, but stealing from his mother was something that she wouldn't tolerate. The brothers turned against him, though there was not one of them who hadn't swindled money form their mother in one way or another. His children refused to talk to him. Gaynor threw him out of his house. He rented a dingy bedsit on the wrong side of town and resigned himself to the fact that, when his case came to trial, he would be going to prison for at least three years. Before his backside ever touched a jail-cell bunk, his creditor's got to him first, mean men who didn't stake their claim through a court of law. He was beaten, left for dead in an alley and found stinking and unshaven by a youth walking his Staffordshire bull terrier.

As John recovered in hospital, his family didn't visit. Even Violet didn't want to see him. Alone in his bedsit, continually hounded by his creditors for his old gambling debts, his decline escalated, drinking as much in the mornings as he would in the evenings, broke, skeletal and depressed. Three weeks after coming out of hospital, two weeks before the date of his trial, John Woods' flat was burned to the ground and a loan shark scored a name from his list. A family in the flat above escaped with minor smoke inhalation and were taken to hospital. John Woods' body was wheeled out on a stretcher and taken straight to the morgue.

Violet was inconsolable. She blamed herself for not visiting him in his hour of need. She never forgave herself. A verdict of murder by arson was carried at the inquest and the perpetrators of the crime were never brought to book. For thirty pieces of silver, Violet could have paid off her son's debts for him again. She always had before. If she had bailed him out this time, he would still be alive. She roamed the corridors of the hotel at night calling out his name and disturbing the guests. Ros left the marital bed and took to sleeping in the guest room in Violet's suite to keep an eye on her.

Chapter Twenty-seven

Two acts of Sabotage caused the temporary closure of the hotel for refurbishment that year. The person responsible, in fact, would have been doing them a favour, had it not been heralding the end of an empire for Mother Duck and her brood. The hotel hadn't had a complete makeover since Violet had bought it. The Halcyon was inviting an older clientele; it was high tea and scones with strawberry jam and clotted cream. It was classic, vintage, boho British, it was art deco, and it was maintained with impeccable cleanliness and taste, but it needed some new life breathing into it.

Every year, a run of bedrooms would be decorated, and every ten years, the reception, lounge and kitchens would be done on consecutive years. The hotel had never been gutted and given a new, fresh feel. It had been in SP's mind for years and the saboteur had given him the push that he needed.

Consuela signed in using a credit card in the name of Grazia Martinez. She wore muted clothing, had her wig of blonde curls pulled back into a knot, applied little makeup and hunched to belie her stature. Her aim to be inconspicuous was impossible—she was the type of woman to be noticed, even when she tried not to be. Her trunk was noted, too. Nobody carried trunks anymore, not in these days of lightweight designer baggage, it was as over the top as she was beautiful. She went directly to her room. Insisting that she bring her own luggage had caused eyebrows to rise at Reception—that's what they employed porters for—but she had timed it to coincide with the arrival of a coach tour of pensioners. They needed a lot of assistance and Connie had managed to tuck into the general mêlée, check in at the desk and drag her trunk to the lift with a minimal amount of fuss. An old dear yelled that she was about to faint in the heat and Connie slipped away while the staff were distracted.

Once inside, she set to work fast. She had chosen her room with care and specifically requested it when she'd booked. It was a large corner suite on an outside wall, but the real beauty of it was that it was directly above the hotel kitchens.

She pulled the large, solid wood wardrobe away from the wall. It was heavy and she struggled, panicking, because time was running out. She was sweating and it took precious minutes to move the furniture far enough from the wall to enable her to work. With a cordless circular saw she cut away two lengths of the skirting board before she dragged the shipping trunk over to the wall. The rats were packed in individual pet boxes so that they wouldn't suffocate under the collective bodyweight. She had ventilated the trunk well, and they'd been in there less than half an hour. She hoped none of them had died, especially the pregnant ones.

Connie opened each of the one hundred boxes and talked softly to the occupants before pushing them one by one into the holes in the skirting board.

She was long gone, riding in a taxi to Lancaster for cocktails, when the first guest screamed.

She rode hot on the heels of that incident, not letting the hotel draw breath before she hit again. This time was easier; she didn't have to be seen at all and had no need of a room. The hotel worked around the clock, night staff manned reception and there was a core of kitchen staff kept on all night, maintained in the small hours to work on the veg prep and other jobs that could give them a head start on the day to come.

Connie was banking on the good old routine, which had kept the hotel moving for thirty years. She laid her bets on the fact that little or nothing would have changed. Between two and three in the morning the kitchen staff took their break and went into the staff room with trays of leftovers from supper service. The kitchen was unattended at this time. It was easy to wait for the night porters to have something to attend and then slip in while they were away from Reception.

It was a hell of a risk, but she wasn't scared of them. Staff lockers were kept in the anteroom of the kitchens; she was banking on the fact that the night workers eating their supper already had everything that they needed. This wasn't the time for one of them to get a craving for horseradish sauce on their pasta.

Consuela slipped in and worked fast. She hit the storerooms first, moving boxes and packing cases to empty her cartons of maggots where they would do the most damage. She dropped cockroaches in cupboards and along the floors where there were gaps in the skirting. She'd only brought a small holdall with her, which was all she needed this time. She dropped another box around the sink area, making sure that the maggots had crevices to burrow into so that they wouldn't be noticed immediately. She opened the catering drums of soup mix, coffee, flour, salt, sugar, gravy granules, pulses and beans, which were already in use and had their seals broken. Working fast, she dug maggots deep into the core of the contents. Anywhere that she could hide maggots and release cockroaches, she did. It had been so easy. Zipping up the holdall with a satisfied smile, she left as inconspicuously as she had arrived.

At nine the following morning, she used her old British accent and called the Environmental Health Agency, explaining that she was a concerned member of staff. She told them that the kitchens at the Halcyon-Woods were alive.

Chapter Twenty-eight

He was a very happy Simon. In the last ten years, life had changed in so many ways and it had been scary at first. And it had been bad. And Simon didn't want to move out of Great Gables. It was his home. And it was his people. And it was his room. And it was his desk with his stuff in it. But it had been a long time now and Simon was happy.

He had his own flat. He was very proud. To get into his flat he had his own key that he kept on a neon green spring that attached to his belt loop so that he couldn't loose it. He had his own flat and his own front door. If somebody came to visit and he didn't want to answer the door, he didn't have to. He did that once when Cheryl, his social worker, called. He just wanted to see what it was like to not answer the door. He'd done answering the door before when people had come to visit and he liked that very much, but he'd never done not answering the door.

Cheryl knocked on the door and Simon sat on his red sofa with a big smile on his face. Cheryl knocked a lot and then she shouted through his letter box, 'Simon? Simon, love? Are you in? Simon, it's Cheryl. Are you all right in there?' And Simon still sat on his red sofa with a big smile on his face not answering the door. Simon heard Cheryl's high heels clicking down the path and he decided that he didn't like not answering the door. It wasn't fun like answering the door was. He wanted to wonder who was there, that was the fun bit before you opened it. Cheryl was his friend and he wanted to see her, he wanted to tell her all about work and Jimmy and all the others. But now he had a big problem, Cheryl was going away and soon she'd get in her blue car and drive away. Simon had to stop her but he had his brown slippers on and you don't wear your brown slippers outside, do you? Brown slippers are for in the house and shiny black shoes are for going outdoors. Outdoors is just another way of saying outside, but Simon likes saying outdoors because it sounds posh in his new flat. Simon had to run down the path in his brown slippers to stop Cheryl. He didn't think he'd not answer the door again. He was out of puff when he ran down the path and grabbed Cheryl's arm. He said, 'How do you do?' because that's a posh thing to say in his new flat. 'Won't you come in.' And Cheryl laughed.

Simon was living in an Assisted Living project. It was very grand. Mr and Mrs Pickering had the last flat on the row; they were wardens and looked after everybody. All the other flats were full of people just like Simon, but they didn't all have brown hair, some of them had blonde hair. And Mr Wright didn't have any hair at all; he was bald and didn't even have any eyebrows. Simon lived at number six and his door was red like his sofa.

Mother didn't visit Simon anymore. She came to his flat once and then said that he was a big man and didn't need her to visit. Simon was glad. She still put money in his bank account and Cheryl or Mrs Pickering would get money out of his account for him when he needed it. Mrs Pickering sat down with him every month when he paid his bills. Simon paid all of his bills himself, but Mrs Pickering had to sit down with him to make sure he did it right.

The other big change in Simon's life was that he had a job. He worked at the Cosy Kitchen café on Bridge Street and had lots and lots of friends. Sometimes the customers teased him. On yestersunday, Jimmy—he's a workman and wears a yellow jacket—put two salts on lots of tables and two peppers on lots of other tables. And then he said a big complaint to Annie, who is Simon's boss. Simon likes having a boss called Annie. He loves her. And when Jimmy said the big complaint, and said that Simon had mixed them all up.

Annie smacked Jimmy with her tea towel and said, 'Get away with yer,' and then she gave the tea towel to Simon, but before Simon smacked him, Billy—that's one of all the others who wears a yellow jacket—showed Simon how to twist up the tea towel first and flick it. Simon ran around the café chasing Jimmy and when he caught him he smacked him with the tea towel and shouted, 'Get away with yer.' Jimmy laughed and gave Simon a pound coin and Simon put it in his tip jar.

Simon has a lot of tips. And he can leave them at work until he wants to take them because the jar says Simon on it, and nobody touches it. Jimmy and Joey and Billy and Jack— they are Jimmy and all the others— tease him about his tip jar. They try to make Simon say that it's his tits jar, but Simon won't say that because it's a bad word. Even if they say they'll give him a pound if he does, because Simon's very clever and he knows that they are going to give him a pound anyway. Simon likes to tell people about all his friends but there's an awful lot of them.

And then the new lady came. She's called Connie. She came in one day and sat at the table by the window. And then she came in every day and sat at the table by the window. She talks funny and is very pretty. Simon was scared of her at first because she was new and Simon is always scared of new customers. Annie said that he had to serve her just like she was Jimmy and all the others, but she doesn't look like Jimmy and all the others. Simon got red. He carried her mug real careful and then went back again for her plate. Annie said Simon was a one-plate-at-a-time kinda guy.

'Here's your latte and your currant bum, be careful because it's bery hot. Can I get you anything else please, thank you.'

The lady, because he didn't know that she was called Connie then, smiled all big at him and said, 'That's perfect, thank you very much. It looks delicious.'

Every day she came in and every day she talked to Simon when he served her. Soon Connie was Simon's friend, too, just like Jimmy and all the others.

One day Simon was walking for the bus. He had his head all the way down because he didn't look up when he was going for the bus. Sometimes people weren't nice and scared him. He heard somebody shout his name but he kept his head all the way down and kept walking. He heard high heels clicking faster to catch up with him.

Sometimes girls with clicky heels on weren't nice, too. It's not just boys who are the horrible people. The voice sounded like Connie from the café, because Connie from the café talks funny but Simon wasn't taking any chances. Simon kept walking. Somebody grabbed his arm.

'Simon, it's Connie. Aren't you talking to me today?'

Simon stopped and turned around. 'Hullo, Connie.' Simon talked to Connie in the café when he served her. Simon did not talk to her on the street when he was going for his bus. Connie had an awful lot of shopping bags.

'Simon, my car's just around the corner. You couldn't be a love and help me to carry some of this shopping?' Simon didn't know if Connie was asking him to help her or telling him that he wasn't allowed to help her. Simon likes helping people. It makes people smile. But Simon likes getting his bus, too. He didn't want to miss his bus and have to wait at the bus stop for another one in case the horrible people came and teased him. Simon didn't know what to do. He didn't say anything.

'Please, Simon. If you could help me it would be doing me a big favour.'

This was bad. 'Miss bus,' said Simon.

'Oh, right, well I'll tell you what, one good turn deserves another. If you can help me carry my bags, I'll give you a lift home, afterwards.'

It was worse, it was even badder. Connie had taken some of her bags and passed them to Simon and his hands had taken them before his mouth said yes. 'Not get in car. No lifts from strangers, not,' Simon mumbled.

Connie laughed and it was a nice laugh, 'Oh, come on, Simon, I thought we were friends; I'm not a stranger, am I? I'm your friend, Connie. You'll hurt my feelings in a minute.'

Simon didn't want to hurt her feeling in a minute or even tomorrow so he walked along the street with Connie, worrying. He got into her black car, worrying. Connie leaned across him and fastened his seatbelt. She smelled very nice. Like flowers. Simon sniffed her hair. He sat without talking nearly all the way home. Connie talked all the time she told him about a place called Spain. Simon thought it must be a long way away. She said that's why she talks funny and then she did the best thing. She winked at Simon and then she spoke to him just like a normal re'glur person. Just like Annie or Shirley who comes in on a Thursday, after the shops. She didn't speak from the Spain place anymore. Simon was so surprised that he forgot to worry. Connie said that it was a secret and he mustn't tell anybody. She tapped the side of her nose. When she pulled up outside Simon's house, she undid his seatbelt and leaned all the way over him to open his door. He sniffed her hair again because she still smelled good.

'Bye, Simon. See you tomorrow,' she called after

him.

Simon didn't look round.

The next day Connie didn't mention giving Simon a lift or about not talking funny. When he put her mug and her currant bun down carefully, she tapped her nose and winked at him.

That night, Simon was walking for his bus. A car slowed down beside him and went very slow. Simon kept his head down. He saw an arm winding the window and he was scared. 'Simon, come on, get in, it's raining,' Connie said to him. He got into her black car. Connie told him that she drove past his house every night and she might as well give him a lift home to save him getting the bus. Simon was still awkward but after a few days he liked going home in Connie's black car. It was even better than getting the bus and the horrible people didn't tease him, or hurt him.

Soon Simon looked forward to going home with his friend Connie. And Annie knew about it, too, because Connie told her that it was on her way and Annie didn't seem to mind Connie taking Simon home. She never told Annie that she could talk normal though, that bit was still the kind of secret that you tapped the side of your nose about. In the car they talked about all kinds of things. Connie gave Simon a money plant. But it wasn't a real money plant, it was just a plant. Simon watered it every week just like Connie told him to and it grew big.

One day they were talking about *High School Musical II*. Simon knew all the songs and could do the dances just like on the DVD. Connie asked him if he'd like to go to the pictures to see it. Simon was very excited and put on his best blue jumper. He didn't have dandruff because Mrs Pickering made him buy Head & Shoulders when they went shopping. Connie said that she'd pick him up at half past seven. Connie didn't come at half past seven. Connie didn't come until seven thirty-nine. Simon thought that she wasn't coming and took his big coat off and hung it up in the cupboard. He was very sad until Connie knocked on the door.

In the pictures Connie bought Simon some popcorn and some fizzy orange that made Simon burp, but she had to hold them when Simon needed to clap his hands to the songs. He knew all the words and sang along. Connie smiled big at him and sang some of the words, too, but she didn't know all the words like Simon did. On the way home, Connie and Simon went to Pizza Hut and bought a big pizza and fries and then Simon had room left for ice cream. Connie said he was going to pop, but Simon hoped not. It was the bestest night of Simon's life. Simon didn't know that Wednesdays could be good.

The next week, Connie came round to Simon's flat. She brought all the ingredients and she said that she'd teach Simon how to bake a chocolate cake. Simon didn't sleep on Tuesday night because he was so excited. Jimmy and all the others teased him because they said that Connie was his girlfriend. They sang Connie and Simon sitting in a tree, k-i-s-s-i-n-g. Simon got red and went into the back room to wash up. Sarah Wallace at

Great Gables was his girlfriend, but Simon thought she might be deaded now because Simon hasn't seen Sarah Wallace for a long time. Connie was his friend.

She didn't come to the café as much any more. She told Simon that she had a business to run and couldn't come for coffee every single day. She still popped in once or twice a week, though. And she was waiting to give him a lift home when he left work most nights. Simon knew that she was a real busy lady and that some nights she couldn't pick him up. He had to get the bus then and he didn't like it. But Annie and Connie told him that it was good for his independence to take the bus sometimes.

The chocolate cake was good. Simon had two slices and Connie said that he mustn't eat too much or he'd be sick and then she wouldn't be able to come and bake with him again because it wouldn't be good for him.

'Shimon not eat more until tomorrow,' he told Connie. 'Shimon be bery good.' And even though it wasn't a secret he tapped the side of his nose and blinked in an attempt to wink.

Connie came to see Simon every Wednesday night. It was their night together. Sometimes they baked cakes, sometimes they watched films and sometimes they went out somewhere. Connie took Simon to the pub. Simon liked the pub. Simon drank half a lager please and it made him burp, especially if he had three half a lagers. Simon sang Elvis Presley's *Teddy Bear* on the karaoke. It was his song. David, who was the karaoke man, said that Simon was better than Elvis Presley, and

Simon swung his hips and got down on one knee to sing. Mostly somebody had to help him back up again though.

Simon took Connie to the Rainbow Club once a month. Cheryl always had to ring up to remind him when it was on, or he forgot. Simon had his own telephone and when he picked up the receiver he said, 'Hello, Woods redisenth. How may I help you?' When it was Connie on the other end she always used to say, 'It's Connie in the bat mobile, you can get the kettle on.' And he always laughed.

Connie liked it at the Rainbow Club. She wore trousers so that she didn't ladder her stockings and no high heels so that she could crawl on the floor. She always brought things for all the people there like Simon. But when they had a disco, Connie danced with everybody and Simon didn't like that. Connie was his friend. He'd sulk in the car on the way home and she'd call him, 'Sulky sod,' but then she'd start singing a song and Simon would join in and then he wouldn't be sulking any more. Wednesday was the bestest day of the week.

One day Simon asked, 'Connie, why Connie normal?' She stopped with a jigsaw piece in her hand. They were working on the edges and Connie said that it was a piece of the chimney pot.

'What do you mean, *Cielo*?'

Simon knows Spanish now. *Cielo* means honey. The horrible people don't know no Spanish and Connie wouldn't call them Cielo at all, not. 'Shimon is normal not, but Connie is normal.'

'Simon, you are a lot of things that other people aren't. You're kind and funny and sweet and a very good singer.'

'Shimon good singer, yes, but normal, not. Connie, why Connie not get normal friend?'

'*Cielo*, I have lots of friends, all different kinds of people, you are just one of them.'

Simon thought about this. He couldn't decide whether this was worthy of a sulk or not. He didn't like Connie having lots of friends. 'Shimon not like Connie have lots of friends, not.'

Connie laughed. 'Well, that's not very nice, is it?'

Simon had thought about it, and he was, definitely, sulking. 'Connie likes normal friends, not like Shimon.'

'Hey sulky sod, I like you lots, like jelly tots. Stop being silly. What if you weren't allowed to see Annie, and Jimmy and Joey, and Billy and all of your friends at Great Gables, you'd be very lonely, wouldn't you?'

Simon didn't answer. He had turned his back on her and didn't want to talk to her. So Connie talked to herself.

'Oh dear, Connie, now we have a problem. See, there was me going to take Simon to the lake to buy an ice cream, but Simon's not talking to me. Do I just buy one ice cream for me? That would be lonely, just like we were talking about, wouldn't it, Connie? But if Simon's sulking and doesn't want to come, I can't bring his ice cream home for him because it will melt, and how on earth will I drive with only one hand. It's a problem,

Connie.'

Simon had turned around with a big grin. He went to the cupboard to get his coat. It was sweltering outside but Simon never went out without his coat. Simon wasn't sulking anymore.

Chapter Twenty-nine

The nearest bus stop was a mile and a half away from the farm. She sorely regretted not bringing her car and just dumping it in bushes somewhere close by. Not only was she trudging up the dirt track in the heat of summer but it was all uphill and she was wearing bloody Jesus sandals. She wore a flowing skirt in purples and reds. It came to her ankles, with bells on a string at her waist that tinkled when she walked. She had on a loose vintage top with no bra and had to admit that part did feel very liberating, but to be authentic she had on no deodorant or perfume. Bloody hippies, why can't they be at least half civilised, I bet there's no champagne on ice when I get there either, she thought. She had developed a taste for the stuff and had become adept at distinguishing which fruit had been used in which label.

When she got to the enormous farmhouse, she gave a low whistle; she wasn't the only one who'd done well for herself. She knocked on the door and was told by a pretty girl with a baby at her breast that Beth was in her studio. The girl pointed her in the right direction.

'Hi there, come on in. Take a seat, if you can find one.'

Beth had aged. Although Connie recognised her immediately, if she had to describe her in one word, it would be passionless. The enthusiasm that she'd had for life had left her eyes. She smiled, but it was just a smile. Beth, like the rest of them, had always looked down her nose at Julie, but she was the best of the lot. They had talked sometimes, and she knew what it was like to be disapproved of by Violet.

Her work had changed too. She still did her fluffy paintings of nature and animals, recorded the changing seasons in oil and watercolour and used the elements for inspiration in her sculpture and pottery, but in amongst the fluff, there was dark art. Pieces of tortured metal, bent and moulded to reflect pain and suffering. Connie bought a lot of art, she knew what was good and what wasn't. Beth was good.

'Connie,' she said, extending a hand.

'Not from around here, then? Spanish, Basque, right?'

'Not bad. Barcelona. I'm just bumming around your island for a few months, heard there might be some work going here. I'm a good worker.'

Beth gave a dry laugh. 'There is plenty of work here. And we can always use a good worker. We don't pay.'

'*Si*, that's fine.'

'Just do what you think your stay is worth and come and go as you please. We don't use locks. I hope you've got a strong back, it's potato picking this week. If you go back to the house, someone there will show you to a dorm and get you something to eat. Good to have you aboard. Welcome, Connie, stay as long as you like.'

Some women buy extravagant Parisian fragrances, in tiny bottles, for vast amounts of money. Connie brought with her Listeria in a tiny bottle, which had cost a fortune. When you have money, you can buy anything. There is nothing that doesn't have a price tag.

She worked in the fields for the rest of that week, until she never wanted to see another potato. In the evenings, she singled Beth out to chat to, showed an interest in the farm and how it operated and wormed herself a week working in the creamery. She was impressed by the size of the operation. Their brand was called *Nature's Riches* and they had an impressive turnover of cheese, milk, cream, yogurt and ice cream. Their cheese in particular had won awards, and was being stocked in the organic section of the leading supermarkets. She had imagined a couple of women turning handles on a churning bucket, but in fact the operation was modern and extensive. The machinery was floor-to-ceiling high and it took the strength of several men to do the manual work. The women were used for packing, labelling and order processing.

This suited Connie's purpose well. She wanted complete control of the placement of stored cheeses. What she planned to do was risky. If one cheese was taken out of rotation she could have the death of many people on her hands. That was never her intention. She wanted to bring down one family, not innocent people, and she didn't want to kill anybody. She didn't blame herself for John's death at all. The people he owed money to got to him; they would have done that with or without the tip off about where he was living. If he didn't owe so much money, he wouldn't have died, it was that simple. What she took credit for was the misery that he died in and the fact that he left this world estranged from his family, that she pushed him into lowering himself to stealing twenty grand from his mother with no means of returning it before he died. He would probably have been killed anyway. The fact that he drew his last breath a lonely man was the revenge that Connie had sought.

Andrew singled her out. He wanted to sleep with her. The last time he'd seen Julie his lip had curled. She disgusted him, though he was civil to her when he had to be. But he wanted Connie. She stirred his blood. His eyes were enflamed with lust. He brushed against her, made excuses to consult with her, did everything in his power to woo her into bed. And she flirted with him. She was disappointed when his obvious desire for her elicited no reaction from his wife. Beth didn't care. They had practised free love since the day they had met. But this was different. The love had left her eyes. She didn't love, need or desire her husband any longer so Andrew slept, at will, with members of their community. Beth slept alone, since the rape. She preferred it that way.

When Connie took Andrew to bed it was because she wanted to. She could have had any man on the farm, and many of the women, but Andrew had captivated her imagination. His body was lean and taut; he was more animal than man. He turned her on, and she found herself watching him, wanting him, and thinking about him while she worked. She wanted to see if he was as good at satisfying a woman as he was at swinging an axe. He was.

She tipped the vial of listeria into the first basin in the production process. Every piece of equipment in the creamery, every utensil, would have to be destroyed. Listeria mainly affects the very young and the very old, and it's dangerous for pregnant women to contract because it's harmful to the unborn. Connie had never had children, but Julie had a little girl, once. She was murdered.

After the tip off, the investigating authorities arrived fast. They locked down the farm and took samples from everything. Connie was sure that none of the contaminated products had left the first storage room, but nevertheless, all of their outlets had to remove the *Nature's Riches* stock from their shelves. It went Nationwide and featured on the evening news. Woods' Kibbutz Farm was finished. Andrew was depressed. He grieved for all the children that he might have killed had it not been found in time. Connie watched his sorrow and revelled in it. He hadn't grieved for Julie's daughter, had he? He was besmirched in the press, his lifestyle laid open for public scrutiny. The intimate details of his sex life were examined with several of his concubines telling their stories. They were raided by the vice squad. A massive cache of drugs were found. Most of the adults in the commune used them, and their high of choice was as varied as a Woolworth's Pick 'n' Mix. That was without the 'crop' that was kept under infra red lights, in the top barn. The haul was all for personal usage, but at street value it was worth hundreds of thousands. Social Services descended on the community to investigate how the members looked after their children. Many of the children, including two of Beth and Andrew's, were taken into care. His family rallied, but he felt their disapproval for besmirching their name again, too.

Andrew smoked less marijuana and more opium. He turned to Beth for solace, but she had none to give. They'd always liked the Cedar tree on the back lawn, where the children played.

It was their children who found him.

Chapter Thirty

She dripped gold and favoured sovereigns, the travellers' currency of old. Her clothing was the best; her shoes Louis Vuitton and her perfume a hundred pounds a bottle. These people, shunned by many in society, knew quality. They wouldn't be fooled by anything less that the best.

It was a semi-permanent site just outside Lancaster. She'd done her research. Her own car was modest so she'd hired an expensive sports car for the day and pulled onto the site in a squeal of tyres. Two men, tending horses by an outbuilding rushed over to her as she alighted.

'This is private property, Miss. You have no business here,' the first man in his twenties said.

'I am here to see the owner of this site.' She spoke with authority.

'Are you from the council?' This was the second man. He was of the same age but thicker set and less attractive than the first.

'Don't be soft, Wilfred, does the 'cil drive a car like that, I ask yer? What are you here for, Missus?'

'Please get me the owner. I am here with a business proposition.'

'We don't do business with Gorgas.'

'Excuse me?'

'Outsiders. We only deal with our own kind.'

The door of a trailer, set in its own courtyard, flew

open and a man strode towards them. 'Can I help you, there? Have you lost yer way, Missus?'

'I don't believe so. Are you the owner here?'

'And who would be wanting to know?'

'As you defend your privacy, so I'm defensive of mine, Mr Lowther. Who I am is not of importance.' He raised an eyebrow. 'Let me convince you that we have business.' She opened her clutch bag and gave him a glimpse of the wad of cash inside.

'Are you alone?' She nodded. 'Junior, Wilfred, why are my horses not on the snaffle? Go and see to my beauties. Stay close to the gate and see that we aren't disturbed.' The men leaned in close, trying to see in the Gorga's bag. 'Begone with you,' Jacob Lowther roared and the two men scattered. 'You'd best follow me, then.' And he led her into the trailer.

He motioned Connie into a seat in the curved bay window. She had done her research on the correct etiquette and respectfully removed her shoes before entering, but she was canny enough to pick them up and place them inside the door where she could see them. The trailer was every bit as immaculate as any home that she'd ever been in. It was tastefully dressed, with porcelain works of art. She had to smile when she saw the same Royal Doulton tea set that Violet was so proud of. It was set in a china cabinet. Violet would have been horrified to know that she shared her taste with gypsies.

'Sheila, get the pibe on, woman.' A voluptuous woman with hair as black as Connie's set about making tea. Neither of them spoke again until Jacob's wife had served them. She didn't ask Connie's taste and the tea was given with sugar and lemon, 'Go on and visit wit yer sister now, begone woman.' Sheila looked Connie over from head to toe. Her eyes flamed with jealousy and she glared at her husband possessively. Jacob raised the flat of his hand towards her in a backhander and with lightning reflexes Connie snatched her own hand out and grabbed him by the wrist.

'That won't be necessary, Mr Lowther.'

'To be spoken to like that in my own home. By a mort, too. I should strike you to the floor, Missus, but you've got balls and you've got my interest, I'll tell yer that much.'

Connie settled back down in her seat and watched out of the window until Sheila had entered a trailer across the yard. She took her time, opened her bag and took out the wad of money. Beside it, with the handle grip facing towards her, she placed a small derringer pistol with a mother of pearl inlaid handle. Jacob straightened in the seat opposite her. He was startled but recovered his composure.

There is ten thousand pounds there, Mr Lowther. If we can strike a deal, I'll be leaving that with you today. I trust and believe that you are a man of your word and if you say that it will be safe in your keeping until you claim it as rightfully yours, then that will be good enough for me. On completion of our business it will be doubled and you will not see me again. If you proved to not be a man of honour, Mr Lowther, I'd hunt you down and shoot you like vermin. Do you believe me?'

Jacob played through a gamut of expressions from anger to affront and finally a broad grin spread across his features. 'Aye, lass, I firmly believe you would. And it'd be a rum fool that'd cross you.' He composed himself and got down to business. 'Talk.'

'I've done my research Mr Lowther. I believe that you and your family engage in bare knuckle fighting?'

He gave nothing away to either confirm or deny this statement. 'Go on.'

'I want a fighter, several, in fact.'

'We don't do security, Missus. Hire a firm.'

'Let me elucidate.' He furrowed his brow in confusion but didn't interrupt. 'What I want is for you to organise a series of bouts, a tournament if you will, to take place over one night.'

'Travellers don't fight for the entertainment of Gorgas.'

'Yes, I know that. I would want some bouts to be amongst your own, for authenticity, but predominantly, I want you to fight an outsider.'

'You've got us wrong, Missus. We don't fight Gorgas. They tend to die. We fight for family name and honour or for prize purses, but always within our own kind. If this is some bookmaking deal, you've had a wasted journey.'

'I think not. You will be paid twenty thousand pounds for running the—shall we call it an event?—for me. I will cover the purse for your fighters. Anything you make on the book will also be yours.'

'Are you mad, woman? For an event like that, the stakes would be thousands.'

'I have no interest in it.'

'This mush of yours must be one hell of a fighter for you to want to put him up against the best in Britain.'

'I don't believe so.'

Jacob looked confused. 'So you're putting up this prize fighter against the best and yet you don't have the faith that he can win?

'My reasons are personal.'

'Hey lady, we don't deal in no hired hits. People die in these fights, sure, but we aint no murderers, if you want to off your old man, get some other sucker to spend the rest of his days in prison for you.'

'He will be a more than willing participant. He has an ego the size of Britain. I think you'll enjoy him.'

'Lady, this day started with me seeing to my hosses and playin' with my grandkids and it's become a strange day of a sudden. I'm a busy man with no patience, so you'd better start talking. You can start with a name. Seems only polite when you're sitting in my home, drinking my tea.'

'My name is of no importance. You can call me Maria.'

'But that's not your real name, right?'

'Here's the deal. I need a location. If you need money to hire somewhere, that's not a problem. I trust you to do what you do and arrange the necessary privacy et cetera. There will be several bouts throughout the competition. The man I bring will fight in three of them. Your men will throw the first two bouts—'

'Wait one minute there, Missus. There will be no fight throwing. We play fair and square. You don't understand this is our pride, our culture, we are a proud people. We don't throw fights. If your Gorga isn't up to it, then you'd better hope that he has some powerful life insurance.'

'Then our business here is finished, Mr Lowther. I am sorry to have wasted your time. She opened her bag and put the money away, rising and walking to the door.

'Hang on.' He licked his lips. 'Leave it with me, I'll find somebody, but it might cost you.'

'Fine.' Connie breathed a sigh of relief. Jacob did so less visibly. 'So, your men will throw the first two fights. Let him win. Let him crow. Then, on the third fight, I want you to beat the living shit out of him. I don't want him walking away at the end of the night.'

'I believe we talk the same language.'

'Maybe, maybe not, there is one more rule. If my demand is not met, then I go back to Spain, and from there I call the authorities and blow you wide open. Do you understand?'

'That's an ugly threat.'

'My final, and most important, rule—he must not be killed. I want him alive at the end of it.'

'So be it.'

'The venue must be arranged on a floating date, cancellable and re-organised at short notice, if he is not willing on the first date.'

'I can put it up and shut it down with an hour either side.'

'Perfect.'

'We will exchange numbers and when I think he's taken the bait, I will be in touch.' Connie spat into her hand and held it out to Jacob.

The deal was made.

Chapter Thirty-one

Her business needed her. Leaving her managers to their own devices for too long would lead to sloppy standards and a decline in honesty. She had good people in place, but every army needs a general and hers was no exception. She'd been home for a week and the second that she stepped foot on Spanish soil, she knew that it was exactly that—home. But she couldn't settle there. Everything was ready for her to step back into the wonderful life that she'd built for herself but her real work, for the time being, was back in England. There was something else back there that she missed. She found that, with being away, she missed Simon terribly. She rang him most nights and knew that sometimes he was so angry with her for leaving him that he didn't answer the phone, but usually curiosity got the better of him. It was good for him to be on his own, sometimes. When he did answer, she always got a buzz out of hearing him say, 'The Woods Redisenth. How may I help you?' She was just sorry that she couldn't answer with, 'I'm in the bat mobile. You can get the kettle on.' So she made do with, 'I'm in Spain, and I'm missing my Simon smiles.'

Simon was over ten years Connie's senior, but he filled a big hole that Vicki had left. Connie had a child-sized crater, and while Simon would never replace Vicki, he filled that hole and spilled out over the sides. She realised that she had taken on the role of a mother figure to him, and she made a conscious decision not to back away from that responsibility. She welcomed it.

Simon had once asked why Connie had befriended him. She was always careful with his fragile and simple emotions. She was cautious not to let him become too attached to her. He had spent many years gaining his independence and the last thing she wanted was to have him forming an unhealthy bond with her despite her maternal feelings towards him.

She was standing in her spare bedroom, looking at the blue Mediterranean tiles and wondering if Simon would be happy there. She would buy him a desk, just like the one he had in his flat, if that's what he wanted. For the first time she let the thought flood in that maybe, when this was all over, she could buy a plaque for his door saying *Sala Simón*, and that he might like to move out here, permanently. But Simon loved his flat and his new friends. He was happy there. He might not want to move to Spain. It was just a germinating idea, something to talk to him about — in the future.

She'd been in Spain for the aftermath of the Andrew scandal, but she was going back. Her flight had originally been arranged for a week later, but she'd brought it forward because, on one of her routine phone calls to Cheryl, she had told her that Simon had to go to the hospital for a barrage of tests to ascertain the long-term damage that had been done to his heart after his attack. He'd panicked and was frightened about it, the attack weighing heavy on his mind, and it had been a terrifying time for him. He'd decided that he didn't like hospitals at all and that he wasn't going to go. And they both knew how stubborn he could be. The women had become friends through their mutual concern over Simon and Connie had, gradually, over two bottles of wine and after swearing her to secrecy, told Cheryl her story, all of it, from beginning to sorry end. The only bit that she hadn't confided, was the story of her ongoing revenge. Cheryl was sceptical of her motives, but Connie made her see that her intentions towards Simon were good, that she cared about him and that she wanted to be a permanent and positive influence in his life.

Connie said that she wanted to be there for the appointment and that she'd fly in and surprise him. She'd meet Cheryl at the hospital and they could speak to Simon's consultant together. Connie knew that having no legal or hereditary right to be there, the consultant would never have spoken to her without the social worker's blessing. Simon had already had one significant heart attack and his life expectancy from here on in wasn't a long one. Connie wanted to make sure that it was good.

She knocked on the door. 'Surprise.'

Simon looked shocked; his eyes were huge in his round, confused face. He ran away from the door and left her standing there. It wasn't the greeting that she had expected. She signed and followed him in to the kitchen.

'Simon, it's me. Aren't you going to say hello?'

'Shush,' he replied, putting one finger up to his lips and spraying saliva all over it. Simon studied his calendar. He had his finger over a tick. Connie saw that it was today's date. Simon ticked it every morning when he got up. The next square had a blue star in it and Cheryl had written, Hospital appointment, underneath for Mrs Pickering's benefit. The next five squares were empty, and then on the day that Connie had been due to arrive back in England, there was a big gold star. She smiled. 'I've come home early, Simon. I've come especially to see you.'

Simon was agitated; he hopped from one foot to the other and pointed to his calendar. 'Not six sleeps, not. Not gold star, not.' He went into the lounge and picked up the telephone handset, because that's how he talked to Connie when Connie was in Spain. He pointed at it. 'Connie in Spain. It's hot and ever body say, "Hola,"' He looked at the handset again, put it to his ear, said, 'Thank you, goodbye,' and hung up.

'I missed you, Simon. I wanted to come and see you. Haven't you missed me?' She put her arms around him and gave him a hug. Simon stiffened. 'Shimon miss Connie in six sleeps,' he said grumpily. Connie sighed; she went into the kitchen with him trailing behind her. At the calendar she carefully peeled off the gold sticker and put it over the last tick. 'Hooray,' she said brightly. 'Its Connie day.'

'Hooray,' Simon agreed, but he didn't look convinced.

* * *

'I swear, Simon, sometimes you're like the fly around a horse's arse.' Simon had to stop and think about that for a little while. He was frightened of horses and didn't want to be a fly, or a horse's arse. 'Put the kettle on, *cielo*,' he said, picking up the kettle and remembering to fill it with water before putting it on to boil. This was his third kettle and Mrs Pickering said she wouldn't buy him another one. She said that he was a liability. Simon didn't know what a liability was, but it had to be better than a fly or a horse's arse. 'Put the kettle on, *cielo*,' he repeated, flicking the switch. This wasn't a request for Connie to make tea, nor was it a term of endearment. He was simply parroting the phrase that Connie always used when she came in, using the same flat monotone that he used when he was coming to terms with changes to his routine. He turned around with an enormous beam on his face. 'Connie, Shimon, go for ice cream in a little minute?'

'Why not,' she agreed, before broaching the delicate subject of the following day's hospital appointment.

Mr Bell, the consultant, looked up from Simon's records. He took a moment to order his thoughts and then looked from Cheryl to Connie and back again. 'The results aren't as optimistic as we'd hoped, I'm afraid. Downs sufferers have a far shorter life expectancy than the rest of us as it is, and with Simon's heart complications, it has just compounded the issue.'

'Is he going to die?' Connie asked. Her throat had dried up and she felt sick with worry.

'We have no way of knowing how long Simon's going to live, Ms Vengarse. His heart attack has seriously affected the function of his aortic efficiency, there's some decline in kidney function, his white cell count is on the low side. The muscles that work his heart are weakened. The best that I can tell you is that he could die tomorrow or, with a good head wind, he could live for another ten or twelve years. I would anticipate that his life expectancy could be somewhere down the middle. The good news is that his weight is down on six months ago. He's lost ten pounds. That's going to help to alleviate some of the pressure on his heart. He doesn't smoke or drink, his little job is keeping him active, and perhaps the greatest thing on his side is that he's a very positive individual. We aren't as happy with the results as we'd hoped, but it could be very much worse. I don't think he's ready to leave us, just yet.' He smiled encouragingly at them.

'Thank you, doctor.' Cheryl offered him her hand to shake. Connie just nodded and attempted a smile. Once released, the tears wouldn't stop. She couldn't bear the thought of losing him—not now. Cheryl took her for coffee in the canteen before they picked Simon up from the day room. She was hard on Connie and told her that Simon wasn't about to die at any second and to pull herself together, for his sake. If she'd had any doubt that Connie's feelings for Simon were genuine, that worry was long gone. Connie was like any mother being told that she was going to outlive her child, a fact that she had known all along, but hadn't done anything about coming to terms with yet.

Chapter Thirty-two

The bar was awful, the staff surly and the clientele a mix of drunken men and loose women on the pull. She'd been watching him for a week and in that time he'd come to this pub twice. It was logical to assume that he'd be back.

When she walked into the bar, everybody turned to stare at her. She was like a peacock in a crow show and would never blend in. She tossed her hair, straightened her shoulders and walked to the bar. 'Gin and slimline tonic, with ice and lemon, please.'

'No slimline, just ordinary. Ice we got. We don't do lemon.'

'That'll be fine, thank you.'

She paid, gave the barmaid a pound tip, took her drink, and turned her back to the bar. It was important that she picked a table that would give her a good view of the door and everything in the barroom. She sat down, aware that every pair of eyes in the place was on her. The two barmaids whispered together and she didn't have to struggle to figure that she was the topic of conversation. The first drink went down quickly. She wasn't nervous or uncomfortable, far from it; she was enjoying herself. Ten minutes after buying her first drink she went to get another.

The girls behind the bar fell over themselves to get to her first. The other one served her this time and her demeanour was curious and greedy, rather than suspicious. 'Same again, love?'

'Yes, thank you.' She paid and gave another tip.

'Not from around here, are you?' Now that she had her tip, only the curiosity remained. 'Gabby, over there,' she gestured with her hand, 'she reckons you're from Eastern European. 'But I says to her, nah, if you was from Eastern European, you wouldn't have a tan like that, not fake tan either, I says. The real kind what you get from the sun.'

'I'm from Spain,' she picked up her glass and took a sip and then put it back on the bar, in no hurry to return to her seat. She hadn't expected ingratiating herself to be as easy as it had been. The girl was looking at her, waiting to hear who she was and why she was there. 'I'm over here for a week or two, visiting friends. They're an elderly couple and, well to be honest, you can only take so much *Coronation Street*, so I thought I'd have a look around and see what the town has to offer in the way of night life.

'Wow, you're brave. Isn't she brave, Gabby? I couldn't walk into a pub on my own. Could you, Gabby? Could you just walk into a pub on your own?'

The first barmaid came over and leaned on the bar. Connie noticed that she'd changed out of her flats and had put on a pair of stiletto heels while they'd been talking. She smoothed down her mini skirt and was brushing at her hair with her hand. 'Shit no, I could never do that. You know what I'm like, Tina, I lack confidence, me.'

Connie laughed. 'All you have to do is hold your

head up high, stick your chest out and say, 'I'm as good as anybody else and if you don't like it, fuck the lot of you.' It's easy.' She smiled, looking at the girls so that she didn't come across as up herself. She had to play it just right. Be interesting enough that they wanted to talk to her, but not too over the top that she alienated herself. She moderated her language to their level. 'I'm Connie, by the way. I like it here. It's a good pub, has a nice feel to it,' she lied. There weren't many customers in the pub, it was still early. A couple in their fifties were the only people sitting at one of the tables, three men and two other women were drinking at the bar. 'I'll tell you what. I fancy a shot. Sambuca, I think. Will you join me? In fact, I'd like to buy everybody one.' It was risky. One, it drew a lot of attention to her, but then she had that cross to bear, anyway. But she didn't want to appear desperate enough to buy people's company. In a place like this, flash wouldn't get you anywhere, except maybe mugged.

The barmaid called Tina expertly lined up shot glasses and filled them with Sambuca. Gabby took a glass each to the couple sitting at the table who nodded their thanks to Connie. When Gabby returned, everybody at the bar counted one, two, three, and then knocked back their shots.

'You know something, you looked like a right snotty cow when you walked in but you're all right, you are.'

And that was all it took. She was accepted, an outsider, not even an acquaintance yet, but she was allowed into the bar under the heading of passing trade—with money—who was all right. The big test was if they'd still be prepared to talk to her when she ordered a Coke for her next drink and forewent the tip. She laughed it off by saying that two G&T's and a sambuka before nine o'clock was not a pace that she could keep up for long. She wasn't snubbed and the staff and locals peppered her with questions and wanted to know all about her. She bought another round at half ten and then the bar staff bought her a double. It didn't look as though he was coming in that night, which was just as well as she needed to have her wits about her when he did. She left the bar, drunk and very pleased with herself.

On Saturday night of the following week, she returned for the fourth time as she'd promised Gabby and Tina that she would.

'Hey Connie, what you having?' Gabby asked, before she'd even reached the bar. 'How's the head?' They had karaoke booked for that night. Connie remembered a girl called Julie who once liked Karaoke bars, but she would only get up and sing with her sisters. The hosts that night were fun and nice people. Like the bar staff, they introduced her to regulars as they came in and bullied her to get up and sing in a good-natured manner. And she found herself having a good time, but she never for one second lost sight of the purpose of her being there.

She was up singing a song when he walked in after

his shift finished at ten o'clock. The unfamiliar voice with the thick Spanish accent was what made him glance at the stage. She sang well, which was a rarity in The Pheasant and Duck. By ten, most of the patrons could barely stand, let alone sing. What made James Woods' mouth drop open was not the way she sang, but the way that she looked. Connie had spent a vast amount of money to look this well designed. She wasn't just good looking, she was extraordinarily good looking. She hadn't only bought her body; she'd bought confidence, class and sophistication, and wore them exquisitely. When Connie wanted a man to look at her, he did — without her having to make him.

James' head turned and with his mouth open he looked like a comical fool. It was only a momentary reaction before he resumed his pace and sauntered over to the bar to order his first pint of the ten that he would consume before either fighting his way out of the door, or being told to go home because they were closing. By the time Connie had finished her song and had returned to the bar, she knew that he had asked about her, and had been given the lowdown that she'd been in several times and was posh, but okay.

She walked to the bar amid applause and high fived with Gabby. 'Way to go, girl, you rocked that one.' She drained her gin, ordered another one and glanced up and down the bar.

She caught James' gaze and smiled at him. It was the smile that you would afford a stranger. '*Gracias*, Gabby, I'm going to sit down and rest my feet for ten minutes, see you in a bit.' She picked up her glass, turned towards James and smiled fleetingly at him a second time. He returned the smile.

She sat at an empty table, on a bench seat, beside a couple at the next table that she'd spoken to a few times. She turned her attention to two young girls who were murdering *True Blue* by Madonna. When they had finished, she applauded warmly.

Every man in the place had flirted with Connie and she had fended them off with grace and a friendly but disinterested manner. She gave off vibes of wanting to be friend to most, lover to none.

She passed a few words with Eddy and Maureen, sitting to her left. In her late fifties, Maureen was a few years younger than him. Eddy was a mouse of a man who wanted two things on a Saturday night—a pint and a quiet life. God knows, he didn't get them the rest of the week. His wife was nice enough to chat to, but Connie realised that spite and venom made up a good part of her blood supply. She was a gossip and had an opinion about everybody. Maureen was never self-obsessed in conversation. She had no interest in talking about herself, she wanted to talk about you, your life, your details, your bits of salacious scandal that she could later impart to a third person. At first glance, she appeared nothing more than a sweet, late middle-aged lady. As the conversation flowed, traits of weasel appeared in her eyes and along her brow line.

Barry Mosley took the mic. He was a large man in his early fifties, more fat than brawn, but his vanity told him otherwise. As a young man he probably had a good voice, but years of karaoke singing had taught him bar singer habits. He could carry a tune but his wail on words was painful to endure. He came over to Connie's table and serenaded her. Connie smiled politely until he was finished and then clapped his performance. As he turned to hand the microphone back to Sharon, Connie felt a dig in her ribs.

'I don't like him, do you?' Maureen had screwed up her nose in distaste. 'Thinks he's God's gift to women, he does.'

'Oh, he's all right, he's just having a good time,' Connie said.

'You won't get rid of him now, you watch.'

'Don't worry; I can soon put him back in his box if he oversteps the mark.'

'Yes, but I wouldn't encourage him too much, that's all.' As far as Connie was aware, she hadn't.

Sure enough, Barry strutted over. 'Connie, my darling, you look absolutely ravishing tonight, as always. Can I buy you a drink?'

Connie motioned to her almost full glass. 'No thanks, Barry. That's kind of you, but I'm okay for now. Thank you, though.'

'Come on now, just a little drink to make an old man happy.'

'Maybe later. Thank you,' she smiled.

'Go on, one drink.'

'No, thank you.'

'I'll have half a lager if you're buying, and he'll

have a pint of bitter,' Maureen said, gesturing her husband and leaning towards Barry.

He ignored Maureen and didn't even acknowledge that she'd spoken. His voice altered. 'I asked you to have a drink with me. I asked politely. Now, in England, where I come from, it's rude to refuse a polite request.'

'And I said no, thank you, just as politely, and in England, where I'm also originally from, it's rude to pester somebody who wants to be left in peace.' She smiled.

'She said no, Barry. Come away and leave her alone, you're making a dick of yourself,' Tina shouted from behind the bar.

He ignored Tina, too. 'You fucking whore.' Spit flew towards her face as Barry spoke. 'Think you're better than me, do you, with your fancy clothes and your money? Not good enough to buy you a drink, am I? Who the fuck do you think you are, coming in here as if you own the joint?'

Before Connie could answer, James Woods was behind Barry. 'Fuck off, Barry. You're getting out of line now, man. Come back to the bar before you upset the lady.'

Barry wheeled around and faced James, his cheeks reddening and anger twisting his mouth. 'And here's another one from the same stable. Another fucking rich bastard, who thinks they're something special just because they've got some money and a fancy job. I'll show you, you twat.' Barry swung his fist towards

James. James' reactions were fast and he caught Barry's fist before it came anywhere close to making contact. He used the other man's momentum against him and twisted Barry's arm high above his back and used it as leverage to walk him out of the pub where he threw him to the pavement and told him not to come back into the pub that night.

James came back in and walked over to Connie. 'Are you okay? I'm sorry about that; I hope it doesn't spoil the rest of your night.' If Connie didn't know him she'd have been impressed, thought him to be a gentleman. He hadn't used excessive force against Barry; he'd only exerted enough dominance to safely get him out of the pub. A far cry from the James she knew, who loved to flex his muscles whenever he got the chance, especially against his poor wife. 'Let me tell you about Barry,' he said, and he sat at her table.

'Oh, there's no need, honestly, it was nothing.'

He smiled and turned up the charm to the max. 'The thing is,' he continued, 'Barry's an all right bloke really. Worked hard all his life until a couple of years ago. He got made redundant from the ship yard. Then his wife left him for somebody with money. It's made him bitter, sensitive, you know?' Connie nodded. 'He's got a mile high chip on his shoulder about people that he perceives are judging him for being on benefits. Now he drinks to forget. He's a proud man. I hope he didn't upset you too much.'

'He didn't upset me at all. And thank you so much for coming to my rescue like that. Perhaps I could buy you a drink to thank you properly.' She gave him the benefit of her immaculate veneers and gazed at him in something that she hoped came across as her being impressed but falling just short of adoration. She had to give his ego something to work towards.

'I wouldn't hear of it. In England, where I come from,' he winked at her, 'ladies do not buy drinks for blokes. Same again? Or am I being too presumptuous?'

'Not at all, that'd be lovely, thanks.'

Chinese whispers at the bar were in full swing when Connie and James spent the next two drinks in each other's company. They were chatting animatedly and both of them laughed and flirted and played the game the way it was supposed to be played.

'And now,' Connie insisted, 'it really is my round.'

'Or,' James looked unsure of himself for the first time since he'd come over. 'Maybe we could go somewhere else. I know a nice bar,' he lowered his voice to a whisper, 'somewhere a lot nicer than this, only a few minutes away. It's a bit like being in a goldfish bowl in here.' He motioned his head towards Maureen who had spent the last half hour hanging on their every word. 'If we hurry we can make last orders.'

Connie agreed and he picked up their glasses to take them back to the bar and say goodnight. Maureen was in like a shot. 'Watch him, he's big trouble. You think Barry was bad, well he's a teddy bear compared to him.'

'Don't worry,' Connie whispered back. 'I've got his card marked.' She tapped the side of her nose and thought of Simon. He loved karaoke and she knew, with absolute certainty that she could never bring him to this bar. He would be laughed at and sniggered about. Simon would never fit in here, and while she'd had a good time and had surprised herself by having fun, neither did she. Connie waved goodbye as they walked out of the door. She wouldn't be back.

In the next pub, James took a sip of his pint and laughed. They were sitting in a secluded booth in a wine bar a few streets away from The Pheasant and Duck. 'Now promise me you won't take this the wrong way. Believe me, cheesy chat up lines are not my style. But you seem familiar and I can't work out why. I've come to the conclusion that you probably remind me of someone on the telly. Ah,' he blushed, 'told you it was cheesy.'

No, thought Connie, you haven't seen me on TV; you've told me in the past a hundred times that I'm ugly, in a hundred different ways, but that was another lifetime. She remembered the sting of his insults and wanted to smash his face in. She wanted to put him in a wheelchair. She wanted to see him bleed. She smiled. 'Do you know, you are a lovely, sweet man.'

The bar was open late and they talked about everything. The drink flowed freely and as he always had, James became a maudlin drunk. This was the stage before he became an obnoxious and violet drunk and she'd be long gone before then.

He told her about his financial worries. His salary was already generous without allowing for what he creamed off the top. But the more money he had, the more he spent, and the more of it he wasted on beer and women. He'd totted up some debts and he whined that his mother, rich beyond her needs, had refused to bail him out. He sank into his self pity, and if she had been a stranger thinking of taking him as a lover, he couldn't have been less appealing than at that moment. 'I just need to find a way of making some fast money,' he moaned.

Connie furrowed her brow as if in thought. He caught the look and it piqued his interest. 'What?' he asked.

'No, no, it's nothing. Ignore me, it's a stupid idea.'

'What? What is? Tell me.'

'It was nothing.'

'Come on now, you can't do that. You have something to say, then say it, don't fucking mess me about.' It was the first time that he'd let his guard slip and the James she knew peeped through his façade of being human.

'I can't tell you. It's one of the ways in which I've made my money in the past, but it's not exactly all above board. Please don't make me say any more.' She touched his forearm. 'I really like you, James, and I don't want you to think badly of me.'

She had him right by his unpleasant, nasty scrotum and she knew it. She could see him working through the possibilities—lap dancer, escort, whore.

His charm was back in place as though he'd straightened a tie. 'Connie.' He took her hand in his and stroked the back of it with his thumb as he spoke to her. 'There's nothing you could say that would make me think badly of you. I think you're an amazing woman. And now, you seem like an amazingly interesting woman. Don't you think one's secrets are an enormous turn on when they're shared with a stranger, such as myself, for instance?' He leered at her and she felt sick. 'Go on, tell me your dark secret, I dare you.'

Connie giggled and crossed her legs to tease him as she spoke. 'I am somewhat of an entrepreneur, back in Spain, and I admit, occasionally here in England, too, I have been responsible for organising,' she halted and took a sip of her drink, letting him see how nervous she was, saying without words that this was difficult for her, that she didn't normally discuss this kind of thing outside of her business circles. 'Promise me that this is strictly confidential. If word got out—' He nodded. 'I organise illegal bare knuckle fights for the top underground organisations in the world. It's made me a rich woman.'

He exhaled and let out the air with a whoosh. 'Fuc—good Lord, I didn't expect that. You are full of surprises, aren't you?' He dropped her hand and his came to rest on the top of her thigh. She gave him a moment and watched a range of emotions crossing his face. 'I want in.' he said.

Connie laughed. 'Out of the question. That's impossible. I'm sorry, I shouldn't have said anything. It was wrong of me. It's a fast way to make a lot of money and my mouth got ahead of me. Believe me, this isn't the way for you.' He'd moved her hair away from her shoulder as she talked and he'd leaned in and was kissing her neck. Connie felt as though a slug was crawling up her throat. She had to hold herself steady so that she didn't visibly recoil.

'We're made for each other, you and me. I knew it the second I saw you. You captivate me. You're the sexiest woman that I've ever laid eyes on. Think bad of you? Darling, what you've just told me has only inflamed my passion for you. You're like nobody in this backwater—Get me into a fight.'

She turned to face him and his wet mouth, stinking of beer, made contact with hers. He slobbered all over her. She wanted to knee him in the crotch. She retuned his kisses enthusiastically. 'I can't, you don't understand.' She was breathless from his kiss, her voice even more husky than normal. Even for an accomplished actress, this role would have been worthy of an Oscar. She felt repulsed by him. 'These men are animals. The fighter's I've got lined up for next Monday are the hardest men in the country. You'd get hurt and I've only just found you, I don't want to lose you now. Kiss me some more.'

He pulled away from her and his gaze toughened. 'I'm hard. I run this town, ask anybody.' He flexed his muscle and presented his biceps for her to feel. He was nothing if not predictable; she was right to attack through his vanity. 'I'm the hardest man around here.' He lowered his voice. 'I've been away for it, you know, in prison. Get me into a fight. I'll make you so proud of me.'

'Are you sure? It's a tough game.'

'I'm a tough man. Let me take you home and I'll show you the animal in me. I'll convince you that I'm all gentleman on the outside and caveman in the bedroom. Take me home, Connie. I want you so much.'

She convinced him that she wasn't that kind of girl. That he'd have to woo her first. She poured iced water on his ardour, raised his ego by telling him that she'd see what she could sort out, and arranged to meet him at five thirty on the following Monday. She told him that he needed to train in the three days left before the fights. She said that sex was definitely off the menu until after Monday, and that blue steak was the order of the day. She kissed him passionately before jumping in a taxi and speeding away. She needed to shower.

Chapter Thirty-three

He'd been training hard all weekend. He'd cut down on the drinking and had been eating lean red meat and drinking raw eggs for breakfast. He could have done with a couple of months to train and he'd had to make do with just two days, but hell, a good right hook is a good right hook and a killer instinct is something that you just have. No amount of gym hours or fancy sweatbands can teach you how to floor a guy with a single punch; it's something you are born with and James had it in abundance. He never wasted a single thought on the possibility that he wouldn't win any of the bouts that he would be entering. He was a lover, he was a fighter and he was a winner. Once he'd taken the purse for the tournament, he fully intended on a little post-fight work down in the bedroom with the lovely Connie. He was out to impress, it wasn't just about the money.

Jacob Lowther strode over to James and Connie. James didn't like the way the man's eyes travelled over her body when she wasn't looking. The way he saw it, this was his woman now and he didn't want any dirty bloody gypsies giving her the glad-eye. He had a low opinion of gypos: thieves and swindlers, the lot of them, fucking pikeys. They were a scourge on society, put on earth for the sole purpose of lowering the house prices of decent folk who paid their taxes. James forgot that he'd once been questioned over tax evasion and it was only the fact that his brother took the fall for the both of them that had kept him out of prison.

He didn't like the way Connie was talking to Jacob. They were discussing the evening and how it was organised. She seemed to have a high level of respect for the sewer rat. She laughed with him and they were familiar with each other. James put a protective arm around her shoulder and she glared at him and shrugged it off. He felt a familiar itch in the palms of his hands; he wanted to make them into fists. He wanted to smash the Gypsy man's face in. He didn't like the way they were talking as though he wasn't there. He didn't like being ignored.

The event was taking place in a warehouse deep in the maze of a disused retail park. Jacob had put a ban on people arriving in vehicles. He laid on buses to ferry people in from the town. The success of the evening relied on discretion. A ring was installed in the centre of the makeshift arena and there was no seating. Hundreds of people from the travelling community were expected to attend and it was standing room only. This was a big-money event and word had travelled fast. There were to be eight fights and James was competing in three of them. He didn't know that. He was expecting to work through the heats to finish overall champion of the night. It was arranged that he'd be taken down in the semi-finals.

Jacob turned to face him. 'So ye recon you can handle yourself, eh, sonny? It's a great honour for you to be here tonight. We don't normally allow Gorgas to our little soirees.' He laughed at his own joke.

James bristled. 'Don't call me sonny, old man. I could take you out any day of the week.' His hands were balled at his sides and he had an ugly snarl on his face. He took a step towards Jacob.

'Save yer energy for the ring, lad, I'm not going to cock fight with yer. The days when I had something to prove are long behind me.' Jacob and Connie shook hands and he indicated where James should go to get changed and prepare for his fight. He didn't offer his hand to James and James spat on the ground in his wake, the fury of being snubbed by a man he considered far beneath him, throbbed with the adrenaline in his blood.

As he came out to fight, the crowd parted. His opponent came from the other side of the ring and was back-patted and egged on by his community. James danced and air punched his way to the ring, sending up an array of cat calls and raucous laughter.

He wore red knee-length shorts and brand new red wrestling boots. He also had on a bright red, satin dressing gown with a white towel around his neck.

Charlie Mcmeakin, his opponent, wore only a pair of cut-off denim shorts and was barefoot.

James did a lap of the ring, punching the air and trying to stir the crowd to his favour. They laughed at him and jeered until the referee approached to go over the rules.

'Right lads, a three second count-in to start the bout. Two minutes. No biting, no eye gouging, no concealed weapons. A knockout or a surrender signals the end of the bout. If you get a knockout, you stand clear of your opponent and he'll be counted out for ten seconds. All clear?' Both men nodded.

'What the hell is that in yer gob, there, laddie?' the ref asked.

James removed his gum shield so that he could speak. 'Just a gum shield.'

'We don't use them here, boy, get rid of it.'

'Fuck off', said James. 'Have you any idea how much I've paid my orthodontist to get my teeth this straight?'

'Ah, let the poncey Gorga have it,' Charlie goaded. 'He's going to need it once I lay into him.'

James lunged for him and Charlie swung in retaliation. James ducked his head and Charlie had him in a headlock, swinging back his fist to hit him in the face before the bout even began.

'Separate, separate, you pair of bleedin' idiots. I've worked dog fights where the opponents had better manners. In your corners.' The ref broke the men up and sent them to their respective corners of the ring.

When he called them out to fight they came out angry. Charlie's pride was hurting him, knowing that he had to throw the fight and couldn't take the Gorga bastard down. Ten grand was a lot of money to the twenty-five year-old. His reputation meant a lot to him, but not ten grand, it was too much to turn down. He couldn't even get many decent digs in; he'd been told that they wanted the Gorga to go three bouts, so he had to keep him pretty. He had a pair of young'uns to bring up and money was tight. It was a hell of a lot of money to him but it was also a hell of a lot of pride to lose.

James came out with an axe to grind. He'd been in many a bar-brawl and this was no different to him. He got the first punch in. Charlie's lip split and he sprayed blood in an arc when he shook his head. He came back at James with a mild kidney punch. James felt his temper burst. He could give it out, but like all bullies, he didn't like to take it. The pain in his side made him see red and he felt the vessels burst in his eyes as his blood pressure rose and the last of his temper exploded. With a roar he tore at Charlie. He hit him with a barrage of punches and Charlie gave little in return. James was flying high. He'd beaten harder men in the local pub. This gypo had nothing about him. He hit him again, and again, and again. Charlie got him in a headlock and they circled the ring. James felt behind him and grabbed Charlie by the balls. He went onto his knees. James swung round and kicked him solidly in the face. He fell onto his back, out cold. The ref told him to break, but James ran forward and kicked the unconscious man hard in the kidneys. The crowd went mad baying for James' blood. It didn't follow the code of conduct to kick a man when he was down. They wanted him disqualified from the competition. The ref knew the score; he'd been bought off, too. He allowed James to qualify to the next round.

James cleaned up after the fight and joined Connie to watch the last contestants in the first round of heats.

He wasn't interested in watching the fighting. He didn't watch to see if the man he was taking on next was still to fight in this heat. He didn't study their strategy or think about his game plan. He was too cocky and convinced of his ability to win. He crowed like a peacock to Connie and she fed his ego, telling him how wonderful he'd been and how the other fella didn't know what had hit him.

The quarter-finals played out much the same way as the first round. James was an easy victor and came away high on his win. He had a split to his right eye that bled and obscured his vision. He was elated and barely even aware of the cut. He did a lap of the ring, skipping and waving his hands above his head. The crowd booed him off. There were several clear calls of 'fix' screamed at the ref, but James took no notice. He was a clear winner and these girl-fighters didn't like it. He crowed to Connie until he had to prepare for his next bout.

His third opponent was a lot smaller and lighter than him.

'Oh, for goodness sake, send me a man. At least let's make this some kind of sport.' He turned to his opponent whose fighting name was Terry 'The Bull' Terrier. 'You're going to get hurt, young man.'

'And if ah hadn't been telt to leave yer breathin. Yer'd be going hame in a coffin fer that kick yer give ter me cousin.'

The fight was about to start. James held out his hand to Terry but Terry snubbed him and spat at his feet before heading for his corner. The ref called him back. 'Shake hands, lad. We'll have a bit of sportsman-like behaviour here. So shake or be up for disqualification.' They shook and Terry glared into James' eyes.

When the ref's hand dropped, James came out fast. He was on the attack, his previous two bouts having made him bold. Terry had studied his opponent in his earlier matches. He knew his weaknesses and his strengths. It was going to be an easy take down, but he was in no rush. Let the crowd have some sport first.

James came at him with a right uppercut. Terry saw it coming and spun out of the way. He did a fast circle of James and could have got three punches in easily, but he didn't. James turned and struck at him again. Terry swerved passed him, ran up the corner post and did a back flip over James' head. The crowd went wild. Terry ran from diagonal corner to corner of the ring every time James came at him with a punch. He hadn't landed one yet, and Terry hadn't thrown one. James was tiring. His feet were stomping heavily on the canvas. He angry, which made him dangerous. Terry squatted to the floor, crossed his arms and did a Kossak dance. James panted, with his fists raised in defence, waiting for Terry to come to him. The bugger was fast.

Terry flew across the ring on his haunches and playfully bit James on the ankle before scurrying into the opposite corner. It was his trademark move and the crowd were pumped with excitement. It took James by surprise and, because he hadn't expected it, he yelped and jumped. The crowd knew that Terry would stop playing now. It was time to start the fight. James roared in fury and ran at Terry, clearly intending to kick him in the face. He was predictable; it's exactly what Terry knew he would do. James swung his leg and Terry rose and grabbed it as he ploughed the kick forward. He twisted James' leg and used it to overbalance him and James sprawled to the canvas. Terry backed away to allow him time to stand. When he was back on his feet he rested his hands on his knees, breathing heavily. Terry leap-frogged him from a squatting position.

'Shall I take him? Shall I take him?' he roared, turning to the crowd.

'Take him. Take him,' they took up the chant.

James was raging. The tendons stood out in his neck like bands and his temper had gone, leaving him out of control and dangerous.

Terry ran up the corner post and took a flying leap at James who was livid and had lost the plot. He landed on his opponent's back and stuck to him with his legs around his waist like a monkey. He leaned forward and pummelled James' face until it was hidden behind a mask of blood. James roared and bent over trying to dislodge his attacker. Terry pulled his feet in and ran up James' back to flip off, somersault, and come to a standing position facing him. He punched him once, twice, three times in the face. He followed with a roundhouse kick to the kidneys. 'That one's fer me cousin,' he yelled. James bent double and Terry kicked him one last time, full in the face. 'And that one's fer me.'

James' head came up with an arced curtain of blood surrounding it. His body followed the momentum of his head and he landed flat on his back in the ring. His skull made contact first with a crunch that bounced back up and then hit a second time. He was out cold.

Later, a stolen white Ford Transit van with false plates pulled up to the doors of Accident and Emergency at Lancaster General Hospital in a squeal of tyres. The back doors flew open and two men launched a third onto the pavement before the van screamed away.

The man, covered in blood on the ground, was barely alive.

Chapter Thirty-four

SP was sulking.

Ros said, 'Please don't drink too much tonight, love. You've been late for work three times this week and it doesn't set a good example for the staff.'

'Stop fucking nagging me, woman. Why shouldn't I have a drink after work? I'm here from first light until two or three o'clock. And let's face it, you're never there to warm my bed, these days.'

Ros had heard it all before, her voice had a sharp edge to it when she spoke. 'Eleven o'clock is hardly first light. And you only stay until the early hours because you're in the bar drinking with that maudlin brother of yours. It can't be much fun for either of you with all that self pity floating around in your whiskey glasses.'

'You never used to be a hard woman, Ros. You've changed.'

'Maybe it's all those nights spent babysitting your mother that's made me bitter. All I'm saying is don't sit up drinking all night with James. Get to bed early.'

'He's broken his neck, Ros. He's in a fucking wheelchair and might never walk again. I think that entitles him to be a little bit angry, don't you?'

'And there's something funny there, as well. Five men just decided to jump him for fun when he was on his way home. He's turned into a self-pitying alcoholic and he's dragging you along for the ride.'

'Oh, go to bed, woman. Leave me alone.'

SP dropped his key card onto the floor and nearly fell over trying to pick it up. It took three attempts to fit it in the slot and get into his room. He staggered to his bed and fell, fully clothed, flat on his back. Within minutes he was snoring.

The cold water brought him round. Somebody had thrown water over him. He felt funny. Not just drunk, but really odd. He couldn't focus, the room was spinning and swirling and twisting inside and outside of itself. Colours became shapes became sounds and he couldn't differentiate one from the other.

And that's when he saw her.

He had been chosen by the Lord God Almighty.

Just like Bernadette, he was a lowly servant, chosen from above to receive a visitation from the Virgin Mary.

She stood at the end of his bed dressed in black and had a golden halo shining above her head. She had chosen to appear to him in the form of an angel, partly extending her resplendent wings and golden dust shimmered in their loveliness. He wanted to get up and fall to his knees but he was paralysed, he couldn't move. He couldn't so much as swallow. He tried to ask her what her message for the world was, but he couldn't speak.

He felt an odd pressure being released on his upper arm. She spoke, but it was in Hebrew. SP instinctively knew that when he woke up the following morning, the message that she had given to him would be clear and he'd know what to tell the world. He was a prophet, just as his mother had always said.

The Virgin Mother walked onto his balcony. It was an uncomfortably hot and muggy night. He'd left his balcony doors open to cool his room so that he could sleep. He didn't see the Mother of God spread her winds and fly away, because he couldn't turn his head. The paralysis restrained him but he wasn't worried about it. He felt euphoric.

He didn't sleep again that night. He watched the magnificent light show that the Virgin had left for him. He was shown the stars right there in his room and all of the planets and the galaxies of God's wondrous creation. An extended tape measure appeared in a corner of the room with a giant apple balancing on the top of it. He watched a caterpillar crawling up the inches to fall back down to the ground before it ever reached the apple. It climbed many times before morphing into a herd of gazelle that ran across his walls and into his bathroom. His mouth had collected with saliva, but he was unable to swallow it. He worried that he would drown. He was aware of his throat, but it felt thick and closed and he had lost the reflex ability to swallow or cough. He dribbled down his chin.

The duck pond was in his bedroom and the beautification turned ugly. A little girl swam towards him and he could see that it was Vicki. She was covered in water weed. He panicked and the swirling colours on this walls turned dark green and deep purple and black. He consciously calmed himself, safe in the knowledge that the Divine Virgin of Virgins would never do anything bad to him. With that knowing, some orange and yellow crept onto the walls. And soon he was smiling, watching the traces of colour swirling from the Lampshades.

Ros found him in bed. After getting Violet up and helping her to dress, she came down early to make sure that her husband was up and had a clear enough head to work. The employees were gossiping about him and she had to stamp down on it before it reached the point of rebellion.

SP was on his bed, sleeping with his mouth open. He'd pissed himself and a wet, stinking stain spread on the quilt beneath him. The smell of urine, stale whiskey and unwashed body in the stifling room was overpowering. She was worried when she couldn't rouse him and went in search of James. His brother came into the room and wheeled himself up to the bed. After trying to wake him he said that he was fine and to leave him to sleep it off.

He appeared shame-faced and sheepish in his mother's quarters at four in the afternoon. He was freshly showered and looked well groomed. When he lifted his tea cup, Ros noticed a tremor to his hand, but otherwise, he seemed fine. Physically, anyway. He told his mother about the visitation from the Virgin Mary and implored her to interpret the vision. Violet fed his mania. She'd known all of her life that she was destined to be a vessel, carrying greatness. She rushed off to tell Clarissa Grainger about the miracle that had occurred in her very hotel. She decided, before she left, that a shrine would have to be built in an arbour on the side lawn, as a more appropriate place for The Mother of God to appear. She said that sooner or later, she'd be sure to catch Simon Peter in a state of undress and that would be most unfitting. Violet told SP that when the Virgin materialised again, he must ask her to appear in the summer house by the lake as a temporary measure, until she'd had the shrine built, and could she please come at a more appropriate hour. 'However,' she said, 'best to avoid three o'clock when the guests will be taking high tea on the lawns.'

Ros, couldn't bring herself to speak to her husband and went downstairs to continue doing SP's job, as she had been all day. When he appeared in the bar after dinner, James said that SP had flipped, and he poured him a large whiskey.

That night, she appeared again. This time, he woke as she stood by his bed. He felt a tightening on his upper arm and then a sharp prick. He was going to ask her what was happening, what she was doing to him, but a feeling of wellbeing washed over him, and shortly after that the colours came.

On the fifth night of her visitations, there was a thunder storm. The rain lashed outside his window. SP hadn't drunk nearly as much; he came to his room semi-sober. He ran to the balcony and shut the doors against the rain pelting onto his carpet. And he sat down in his winged armchair to wait. Since the first night, and after much ribbing, he'd stopped talking about the visitations. He'd made it to work on the second morning of Our Lady's personal appearances, but not the third or fourth. He was distracted, his concentration poor. He felt nauseous all day and his appetite was ruined. He had to be forced to eat. He had tremors, and towards the evenings he burned with a fever that he dulled with the help of whiskey.

That night he waited. She didn't come.

As the clock turned his condition worsened and he was delirious. He moved to his bed and crawled beneath the sheets. Within minutes they were soaked with sweat. SP lay shivering and burning until, instead of the Virgin Mary, the sickness and diarrhoea came to him.

Ros found him the following morning. His bed was covered in excrement and vomit. He was sodden with sweat and burned with a fever. He told her that he was dying. He asked repeatedly what was wrong with him. Ros hated him as she helped him into the shower and turned the hose on him. Her cheeks burned with shame as she took his soiled sheets and fastened them in rubbish sacks to go in the refuse. She dealt with it, while he lay in bed feeling sorry for himself.

She fed him weak broth and rang for the family doctor. He asked if SP had taken anything. She assured him that he hadn't. Ros told him about the whiskey that he and his brother were consuming nightly. The doctor knew addiction when he saw it and this wasn't just alcohol. He suspected heroin, but took a blood test and kept his mouth shut until he knew for sure.

That night she came.

Ros missed her by seconds. She was going backwards and forwards between Violet and her husband's room and was exhausted. She had settled Violet and wanted to sit with SP for a couple of hours before morning. When she went to him, the tremors had stopped, the fever was broken. He had a smile on his face— and he was out of it.

A needle hung out of his arm, its plunger spent, and a drop of blood had settled in the carriage. The tourniquet was still fastened to his upper arm. Ros sank to her knees and cried.

When Connie had first come back from Spain she'd done her homework. Her research made her angry. Phil had remarried four years ago. He had two sons, Thomas, three, and the baby, Oliver, who was just a few months old. She followed him, watched him, stalked him. He was happy. His wife was a mouse, pretty enough in her own way, carrying some baby weight. His children seemed happy, too, but then, to the outside world, so had Vicki.

Sometimes she thought about taking the two boys. She fantasised about taking them with her to Spain and keeping them for her own. At other times, in her darkest hours, she imagined killing them, the way that her Vicki had been killed, watching them drown, and knowing that Phil would suffer. The sins of the father shall be visited upon the son a thousand times.

But Vicki had been an innocent child, just as those

two boys were. They had done nothing to deserve vengeance. They were beautiful boys. Connie felt as though she came to know them. She watched them playing, listened to Thomas' games and saw Vicki's features in their faces. One day, Thomas pretended that he was a spaceman and walked up and down his garden as though he was walking on the moon. She could picture Phil, the first time the little boy had shown an interest in space travel. He would have lectured the boy, forced him to look at pictures and documentaries beyond his years. But he hadn't killed the child's love of space, or his imagination—yet. Connie would not hurt their father through the boys.

She considered all of the things that she had done to date. Two men were dead and another one in a wheelchair. John and Andrew wouldn't be dead if it hadn't been for her involvement. But she hadn't killed them, she hadn't put James in the wheelchair, he had done that himself. His vanity put him there; all she had done was presented him with an idea. He took it. He ran with it. He'd wanted it and welcomed it.

John's greed and Andrew's loose lifestyle had led to their deaths. She felt only a small responsibility for them. They both could have turned away from their choices and could have altered their ways. They chose not to. Therefore whoever resists the authorities resists what God has appointed, and those who resist will incur judgment.

It was true that she had made SP a heroin addict. She had assaulted him while he slept and pushed the needles into his veins without his consent. She regretted that. She would rather have had him accept it through choice, as the other's had chosen their paths. But she had righted that by giving him choice on her final visit. It was only a very new addiction and could be cured with a short period of rehabilitation. He could have easily put it right. On the fifth and final time, after injecting him with heroin, she left his next needle, filled and ready for use, on the dressing table, beside it she left an appointment card for a five day detox in a private clinic that she'd pre-paid for. All he had to do was ignore that needle and turn up for the appointment.

But he was weak.

SP knew when he saw the syringe that his visitations weren't from the Virgin Mary. He had been so fucking stupid. He thought Ros had done it to him. Somebody had. He rang the clinic, was told that a lady had booked the appointment with a credit card. The name was false and the card led to a dead end and was untraceable.

He knew what he was doing when he depressed the plunger. He was a weak man. He yearned for the pretty colours. Six months earlier, a member of his staff had been sacked for drug use on the premises. He went through the hotel staff records to hunt him down. The junkie became SP's supplier.

A month later SP admitted that he was unfit for work. He couldn't hold down his job. His wealth meant that his addiction had grown fast and he spent almost all of his waking hours incapacitated. He was unwashed and dirty. He kept himself away from the public areas and avoided the guests.

Philip was called to run the hotel, but he wasn't up to the job. It was decided that he shouldn't give up his own job to run the hotel further into the ground.

For the first time since the family had taken the Halcyon Woods Hotel, Ros had to hire an outsider as hotel manager. The empire had crumbled and was on its knees. James still oversaw the running of the kitchen from his wheelchair, but he only went in a couple of times a day and yelled at everybody for five minutes. The Empire was a damaged wreck, and Violet's ducklings we no longer in charge.

Chapter Thirty-five

He was working the back shift, from three till eleven. She'd watched him leave home at two-thirty on Monday, Tuesday and Wednesday. He returned each of those nights at 23:18. He had moved from the old house, from *her* house, and he'd bought a much bigger detached property with stables for his new wife's horses and large gardens, on the Roan Head road. It suited Connie's purpose well.

The road he came along on his return from work was little more than a country lane. There were no street lights and traffic after eleven o'clock at night was light. She paid a visit to her old gypsy friend Jacob. Money changed hands, and for this business venture they would use Wilfred because he ran faster than his brother, Junior.

Consuela Vengarse walked along the secluded road. She had a kitbag of expensive photographic equipment and a high-end Cannon on a webbing strap around her neck. In this incarnation, she was a keen and accomplished photographer, commissioned to take scenic shots for *Country Life Magazine*. At her studio she had easels set up with arty prints to confirm her story should she ever find herself entertaining there. In reality, every photograph that she'd ever taken had its subjects decapitated or out of focus.

At eleven fifteen, a man jumped out of bushes at the roadside and grabbed her. They were beside a gate leading into a field of cows. He rammed her into it and brought his body up against her. He had three day's growth and kissed her brutally to ensure that she had swollen lips and an inflamed stubble rash when she was rescued. He pulled at her top, tearing open the zipper on her fleece and ripping apart her blouse. Two buttons flew off as he exposed her cleavage and lacy, teal-coloured bra. 'Nice,' he murmured, before burying his coarse lips into her breasts and neck. He sucked her flesh until it bruised and left marks on her arms where he mauled her.

She smiled when she felt his erection. 'Pull the camera strap around my neck and twist it tight.'

He stopped groping her. 'Missus, I'm good with all the kisssin' and the cuddlin'. Hell, I'm enjoying that, but I don't hurt women. Never have, never will—'

They heard a car. She pulled one arm free and struggled wildly. He fastened his mouth back on hers and kissed her brutally. Then he moved his mouth to her neck leaving her free to scream. She thrashed and screamed twice, once as the car approached and once when it was level with them.

Before it had a chance to stop, the attacker broke away and ran down the road, pumping his arms and legs as he went, to cover ground fast. Consuela, weak in the legs, wilted to the floor and sobbed as the car screeched to a stop and a man ran towards her.

'Are you all right?' He knelt beside her and she turned tear-stained eyes towards him and nodded. The tears were genuine. In the time between Wilfred running away and Phil stopping the car, she had tightened the camera strap around her neck and strangled herself. It had only been for a few seconds, but she'd been aggressive and was sure that it would bruise. The inside of her throat was raw. She'd bitten her lip at the same time and it bled. When Connie made eye-contact with her ex-husband for the first time in ten years, she almost lost control of the hatred and had to suffocate the need to kill him.

'Can you stand?' he helped her to her feet, but she made no attempt to move. 'Stay there, I've got a blanket in the car.'

'Don't leave me,' she screeched, terror in her voice.

'Okay, okay, I'm here. I won't leave you.'

She flung herself into his arms. Her blouse was open and her exposed cleavage pressed against his chest. He might be a loyal man and faithful to his wife, but she knew his body would respond. He was, after all, addicted to sex.

Because of her surgery she was unrecognisable, but he had altered remarkably little. Time had been good to him and she was repulsed to find that he was like a memory foam mattress that fitted against her perfectly. He looked the same, smelled the same. She was sobbing into his neck and she could feel his heartbeat through his shirt. She moved her body to the side as though she'd been suffocating in his neck and her breast pressed against his arm with each inhalation. She had fucked this man a thousand times and knew how to arouse him. That was all that she needed, for now.

'Thank you. You saved my life.'

He laughed. 'Anybody would have done the same.' She remembered he'd used the same line the first time that he'd rescued her from danger, on the day they met. 'I live just down the road. Don't worry, my wife's in. It's perfectly safe. She'll look after you and then we can call the police and get you to the hospital to be checked over.'

She smiled at him. 'I've been enough of a nuisance already, I'm okay now. It was just the initial shock. I'm not badly hurt, just bruised. I can walk home now. Thank you.'

'Rubbish, you can't walk home on this lonely road in the dark. What if he comes back to finish what he started? I don't want to scare you, love, but you've got a nasty bruise on your neck. At least let me take you to A&E. I can have you there in five minutes.' Hero on the outside, bastard within.

She fingered her throat and winced, it was agony and when she spoke her naturally husky voice was raspy and hoarse. 'I don't want to be any trouble.'

'It's no trouble, my dear,' he said, his hand already under her elbow. He helped her to her feet and guided her to the car. 'I'll ring my wife from the hospital to let her know what's happening.'

His phone rang. 'Hello. Yes—something's come up. I'll ring you back in a few minutes and tell you all about it, darling. Yes. Put it in the oven and I'll have it when I get back. Won't be long. Yes. Yes. Love you, too.' He made pathetic kissing noises. He had never done that with her. Bastard. He was close with the new wife. Connie had known that. He seemed to be in love with her. Getting her ex-husband into bed again wasn't going to be easy, but at least he made the next part simple. She didn't even have to play up to him.

After being examined by the doctor and filling a prescription for painkillers at the pharmacy, Phil insisted on driving her home from the hospital. He explained that he'd rung his wife while she was being seen by the doctor and he'd brought her up to speed on what was happening.

He guided her into the passenger seat and she gave him directions to the flat that she'd rented for the times she stayed in England. This was the first of the brothers, except Simon, that she'd had in her home and she hated opening her front door to him, but it was necessary. He didn't suggest buying brandy for the shock, so she suggested it even though she had a bottle of Courvoisier Brandy in her small bar. It was a calculated move. She wanted to recreate their first meeting of twenty years earlier, though this time she had lead crystal glasses instead of chipped Easter bunny mugs.

When they arrived, he didn't take over or put her to bed as he had done the first time. He was intimidated by her and her surroundings. He was uncomfortable and his manner was completely different than had been with Julie.

She poured their drinks and excused herself to change in the bedroom. She contemplated lingerie, but Phil was already squirming and she didn't want to frighten him off. She opted for a skirt that finished respectably just above the knee and a simple fitted T-shirt. He'd already had a good look at her bra so she did away with it. She checked her appearance in the mirror to ensure that the T-shirt wasn't overtly sexual—she was aiming for irresistible, not slutty. The seduction, when it came, had to be his idea. No matter how much he was the loyal and faithful husband, she would see to it that he came to her willingly. Before returning to him she gave her nipples a tweak. She had paid a lot for them; it was about time they earned their keep. She ensured that they were prominent enough to get his attention.

She offered him another drink when she noticed his glass was empty. He was driving and although she tried to tempt him he would only have a soft drink. Sitting next to him would have been too obvious, so she took the armchair facing him. She crossed her legs slowly and made sure that he got a flash of thigh. Her skirt had ridden up when she sat down so she pulled at it modestly, but it was trapped beneath her and sat at mid-thigh. While his eyes were fixed on her, she pulled at the barrette holding her hair in a loose bun. Her black hair fell in long curls to frame her face and spill over her shoulders. He cleared his throat and crossed his legs.

She pandered to his ego and cooed about how he'd rescued her from the clutches of death. 'You were so brave; I can't believe you came along just when I needed you. Like a knight in shining armour,' she laughed beautifully. 'I can never repay you. But I need to think of something to show you my appreciation. In Spain it is a matter of honour to refund kindness when it is given to you.' She made sure that this was implied as a financial proposition rather than a sexual one.

'Oh, honestly, there's really no need. In fact, this isn't the first time I've come to the aid of a damsel in distress, so to speak,' he laughed. 'I once threw a pint over a young lady in a restaurant who had spilled a bowl of boiling hot pasta all over her. It could have been nasty otherwise. She'd have been scarred for life. I'm a first aider you see, so I knew exactly what to do.'

'Really? How fascinating. Was she all right?'

'Yes, thanks to my quick thinking she was perfectly unharmed. In fact, I married her.'

'Oh, it was your wife.'

'Not this one. I've been married twice,' he blushed. 'Danielle's my second wife. Second time lucky, eh?'

'Do they? I thought it was third.' She gave him a coquettish smile. 'So was the first one a demon, then?'

He laughed, pleased with the description of his first wife. 'Oh, I wouldn't necessarily go that far, but she was highly strung, let's put it that way.'

'You don't miss her, then?'

'Cor, hardly. Danni's ten times the woman that she was.' He looked her straight in the eye, 'We're very happy.'

She changed the subject. 'So what do you do for work, Philip?'

'Please, call my Phil. My mother's the only person who calls me Philip and, trust me, you are nothing like her.' He laughed again, flirting. 'I'm an HR manager for a large car manufacturer.'

'Impressive. Do you like it?'

He sat back, relaxed. He always did like talking about himself. 'I used to. I worked my way up from the shop floor. Took this particular position about nine years ago. But I'm bored of it now. I've taken it as far as I can go. I'm at the top of the ladder in this company, and to improve my status I'd have to leave and go somewhere else. That would be too much of a gamble. You know what it's like, the pay's good and I'm comfortable. I can provide well for my family and although the company shows me no personal appreciation, my salary reflects that I'm valued.'

'Sounds grim. But if all the circumstances were correct, you'd love a new challenge?'

'Oh God, yes. I used to go into work every single day with such a buzz from doing a good job, but now it's just work. I'd love something to get my teeth into, but I'll stay where I am and plod along, probably until the day I retire.'

'You've got twenty good years in you yet. Could you really stand that?'

'I'll probably take an early retirement option when it's offered. If the payout is good enough.'

'Interesting.' She went quiet and ran a manicured fingernail around the rim of her glass. She caressed the bowl of the snifter, then slowly wanked the stem. She made love to the brandy glass with her fingertips, feigning distraction, knowing full well that he was thinking about sex. He was thinking about having sex with her.

'Well, I'd better be going, I suppose. Danni will be wondering where I've got to.'

'Will she have waited up for you? She must love you very much.'

He laughed again. 'And I love her very much. I doubt she'll have waited up, it is very late now, but she's a light sleeper and she won't settle properly until she knows I'm home safe.'

It was now or never. She stopped fingering the glass and went in for the kill. 'Give me just five more minutes of your time. I have a business proposition for you, which I think you'd be a fool to turn down.' He'd listen and he'd accept. He wouldn't want to be seen to be a fool in her eyes.

'I own a large company. I am based primarily in Spain, just outside Barcelona to be exact. However, I have eleven subsidiary businesses here in England. I'm constantly flying over from Spain to oversee them. I have been on the lookout for a trustworthy businessman to run my British operation. It's a big deal. Do you think you would be up to it?'

'Me? Wha—are you offering me a job?'

'No, I'm a businesswoman, Phil, not a fool. I'm offering you an opportunity to apply for a job. And not just any job. A massive job. So I repeat, are you up to it?'

'Yes. Yes of course I am. I have almost twenty years in managerial experience. I've—'

'Save it for your CV. As you say, it's late. She took a

pen and paper from her writing desk and scribbled down an email address and mobile number. 'Here. Email me your CV. I need two references and I want you to write down why I should hire you. Why are you the best man for my operation?'

'I'm very flattered, thank you. But I don't know.'

'What are you earning?'

'A hundred and ten thousand, plus a new car on contract, every two years.'

'If you are the right man to run my office, it pays a hundred and sixty and, within reason, your choice of car, not on contract. I'll replace it every five years, and you get to keep the old one.'

'Why would you do that for me?'

'Because, you possibly saved my life, Philip. I told you, in my country that is a debt of honour. But you haven't got the job yet. You still have to prove yourself worthy. This is the job of a lifetime, Phil. Don't let it pass you by.' She had led him towards the door. She extended her hand for him to shake. Instead he took it and kissed the back, maintaining eye contact with her the whole time.'

She was in business mode. She didn't flirt with him. She wanted him to go away thinking about her offer first, and sex second. But she knew that when he got home to his wife, he'd wake her and force her into hard sex, and she knew, with one hundred percent certainty, that in his imagination his cock would be pounding an exotic Spanish woman called Consuela, not his mumsy wife.

Chapter Thirty-six

Things moved quickly. Faster and better than she could ever have hoped for. While Phil was serving his months' notice, she had set up the business ready for him to walk into. She spent her weekend's barbequing with Philip and Danielle. The second time that they invited her to the house, Philip told her that his mother, two brothers and their families would be coming. Consuela said that she was looking forward to it, but when the day came, she had unfortunate and unavoidable business that took her away from the country for the weekend. She knew that she would be discussed at the gathering and hoped that not too much was made of her nationality. But she felt safe because SP had never spoken to his vision. She hoped that, in moments of lessened clarity, he still thought that she was the Virgin Mary, or that she had been a figment of his imagination and that he'd been spiked with the heroin by somebody unknown. James had met a Spanish gangster's moll, a far cry from the high flying business woman who Phil would be working for.

Far from a simpering mother, she found Danielle to be likeable. The women were friends and Consuela was truly sorry that she was going to have to hurt the woman. She liked her, but in taking down her ex-husband sacrifices had to be made. His boys were sweet. Thomas could be a sulker, and petulant like his father, but he was mostly a good kid. Oliver was just a little sweetheart and loved his Auntie Con-con. On the third weekend, when it was just the five of them, Connie wished that she could have brought Simon. He would have got a buzz out of it and would have loved playing with the two boys. Phil was the only one of the Woods' brothers who knew about Simon. He'd seen him going from the bus to his school once. Connie had read about it in his diaries. Phil had written that Simon was ugly and stupid, 'Deeply entrenched in his disgusting mongolism,' he'd said. Connie wanted to kick him in the balls just for that one statement.

The office set up, went well. She rented property in a designer complex with air conditioning and plate glass windows. She had eleven subsidiary branches of Victoria's Kitchen in England. She was shutting three of them, they weren't doing well and she brought over enough of their business to make the Barrow office appear valid. It was Connie's idea to give Danielle a job. She took her on as receptionist from ten until three Monday to Friday, with total flexibility for illness and school holidays. She was generous and gave her a twelve grand a year salary with no deductions for time taken off for necessary child care.

As Philip was officially her Head of Operations, they interviewed for the rest of their staff together. Phil surprised her. She had wanted to take on a plain woman of dim intelligence to be his PA. He fought her bitterly and said that he wouldn't be able to work with a woman like that. Connie gave her reasons for wanting to hire her. She said that she was likely to be honest and that she seemed reliable. Her references were adequate. Phil said that she had no drive. He fought her to hire a man in his late twenties called Max Oaks. Phil said that he had drive, ambition and balls. He felt that he could work with him and said that even his name sounded steadfast and reliable. He stood up to her, wouldn't back down and backed his horse well. She was impressed. Max was exactly the man that she would have taken on had she been hiring for real. To complete their staff, they hired a general assistant who would be responsible for all the mundane admin and odd jobs. She was an ordinary girl, more than capable of the job, called Debra Thomas. Their team was established.

The surprises didn't stop there. In his first week Phil insisted on going in person to meet with all the staff at the three factories that he would be brining up from their knees. Connie hadn't anticipated this. It was too close for comfort and too close to home, but Phil was determined to do a good job. He came back from his week away brimful of ideas. Most of them were good ones and Connie had a new found grudging respect for the way that the man did business. If things had been different, if he had seen her potential when they were together, and if she had seen his, they could have been formidable in the business world. His aptitude and enthusiasm only made the thought of bringing him down sweeter.

In the ten years since she'd seen him, time hadn't been too hard on him. He'd spread a little across the middle and he had some greying at the temples, but he still had a head of predominantly black hair. Whereas she had grown four whole inches, he was still short. She had had her legs broken in Russia and rods inserted and grafted into the bone to gradually, over six painful months; lengthen her legs so increasing her overall height. Philip's stature remained the same. He still wore white sports socks that had, and still did, infuriate her. She remembered having sex with him and staring at the socks, still on his feet as he hammered into her. She remembered the white socks with sandals when they had been abroad. She remembered his small cock and the way he'd sweat all over her, dripping perspiration from his forehead into her eyes, stinging them and making her ball her fists and prop them under her backside to stop her from punching him while he rode her. She remembered all this while she watched him at his desk in his crisp white shirt.

While his wife was mere yards away at the reception desk in the foyer, she'd flirt with him. There were days when his hard on would almost be lifting his desk. She knew him, she knew how to lean over him, how to display her body when she was reaching for something. She knew how to accidentally brush against him in passing and how to innocently insert images, ideas and fantasies into his brain. And she knew that he got off on thinking about having sex with Consuela while is wife was working in sweet oblivion. She tortured his imagination.

The office was only ever going to be in operation for one month. It was a shame, given time Phil and Max could have turned all three of the failing businesses around. They worked well together and Phil was hard to the point of brutal in implementing changes and making things work.

They had been working together for three weeks and they had known each other coming up eight weeks when Connie told Phil that she needed him to accompany her on a trip to Spain. Danielle was the needy type, she didn't like him being away from home, she sulked for a while until Connie promised that she would take very good care of him and that, if they got on with the job and made good time, he might only be away for a couple of days. Connie knew it would be a week.

Danni drove them to the airport and cried when she waved Phil away. Despite leaving his wife in tears Phil was in good humour. She knew that he liked travelling; they'd done enough of it together. They had fond memories of Barcelona. He was more than happy to have a working holiday away from his family. On the plane, he was in excellent mood and when the drinks trolley came around they ordered two whiskey and cokes each, all on company expenses. They travelled First Class and had plenty of leg room to stretch out. After the excellent in-flight meal, Connie feigned sleepiness and dosed as the plane prepared for descent. As she pretended to sleep she let her head fall onto Phil's shoulder and was mildly surprised when he allowed it to rest there. Through slitted lids, she saw him peer down her top and when she nuzzled contentedly into his body she saw the definition of his erection through his suit pants.

When they came into land, Phil woke her gently. She pretended embarrassment for resting on him and he gallantly swept her apology away. Max had booked them into single rooms in the Hotel Omm. Connie manipulated him into believing that it was his idea that they stay instead at her villa. It would be less awkward if they needed to work late into the night, or very early in the day. It was more convenient geographically to the hub of her enterprise. They could eat when they wanted to and not be disturbed by other diners. All ideas that she had insinuated into his head but that he thought he had come up with. He rang Danni as soon as they dropped their cases in their rooms to let her know about the new arrangements. Connie had expected fireworks, but Danni trusted her husband and she accepted the changes without complaint. Her beef was that he was away from home, who he was away with was never an issue.

They freshened up by taking turns to use the shower room. Connie went first because she couldn't bare the thought of stepping into the shower immediately after Phil had been in there. He would almost certainly masturbate under the hot water and the thought of it turned her stomach. They were working from home that afternoon. Connie had arranged meetings at some of her plants for the following day and throughout the week. The blistering temperatures suited her purpose well. She wore a gold bikini with a sheer kaftan over it to work in. The kaftan was see through and covered nothing, but it did add titillation to the effect. She had long since lost the need for sun cream, she had a Mediterranean tone and her skin had adjusted to the Spanish sun, but she wanted to evoke memories. She used the same coconut sun cream that she had when they were together. She knew that the smell of it turned him on. In Ibiza, on their fourth wedding anniversary, he had bought her a perfume that was branded especially for the island. It was cheap; nothing like what she wore now, but it was a scent that he associated heavily with sex. She'd had some delivered to use that week. She pulled her mane of thick black hair into a single plait that left her shoulders bare. She intended to spend the afternoon driving him insane.

Her housekeeper and cook, Anita Castillo, had been given her hours for the following week. When Connie was in England, Anita came in regularly to water the pants and clean the villa and when Connie was home, they worked her hours accordingly. Anita produced a fantastic lunch of grilled salmon with a light salad and baked potatoes. Desert was fresh fruit, much of it from Connie's own garden. They washed their meal down with a bottle of La Rioja Alta.

She worked him hard in the brutal sun from one until four. She had had one glass of wine, he had drunk three. The effects of the alcohol told on him and she could see him striving to maintain a professional demeanour. He wore shorts and a t-shirt and he was quickly covered in a sheen of perspiration, his shirt stained with wet dark patches. He repulsed her. The office was fully air conditioned but the windows were open and the scent of mimosa and oleander came in with the sun's heat. She was brusque and businesslike as she swished around the office and his eyes followed her like a hungry predator.

At four, she suggested that they take a break. She called for Anita to bring them iced tea on the terrace and they went out into the sun. He complimented her on the garden as they sat in comfy furniture beside an oak table. She never tired of looking at her garden; every week there was something new to see throughout the year. The bougainvillea covered the back of the villa and trailing Wisteria hung in grape like bunches of blooms over a trellised arbour that led to the pool. Rich scents hung in the air and the colours were magnificent. She was truly blessed. She only needed two more things to make her life perfect. She needed to avenge the death of her daughter, and she needed to have Simon out here with her for at least part of the year. When they talked about her garden, he mentioned that his first wife had been a keen gardener.

They sipped their tea and relaxed in the afternoon haze when, without a word, Connie rose and took off her kaftan. She let if fall to the chair in a shimmer of gauze and stood before him in just a skimpy bikini.

'Come on then,' she said in invitation before leading the way to the pool. She stood on the edge and gracefully dove in. She had surfaced from under water by the time he had made the edge of the pool and had got rid of his pathetic sandals, white socks and wet shirt. He dove in quickly and without elegance, but not before she'd see the bulge in his shorts and not before he'd seen her rise with her nipples erect and goose pimples on her breasts from the cool contrast of the pool against the afternoon heat.

She swam underwater and came up to playfully duck him. They swam and frolicked in the water, both of them laughing like children. She remembered past times of playing in pools with Vicki and she wanted to hold his head underneath the water and watch the bastard die.

She ensured that there was plenty of skin on skin contact. At one point she came up in front of him and he grabbed her roughly. His face was inches from hers, water dripping from his fringe. He was going to kiss her. His head moved in towards her. She opened her mouth a touch and then in the second before their lips met, she splashed him with water and swam away. It was too soon. They would kiss, he would be eaten with guilt and remorse, and that would be it. When Connie took Philip Woods to bed again she wanted him good and ripe to explode so that there could be no going back.

She pretended that she hadn't been aware of his intentions. She played with him in the pool as though nothing had happened. The next time she floated up behind him. She wrapped her legs around his body before pushing him under water and swimming a length of the pool with him without either of them coming up for air. At the deep end they rose against the edge. To get to the ladder she had to pass in front of him, she could have swum clear but she clung to the edge taking her hand across his body to grab again on the other side of him. Her knee came up with the buoyancy in the water and brushed gently against the front of his shorts. His cock was like iron and stuck straight out in front of him. Her fingers travelled across his chest, a red talon grazing his nipple as she transferred from one side of him to the other in the deep water. The touch had been nothing more than a brush, but when her leg made contact with his cock, he gasped, and when the pressure was lifted, he groaned, unable to stop himself. She was satisfied with this opening gambit and swam to the ladder. As she pulled herself out of the pool, the water cascaded off her body in pearl droplets against the barrier of the sun cream. The weight of the water captured in her bikini bottoms pulled them down slightly showing him that she had no tan lines at all. If he noticed her perfect scarring, he never made comment. He stayed in the pool. When he joined her back in the office, he was calm and in control of himself. She knew that he'd ejaculated. She'd been with him almost ten years; she knew that when he was horny nothing would calm him until he'd had sexual release. She only hoped that he'd gone to his room to do it and hadn't contaminated her water. He was freshly showered and dressed in a clean shirt and shorts. They worked steadily until dinner time.

Dinner was served at eight. They ate fresh fish with vegetables followed by a dessert of mangos in a light torte. Their wine selection included a vintage Marques de Caseres, followed by sangria on the terrace and ending the night with vodka and brandy. They stayed up late and talked about work, about family and life. He'd changed a lot. He was a better man, but she still hated the man that he'd been and Vicki hadn't been offered any second chances, why should he be? She was going to destroy him. They were both drunk. When he kissed her goodnight she allowed him to kiss her on the lips, not on each cheek as would be normal. She let his lips press against hers for a fraction of a second longer than was polite, before she was the one to pull away. He dropped his hands quickly to cover the inevitable erection.

The next morning he was all business. She knew from the efficient way that he spoke to her, that the kiss was at the forefront of his mind. He felt guilty. Since kissing her on the mouth, he would have blown sweet kisses down the phone to his wife.

They had a busy day. She listened to what Phil had to say. The meetings were pure staging, the trip a fabrication; she didn't need him out there. But as with the business in England, a lot of what he had to say made sense. She saw ways of cutting costs and increasing productivity without alienating her workforce, who she greatly valued and treated well in return for loyal employment. She intended to use some of Phil's suggestions going forward.

That night, after returning to the villa to shower and change, they went out. Connie took him to an excellent Cantonese restaurant and then they went bar-hopping before falling into a club and dancing until the early hours. Connie kept fit with Zumba DVD's. She wasn't fanatic about them, but once or twice a week, she found it a great release of work tension to dance to them. She was lithe and danced well. She was sexy without being slutty, outstanding without being exhibitionist and Philip strutted like a king dancing next to her. Every man's eyes in the room were on the woman that he was out with. Connie doubted that he thought about his wife once.

When the music slowed he took her in his arms and they swayed into a rhythmic waltz. After a few bars she dropped his hand and let her arms slide around his neck. She pressed her body against the length of his. Hello, how did I know you'd be there? She swayed her hips left to right, with each sway her pelvis brushed against his cock. Her head was against his shoulder and she sang softly in Spanish as they danced. She was driving him wild and his breath, hot against her ear, was raspy and uneven. He was drunk. His inhibitions were compromised with alcohol and his feeling of well being. She hadn't pushed him away and he was being led by his cock. He didn't try to hide his hard on. He knew that she'd felt it and he knew, at this point, that he was being played with; he was just powerless to resist.

As they danced he was bolder. He let his hands drop from her waist to her bottom. When she didn't resist he increased the pressure under his hands and pulled her in to him while thrusting his pelvis into her body. They wore thin clothing, she a sun dress with no bra and only a tiny thong, him a pair of linen trousers and a dress shirt. She was aware of every vein and contour of his cock as it thrust against her. She maintained the rhythm of her dance while he dry humped her on the dance floor. His breath was in full sexual flow, he moaned twice when his sensitive glans rubbed against her pubic bone. He even dropped a couple of disgustingly wet kisses onto her neck. The dirty bastard was going to come in his shorts if she didn't pull away. Luckily, for her the song came to an end before he did. 'I think we'd better go and get a drink to cool down,' she muttered into his ear.

'Oh just one more dance,' he whined.

Just one more molestation was closer to the mark. 'I think we've had too much alcohol,' she laughed. 'We need a soft drink to allow the—er mood to soften, don't you think?'

He looked up at her and blushed. She was cool and perfectly in control of herself. He was erect, hot, sweating and on the point of losing his load in his pants. He managed to gain some control as they walked to the bar. His erection dwindled and he wiped his sweaty face with a hanky. But his mind and his imagination were still turgid, she knew that. Danni was the last thing on his mind and on that second night, she could have had him if she'd wanted to. She didn't, not yet.

He tried to paw her at the bar, in the taxi on the way home and in the living room when they arrived back at the villa. She laughed him off, continuing to flirt with him while keeping the mood light, and him at arms length.

The following morning he arrived at breakfast shamefaced and sheepish. She was the first to speak. She touched his arm lightly as he sat at the table. Anita was in the kitchen but she kept her voice low. 'I want to apologise to you for my appalling behaviour last night. My only excuse is that I was drunk. It's been a long time since I had a strong, virile man in my arms and I'm afraid I got caught up in the moment. If you want to cut the trip short I can book you a flight home today, but I can assure you, it won't happen again.'

He let her take sole responsibility of the blame, the utter bastard. 'Oh, think nothing of it. Of course I don't want to leave before the work is finished. We came out here to do a job and that's what I want to do. We'll just make sure that you have one less vodka tonight.'

She knew that he'd be plying her with as much alcohol as he could get down her throat. Like a hypnotists she had inserted triggers into his brain. He had all but forgotten that he had a wife apart from the pathetically insipid nightly phone calls home. His master was lust and he was firmly in his master's grip. All she had to do was wiggle her hips and his dick would begin to drip like a tap. She was ready to take him.

She managed to fend off his advances until their

last night in Spain. She couldn't bear the thought of more than one intimate night with him. By the time that dinner was finished and Anita had left for the night, she had him panting like a dog. She didn't need to brush against him any longer. He did enough of that for both of them. She was pouring after dinner drinks when he came up behind her. She wore a backless evening dress and she felt his fingers on the bare flesh across her shoulders. He mistook her shudder for one of arousal. She leaned back into his hand giving him the encouragement that he sought. Bingo! His lips dropped to the nape of her neck. When they lifted he left a saliva imprint of his mouth on her skin. As he'd kissed her she'd pushed her bum into his groin. His hand came around to the front and grabbed her between the legs. He was raising her skirt with his other hand. He hadn't learned any finesse in the years that they'd been apart, whereas she had become an excellent lover with no shortage of partners to hone her abilities. He was going to take her right there over the drinks trolley.

She swung around and kissed him full on the mouth. His instantly filled with saliva and it dripped from his mouth into hers. She fought the urge to gag. Vomiting into his mouth would have been repayment in kind, and would undoubtedly give her immense satisfaction, but was probably not the way forward when she had sex in mind.

She led him into the bedroom where the cameras and recording equipment were already set up and filming.

416

Chapter Thirty-seven

Simon had folded his underwear, his six pairs of shorts and six vests and six t-shirts and two hats and one pair of sunglasses and two pairs of sandals, and six pairs of underwear and six pairs of shorts and six pairs of underwear and six pairs of socks and six t-shirts and six pairs of underwear and six pairs of socks. Simon worried that he wouldn't have enough clothes to wear in Spain. Connie told him that she does have a washing machine; you know, and wanted to take nearly all of Simon's clothes back out of his suitcase. They had a big argue. Simon had a seizure. Simon won. Simon was worried that he wouldn't have enough clothes to wear in Spain. Connie worried about breaking her back. She had taken him shopping because they were going on a big plane to Spain the next day, but first they were going to a really posh party that night and it was very special. Simon sang, 'Oh my dear I'm ob to summy Spain, Eh biba Esbanya,' until Connie told him that if he sang it just one more time, she'd put him on a different plane and book him into a different villa. But Simon knew that she was only joking. He was very excited. Connie had her own swimming pool and Simon could swim in it every day. Connie told him that she'd shout at him if he peed in it. He sometimes peed when he went swimming in the sea and he sometimes peed in the shower, but he didn't tell Connie that. He'd never been on a big plane before and he was going to go right up in the sky and Connie said that he'd be all the way up above the clouds and when he looked out of the window, the clouds would be on the bottom of him and not on the top. That was very strange indeed. Connie said that he'd have to sit on his head in the plane to make the world come the right way up again, but Simon didn't think that was true, he thought it was another joke, but he packed a cushion to put under his head, just in case. Connie took the cushion out of his suitcase and told him that he wouldn't need it, and that he wouldn't need all of his big cardigans and jumpers and that he wouldn't need his parka coat. She said that she'd buy him lots of new Spanish clothes, in lovely bright colours, when they got there.

Simon was big excited about going to Spain on the big plane and he was big excited about the posh party tonight and he had all this big excitement inside his tummy getting all mixed up so that he didn't know which excitement was plane and which excitement was party. He farted and his tummy felt better and Connie called him a serdo sucio, which means dirty pig. Simon was a bit sad because when he was younger there were a whole lot of people that he'd like to have said serdo sucio to. But now he only knew people who were always nice to him. He had a brand new thing to say to the horrible people, but the horrible people had all gone. Connie laughed and said that he worried about the strangest things. Then she said, 'It's like rain on your wedding day, it's a free ride when you've already paid,' but Simon didn't know what she was talking about. He didn't think he was getting married. So he sat down when he was supposed to be packing and he had a big think about it. Connie told him that he'd have his choice of serdo suckios to choose from that night. Simon was worried then and he hadn't even finished worrying about not having enough clothes to wear in Spain, yet. Was it going to be a bad party with horrible people? See, maybe with being Spanish, Connie didn't know what a party was. Simon was good at knowing parties; he'd been to lots of parties. He knew jelly and ice cream and party hats, and balloons that made you spit when you tired to blow them up—but they never went up. Shimon didn't want to go to no place where Horrible People meant Party in Spanish.

Connie had spent a lot of time telling Simon exactly what she wanted him to do at the party. They had been practising for ages. She made him happy by telling him that they were going to do a kind of play and he was going to be the main actor man. She said that they were going to have a wonderful time and if there were any horrible people there, it didn't matter, because they'd be together and they'd laugh at the horrible people and make them go away. Simon had never laughed at horrible people but with Connie he could do it in a kind of play, when he was the main actor man, he thought.

Connie laid out his black thirty-six-inch-waist trousers that had to go back to the shop and be exchanged for new ones, and now they weren't a thirty-six-inch-waist trousers anymore, they were a thirty-eight-inch-waist trousers, but they were still black. And she laid out his new blue shirt with silver pin stripes. And she told him to make sure that when he got in the shower he washed all of him and didn't try to get away with one of his two minute cat licks.

Simon didn't want a shower. He was going to have a long bath and he was going to put soft bubbles in it. They were peach and when they were in the bottle, they were a kind of orange and pink colour mashed together like ice cream. He was going to use his blue shower gel and his shampoo and conditioner. And then he was going to put aftershave on and his silver chain and his black shoes that were shiny and good for dancing in. Connie would say that he looked good enough to eat and that she was proud of him and then she'd call him cielo.

Simon was ready to go to the party at Four o'clock. He knew that was a long time until half past seven when Connie was coming to pick him up. He said oops and sat very still so that he wouldn't crease his new shirt and trousers with the thirty eight inch waist.

It was the day of the garden party and Phil was in the bad books as he left the house for work. Danni had wanted him to take the whole day off to be with her and the boys but he had a backlog of work on his desk and had insisted on going in until lunch time. When he got to work, and pulled his car into his own parking space, with his name painted on the floor, he found that his was the only car there. The blinds were still drawn on the office windows. Max and that dim admin girl were supposed to be in from eight and it was just short of nine o'clock. He put his key in the lock and found the place empty. Literally empty. There was neither a potted plant nor a stick of furniture in the building. Desks, computers, filing cabinets and white boards — they were all gone. He thought that they'd been burgled. Until he saw the note pinned to the toilet door.

> *My Darling Philip. Your services are no longer required. I have dispensed with the staff and have cleared the office. Your employment has been terminated, effective immediately. On a personal note, I should return home straight away, if I were you, your world is about to come crashing down and your wife needs you.*
>
> *Vengeance will be mine, Goodbye.*
> *Yours never, Conseula xxx*

His mind was racing. At first he thought it was an elaborate practical joke. Connie wasn't answering her phone. It rang with the discordant tone of a phone that had been withdrawn from service. His mind was reeling. He'd never been a man of keen wit, subtleties of Connie's joke on him trickled into his mind drop by acidic drop. He realised that his world had just turned upside down.

They had arranged for Danni and the boys to go to the hotel early. Phil was worried sick when he turned into their drive and saw her car parked there.

In his haste to find out what was wrong, his key got

stuck in the door. Danni had promised that she would go to the hotel when she got the boys sorted, to help with the last minute arrangements. She was very good at organisation. She was also very reliable, Violet liked her. She would never have let her mother-in-law down and had to face her disapproval, unless something was wrong. Phil's first thought was that something had happened to one of his boys. He felt cold dread griping in his stomach. 'What is it? What's the matter? Are the boys all right?' he yelled, bursting into the lounge. The children weren't there. Danni sat alone on the sofa, her face red and swollen with crying, tears coursing down her face. She didn't say a word.

A DVD had been running on the recorder when he'd gone into the room. Danni stopped it, pressed rewind and set it playing again. He stood as though frozen to the floor, He was transfixed on the screen, horrified. She pressed stop, rewind. The movie halted and then ran backwards and Phil saw the foul images running in reverse for a few seconds. She hit stop and play. The same section of the movie played again.

Phil was lying on a bed. It was clearly him. His mind was racing, wondering if he could say that it was a super imposed image of his face on somebody else's body, but he knew that he couldn't. It was him and there was no escaping that fact.

Phil lay naked on a bed with Connie's head between his legs sucking him off. He was bending forward so that he could watch her mouth bobbing on his cock. His face contorted in ecstasy. His wife was watching the exact moment when he came and Connie pulled her head away at the last second so that he exploded all over her face and tits. Danni didn't say a word. She pressed stop, rewind. She hit stop and play and the sequence began.

'Honey, it meant nothing. I can explain.'

Danni spoke as though she was a robot. Her voice sounded as though her larynx was made of metal. 'Get your things and get out.'

He saw the note from Connie on the arm of the chair. Presumably it had come through the post with the DVD. It was a note informing her that her employment had been terminated and that her husband was crap in bed. Philip couldn't take it in. He wanted his Mother. She'd tell him how to make it all right with Danni.

'It's Mother's garden party,' he said in a small, pathetic voice. 'You need to get ready. You're not dressed yet.'

'Get out.'

Philip left the house without another word. He'd go to the party; he wouldn't say anything today, it would spoil Mother's big event. Danni needed time to calm down and then they could move forward and put all of this behind them. He'd pretend that everything was fine. It would be fun. He'd have a laugh with James. He could pretend. He could do that. Danni would be okay and he'd deal with her tomorrow. Connie had shown him that Danni was boring anyway. It had been fun up to now, but if it was all going to get heavy —like the last one, then maybe he was better off. Phil liked being single. He was more worried about his job than his marriage. He felt that he may have a nervous breakdown. But it could all wait until tomorrow.

Chapter Thirty-eight

When Connie picked Simon up, she took him to Burger King, which was one of his favourite places on earth. She wasn't sure that they'd be at the party long enough to get anything to eat. While he grinned from behind a massive burger, Connie delved in her bag for baby wipes and adjusted the serviette at Simon's chin to make sure that he didn't spill down himself. She wasn't going to give that family any excuse to mock him. Simon was happy and nothing was going to fracture that happiness.

In the limousine on the twenty minute drive to Windermere, Connie broached the subject of Violet. She'd been picking her moment to tell him. She had to prepare him for seeing his mother but she didn't want him going into meltdown and had to handle it delicately. She had too much at stake in this night to risk Simon blowing his stack and making a holy show of them. When he faced his family, she wanted him to do it tall and proud. A man with dignity, just as they'd practised.

'Simon I've got another surprise for you.'

His face lit up and he turned towards her. 'Connie, Shimon's all full up with Burger King and shurpridis. Shimon's gonna go pop. What's Shurpride?'

Connie laughed, but anybody who didn't have Simon's simplistic view of the world would have noticed the tremor and nervousness. 'Your Mother's

425

coming to watch our play. Isn't that fantastic?' It broke her heart to see his face fall. He hadn't seen Violet in two years and those had been the happiest years of his life.

'Shimon not know, not.' He spoke sadly. 'Shimon miss Mummy, some little times, but all some big times, Shimon not miss Mummy. Shimon scared.'

She put her arm around him. 'Simon, you don't have to be frightened. We are going to do the play and you are going to be the star of the show, just like we said. Yes?'

'Yes,' his eyes were solemn, 'Shimon Scared.'

'When you stand in front of all of those people and do your play, your mummy is going to be so proud of you.'

Simon smiled but looked doubtful.

'I know, let's go through it again, just how it's going to be, so that you are happy that you can get it right and make your mummy proud.' And mainly to distract him from thoughts of his mother, Connie took him through what was going to happen when they arrived at the hotel.

The party was in full swing when they got there. It had been going since eleven that morning. A tradition that had built up over the years was the Halcyon Woods Summer Garden Party, second only to the Queen's garden party, and coming second place even to that was debateable in Violet's eyes. The day had built to be *the* event in the Windermere calendar, everybody would be there.

During the day, everybody with a wallet was welcome. There was entertainment, stalls and food all at a healthy financial premium. They had tournaments, archery, it's a knockout, the X-Factor, face painting, donkey rides and food enough to sink a ship.

The evening was a genteel affair with the Windermere elite staying on to dine in the banqueting hall, an elaborate sit-down meal with after dinner speeches, followed by a string quartet and then a ceilidh for the lively who wanted to dance.

Connie had timed it so that they would arrive in the middle of the speeches. The delivery arrived on time and while everybody was occupied inside the banqueting hall, at the back of the hotel she talked to the pallbearers and explained what they would do. It was a shame that the grand arrival of the four black stallions pulling the white casket, had gone predominantly unnoticed. Giving a cursory glance at the coffin and the flowers, she made sure that everything was in order.

She peeped through the door, waiting for the moment when Violet had positioned herself behind the podium to deliver her speech. Mother duck was at the head of proceedings, in a prime position to see—and be seen.

Connie pressed the button on the ghetto blaster that she had on a wheeled trolley, and gave the nod to the four men holding the tiny coffin.

As it had on the day of the funeral all of those years earlier, the strains of *All Things Bright and Beautiful* played out among the people assembled. She had gone to great pains to recreate everything exactly as it had been on that day. The flowers were identical. The brass plaque on the top of the white coffin with gold furniture read, *In memory of our lovely angel.* And the sandbag inside the coffin was similar, if not identical, to the one giving weight to the proceedings on that day, long ago.

The pallbearers walked a slow, dignified death march down the centre aisle of the banqueting hall. At the head of the central walkway they stopped, and waited for Connie to catch up with the trolley. She removed the ghetto blaster, smiled at an old crone at the top table, and put the radio beside her. She turned the music off and there was a deadly hush in the room. You could hear a pin drop.

'What's going on? What is the meaning of this outrage? Who are you?' Violet was red in the face and seething with rage. She hadn't grasped the implications of what was happening and, as she did, the colour drained from her face.

'Hey that's Maria Callas' James shouted.

'Connie, what are you doing here?' said Philip, jumping to his feet.

Connie waved him back down and he sat like an obedient puppy. 'I need to talk to you, you bitch,' he hissed from a seated position, 'You've ruined my marriage.'

'You got off lightly, mate,' James screamed.' She put me in a fucking wheelchair.'

Connie held up her hand for silence and

everybody, Violet included who had been blowing hard out of her mouth like a distended fish, stopped speaking.

From a shelf underneath the trolley Connie brought out a large frame protected with a midnight blue velvet cover. She took her time revealing the portrait before kissing it. She showed it to the audience and then placed it on top of the white coffin, facing Violet.'

The colour had left the older woman's face. She was bleached of tone and bluster, the makeup standing out starkly on her cheekbones. She stared at the portrait of the handsome man, horrified. Groping behind her for the stability of the chair, she wilted into it in a swoon. Connie thought that, on this occasion, Violet's dramatics were entirely genuine. She felt a thrill of excitement as the culmination of her plan came to fruition. There was no pity in her heart for these people.

The crowd, who had enjoyed their day, feasted at the meal, and resigned themselves to the inevitable speeches, turned to each other asking in confused whispers, what was going on. SP went to Violet and was bending down beside her. The crowd were thrilled by the new and unexpected entertainment; you could always rely on them Woodses for a bit of scandal. Connie held up her hand for silence and a reverent hush fell on the room.

'Some of you here will remember attending a funeral on the third of November nineteen sixty.' There was a whoosh of whispers around the room and a few of the older people nodded their heads, wondering

429

what the hell was going on.

Violet Woods was very young, then. She'd just had her first child, a boy, born within wedlock, but only by a matter of weeks. He was stillborn and some of you attended his funeral.' She indicated the coffin with her hand.

'Jesus, sweet mother of God, she's only gone and dug `im up.' One of the locals announced, drawing the sign of the cross on her body as she spoke.

SP was helping Violet to her feet; he was going to take her to her room for a lie down. He called out to Ros to come and assist. Connie swung on them angrily, 'Leave her alone. Sit back down. She's not leaving this room until I've had my say.'

'The woman's mad,' whined James, she put me in this wheelchair. Somebody call the police.' Nobody moved.

Connie walked to the coffin and rested her hand on it. 'In memory of our lovely angel,' she read. She picked a bloom from the wreath arranged to form the word *SON* and brought it to her nose to smell it. She smiled, taking her time before speaking again. Not a single person in that room moved.

'Ladies and Gentlemen, you must be wondering what this is about. I'm here tonight to introduce you to the baby that was buried back in nineteen sixty three. Of course he's not a baby any longer, he's a fine man. It is with great pleasure that I introduce to you the eldest child of Donald and Violet Woods. I give you, Mr Simon Peter Woods.'

The doors at the end of the great room opened with a creak and Simon walked through them. He was beaming and stood very straight, just as Connie had teached him to do. He held the white, word flowers, which Connie had told him spelled out MOTHER. He walked very carefully and very slowly counting, one elephant, between each step. It had taken him a long time to stop saying, 'One elephant,' out loud and he had to walk up and down his living room a lot of times until he remembered not to say it. His feet hurt him a lot and he worried that all that walking up and down on his nice carpet would make there be no nice carpet left. He was walking on a wood floor now, like his name. That was funny, but he didn't laugh because that wasn't part of the play, not. His feet made a big click click click noise, but he wasn't worried about it because Connie had told him that it might be quiet in there, and that it was good if his shoes made a big noise because that was dra-mat-tic for the play. He was worried because in the car Connie had changed it. He was supposed to put the white flowers that spelled the word MOTHER on the white box. But now she said that he had to walk up to Mummy and give her the flowers. If she didn't take them off him, he had to just put them in her lap and it didn't matter, not, if she threw them down on the floor 'cause that might be part of the play, too.

Simon walked up to his mother and offered her the wreath. Violet made a strangled noise in the back of her throat and lifted her hands up in the air, as if the flowers were a snake. Simon was beaming at his mummy. He wanted to make her proud. He really wanted to say hello to her, but Connie was very strict about that. She said that he wasn't allowed to say anything unless she spoke to him a direct question. That was part of the play. Just like he was told, he turned around by putting his heel down on the floor and lifting his toes up and spinning on his heel. He liked doing that, it was the best bit of the play and very dra-mat-tic. He walked over to Connie but he couldn't remember if he had to count, one elephant, or not. He was going to get worried and if he got worried, he'd throw a fit and ruin the play. But before he got worried, he had an idea. He would count, one kangaroo, instead, because they were smaller than elephants. He nearly ruined the play because he was used to counting elephants and wasn't used to counting kangaroos, so he counted them out loud and most of the people watching the play laughed, and some old ladies gave him a big clap and so he did a big bow. Then Connie came over and took his hand and calmed him down and walked with him to the white box.

Simon beamed.

When Connie had announced him as Simon Peter, SP stood up and demanded to know what the hell was going on. Connie told him to have patience and that all would be revealed. Then she spoke to the crowd.

'This man, Ladies and Gentlemen, is Violet's first born child, but as you can see, he isn't dead. Look at him, Ladies and Gentlemen, he's magnificent.'

The row of three old ladies clapped again and

Simon felt very important. It was a very good play and he was a very good actor as well as a very good singer.

'So let's see who, exactly, is in the casket, shall we?' there was a collective gasp around the room. The replica coffin hadn't been nailed shut and opened easily. Connie swept the flowers from it and opened the lid. Several people seated at the back of the room, stood up to get a better view.

Connie lifted the bundle of white lace from the casket and a woman five rows back fainted. From the Christening gown, Connie pulled a 2lb sandbag and held it up for the people to see. 'This ladies and gentleman is what Violet Woods buried that day. This is what was in the grave that she has lovingly tended for the last forty years. And this fine man,' she pointed at Simon who grinned even bigger, 'is the son—that Violet was so ashamed of—that she packed him off to an institution, where he has spent most of his life. He has a condition that I'm sure you are all aware of. Simon has Downs Syndrome,' Simon mouthed the words along with Connie. It wasn't part of the play for him to say them too, but he liked saying that he was a fine man with Downs Syndrome so he said those words when she did.

'Simon has a condition that makes him different from other people, but if wealth could be measured by the good attributes in a human being then Simon could buy and sell any one of that Woods lot, a thousand times over.' Simon didn't understand all of those words but he knew that it was a very important part of the play. The old ladies clapped a lot this time and one of them shouted, 'Hooray.' Simon thought that the old ladies liked him very much. Maybe they would invite him to their house one day for tea and cakes because he was such a good actor.

Now they were getting to the next bit of the play. Simon thought this part was a boring bit and had suggested an awful lot of times that Connie let him sing a song, instead of this bit. He wanted to be centre stage but he didn't have a big bit in the play again until the end. All he was doing now was passing pictures back and forth to Connie. Anybody could do that. You didn't need to be a good actor to do it. He wanted to sing a song, but Connie brought a chair over for him to sit on until it was his time to get up again. Simon was sulking but the old ladies kept smiling at him. The man in the wheelchair, like the one that Bernie Roberts had at Great Gables, kept staring at him. He looked really mad at Simon, so Simon didn't look at him at all. Maybe he wanted be a great actor man, too, and to get up at the front and do the play, but he couldn't on account of being in the wheelchair. That was sad.

Connie pulled four pictures out of the cloth. They were a lot smaller than the picture of Simon. Connie said that's because Simon's picture was special. She showed the pictures to the people before giving them to Simon to hold.

The man in the wheelchair, and the man who was already standing beside Mummy, and another man who was drunk, and some ladies, were arguing with

Mummy about the baby what didn't die, and about Simon. Simon was confused. Connie didn't tell him if this was part of the play or not and Simon needed to know. People shouldn't argue in the middle of the play, not. That was rude. And if they were being rude, Simon wanted to tell them to shut up. But he didn't know if it was part of the play. Simon decided to tell them to shut up anyway, so he put his finger over his lips. He looked at all the people arguing with Mummy and made a loud shush noise without getting too much spit on his fingers. The old ladies clapped. Simon wanted to see if they would clap if he did something else. So he got the pictures of the boring people that he was holding, and he jiggled them on his lap to make it look as though they were dancing. The old ladies clapped like mad and beamed. Simon beamed at them. Connie came over to whisper in his ear that he was spoiling the play. Simon thought that was not fair, not. The people arguing with Mummy were making a lot of bad noise and she didn't shout at them. Connie whispered that it was her bit now. She held her hand up to him and said, 'Ah ah,' when he was going to argue, so he didn't and shut his mouth. Connie said that if he did anything else that they hadn't practised he wouldn't be able to stand up again at the end, and that's when he got to take a big bow. Connie told him to act out 'sitting quietly on a chair.' And then she went back to the people.

Connie took another large picture from the cloth and held it up to the people. This one wasn't framed like Simon's picture was, so Simon thought that it might be a little bit special. Connie held the picture in front of her.

Suddenly every trace of the Spanish accent disappeared from her voice. She spoke in her old voice. She spoke as Julie Spencer. She saw it as Julie making a cameo appearance into her life, for the last time, before she was banished forever. Her voice was deeper than it had been before, but those who had known her as Julie in the past, recognised it for what it was.

'Some of you will know the person in this picture. Her name is Julie Woods and ten years ago she was married to Philip Woods. He was a bad husband and a bad father. He took their little girl and murdered her.' She wheeled on Philip and screamed at him, 'You killed our daughter, you murderer.'

Nobody understood what was going on. The drunken man came over and grabbed the picture out of Connie's hands and looked from it, to her.

'You're not Julie. It's impossible. He was hearing but not believing what was in front of him. You look nothing like her. You can't be. You're taller.' He motioned with his hand how tall Julie had been.

'I have had twenty seven operations to look like this. I lay in traction in a Russian clinic for six months to gain four inches in height. I've had my larynx operated on, almost every part of my body. I learned to speak a new language and I became somebody new, somebody who I like. When you were unfaithful to your new wife, three nights ago, and had sex with me, rutting in my

436

bed like a disgusting animal, you had no idea that you were sleeping with your ex-wife.'

The crowd gasped. This was the best thing they'd seen in the long, scandalous run of the Wood's time in the village.

The brothers were intrigued, they wanted to hear what she had to say before deciding what to do with her. When Connie told them to bring 'her,' –she couldn't speak Violet's name— down to the front of the room where they could see and hear what was being said, they agreed. James shouted obscenities but he wanted to know what this was about as much as the rest of them. SP had taken heroin that morning to get him through. He'd retreated to his room at lunchtime to top up and aid alcohol in carrying him through to oblivion. The image he'd seen in his room was indistinct in his memory, but he had a feeling, creeping though his addled brain cells that he'd seen the woman with the coffin before. With being high, he was having greater trouble than the others in grasping what was happening and was happy to sit in an addled daze. Philip was drunk and in shock, like James, he shouted the odd comment from the peanut gallery, but for the most part he was sullen and silent waiting to hear what the woman who had wrecked his life—again—had to say.

Simon arranged the photographs in order and passed Connie the one of the man with the black glasses, first.

'Simon Peter the second, Ladies and Gentlemen. A fine upstanding pillar of society—wouldn't you agree?'

437

The crowd turned to look at SP. His head had slumped to one side, he was trying to focus and concentrate on what was being said but her moving hands were creating tracers and it was difficult.

'He was born an imposter. He was given the title of heir to the Woods' estate. A title that wasn't his to own. What kind of sick woman gives her second child the same name as that of her disabled first born? Simon Peter raised, educated, and groomed throughout his childhood to take over the family business. Simon Peter has taken the right of his older brother's inheritance. He's taken his name. And while he has lived life with his mouth around a silver spoon, the original brother has mouldered away in a facility away from prying eyes. Simon has never known one moment of maternal love. His mother visited once a week out of a sense of guilt and duty. She resented him for it. Hated him for what he was. Look at the second Simon Peter and compare him to the man sitting over there.' She pointed at Simon. Every head in the room turned to look at him, except Violet, who had her head hung in shame. It was supposed to be her special day of the year. She was in shock and she hummed a hymn to herself.

Simon beamed with pride, but it was strange hearing Connie talking in the funny voice. He had to concentrate very hard not to laugh

'Which one, do you think, is the thief, Ladies and Gentlemen? Which one has been stealing form the business for years? Which one is a pathetic heroin addict? And which one do you think is a son that any mother could be proud of because he's sweet and funny and kind? Which one of them is a good man, would you say?'

'Hey hang on,' SP slurred, trying to get to his feet and failing, 'that's slander.'

'Shut up, or get out,' Connie spat at him. 'You are a worthless human being. What kind of husband have you been? What kind of man?' SP sank into his chin, his outburst had taken the last of his energy and he had no more to say. James shouted in defence of his brother but Connie told him to be quiet or she'd have him wheeled out of the room.

Connie handed the photo of SP back to Simon and he passed her the next one. This one had a red jumper on.

'John Woods,' Connie began, 'Thief, gambler, swindler, and womaniser. Are we seeing a pattern emerging? He conned his mother out of thousands over the years. She bailed him out of trouble when his gambling got out of control, time and again. What kind of father was this man when he was out bedding hundreds of women during the course of his marriage? He's dead now. And good riddance.'

The next picture was the one of the man with the long hair and the beard.

'Of the five Woods' boys who were allowed to grow up in the wealth and splendour of the family home, Andrew is the best of the rancid lot of them.' Several of the crowd nodded and some muttered their agreement. 'He's no longer with us, but the world is a better place without him.' Somebody made a comment about not speaking ill of the dead, but Connie continued.

'This man was a thief, also. He forged clocks and watches and made vast amounts of money with his forgeries. He was involved in gang crime, the money that he brought to the mafia from his crime spree bought arms and drugs. He was a drug addict. He brought his children up in a commune, sleeping with women who weren't his children's mother. He grew drugs on his property; all bought from his illegal gain, lived a live of loose morals, and immersed himself in crime until the day he died'

Philip wept for his dead brothers as though Connie had read out a sweet eulogy. 'Andrew was a good man,' he shouted to her belligerently.

She took up the second to last photo and glared at James. The crowd looked at him too. 'This man is a thug. He has gone through life beating his wife and brawling, when he thinks that his evil temper will carry him through. He has bullied, often to the point of breaking people with a weaker character than his own. He has driven people to suicide. He has to wear a dress to come down from the stress and pressure of always being the hard man, bawling people out, fighting. Inside he's just a frightened little boy. Every time he's hurt somebody, Mummy has signed a cheque and got him off the hook. He's scum, pathetic.'

'You put me in this wheelchair, you fucking bitch.'

'No, you fool, you put yourself in it. Did I force you

into an illegal backstreet brawl with a Neanderthal thug? No, you begged me to set it up for you, you vain, egotistical, pathetic, human being.'

She replaced James' photo with Phil's, and Simon playing to the audience in general, and his old ladies in particular, spread his hands to show that they were empty because he'd been putting the used pictures under his chair so that they didn't get mixed up. When he spread his hands and made a surprised face, he looked at his ladies, but they didn't clap. They were all staring at Connie, listening to every word that she said. Simon went into a big sulk. If they weren't going to give him no more big claps, he might not even bother getting up and doing the great acting in the play. He might not even take his big bow at the very end. And when they send the invitation to go to their house for tea and cakes, he might just tell them, 'No thanks you,' and not go— but that all depended on what kind of cakes it was.

Connie studied the picture of Philip and then looked from that to the man, in person, before turning the photograph around for the people to see. 'Thank you for bearing with me because, you see, I've almost saved the best until last. I've run out of photos but there's still one left to tell you about after Philip Woods, my ex-husband. Philip Woods,' she repeated the name as though she was tasting the words in her mouth. I've already told you that he took my little girl and killed her. She drowned in the pond a few feet away from where you're sitting. Accident, they all said. It was no accident. It was murder by way of neglect.'

Phil jumped out of his seat and although he'd sobered since Connie's entrance, he staggered and almost fell over. 'You're evil. You're nothing but evil coming here with a coffin and all your games, that's just sick.'

'And who made me sick, Philip? Who spread the evil and infected me with it? Who took sweet little Julie Spencer and turned her into somebody filled with hatred and rage? You did, you bastard.'

Simon did the surprised face and covered his mouth with his hand, it was partly because he wanted to get in the play, but it was more because Connie used the dirty word. 'Dirty word,' he shouted loudly and some people laughed. That made him feel better, but most people were still looking at Connie and the drunk man. 'Dirty word, dirty Bird,' he shouted, trying for another laugh.

'Be quiet, Simon,' Connie said, and she sounded annoyed with him so he put his head down and thought about going on a big plane to Spain and then he forgot all about being in a sulk. She turned her attention back to Philip.

'That's not all you did though, is it Phil. Should we tell Mummy about the blackmail?'

Phil's eyes darted around the room. For a second, Connie thought he was going to make a run for it rather than have her saying anymore. He was more worried about conning a few quid out of his mother than he was about taking his daughter's life. 'Shut up, and get out of here, you evil witch. Haven't you upset my family enough?' He didn't stop to wait for a reply, which Connie felt was a great shame because she had an answer ready for him. '

'Yes, make her go away, Philip. I don't like her' Violet spoke for the first time and raised her head as she spoke as though examining Connie to see if she really was that awful Julie creature from the past.

'That was the problem, you old demon, you never did like me, did you. You never gave me a chance. You looked at my background, found me lacking and did everything within your power to stop Philip from marrying me.'

'Simon Peter, Philip, she's being nasty to me. Make her stop.'

'Oh shut up, I'll get to you, in a minute.'

'What does she mean? Why's she saying that she's going to get to me? I don't know her.'

'Shush mother and listen,' said James. 'This is just starting to get good.' Philip glared at his brother and SP was beyond caring, he had passed out in his chair.

'You always did like confrontation, didn't you, James? Always there waiting to stick the knife into me. You were the one with a hateful remark about my figure.' James was still having a hard time equating the stunner who'd shafted him, with his weedy little ex-sister-in-law.

'What figure? You didn't have a figure, love; you

were an ugly little weeble. Mind, I've got to say you look fit enough now. And you see me here in this wheelchair? I can still smash your plastic face in and put it back how it used to be. Think I won't?'

She turned an icy stare onto James and made a point of looking down on him in his chair. 'I have no doubt for one second that if you had the intelligence to find me that you wouldn't hesitate in inflicting violence on me. After all, that's what you're good at, hurting women. But come on, James, let me play. You like a bit of salacious gossip, don't you. I bet you a fiver, you want to know what your little brother's been up to.'

James smiled equally coldly, but gestured with his hand to give her the floor. She took it. 'Philip has known about Simon for a long time.'

Violet's head shot up. Connie had her attention. And Violet was still shrewd enough to be able to pull herself out of her weakening mind when she had a need to. She stared at Connie with rapt attention.

'Philip's thing was watching people, listening at doors, spying and turning his nasty, sly little character into an object for poking into other people's lives. Violet used to visit Simon religiously, every Wednesday afternoon.'

Simon sighed; he was bored with this. He didn't expect the play to be this long, but he couldn't stop himself form piping up, 'Shimon no like Webnudsday, not.'

'Wednesday's weren't pleasant for him. His mother was cruel and bullied him.'

'Oh you wicked girl. I most certainly did not. I always did what I could for the boy. How can you say such a horrible thing?'

One afternoon, Philip followed Violet to see where she went every week. He did some digging, asked some questions and learned everything that he wanted to know. He knew from being a teen that he had an older brother with Downs Syndrome. He even hid outside the home one day and watched Simon getting on his school bus.'

'Is this true Philip, and have you really been having an affair with this vile woman? Is that why Danielle is not here?' Violet asked?'

Connie continued to talk over her, doing Philip the favour of not having to answer his mother. 'When Philip found out that he had another brother, did he confront his mother and beg her to bring the lad home, so that he could be with his family where he should have belonged, but never did? No. Like Violet, he was ashamed of what Simon was. But he didn't just ignore it. He used the situation to blackmail his mother. It's all in the diaries Violet. Philip was the one who was blackmailing you to keep your dirty secret, all those years ago.'

'That can't be true. It was a professional blackmailer. It was somebody who threatened to ruin me.'

'And that's exactly what your youngest son became. You weren't his first; John had used a poor girl in his class at school for sex. Afterwards, Phil blackmailed her; it's all in the diaries, those and hundreds more. Unbeknown to anybody, Philip has been blackmailing the people of this town for thirty years.

Pennies dropped all over the room and customers from present and past, hearing who their blackmailer was, rose from their seats. Phil ran from the room with half a dozen men behind him. Violet was weeping. James who was evil to the point that it reached his brain, was grinning. Sensing a fight and still fancying his chances, despite the chair, he wheeled himself to the door in Phil's wake. Connie looked around the room, she recognised several other people from the blackmailing diaries, sitting next to their spouses, looking terrified. They didn't move or say a word. She caught the eye of them all and empathised with them.

SP was unconscious; the brothers were either dead, passed out, or out of earshot. Ros was there, and a couple of Andrew's grown up kids, but for the final showdown, it was just Connie and her nemesis.

Connie looked Violet in the eye and the other woman looked away.

'Why are you doing this to me?' Violet sounded pathetic.

'Come on Violet. Don't make this a battle of the weak against the strong. You might have this lot fooled, but I know that there isn't a weak bone in your body. You're as tough as old boots, so let's see you give me a fight, eh?'

'I'm an old woman.'

'You're an old fool.'

'Do you know, Violet, your reputation has always meant everything to you. It was more important than any of your children, than your marriage, maybe even than your God, but do you know what you are? What you have always been? You're a joke. People in this town laugh at you. They always have done. Mother Duck and her five ugly ducklings. Nobody ever knew that there were six, did they?

'People don't laugh at me. I'm highly respected in this town.' There were a few bold titters. And somebody shouted, 'Quack. Quack.'

Simon liked doing farm animals and he took up the quack and quacked several times more, before dropping into a deep moo. Connie didn't bother to shut him up.

'When I met Phil, I was only a kid myself. I thought that I was in love. You were right about one thing. I never did love him. He was an impossible man to love. You decided before you'd even met me, that I wasn't good enough for your son. In fact, it didn't even have anything to do with Philip. You decided that I wasn't good enough for you, and you were vile to me. You made my life a misery. You called me a heroin addict, when I'd never touched drugs in my life. Well, Violet, look at your son passed out and dribbling there. That's what an addict looks like. Did you ever once see me like that? You called me a prostitute. Didn't your precious James get done for prostituting himself to men, in a dress? You called me a gold digger. Your children have dug gold from you from the moment they could walk.

447

Maybe that's the reason you never breast fed, they'd have had the silver out of your fillings while they sucked.'

'You filthy woman. See everybody. See what she is, with her dirty mouth?'

'Go`arn, lass,' one of the men said.

'You were nothing when my son met you.'

'That's right Violet, you said he picked me out of the gutter, didn't you?'

'And so he did. He should have left you there to be eaten by rats.'

'Look at your own family, Violet, and then look at mine. You've got money, but pound for pound you've got a hell of a lot more gutter than I have.' Some of the crowd laughed.'

'She tried it on with my dear departed husband once,' Violet shouted. 'She exposed herself to him.' that shocked the crowd and they straightened up to see what the outcome of the allegation would be.

Connie hadn't a clue what she was talking about, and then realisation dawned. She laughed. 'I breast fed my child in his presence.'

'Ah,' the crowd said, disappointed at the anti-climax.

'So what have you come here for Julie, just to exact your warped revenge?'

'No. I have a clearer reason. But Julie isn't here Violet. She died when her daughter did. My name is legally Consuela Vengarse. You can call me what you like, but I know who I am.'

'You're a trollop and a hussy. That's what you are.'

'That's as maybe but you asked why I've come back.' She called Simon over and he stood up beside her. She held his hand.

At that moment the doors at the back of the room swung open and a tall lady in a tailored suit and high stiletto heels walked up to Violet. The lady was called Monica Dupont. She was a solicitor, a ballbreaker, who usually only went after men, but on this occasion she was happy to take this family out from the rotten matriarch, to every putrid apple on the tree. In ten years, she had never forgotten the story that Julie Woods had told her about her marriage, and the way that the family had treated her. Monica had looked down on Julie. She had thought her weak. She had turned her business away because she wouldn't financially destroy her husband. Monica had been wrong and that was a seldom felt experience for her. She was astute when it came to people and was used to being right. The women had become friends, and Monica admired Connie for what she'd made of herself, despite the Woods' repression.

'Mrs Violet Woods?'

'Yes, and who are you?'

Monica handed her the envelope. 'Of course you can open that privately later, but just to let you know what it contains. That is a summons for you to appear in court two weeks from today. I am representing Mr Simon Peter Woods,' she paused— 'the elder,' she finished. There were some titters around the room. 'We are bringing a case against you to have Mr Woods affirmed in his rightful title as heir of the Halcyon Woods Hotel. We will bring an independent injunction against you granting that Mr Woods does receive his one sixth share, of all assets, on the event of your death, further to this, we are seeking to claim a likewise amount, based on a rough average approximation of everything that your other sons have had over the years to be paid to Mr Woods, immediately. You will find all the paperwork and reports relevant to our case, inside the envelope.

Violet smiled, and looked around the assembled people smugly. 'My dear woman. I would like to see the credentials that declare you a competent solicitor. Surely, you must know that you can't possibly represent that man in court. He's—'Connie cut in. 'He's your son Violet. Say it. Say that he is your son.'

'That man is no son of mine. I denounce him.'

'You wicked bitch,' somebody shouted.'

'And as I was about to say before the guttersnipe interrupted me, you can't represent him in court because he isn't of sane body and mind. He is incompetent and not capable of knowing what's in his best interests. That, my dear is why, I am his legal guardian.'

'Yes, you've got me there Mrs Wood's, that's true, you are. But last Tuesday Senora Consuela Vengarse applied to the court and laid before them the extenuating circumstances of Mr Woods' maternal neglect and cruelty. She applied for, and was granted, the position of Guardian ad litem to Mr Woods. A guardian ad litem is an independent person, who is appointed only to take into account the best interests of her ward. Ms Vengarse is responsible for Mr Wood's welfare, that includes his financial welfare. So I think you'll find that, as well as my excellent credentials for the post that I hold, everything in that envelope is legal and above-board. Ten years ago I wanted to take your weasel of a son for everything he had. Connie wouldn't let me have him, so I've waited a long time for this Mrs Hoity Toity hotel owner. I'm going to take you for everything that I can legally get on behalf of Simon. And when I've finished with you, I'm going to spit you out like a dirty rag. I've been looking at every loophole in the law. At the moment, it stands that your assets must be split six ways, between your living sons, and the surviving offspring of your dead ones. But believe me, lady, if there is any way possible that I can take this whole pile of rubble for my client. I'm going to find it, so you'd better have yourself a good solicitor because I'm looking forward to meeting him.' With that Monica took a deep breath. It had been one hell of a speech. She hugged Connie, high fived with Simon, and left the room with her high heels tap tapping her, all the way out of the door.

Connie smiled. Violet looked done in. And the people who had paid ticket money for entertainment that night, weren't disappointed. 'Thank you for your time and patience everybody. I'm going to leave now, but I think I'll let Simon have the last work, if you don't mind.'

This was Simon's big moment; He stood with a huge grin on his face and looked around at all of the people. Mummy didn't look very proud of him yet, but she would be when he'd done his great acting.

'Shimon Woods is I?' he began.

'I am Simon Woods,' Connie whispered, correcting him.

Simon cleared his throat and started again. 'I am Shimon Woods. Shimon is a very great singer. Shimon is a very great actor. Shimon is always good to other people. Shimon is a fine man.' He stopped and puffed up his chest. He put one arm behind his back and bowed low. When he rose he shouted out above the noise of the crowd clapping him and whistling…

'I am Shimon Woods.'